THE WOOD BEYOND THE WORLD

broadview editions
series editor: L.W. Conolly

William Morris. Photograph taken by Emery Walker on 19 January 1889; Frederick Hollyer/Hulton Archive/Getty Images.

THE WOOD BEYOND THE WORLD

William Morris

edited by Robert Boenig

broadview editions

Library and Archives Canada Cataloguing in Publication

Morris, William, 1834-1896
The wood beyond the world / William Morris ; edited by Robert Boenig.

(Broadview editions)
Includes bibliographical references.
ISBN 978-1-55111-982-3

I. Boenig, Robert, 1948- II. Title. III. Series: Broadview editions

PR5079.W6 2010 823'.8 C2010-901935-0

Broadview Editions
The Broadview Editions series represents the ever-changing canon of literature in English by bringing together texts long regarded as classics with valuable lesser-known works.

Advisory editor for this volume: Betsy Struthers

Broadview Press is an independent, international publishing house, incorporated in 1985. Broadview believes in shared ownership, both with its employees and with the general public; since the year 2000 Broadview shares have traded publicly on the Toronto Venture Exchange under the symbol BDP.

We welcome comments and suggestions regarding any aspect of our publications—please feel free to contact us at the addresses below or at broadview@broadviewpress.com.

North America
Post Office Box 1243, Peterborough, Ontario, Canada K9J 7H5
2215 Kenmore Avenue, Buffalo, NY, USA 14207
Tel: (705) 743-8990; Fax: (705) 743-8353
email: customerservice@broadviewpress.com

UK, Europe, Central Asia, Middle East, Africa, India, and Southeast Asia
Eurospan Group, 3 Henrietta St., London WC2E 8LU, United Kingdom
Tel: 44 (0) 1767 604972; Fax: 44 (0) 1767 601640
email: eurospan@turpin-distribution.com

Australia and New Zealand
NewSouth Books
c/o TL Distribution, 15-23 Helles Ave., Moorebank, NSW, Australia 2170
Tel: (02) 8778 9999; Fax: (02) 8778 9944
email: orders@tldistribution.com.au

www.broadviewpress.com

This book is printed on paper containing 100% post-consumer fibre.

Typesetting and assembly: True to Type Inc., Claremont, Canada.

PRINTED IN CANADA

Contents

Acknowledgements

I wish to acknowledge the help of my research assistant, Gabriela Rios, and the generosity of the Graduate English Program of Texas A&M University, which made her help possible. I am grateful to Stephanie Elmquist and staff members of Cushing Library, Texas A&M University, for help with digital imaging.

Introduction

Constructing Something Like the Middle Ages

In the last eight years of his life and in failing health, the Victorian poet, designer, and political activist William Morris tried his hand at something new, something different. He returned to his Pre-Raphaelite roots and to his early love of the Middle Ages by writing a series of eight narratives, usually termed his late prose romances, that enormously influenced the later genre of the modern fantasy novel. What constitutes fantasy, of course, depends on one's definition of it. Elements incorporated into fantasy novels have been around since the time of Homer, and a case could be made for classifying almost anything that does not strive hard to represent "real life" as a fantasy novel. We can be sure that George Eliot's *Middlemarch* or Jane Austen's *Pride and Prejudice* are not fantasy. But under the right definition George MacDonald's *Phantastes* or Mary Shelley's *Frankenstein* could be. For that matter, so could Horace Walpole's *The Castle of Otranto*, Edmund Spenser's *The Faerie Queene*, or even Thomas Malory's *Morte D'Arthur* (see Appendix A3). But with Malory, at least, we have receded far enough away from what the word "modern" represents, for he was writing in the last stage of medieval chivalric romance, the genre that spawned the later fantasy novel. Fantasy, at least in its most recognizable mode, is medievalistic rather than medieval.[1]

A definition I find compelling of the modern fantasy novel might be resisted as special pleading—crafting a description so that it fits Morris's works. But there is an argument, I feel, that saves it from this pitfall. Here is my working definition:

> The modern fantasy novel is a prose work written in an industrial age that is uneasy with its own achievements. It evokes the Middle Ages by creating a world medievalistic in nature yet unrelated to that historical period. The genre is also structured around an individual quest, where the main character goes off into a geographically vague landscape to accomplish a deed against formidable odds. It moreover employs the supernatural, the marvelous.

---

1 For an analysis of modern medievalism, see Michael Alexander, *Medievalism: The Middle Ages in Modern England* (New Haven, CT: Yale UP, 2007).

What saves this definition from the charge of special pleading is that the work of the acknowledged master of the genre, J.R.R. Tolkien, not only embodies these criteria so well but he also acknowledges his debt to Morris, as does C.S. Lewis, whose children's books are almost as important as Tolkien's works in establishing the genre.

The novel edited for this volume, *The Wood Beyond the World* (1894), along with Morris's earlier *The Glittering Plain* (1891), is the first that meets all of these criteria. The two books are, however, not the first of Morris's eight prose romances; the two preceding them—*The House of the Wolfings* (1888) and *The Roots of the Mountains* (1889)—measure up to some but not all these criteria. One of his prose romances subsequent to these two, *Child Christopher and Goldilind the Fair* (1895), also does not measure up to them all. If you have been keeping up with the math, that means five of Morris's eight prose romances qualify. *The House of the Wolfings* and *The Roots of the Mountains* purport to have roots in real history, in the conflicts of the Germanic tribes against the Romans and the Huns, respectively. *The House of the Wolfings*, moreover, lacks an individual quest (though there is a main character who does heroic deeds). *Child Christopher and Goldilind the Fair*, an adaptation of the early Middle English poem *Havelok the Dane*,[1] carefully avoids the marvelous and lacks a fully developed quest.

Both *The Wood Beyond the World* and *The Glittering Plain* show uneasiness about the modern world. In brief, the main characters effect a retreat into a marvelous world that stands in opposition to the "real" world of each novel's outset, and the contrast between these competing worlds generates an implied criticism of Morris's own world. In both of these novels, moreover, the fictive worlds, though unrelated to anything historical, are recognizably medieval: there is nothing in the way of technology, the weapons of choice are swords, the mildly archaic language evokes

1 For Morris's adaption of that poem, see May Morris, *The Collected Works of William Morris with Introductions by his Daughter May Morris: Volume 17: The Wood Beyond the World, Child Christopher, Old French Romances* (London: Longmans, Green and Company, 1913), xxxix. See also Norman Talbot, "'But he were king, or kinges eyr ...': Morris's Re-telling of *Havelok*," *Journal of the William Morris Society* 10.4 (1994): 28-39; and Richard Mathews, *Worlds Beyond the World: the Fantastic Vision of William Morris* (San Bernardino, CA: Borgo Press, 1978), 48.

medieval English, and the societies depicted in each have analogues to real medieval social structures. Both main characters go off on individual quests; that is, they leave their societies and the entanglements that these societies involve for urgent journeys into the unknown to accomplish specific tasks. And both heroes encounter the supernatural along the way. The last three of Morris's late prose romances—*The Well at the World's End* (1896), *The Water of the Wondrous Isles* (1897), and *The Sundering Flood* (1898)—are longer than these two; they not only exhibit all these characteristics, but they also perfect them.

If a fantasist wishes to construct something that looks like the Middle Ages but really is not, things have to be omitted as well as included. Morris is not interested, for instance, in medieval religion. In *The Well at the World's End*, though we occasionally encounter monks and abbeys, they are far in the background. In *The Wood Beyond the World* even that ghost has fled. Morris is likewise uninterested in the world of medieval learning, including, surprisingly, the craft of making books (he himself experimented with producing hand-illuminated manuscripts and was an enthusiastic collector of such manuscripts produced in the Middle Ages). He similarly was not drawn to medieval dynastic politics, and though he flirts with Courtly Love, especially in *The Water of the Wondrous Isles*, he prefers to depict interpersonal relationships that are much more complex than is the norm in medieval narratives, even in Malory's *Morte D'Arthur*. How he sifts through medieval romance is discussed below (see pp. 28-31).

It is, moreover, the thesis of this Introduction that the events of Morris's life and the enthusiasms he had for things as disparate as art and politics emerge in his late prose romances in perhaps odd but still recognizable ways. As a professional artist and designer, he had a highly developed sense of the visual, particularly color, and in consequence he often writes scenes with a painterly eye. His own marital troubles loom transformed but nevertheless large in the opening chapters of *The Wood Beyond the World*. He began writing his late prose romances at the height of his commitment to revolutionary socialism (see Appendix B), and in them we can perceive ways in which he theorizes about society and its effect on the individual that were perhaps not appropriate for a socialist podium or in the pages of *Commonweal*, the socialist periodical he helped found. Consequently, this Introduction looks briefly at the events of his life.

Morris's Life

William Morris, the first of nine children, was born on 24 March 1834 at Elm House, Walthamstow, Essex.[1] His father was a partner in a bill-brokering financial firm in London who subsequently invested in a lucrative copper-mining business in Devonshire. In 1840 the Morris family moved to what we would now call an upscale estate—Woodford Hall, near Epping Forest, also in Essex. The move not only heralded the family's increasing wealth, but it also gave the young Morris access to the forest as a playground. This fostered in him a love of nature and also provided him a space in which to reenact in play scenes from Sir Walter Scott's medievalistic novels, which he began reading at an early age. Victorian Britain was all a-flutter with the Middle Ages. Gothic Revival architecture was beginning to flourish, and the Oxford Movement in theology was turning religious sensibilities in a medieval direction. Scott whetted the appetites of the mostly middle-class reading public for narratives evocative of the Middle Ages. In 1842 Morris's father, William Sr., took him on a visit to Canterbury Cathedral, where he was exposed for the first time to medieval art. It is a good guess that his lifelong devotion to visual art, particularly that of the Middle Ages or influenced by that era, began at this point.

Morris's idyllic childhood was disrupted in 1847, when his father died at age 50. The death, which happened at a time of economic recession, adversely impacted the family's finances, though they did remain quite wealthy. There were soon rumors of other problems. In 1848, when Morris was 14 years old, there was widespread revolutionary unrest and rioting throughout the

1 The standard biography of William Morris is Fiona MacCarthy, *William Morris: A Life for Our Time* (London: Faber and Faber, 1994). There were two notable early biographies of Morris: Aymer Vallance, *The Life and Work of William Morris* (London: George Bell and Sons, 1897); and J.W. Mackail, *The Life of William Morris* (London: Longmans, Green and Company, 1899). This last was in a sense the "authorized" biography, for Mackail was a son-in-law of Edward and Georgiana Burne-Jones, Morris's closet friends. A full and very helpful chronology of the significant events of Morris's life is Nicholas Salmon with Derek Baker, *The William Morris Chronology* (Bristol: Thoemmes Press, 1997). The following sketch of Morris's Life is indebted to these works. For an online chronology of Morris's life, see Robert Boenig, "William Morris Lifeline," <http://www.litencyc.com/php/newlifeline.php?id_author_0=3210>.

Continent. Though Britain was mostly spared and order was soon restored, the troubles of 1848 left Europe looking for political change. This was the year that Karl Marx's *Communist Manifesto* was published (see Appendix C1), and that book sowed the seeds of the socialism that figured so very prominently in Morris's later life.

1848 was also the year of two significant events in Morris's personal life. In September his family moved to Water House, a home smaller than Woodford Hall, situated in the same town of Walthamstow. The move was made in response to their new financial circumstances. Water House was a home suitable enough for a well-off family, though not as grand as what they had grown accustomed to. More important, in February of that year Morris matriculated at Marlborough College. Morris's time at Marlborough was not a happy one, due largely to the school's mismanagement. While there he was only an average student but enjoyed the proximity to the mysterious Neolithic sites of Avebury and Silbury Hill, strong stimuli to his imagination. Morris's later critique of the British educational system dates from his uncomfortable years at Marlborough.

Also in 1848, a group of young painters, including Dante Gabriel Rossetti, John Millais, and William Holman Hunt, founded what they termed the Pre-Raphaelite Brotherhood.[1] Its aim was to change the course of British painting by rejecting the formal conventions of the established artists of the previous generation and by emphasizing precise representation and narrative themes drawn from literature, particularly that of the Middle Ages. About a decade later Morris would become close friends with Rossetti and launch a career in the visual arts whose foundations were the principles of the Pre-Raphaelites.

On 17 March 1849 Morris was confirmed by the Bishop of Salisbury into full membership in the Church of England. Early in his life he was devout, with doctrinal leanings towards the neo-medieval church of the Oxford Movement. In fact, during his undergraduate years he originally intended to be ordained and pursue a clerical career, but his faith quickly enough waned—though his love for church architecture and its decorative arts like stained glass and embroidery never did. For most of his life he professed no belief in organized religion, that is, until in the early

---

1 For a history of the artistic movement they founded, see Timothy Hilton, *The Pre-Raphaelites* (London: Thames and Hudson, 1970).

1880s he converted to socialism[1] and devoutly followed it as a surrogate religion.

In 1851 the so-called Great Exhibition was mounted in Hyde Park in London. It was housed in a structure that came to be called the Crystal Palace, and its purpose was to showcase British trade and industry. Morris attended but then refused to enter the building, for he was appalled by what he perceived as the shabby tastelessness of British art. From this point on, he associated modern culture with everything cheap, tawdry, and oppressive, often remarking that he was born in the wrong age. The Middle Ages that he constructed in his imagination, one democratic and filled with people doing honest work,[2] and his later fabrication of a future socialist society, expressed so eloquently in his utopian novel *News from Nowhere* (1890), suited him better than the crass capitalistic Victorian age.

In the late autumn of 1851, not long after his disappointment at the Crystal Palace, a violent student rebellion that began on Guy Fawkes Day (5 November) severely disrupted the operation of Marlborough College. Morris's mother responded by withdrawing him from that school. Thereafter he was tutored privately in preparation for his matriculation at Oxford. On 2 June 1852 he took his entrance exams. Also taking exams that day was a thin and impoverished young man from Birmingham who was also considering a career in the Church, Ned Jones, who later would style himself Edward Burne-Jones.[3] The two became friends—a lifelong relationship that had significant consequences for the development of late Victorian art and literature. While at Oxford the two were greatly influenced by the writings of John Ruskin and developed a love for the Arthurian romances of Sir Thomas Malory. Together Morris and Burne-Jones drifted away from the Church towards a life devoted to art, particularly paint-

---

1 For a critical biography of Morris emphasizing his socialism, see E.P. Thompson, *William Morris: Romantic to Revolutionary* (Stanford, CA: Stanford UP, 1955). For a summary of Morris's engagement with the socialist cause, see the Introduction to Stephen Arata, ed., *News from Nowhere* (Peterborough, ON: Broadview Press, 2003), 11-44. For analyses of Morris's literary works in terms of socialism, see Florence S. Boos and Carole G. Silver, eds., *Socialism and the Literary Artistry of William Morris* (Columbia, MI: U of Missouri P, 1990).

2 See Lee Patterson, *Negotiating the Past: The Historical Understanding of Medieval Literature* (Madison, WI: U of Wisconsin P, 1987), 10.

3 For a biography of Burne-Jones, see Penelope Fitzgerald, *Edward Burne-Jones*, rev. ed. (Stroud: Sutton Publishing, 1997).

ing and architecture. At this time Morris began writing poetry, mostly based on Arthurian romance and the *Chronicles* of the late fourteenth-century courtier Jean Froissart.

1855 was an eventful year for Morris. When he turned 21 in March, he received control of his inherited share of his father's copper-mine investments. This made him independently wealthy. Though years later the shares would devalue substantially, by that time he had established his lucrative business as a decorator. Morris remained quite well-off for his entire life. In June 1855 Morris and Burne-Jones viewed a number of early Pre-Raphaelite paintings at the Royal Academy in London and were impressed by them, and during July and August the two friends traveled to northern France to see some of that region's famous Gothic cathedrals. It was during this trip that Morris and Burne-Jones together decided to give up their plans for careers in the Church in favor of ones devoted to the visual arts—Burne-Jones in painting and Morris in architecture. In October Morris took a pass degree at Oxford.

In January of the next year the first issue of the short-lived *Oxford and Cambridge Magazine* was published. Morris and a number of his college friends had been planning the magazine for several months. Morris was its first editor and its chief financial backer, and he was also a frequent contributor; his tale, "The Story of the Unknown Church," and a poem, "Winter Weather," appeared in the first issue. The magazine ceased publication after only 12 monthly issues, but it was the venue in which Morris launched his literary career.

Also in January 1856 Morris was articled to G.E. Street's Oxford architectural firm. He joined this office to learn the trade of architecture with the intent of one day setting up on his own. Street was a prominent architect who specialized in Gothic Revival buildings, particularly churches. While working for Street, Morris met Philip Webb, then a member of Street's firm and later a famous architect in his own right. Webb became Morris's lifelong friend and, with Burne-Jones, one of his most significant artistic collaborators. In July 1856 Morris met Rossetti. The meeting was arranged by Burne-Jones, who had met Rossetti shortly after he moved from Oxford to London to begin his career as a painter. Rossetti encouraged Morris to try his hand at painting as well, and Morris accordingly left Street's firm, since he had been dissatisfied with some of the drudgery associated with working in an architectural office. At the urging of Rossetti, Morris and Burne-Jones moved into rooms at 17 Red

Lion Square, Bloomsbury, London, where they set up a joint studio, with Morris commissioning for it furniture designed by himself in the medieval style. As this early design work indicates, Morris never focused solely on painting.[1] He quickly began experimenting as well with textile designs, initially patterning his work after medieval originals. Sometime in 1857 he produced his "Bird and Tree" and "If I Can" embroideries; they mark his first efforts at textile production and pattern designing.

In July 1857 Morris and Burne-Jones temporarily returned to Oxford to help Rossetti paint murals for the Oxford Union. Rossetti gathered a number of his friends for this project, which occupied the rest of the summer and lingered into the following few months. They painted frescoes based on Malory's Arthurian tales in the bays among the Oxford Union's upper windows; Morris's bay had as its subject the love triangle between Tristan, Iseut, and Palomydes. Morris finished his fresco first and then devoted his time to producing patterned decoration for the Union's ceiling. Rossetti himself abandoned the project in November because of the illness of Lizzie Siddal, his fiancée, but work was continued until the following March, though the project was never completed. For a number of reasons, the frescoes quickly deteriorated; the artists' ignorance about how to prepare the surface to receive the paint was the main culprit. In the 1870s Morris directed his artistic firm, Morris and Company, to restore the work.

While Morris was at work on the Oxford Union he met Algernon Swinburne, who became an early admirer of Morris's poetry and for a number of years was often in the circle of Morris's friends. But more importantly, it was at this time that he also met his future wife. Rossetti had convinced Jane Burden, a teen-aged

---

1 For assessments of Morris as a visual artist, see Linda Parry, *William Morris Textiles* (New York: Crescent Books, 1983); Elizabeth Wilhide, *William Morris: Decor and Design* (New York: Abrams Publishers, 1991); Ray Watkinson, *William Morris as Designer* (London: Trefoil Publications, 1990); and two books edited by Linda Parry with various contributors, *William Morris: Art and Kelmscott* (Woodbridge: Boydell and Brewer, 1996) and *William Morris* (New York: Abrams Publishers, 1996). For the related impact Morris had on British domestic gardening, see Jill, Duchess of Hamilton, Penny Hart, and John Simmons, *The Gardens of William Morris* (New York: Stewart, Tabori, and Chang, 1999). For the interplay between gardening and the floral designs of Morris, see Derek Baker, *The Flowers of William Morris* (Chicago: Chicago Review Press, 1996).

daughter of a working-class Oxford man who looked after stabled horses, to sit for him as a model. Morris soon met her, fell in love with her, and began courting her and also using her as a model. She later admitted that she had never loved Morris, agreeing to his proposal of marriage for economic reasons. They became engaged in February 1858, and on 26 April 1859 they married. Their marriage was a notoriously unhappy one, largely due to Rossetti, for Morris's wife and friend began a long-lasting affair sometime in the 1860s. The marriage took place at St. Michael's Church, Oxford and was performed by R.W. Dixon, a young Anglican priest and an undergraduate friend of Morris. Canon Dixon became a poet in his own right, later befriending Gerard Manley Hopkins.

In February 1858, the same month of his engagement, Morris issued through the publishers Bell and Daldy *The Defence of Guenevere and Other Poems*. This was his first book and also the first book of poems published by any of the Pre-Raphaelite poets. It contains 30 poems, most narrative in nature and some heavily influenced by Robert Browning. The book received little critical acclaim at the time, and this contributed to Morris largely abandoning for a number of years his efforts at writing poetry.

In June 1860 Morris moved to Red House in Bexleyheath, near London. For the year since they were married, the Morrises had lived at 41 Ormond Street, London. During this time contractors were building Red House, the home Philip Webb designed for him. Named after the bright red color of its brick walls, the house was loosely patterned after thirteenth-century buildings. Morris's two daughters, Jenny and May, were born there.

Over the next couple of years Morris and his artistic friends did much to decorate Red House with paintings, embroideries, and furniture designed in a neo-medieval style. It was so innovative in its departures from the prevailing Victorian norm that it helped to set a new direction in British domestic architecture. The design work done there so animated Morris and his friends that they decided to make a living out of it, and on 25 March 1861, Morris, Marshall, Faulkner, and Company commenced business. Familiarly known as "the Firm," Morris's company specialized in home and church decoration. It originally had seven partners—Morris, Burne-Jones, Rossetti, the painters Ford Madox Brown and Arthur Hughes (who soon withdrew), and two of Morris's friends who had the ability to handle the business end, Peter Paul Marshall and the Oxford mathematician Charles

Faulkner. The purpose of the Firm was not only to make a profit but also to change Britain's artistic tastes.

The first workshops were in London at 8 Red Lion Square. In 1862 the Firm took two stands at the International Exhibition at South Kensington Museum (now the Victoria and Albert Museum), one for stained glass and the other for embroidery and painted furniture, and both won medals. The Exhibition in effect launched the Firm's considerable financial success. Morris restlessly pursued one craft after another throughout his life, often reviving older, sometimes lost ways of production. Wallpaper design rivaled stained glass and textile production as the Firm's major producer of income. Morris's first wallpaper design, *Trellis*, was produced in November 1862; its birds were designed by Webb, though Morris did the background. This is one example of many of how Morris preferred cooperative rather than individualistic design.

In November 1865 Morris suddenly abandoned his beloved Red House and moved to London. The abandonment was the result of a number of circumstances: the necessity for him to be in London close to his business, Burne-Jones's refusal of an offer to move with his growing family into a proposed new wing of Red House, and possibly the beginnings of the affair between Jane Morris and Rossetti. The Morrises moved into rooms in 26 Queen Square, Bloomsbury, London, the building that then housed the operations of the Firm. Among its early commissions was one received in September 1866 to decorate the Armoury and Tapestry Room at St. James's Palace. That the royal family would thus commission the Firm to design these two prominent rooms is an indication of Morris's growing reputation as a designer. Other important commissions were for the Green Dining Room at the South Kensington Museum and Jesus College Chapel, Cambridge.

In August 1866 Morris and Burne-Jones drew up plans for illustrations of what would be a massive new poem of Morris's creation, *The Earthly Paradise*.[1] The edition was originally meant to contain woodcut illustrations by Burne-Jones. Though the illustrated edition never came to fruition, the composition of the poem occupied Morris over the next four years. It is a long "framework" collection of 24 individual narratives partially patterned after Geoffrey Chaucer's *Canterbury Tales* and intended as

---

1 For an analysis of this proposed book, including reproductions of the surviving illustrations, see Joseph R. Dunlap, *The Book that Never Was* (New York: Oriole Editions, 1971).

homage to that greatest of all English medieval poets. Published in several volumes, *The Earthly Paradise* secured Morris's reputation among his contemporaries as an important poet. In May 1867, though, preceding the publication of its first volume, Bell and Daldy at Morris's expense published his *The Life and Death of Jason*, a long narrative of the classical myth of Jason and the Argonauts. It was originally intended as a section of *The Earthly Paradise*, but it was too long and thus had to be published separately. Among its favorable reviewers over the next several months were Swinburne, the American scholar Charles Eliot Norton, and Henry James. Browning wrote Morris to commend his work. The success of *The Life and Death of Jason* paved the way for the greater success of *The Earthly Paradise*.[1]

In August 1868 Morris met the Icelander Eírikr Magnússon, who began to tutor Morris in Icelandic, a modern language that had changed little from its origins in the Middle Ages as a dialect of Old Norse. The medieval sagas of Iceland interested Morris greatly, so in collaboration with Magnússon he began translating a number of them. Morris's method of translation was to have Magnússon prepare a literal prose translation which Morris would then mold into an artistic translation. (Morris would use this same method near the end of his life when with the Anglo-Saxonist A.J. Wyatt he translated the early English epic *Beowulf* [see Appendix A1].)[2] The resulting translations of Old Icelandic sagas were the first ever published in English; the most important were *Grettis Saga* (1869) and *The Volsunga Saga* (1870), which he later reworked into a long poem, *The Story of Sigurd the Volsung and the Fall of the Niblungs*, published in 1876 (see Appendix A2). In these works Morris first employed the archaizing prose style so evident in *The Wood Beyond the World*, one in which he incorporated medieval vocabulary and occasional grammatical inversions. The German composer Richard Wagner, a contemporary of Morris, was also attracted to the story of the Volsungs and Niblungs, for about this time he was crafting the Old Icelandic story into his famous series of operas, *The Ring Cycle*. Iceland

---

1 For analysis of *The Earthly Paradise*, see Blue Calhoun, *The Pastoral Vision of William Morris: The Earthly Paradise* (Athens, GA: U of Georgia P, 1975); for the centrality of the theme of the Earthly Paradise for Morris's work as a whole, see Roderick Marshall, *William Morris and his Earthly Paradises* (New York: George Braziller, 1979).

2 For an analysis of Morris's translation of *Beowulf*, see Robert Boenig, "The Importance of Morris's *Beowulf*," *The Journal of the William Morris Society* 12.2 (1997): 7-13.

itself also captured Morris's interest, and he made two trips there with Magnússon and some others in the early 1870s. Its landscape figures prominently in several of his late prose romances, notably in *The Glittering Plain* and *The Well at the World's End*.

Like 1855, 1871 was an eventful year for Morris. In March there was a short-lived socialist revolution in France, known to historians as the Paris Commune. Morris's sympathy with the cause of the rebels eventually facilitated his conversion to socialism. More important, though, was his personal turmoil. The affair between Jane Morris and Rossetti had become so blatant that to remove it from public view Morris agreed to take a joint lease with Rossetti on a home away from London so the lovers could spend time there in seclusion. This arrangement was in effect a capitulation, an emotional distancing of himself from the situation. Morris and Rossetti settled on terms for a joint tenancy of Kelmscott Manor on the upper reaches of the River Thames, a beautiful building fashioned in the sixteenth century and added to in the seventeenth. It survived its early association with the love affair to become Morris's most beloved home, a substitute for the lost Red House. After Jane Morris and Rossetti established themselves there, Morris left the field, as it were, and went off on the first of his journeys to Iceland. He, Magnússon, Faulkner, and an acquaintance named W.H. Evans traveled about the wilds of that starkly beautiful country on horseback to visit places mentioned in the Icelandic sagas. Morris kept a journal full of vivid descriptions of the countryside and his experiences there, and eventually it was published as part of his *Collected Works*.

After his second trip to Iceland, which took place in the summer of 1873, Morris returned home with a sense of resolve. He forced Rossetti out of his share of the lease on Kelmscott Manor and then reorganized the business terms of the Firm, again forcing Rossetti out, together with a number of partners and associates who had not been carrying their weight. The Firm was reconstituted as Morris and Company. The new set-up was not only advantageous to Morris financially, but it also offered him increased artistic freedom. He began experimenting in organic methods of dyeing and weaving, initiated a line of carpets, and increased the Company's output in wallpaper. This all signaled a shift away from the ecclesiastic to the domestic. For a long time Morris had been disturbed about the damage to old churches that were undergoing renovation, and in 1877 he founded the Society for the Protection of Ancient Buildings and even began refusing commissions to restore old churches. At about this time he also took an interest in politics, joining a liberal protest against a Tory-backed intervention in a conflict between the Turks and the Russians. He soon became disillusioned with left-leaning politics and began moving towards political radicalism.

In the summer of 1878 Morris took a lease on a new London home, a house in Hammersmith on the banks of the Thames known as "The Retreat." He took over this lease from George MacDonald, the novelist and fairy tale writer, renaming the building Kelmscott House in honor of his country home, Kelmscott Manor. Kelmscott House became Morris's main home for the rest of his life. In the early 1880s he made two river journeys with his family and friends from Kelmscott House to Kelmscott Manor, later fictionalizing such a journey in his 1890 socialist Utopian novel, *News from Nowhere*.

In 1882 Rossetti died. He had been in decline both physically and mentally, largely due to his addiction to chloral, a drug used to induce sleep. His affair with Jane Morris had long since ended, in partial response to his substance abuse. Morris had overcome the emotional turmoil of the affair, and, aided by his friendship with Burne-Jones's wife Georgiana, who became his confidant, he reached some measure of personal peace. He consequently evolved a strong friendship with his unfaithful wife based on family concerns, especially Jenny Morris's debilitating epilepsy and the stormy personal life of May Morris, whose relationship with George Bernard Shaw in time disrupted her own marriage.

At this time socialism became Morris's main preoccupation. Early in 1883 he joined H.M. Hyndman's Democratic Foundation, and in the spring of that year he first read Karl Marx's *Das Kapital* in a French translation. In the summer he began hosting socialist meetings in the carriage house at Kelmscott House, and such meetings became regular features of life there. It became the custom to gather on Sunday mornings; among the many who attended were Shaw, Oscar Wilde, H.G. Wells, the composer Gustav Holst, and W.B. Yeats, whose sister Lily was employed in the embroidery section of Morris and Company. After his declaration of socialism, Morris began to give frequent lectures in support of the cause, some of which, like a socialist demonstration in Hyde Park in July 1884 and the famous "Bloody Sunday" demonstration at Trafalgar Square on 13 November 1887, turned violent. On 21 September 1885 Morris was arrested for assaulting a policeman. The altercation happened at Arbour Square

Police Court, where he was attending a legal proceeding involving a number of his socialist colleagues, and there was some scuffling, leading to Morris's arrest. He was eventually acquitted, probably in deference to his class and fame as a poet and visual artist.

In the mid-1880s Morris began to write socialist propaganda and also serious works that offered a socialist message. In consequence he gave over much of his artistic work for Morris and Company to colleagues and assistants, notably his daughter May, who was a formidable artist in her own right specializing in embroidery, and also J.H. Dearle, a younger man whom Morris had trained in pattern design. A few famous pattern designs long attributed to Morris were actually done by others—the second *Honeysuckle*, designed by May Morris, and both *Iris* and *Compton*, designed by Dearle. Morris was busy editing, funding, and contributing to the socialist periodical *Commonweal*. His serious literary production for the socialist cause includes *A Dream of John Ball* (1887), a narrative of the medieval Peasants' Revolt, and the enormously influential *News from Nowhere*, which depicts his version of a peaceful socialist future.

It is unclear when Morris's health began to fail, but by the early 1890s he was curtailing some of his socialist activities. It is also unclear what ailed him, though diabetes combined with cardiac problems is possible if not certain. Though increasing ill-health is doubtless the main cause of his retreat from socialist committees and podiums, the bickering factions and irreconcilable differences among his socialist colleagues were likely causes as well. The last eight years of his life, though, were by no means a time of total withdrawal and rest. He summoned up a last, huge burst of creative energy and devoted himself to two separate but related projects.

The first was the establishment of the Kelmscott Press, which pioneered the artistic hand-printing that so characterized the Arts and Crafts Movement of the first half of the twentieth century.[1] Under Morris's direction and with his design work on typefaces, capital letters, page layout, and borders, the Kelmscott Press produced in the 1890s a remarkable run of very beautiful

---

1 For a history of the Kelmscott Press, see William S. Peterson, *The Kelmscott Press: A History of William Morris's Typographical Adventure* (Oxford: Clarendon Press, 1991). For an early assessment of Morris's achievement as a printer, see H. Halliday Sparling, *The Kelmscott Press and William Morris, Master Craftsman* (London: Macmillan, 1924). Sparling was Morris's son-in-law.

books. Burne-Jones, together with others such as Walter Crane, often provided designs for woodcut illustrations. The greatest masterpiece among many was *The Kelmscott Chaucer*, a decorated edition of the complete works of that great medieval poet.[1] Published in 1896, the year of Morris's death, it has sometimes been termed the most beautiful of all printed books.

The second project was the remarkable series of eight prose romances that in effect invented the genre of the modern fantasy novel. They were all published by the Kelmscott Press (though the first three were first published by Reeves and Turner). In order of composition, they are *The House of the Wolfings*, *The Roots of the Mountains*, *The Story of the Glittering Plain* (the first Kelmscott book), *The Wood Beyond the World*, *Child Christopher and Goldilind the Fair*, *The Well at the World's End*, *The Water of the Wondrous Isles*, and *The Sundering Flood*. The last two were published posthumously. Morris was working on the last chapters of *The Sundering Flood* on his deathbed, too weak to write them out in his own hand, and so dictating them to Sydney Cockerell, his secretary, who subsequently became Director of the Fitzwilliam Museum, Cambridge. Morris died on 3 October 1896 and was buried three days later in the yard of St. George's Church, Kelmscott, the location of the concluding scene of *News from Nowhere*.

Morris's Prose Style

In his 1640 *Timber, or Discoveries*, Ben Jonson took issue with the archaic, medievalized language of *The Faerie Queene*, writing his famous half-sentence put-down, "Spenser, in affecting the ancients, writ no language...." From at least that year, many have rejected the conscious evocation of the past in one's prose style as awkward, escapist, or silly. Morris did not. Early on in his career he began crafting a style that was meant to evoke that of the Middle Ages, though he would not use it for everything he wrote. We detect some archaic words in his earliest volume of poetry, *The Defence of Guenevere and Other Poems*, which he published in 1858, when he was in his mid-twenties. The archaism deepens in his multi-volume *The Earthly Paradise* of the late 1860s and early 1870s, and he perfects it for his translations from the Old Norse

1 For the achievement of *The Kelmscott Chaucer*, see Duncan Robinson, *William Morris, Edward Burne-Jones, and* The Kelmscott Chaucer (London: Gordon Fraser, 1982); and Fridolf Johnson, *William Morris: Ornamentation and Illustrations from* The Kelmscott Chaucer (New York: Dover Publications, 1973).

Edward Burne-Jones and William Morris at the time of their initial collaboration on the Kelmscott Press. Photograph taken on 27 July 1890 by Frederick Hollyer; Hulton Archives/Getty Images.

sagas he produced with the help of Eírikr Magnússon shortly after that. The style is very much in evidence in *The Wood Beyond the World* and his other late prose romances.

This archaic style is characterized by several things. First, there is the seemingly frequent use of obsolete words drawn from late medieval literary English stock, particularly that of Sir Thomas Malory, whom Morris in part imitates. (How close an imitation may be gauged by reading the selections from Malory included in Appendix A3.) Second is Morris's preference for modern words of Anglo-Saxon origin that are monosyllabic rather than Latinate and polysyllabic. Third is his frequent rejection of Modern English idiom, and fourth is his tendency on occasion to use non-standard word order, particularly in inverting normal subject-verb syntax. Here is a short passage from *The Wood Beyond the World* in which we see Morris doing all these things. At the beginning of the book its hero Walter tells his father of his desire to go on a journey so he can escape his failed marriage to an unfaithful wife:

> So on a day as he sat with his father alone, he spake to him and said: "Father, I was on the quays even now, and I looked on the ships that were nigh boun, and thy sign I saw on a tall ship that seemed to me nighest boun. Will it be long ere she sail?"
>
> "Nay," said his father, "that ship, which hight the Katherine, will they warp out of the haven in two days' time. But why askest thou of her?" (p. 48)

The archaic words are easy to spot. The obsolete second-person pronoun "thou" with its grammatical requirement of a verb ending in –est is there, as is the old allomorph for "spoke"—"spake." "Nigh," still marginally attested in Modern English as a synonym for "near" or "nearly," together with "boun" ("prepared"), "ere" ("before"), "hight" ("named"), and "warp" ("haul") give ample evidence that this is not a conversation a late nineteenth-century (or early twenty-first-century) son would have with his father. The prevalence of monosyllables is evident throughout the passage. "On a day" is not in accord with Modern English idiom. Neither are the phrase "even now" or the subjunctive mood of the verb in "ere she sail." "But why askest thou of her" and "will they warp" invert the normal order of subject and verb.

Much more significant than this list of the passage's archaisms is the fact that almost none of them hinder immediate understanding of what is being said, even for those with no exposure to late medieval English. The use of the "thou" family of pronouns in older translations of the Bible and in some religious contexts (where "spake" is also well attested) helps. Inversion of subject and verb usually causes no difficulty in comprehension. "On a day," though not idiomatic to us, is close enough to "one day," as is "even now" to "just now." Perhaps most helpful is Morris's use of archaic vocabulary in contexts where it is almost always self-defining. "Boun" clearly means something like "ready" or "loaded," while both "ere" and "hight" can mean nothing else than "before" and "named." The only potentially troublesome word is "warp," particularly for generations who have grown accustomed to its use in science fiction ("warp-speed"). "Warp" is a particular nautical term meaning "to haul with a rope." Ropes are constructed of twisted fibers, and the Old English verb *wearpan* means "to twist, to turn," as the Modern English participle "warped" ("distorted") means "twisted." In nautical jargon "warp" actually refers to the rope itself, but in old English it was employed verbally when a boat was being hauled by a rope. Though we do not, we could say, "They will rope it out of the harbor." But that said, Morris's context makes clear the general idea if not its specifics: the ship will soon be moving out of the harbor.

In spite of the presence of these archaic words, a statistical analysis of this or any passage in Morris's prose romances would indicate a surprisingly low percentage of them. Morris uses archaic words sparingly, less than one thinks, but they stand out because of their strangeness. In the passage's first sentence, for instance, there is only one ("spake"), while the second has just two ("nigh boun" and the phrase's superlative).

The artistic effect of the archaizing becomes evident if we remove it. Here is the passage rewritten into perfectly modern, perfectly idiomatic English:

> So one day as he sat with his father alone, he said to him, "Father, I was on the docks just now, and I looked at the ships that were nearly loaded, and I saw your sign on a tall ship that I saw almost ready to go. Will it leave soon?"
>
> "No," his father said, "that ship, which is called the Katherine, will leave the harbor in two days. But why do you want to know?"

My version is pedestrian, and were I the author of a book full of such dialogue, I would not blame you for leaving it unread.

Morris's game is to evoke a longing for the past, and though his style is not his sole means of doing so, it helps.

Morris's style can be taken to extremes, however. Here is a passage from the translation of *Beowulf* that he made with the help of the Cambridge Anglo-Saxonist A.J. Wyatt (see Appendix A1) at approximately the same time he wrote *The Wood Beyond the World*:

> By Finn's sons aforetime, when the fear gat them,
> The hero of Half-Danes, Hnæf of the Scyldings,
> On the slaughter-field Frisian needs must he fall.
> Forsooth never Hildeburh needed to hery
> The troth of the Eotens; she all unsinning
> Was lorne of her lief ones in that play of the linden,
> Her bairns and her brethren, by fate there they fell
> Spear-wounded. That was the all-woeful of women.

Morris's *Beowulf* is in many ways a very remarkable achievement, for he manages to translate each line with surprising accuracy and with some rhythmical and alliterative success. But the percentage of archaic words is far too high, and, most importantly, the context often fails in making them self-defining. Morris's methods of translating likely caused this. He would collaborate with people more adept at the original languages than he (Wyatt for *Beowulf* and Eírikr Magnússon for Old Norse works), and they would provide him with a literal prose translation, which he would then work up into literary, archaic English. For his *Beowulf*, he was likely seduced by the strange and beautiful language of the original into using too many Anglo-Saxon words only lightly modernized. Cut off from a seductive original while he crafted *The Wood Beyond the World*, he exercised the restraint necessary for successful archaizing. As with the use of habanero sauce in cooking a Mexican meal, less is more.

One must, of course, realize that Morris's archaic style is part of an aesthetic experience larger than just that of the style alone. The story of *The Wood Beyond the World* evokes a world not dissimilar to that of the Middle Ages. The Kelmscott Press edition of the book, moreover, is a magnificent work of visual art that is meant to evoke an ornamented medieval manuscript. There are elaborate floral borders and capital letters designed by Morris, along with a beautiful frontispiece done by Edward Burne-Jones in which the Maid walks through a field of flowers; its many flowers evoke late medieval *millefleur* tapestry similar to those that

Morris and Burne-Jones designed. Each of the components evokes the medieval, and when they are combined their synergy is remarkable. In the end, enjoying Morris's archaic style is perhaps a matter of taste, but for those not predisposed against it, it offers something very rich and sweet.[1]

The Wood Beyond the World and Medieval Narrative

As a student in the 1850s at Exeter College, Oxford, Morris, like so many educated young men of his generation, was swept away by all things medieval, particularly Arthurian romance. The stories of King Arthur and his knights contributed to an ideology shared among the group of university friends that gathered around the charismatic Morris. After graduation, the group expanded to include the painter Rossetti and other Pre-Raphaelites. While at Oxford, Morris, Burne-Jones, and some of their other friends had considered founding a semi-monastic, semi-chivalric religious order, and many of Morris's early poems, written while he was an undergraduate, were based on Malory's *Morte D'Arthur*. Notable among them is the title poem to Morris's *The Defence of Guenevere and Other Poems*. In it Guenevere poses as a Pre-Raphaelite model and descants on the complexities of love and betrayal. Shortly after graduation, as mentioned earlier, Morris and Burne-Jones joined Rossetti and others in collaborating on painting frescoes in the bays between the upper windows of the Oxford Union; the frescoes were based on stories from Malory. The bay assigned to Morris took as its subject the lament of Sir Palomydes over his unrequited love for Iseut, whose adulterous passion is directed at Tristan rather than himself. After his marriage, Morris collaborated with some of his artistic friends in decorating his newly built home, Red House, with depictions in various media of scenes drawn from medieval narrative, including Malory's great work.

The second half of the nineteenth century was the first golden age of the widespread dissemination of medieval texts. The thirteenth-century English poem *Havelok the Dane* (edited by Fredrick Madden and published by the Roxburghe Club in 1828 and reedited by W.W. Skeat for the Early English Text Society in 1868) became the source for Morris's *Child Christopher and*

1 For a defense of Morris's archaizing style, see C.S. Lewis, "William Morris," in *C.S. Lewis: Selected Literary Essays*, ed. Walter Hooper (Cambridge: Cambridge UP, 1969), 220-21.

Goldilind the Fair. The newly founded Early English Text Society began its still flourishing run of editions of medieval and early modern texts; its earlier numbers customarily included brief marginal summaries of plot to help readers cope with the often difficult language. Morris imitates this practice in a number of his works, including *The Wood Beyond the World*. This period also saw the publication of the first great modern edition of Chaucer—Skeat's multi-volume work—one which heavily influenced Morris in the production of his great artistic masterpiece, *The Kelmscott Chaucer*. Morris relied on original manuscripts as well as editions. As a wealthy man, he purchased a fairly large number of them, though he sold a portion of his collection to support socialist causes. The British Museum, not yet separate from the British Library, occasionally called him in as a consultant to date medieval manuscripts it had acquired.

Though he wrote other things, the retelling of medieval narrative was for Morris a dominant mode of literary composition. Individual poems in *The Defence of Guenevere and Other Poems* retell portions of Malory and also Jean Froissart's late fourteenth-century *Chronicles*. The framework of Morris's *The Earthly Paradise* imitates that of Chaucer's *Canterbury Tales*, while half of its 24 tales are retellings of various medieval stories. As we have seen, he translated a number of Old Norse sagas with Eírikr Magnússon and later worked up his own poetic version of *The Story of the Volsungs and the Fall of the Niblungs* as *Sigurd the Volsung* (see Appendix A2). With A.J. Wyatt he translated *Beowulf* (see Appendix A1).

With the exception of *Child Christopher and Goldilind the Fair*, Morris's late prose romances are not direct retellings of medieval narratives, although they evoke the Middle Ages in different ways. One could argue that *The House of the Wolfings* depicts a pre-medieval era, for it recounts a war between the Goths and an invading Roman army. Though its setting is the first century BCE, we never get close enough to the Romans to see their civilization; the action is mediated through the point of view of the Goths, whose civilization is the heroic one familiar to students of the early Middle Ages. *The Roots of the Mountains* depicts the struggles the Goths have in a later generation against invading Huns. *The Story of the Glittering Plain* evokes a medieval Norse tribal society, while *The Sundering Flood* recreates the culture of their descendants, the agrarian Icelanders in the later Middle Ages. In *The Water of the Wondrous Isles* Morris reformulates the chivalric and courtly culture of the High Middle Ages, while the longest of his prose romances, *The Well at the World's End*, evokes a later medieval culture where merchants vie in importance with knights.

The Wood Beyond the World presents a mix similar to that of *The Well at the World's End*. Its hero Walter is the son of a rich merchant, and his quest begins on a voyage of a merchant ship, the *Katherine*. By the end of the book, he has become the king of a chivalric society. Along the way Morris employs many of the themes we customarily encounter in medieval romance—the quest, the surpassing beauty of hero and heroine, the vague and therefore mysterious geography, and the use of the marvelous and the supernatural.

The medieval narrative elements that the book avoids, however, are even more significant that those it uses. There are no battles, and there is relatively little in the way of hand-to-hand combat except for Walter's conflict with an evil dwarf and a second-hand account of a bloody conflict that claims the life of his father after Walter's quest has begun. Medieval narratives typically invest heavily in violence, and so do Morris's other prose romances, where battles abound and individual fights sometimes occur. Pre-chivalric medieval narratives such as *Beowulf* and *The Song of Roland* are structured around battles and fights. Chivalric romances normally employ strings of individual jousts as knights wander through their quests. Walter's quest is largely an emotional rather than physical one, taking him from his failed marriage through temptation to emotional fulfillment. He has adversaries among the book's characters, but a case can be made that his real enemy is his misplaced desire. In other words, the things that happen in Walter's mind and also in the mind of the Maid are in some ways more important than the book's external events.

Morris seemed to gravitate towards the medieval narratives that were most complicated morally and emotionally. A reading of the "Finnsburg" section of *Beowulf* (Appendix A1), with its complicated web of loyalty and betrayal surrounding the dynastic marriage of its heroine Hildeburh, convinces us of the large moral ambiguities of the poem as a whole. Morris's assignment of the Oxford Union frescoes was Palomydes's lament (Appendix A3), which gives voice to his entanglement in one of the most famous and complex of medieval love stories. Guenevere's own defense in Morris's early poem opens a window to another famous medieval sexual tangle: that of Sigurd, Brynhild, Gudrun, and Gunnar—a narrative to which Morris was twice drawn, first for his translation of *The Story of the Volsungs and the Fall of the*

Niblungs and then for his poetic retelling of it in *Sigurd the Volsung* (Appendix A2). That Morris's own life had its moral and erotic complexities is worth remembering when we chart his engagement with medieval narrative and when we read *The Wood Beyond the World*.

The Wood Beyond the World and Visual Art

By the time he wrote *The Wood Beyond the World*, Morris had been a professional visual artist for over 30 years. He shared with his fellow Pre-Raphaelite artists an enthusiasm for literature and an impulse to set the one art in dialogue with the other. Several Pre-Raphaelite visual artists, most notably Morris and Rossetti, wrote poetry; Rossetti sometimes wrote poems to accompany his own paintings, and two poems that Morris included in *The Defence of Guenevere and Other Poems* are evocations of paintings by Rossetti, *The Blue Closet* and *The Tune of the Seven Towers*, that he himself had purchased from his friend. How visual a writer Morris could be when he deemed it appropriate is evident from the opening lines of "The Defence of Guenevere":

> But, knowing now that they would have her speak,
> She threw her wet hair backward from her brow,
> Her hand close to her mouth touching her cheek....

Guenevere is here carefully posed like a Pre-Raphaelite model.

Morris published this poem as a young man in 1858; 36 years later he was still capable of posing a character on a canvas as if for a Pre-Raphaelite painting. Here is the passage from Chapter X of *The Wood Beyond the World* where Walter first encounters the Maid in "real life" (he had already seen visions of her):

> After he had gone a while and whenas the summer morn was at its brightest, he saw a little way ahead a grey rock rising up from amidst of a ring of oak-trees; so he turned thither straightway; for in this plain land he had seen no rocks heretofore; and as he went he saw that there was a fountain gushing out from under the rock, which ran thence in a fair little stream. And when he had the rock and the fountain and the stream clear before him, lo! a child of Adam sitting beside the fountain under the shadow of the rock. He drew a little nigher, and then saw that it was a woman, clad in green like the sward whereon she lay. She was playing with the welling out of the

water, and she had trussed up her sleeves to the shoulder that she might thrust her bare arms therein. Her shoes of black leather lay on the grass beside her, and her feet and legs yet shone with the brook. (p. 78)

He first sets the overall level of light for this "painting," for he depicts a summer morning "at its brightest." We next get a landscape detail, "a grey rock rising up from amidst of a ring of oak-trees." Pre-Raphaelite painters were fond of focusing on seemingly inconsequential details, depicting them with meticulous detail. Our eye in this passage is captured by this rock, which has no particular significance for the story. We even see the spring ("fountain" in its pre-modern sense) that emits from it and the stream that this spring spawns. It is only after the setting has been sketched that we notice the painting's main subject, the Maid. She is partially in shadow, and after Morris shifts perspective somewhat as Walter draws near, we see that she is dressed in the same green color as the grass that surrounds her. We also see another seemingly inconsequential detail when we notice that her sleeves are rolled up and that she is playing with the stream of water. Her shoes, lying off to the side, are black, and her bare feet and legs glisten with water. Though some of these details can endure a symbolic reading (she is clad in green, appropriate for her later role as a nature goddess among the people of the Bears, for instance), it is the visual, pure and simple, that dominates. Morris at age 60 was still a Pre-Raphaelite artist. One can read *The Wood Beyond the World* as a gallery of his paintings.

The book itself as a physical object, at least in its Kelmscott Press edition, is also a work of art, though the first trade edition, published in 1895 by Lawrence and Bullen, is not. The 1895 edition was issued in plain maroon cloth boards with gilt lettering on the spine for its title and the author's name. Lawrence and Bullen used neither typeface that Morris himself designed, "Troy" and "Golden" ("Chaucer" is a reduced version of the black-letter "Troy"). The print is rather large and plain, and this edition lacks the marginal summaries that are found in the Kelmscott edition. The publishers used a small yet pleasant woodcut on the title page, one that had been designed some years earlier by Alfred Crowquill (a pseudonym for Alfred Henry Forrester), a Victorian illustrator who had died in 1872. The contrast with Morris's Kelmscott edition is great.

Kelmscott books were usually printed on high-quality rag paper, which resists decay and typically seems fresh and appears white today, over 110 years after the last of the press's books was printed. Runs usually included a number printed on vellum, many of which Morris gave as presentation copies to his friends. The run for *The Wood Beyond the World* totaled 350 paper copies and eight done on vellum. Kelmscott covers were normally of limp vellum with silk ties, a cover that Morris intended as temporary, assuming his clients would rebind the books at one of the high-end artistic binderies, such as the Doves Bindery. Most copies of the Kelmscott *The Wood Beyond the World* today retain the vellum binding.

For the text, Morris used his "Chaucer" typeface, the reduction of "Troy," which he designed to evoke the black-letter typefaces of the earliest printed books. The summaries in the upper margins of most pages are printed in red ink, as are the titles to chapters. Large Morris-designed wood-cut capital letters begin the chapters, while smaller ones often signal paragraph breaks. Other paragraphs have no breaks, just small decorative oak leaves placed within the text-block where a paragraph should begin. Morris omits quotation marks (as does the Lawrence and Bullen edition, though the edition included in *The Collected Works of William Morris,* edited almost 20 years after his death by his daughter May Morris, includes them). Chapters are moreover heralded by floral tendrils in the margins, also designed by Morris. The very elaborate opening page-spread has a full floral border for both sides. On the right page of the spread we find Morris's most elaborate capital letter (an "A") drifting down to the tenth line of text.

On the left side of the opening spread, Morris includes a woodcut designed by Burne-Jones that depicts the Maid. She is one of that artist's most graceful creations. She walks towards the right, that is, towards the text on the facing page, thus inviting us to begin reading. She walks, appropriately, through a wood. Bare branches stretch far in the background—a slight touch of the menace to be encountered in the Wood. But she walks barefoot (long abandoning her black shoes) through a delightful field of flowers and grasses that does much to mitigate this menace. The effect is not dissimilar to that found in late medieval millefleur ("thousand-flower") tapestries and in their masterful imitations, the neo-millefleur Morris and Company tapestries, such as *Pomona* and *Flora,* designed by Morris and Burne-Jones. Like all young women found in Pre-Raphaelite visual art, the Maid has a long neck and abundant hair. Her smock flows like a rich gown as she swings her arms, and her body imitates the S-curve that

Opening page spread of *The Wood Beyond the World* (Hammersmith: Kelmscott Pre
1894); editor's collection.

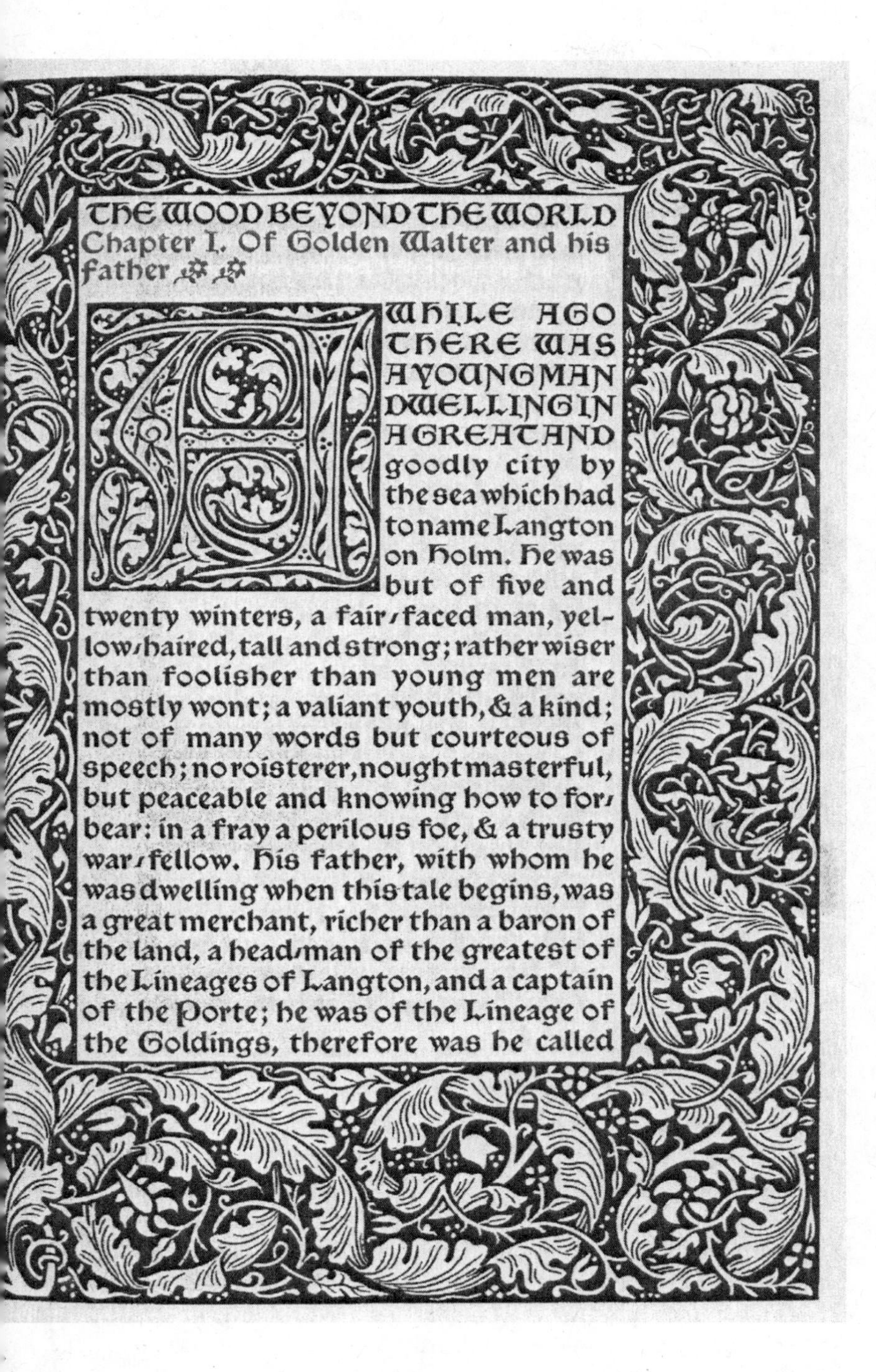
THE WOOD BEYOND THE WORLD

Chapter I. Of Golden Walter and his father

A WHILE AGO THERE WAS A YOUNG MAN DWELLING IN A GREAT AND goodly city by the sea which had to name Langton on Holm. He was but of five and twenty winters, a fair-faced man, yellow-haired, tall and strong; rather wiser than foolisher than young men are mostly wont; a valiant youth, & a kind; not of many words but courteous of speech; no roisterer, nought masterful, but peaceable and knowing how to forbear: in a fray a perilous foe, & a trusty war-fellow. His father, with whom he was dwelling when this tale begins, was a great merchant, richer than a baron of the land, a head-man of the greatest of the Lineages of Langton, and a captain of the Porte; he was of the Lineage of the Goldings, therefore was he called late medieval artists found so attractive. Her waist, bosom, and hair are adorned by the garlands of the flowers that she will animate and so impress the people of the Bears, who thus will deem her a goddess; the flowers are not withered but have already become fresh through her magic. Her face is serene with a very slight hint of the uncertainty she initially feels when she worries about Walter's love for her. She lacks the iron ankle ring that Morris provides for her as a sign of her servitude to the Lady, but sprigs of leaves play about her feet. The opening page-spread is inviting and visually most impressive, informing us that this book is a work of art as well as a compelling story.

The Wood Beyond the World and Socialism

Morris wrote *The Wood Beyond the World* shortly after his most active period of socialist commitment. He had thrown himself into an exhausting round of attending committee meetings and traveling to deliver socialist speeches, but by the early 1890s the factionalism of his socialist colleagues and his increasing ill-health had caused his partial withdrawal from these rigors. He nevertheless considered himself a socialist to the end of his life and occasionally made appearances at socialist affairs. Much of his writing leading up to *The Wood Beyond the World* is overtly socialist, particularly his two fictional arguments for the cause, *A Dream of John Ball* and his utopian masterpiece *News from Nowhere*. Many of those who read Morris primarily for his forceful presentation of socialist ideas sometimes find his late prose romances escapist, for their medievalesque world seems far distant from the pressing economic inequities that socialism would redress. But others find ways to invest them with socialist meaning, especially *The Wood Beyond the World*.

Perhaps the most compelling way to interpret the book in this way is by developing a socialist allegory. Walter must choose between the rich Lady and the Maid who serves her. The Lady, though beautiful and capable of inciting Walter's desire, is treacherous, deceitful, and evil. The Maid, though poor, offers him genuine love and is capable of leading him to freedom. To augment the allegory of the Lady as Capitalism and the Maid as Socialism, the evil dwarf can be seen as representing the vicious and morally stunted means by which Capitalism operates and the King's Son as a mirror for the complicity between the capitalists and the royalty of late nineteenth-century Europe. Morris was no fan of the British monarch, particularly after 1875, when Queen

Victoria set herself up in the tapestry-making business as rival to Morris and Company.

There are many specific details of the book that support such a socialist interpretation. The Lady's House, for instance, is a dwelling fit for a capitalist magnate, as this passage from the beginning of Chapter XI attests:

> So an hour before sunset he saw something white and gay gleaming through the boles of the oak-trees, and presently there was clear before him a most goodly house builded of white marble, carved all about with knots and imagery, and the carven folk were all painted of their lively colours, whether it were their raiment or their flesh, and the housings wherein they stood all done with gold and fair hues. Gay were the windows of the house; and there was a pillared porch before the great door, with images betwixt the pillars both of men and beasts: and when Walter looked up to the roof of the house, he saw that it gleamed and shone; for all the tiles were of yellow metal, which he deemed to be of very gold. (p. 85)

The Maid, however, is poor, for she usually appears dressed in a smock, not an opulent gown, and Morris often calls our attention to the iron ring of servitude she must wear around her ankle.

There was, as May Morris tells us,[1] a discarded first draft of the book, entitled *The King's Son and the Carle's Son*, with "carle" Morris's archaic word for "peasant." He completed 65 pages of it and outlined the rest. The original social contrast was between the peasant's son (later transformed into the rich merchant's son Walter) and the King's Son, who figures more prominently in this first draft than in the published romance. According to May Morris, this original version of the King's Son is "weak and not ill-meaning," making him a morally better person than Otto, the King's Son of *The Wood Beyond the World*. Even though this pairing of the two male characters is more difficult to turn into a socialist allegory, it is clear that Morris's original involved some sort of point about social difference.

When a reviewer in *The Spectator* interpreted *The Wood Beyond the World* along socialist lines, suggesting the allegory of the Lady as the rich capitalist and the Maid as the worker, Morris force-

---

1 See May Morris, *Collected Works* Volume 17, pp. xxxvii-xxxviii. She summarizes the plot of the early version, explaining that her father grew dissatisfied with it and began the story anew as *The Wood Beyond the World*.

fully rejected this interpretation, claiming that the story had been "made for a tale, pure and simple." He may have done so because authors usually bristle at interpretive schemes that are reductive, as this one clearly is. Perhaps Morris intended the socialist allegory when he first plotted out the book, but then the romance took on a life of its own. Autobiographical content not given to socialist interpretation interposed, with Walter like Morris himself facing the anguish of being married to an adulterous wife, thus shifting the erotic complexities of the main characters to the forefront. It is notable that Walter and the Maid end up as king and queen—not suitable roles for young socialists to emulate. In the end *The Wood Beyond the World* is uniquely itself—a medievalesque romance and proto-fantasy novel whose narrative wanderings produce in us a sense of wonder.

William Morris: A Brief Chronology

1834 On March 24, Morris is born at Elm House, Walthamstow, Essex, to wealthy parents.

1842 Morris's father takes him on a visit to Canterbury Cathedral, where he is exposed for the first time to medieval art.

1847 Morris's father's death adversely impacts the family's finances, though they remain wealthy.

1848 Widespread revolutionary unrest and rioting throughout the Continent; though the established order weathers this storm, the troubles leave Europe looking for political change.

1848 Morris matriculates at Marlborough College.

1848 The Pre-Raphaelite Brotherhood is founded by John Millais, William Holman Hunt, and Dante Gabriel Rossetti.

1852 Morris takes matriculation exams for Exeter College, Oxford, where he meets Edward Burne-Jones, who becomes his lifelong artistic collaborator and friend.

1853 Morris matriculates at Oxford.

1855 Morris comes of age, receiving control of his inherited share of his father's copper-mine investments, which makes him independently wealthy.

1856 The first issue of the *Oxford and Cambridge Magazine* is published. Morris is its first editor, frequent contributor, and financial backer. His tale, "The Story of the Unknown Church," and poem, "Winter Weather," appear in the first issue. The magazine ceases publication after 12 monthly issues.

1856 Morris joins the office of G.E. Street, a prominent Gothic-revival architect in Oxford. There he meets Philip Webb, a member of Street's firm, who becomes another lifelong friend and artistic collaborator.

1856 Shortly after Morris moves from Oxford to London, he meets Rossetti through Burne-Jones, who had met him earlier. Rossetti urges Morris to be a painter rather than an architect. Morris and Burne-Jones set up a studio together.

1857 Morris and Burne-Jones temporarily return to Oxford to help Rossetti paint murals in the Oxford Union; they rent rooms in High Street. Morris meets Jane Burden, his future wife.

1858 *The Defence of Guenevere and Other Poems*, Morris's first book, is published.

1859 Morris marries Jane Burden. A year later they move into Red House, the home Webb designed for him.

1861 Morris, Marshall, Faulkner & Co. commence business.

1865 Morris moves back to London, abandoning Red House.

1866 Morris and Burne-Jones plan an illustrated edition of a massive new poem, *The Earthly Paradise*. Though the collaboration never comes to fruition, the poem occupies Morris over the next four years and secures his reputation among his contemporaries as an important poet.

1867 Morris's *The Life and Death of Jason* is published.

1868 Morris meets Eírikr Magnússon. They soon start publishing joint translations of Old Icelandic sagas.

1871 Morris and Rossetti take a joint lease on Kelmscott Manor. In the summer of this year, he makes the first of his two visits to Iceland.

1874 Rossetti leaves Kelmscott Manor because of Morris's resentment of his affair with Jane.

1875 Morris forces Rossetti and his other business partners out of the Firm and reconstitutes it as Morris and Company.

1876 Jane Morris ends her affair with Rossetti. Morris begins political activity in support of the Liberal opposition to Britain entering a conflict between Turkey and Russia.

1877 Morris founds the Society for the Protection of Ancient Buildings.

1878 Morris leases a house in London from George MacDonald, the novelist and fairy tale writer, giving it the name Kelmscott House in honor of Kelmscott Manor. It remains his home for the rest of his life.

1882 Morris raises public concern over a famine in Iceland.

1883 Morris joins the Democratic Federation, an important step in his conversion to socialism. Attending Sunday morning socialist meetings in Kelmscott House's coach house are George Bernard Shaw, Oscar Wilde, H.G. Wells, W.B. Yeats, and the composer Gustav Holst.

1885 Morris is arrested for assaulting a policeman at the Arbour Square Police Court, during a legal proceeding involving a number of his Socialist colleagues. He is acquitted, probably in deference to his class and fame.

1886 Serialization of Morris's *A Dream of John Ball*, a narrative of the 1381 Peasants' Revolt, begins in the Socialist periodical *Commonweal*.

1887 Morris is one of the speakers at a Socialist demonstration in Trafalgar Square that is violently disrupted by the police. Three people are killed and more than 100 injured on what becomes known as "Bloody Sunday."

1888 Morris's *The House of the Wolfings* is published.

1889 Morris's *The Roots of the Mountains* is published.

1890 Morris's *News from Nowhere* begins its serialization in *Commonweal*. Soon published in book form, it is a utopian novel about a future England in which socialism has triumphed as rural and craft-oriented rather than governmentally totalitarian.

1891 Morris sets up the Kelmscott Press. His *The Story of the Glittering Plain* is its first book.

1894 Morris's *The Wood Beyond the World* is published by the Kelmscott Press.

1895 Morris's translation of *Beowulf* and his prose romance *Child Christopher and Goldilind the Fair* are published by the Kelmscott Press.

1896 Morris's *The Well at the World's End* is published by the Kelmscott Press.

1896 *The Works of Geoffrey Chaucer* is published by the Kelmscott Press. It is the Press's masterpiece, a large and lavishly decorated and illustrated edition of Chaucer's works, and Morris's last collaboration with Burne-Jones.

1896 On October 3, Morris dies and is buried at St. George's Church, Kelmscott.

1897 Morris's *The Water of the Wondrous Isles* is published posthumously by the Kelmscott Press.

1898 Morris's prose romance *The Sundering Flood*, written between January and August 1896 during his last illness, is published posthumously by the Kelmscott Press.

A Note on the Text

There are three early texts of *The Wood Beyond the World*—the edition Morris published at his Kelmscott Press in May 1894; the first trade edition, published the next year by Lawrence and Bullen (and transferred to Longmans, Green in 1900); and the version published in 1913 as part of Volume XVII of May Morris's *The Collected Works of William Morris*. The Kelmscott edition, as did each of that press's books, had a limited run—350 copies with eight done on vellum and the rest on rag paper. The Lawrence and Bullen edition had an even smaller run of 50 copies. Its Longmans, Green incarnation, though, was a true trade edition, running into a second printing in 1904 and a third in 1911. *The Collected Works of William Morris* was issued in a run of 1050, of which 50 were presentation copies.

I have produced a critical edition of *The Wood Beyond the World* that takes into account variant readings from each of the three early texts. I chose the edition in *The Collected Works* (CW) as my base text, for it alone punctuates the characters' speeches with quotation marks (except for characters' inward thoughts, which lack them). Kelmscott (K) omits the quotation marks, doubtless because of Morris's efforts to make the book visually akin to a medieval manuscript or a fifteenth-century printed book, both of which do not employ them. The Lawrence and Bullen edition (LB) follows K in this. The three texts are remarkably stable; the variant readings among them are almost all very minor, with only a very few affecting the sense of what is going on in the narrative. Where there are differences, I have preferred K to the others unless CW and LB present cogent alternatives. The textual notes at the bottom of pages offer the details.

LB probably used Morris's original manuscript when it was being set. The interval between the publication of K and LB is one indication of this, for it is about the right amount of time for sequential use of the manuscript by both presses. An even stronger indication of this is that LB follows K very closely, and when there are variants, the two usually align against CW. May Morris likely consulted both K and LB when she was preparing CW. She includes K's marginal summaries, whereas LB omits them. Morris's manuscript omitted them, and they likely were composed after the main text for K had been set. K deploys marginal summaries regularly at the top outside margin of pages where there is no chapter break (though a few of those pages do include them). CW, which does not follow the pagination of K, places them at varying points in the margins near the words next to which they were placed in K and not therefore at the top of each page, for CW's pages do not fall as they do in K. Of necessity, I follow CW in their placement, though for the present edition the marginal summaries are shifted into the body of the text to serve as headings. Occasionally they are shifted a few lines upward or downward to align with paragraph breaks. CW also adds the periods to the end of chapter titles that LB first supplies. I have followed K in this by omitting them. LB moreover occasionally hyphenates words at the end of lines where K supplies unhyphenated compounds; CW at times adopts the hyphenation, even when the word does not occur at the end of a line, even in the face of its tendency to remove many of the hyphens in other places in the text. CW follows LB's lead in correcting the misspelling "befel" in the second chapter of K, altering it to "befell." CW also follows the paragraph breaks of LB; K omits paragraph breaks in favor of medievalesque ornate capital letters flush against the left margin and little decorative oak leaves scattered in the block text of almost every page where paragraph breaks should fall.

THE WOOD BEYOND THE WORLD

Frontispiece to the Kelmscott Press edition of *The Wood Beyond the World*; editor's collection.

Chapter I. Of Golden Walter and His Father

A while ago there was a young man dwelling in a great and goodly city by the sea which had to name Langton on Holm.[1] He was but of five and twenty winters, a fair-faced man, yellow-haired, tall and strong; rather wiser than foolisher than young men are mostly wont; a valiant youth, and a kind; not of many words but courteous of speech; no roisterer,[2] nought masterful, but peaceable and knowing how to forbear: in a fray[3] a perilous foe, and a trusty war-fellow. His father, with whom he was dwelling when this tale begins, was a great merchant, richer than a baron of the land, a head-man of the greatest of the Lineages of Langton, and a captain of the Porte; he was of the Lineage of the Goldings, therefore was he called Bartholomew Golden, and his son Golden Walter.

Of the wife of Golden Walter

Now ye may well deem[4] that such a youngling as this was looked upon by all as a lucky man without a lack; but there was this flaw in his lot, whereas he had fallen into the toils of love of a woman exceeding fair, and had taken her to wife, she nought unwilling as it seemed. But when they had been wedded some six months he found by manifest tokens, that his fairness was not so much to her but that she must seek to the foulness of one worser than he in all ways;[5] wherefore his rest departed from him, whereas he hated her for her untruth and her hatred of him; yet would the sound of her voice, as she came and went in the house, make his heart beat; and the sight of her stirred desire within him, so that he longed for her to be sweet and kind with him, and deemed that, might it be so, he should forget all the evil gone by. But it was not so; for ever when she saw him, her face changed, and her hatred of him became manifest, and howsoever she were sweet with others, with him she was hard and sour.

---

1 In Old English, the name of the city means, "the long town on the sea." At the time he was working on *The Wood Beyond the World*, Morris was studying Old English with the Cambridge Anglo-Saxon scholar A.J. Wyatt in preparation for their joint translation of *Beowulf*, published by Morris's Kelmscott Press in 1895.

2 Partygoer.

3 Battle.

4 Guess, judge, think, estimate.

5 The circumstances of Walter's marriage resemble to a certain extent Morris's own; his wife, the Pre-Raphaelite model Jane Burden Morris had successive long-lasting affairs with the Pre-Raphaelite painter and poet Dante Gabriel Rossetti and then the poet Wilfred Scawen Blunt.

Of father and son

So this went on a while till the chambers of his father's house, yea the very streets of the city, became loathsome to him; and yet he called to mind that the world was wide and he but a young man. So on a day as he sat with his father alone, he spake to him and said: "Father, I was on the quays[1] even now, and I looked on the ships that were nigh boun,[2] and thy sign I saw on a tall ship that seemed to me nighest boun. Will it be long ere[3] she sail?"

"Nay," said his father, "that ship, which hight[4] the Katherine, will they warp[5] out of the haven in two days' time.[6] But why askest thou of her?"

"The shortest word is best, father," said Walter, "and this it is, that I would depart in the said ship and see other lands."

"Yea and whither, son?" said the merchant.

"Wither she goeth," said Walter, "for I am ill at ease at home, as thou wottest,[7] father."

The merchant held his peace awhile, and looked hard on his son, for there was strong love between them; but at last he said: "Well, son, maybe it were best for thee; but maybe also we shall not meet again."

Walter is to depart

"Yet if we do meet, father, then shalt thou see a new man in me."

"Well," said Bartholomew, "at least I know on whom to lay the loss of thee, and when thou art gone, for thou shalt have thine own way herein, she shall no longer abide in my house. Nay, but it were for the strife that should arise thenceforth betwixt her kindred and ours, it should go somewhat worse with her than that."

Said Walter: "I pray thee shame her not more than needs must be, lest, so doing, thou shame both me and thyself also."

Bartholomew held his peace again for a while; then he said: "Goeth she with child, my son?"

---

1 Docks.

2 Prepared, ready.

3 Before.

4 Is named.

5 Haul.

6 Medieval merchants typically sent ships loaded with goods to sell and trade to far-off places and expected the ship to return with goods to sell at a profit at home.

7 As you know.

Walter reddened, and said: "I wot[1] not; nor of whom the child may be." Then they both sat silent, till Bartholomew spake, saying: "The end of it is, son, that this is Monday, and that thou shalt go aboard in the small hours of Wednesday; and meanwhile I shall look to it that thou go not away empty-handed; the skipper of the Katherine is a good man and true, and knows the seas well; and my servant Robert the Low, who is clerk of the lading,[2] is trustworthy and wise, and as myself in all matters that look towards chaffer.[3] The Katherine is new and stout-builded, and should be lucky, whereas she is under the ward[4] of her who is the saint called upon in the church where thou wert christened, and myself before thee; and thy mother, and my father and mother all lie under the chancel[5] thereof, as thou wottest."

Therewith the elder rose up and went his ways about his business, and there was no more said betwixt him and his son on this matter.

Chapter II. Golden Walter Takes Ship to Sail the Seas

When Walter went down to the Katherine next morning, there was the skipper Geoffrey, who did him reverence, and made him all cheer, and showed him his room aboard ship, and the plenteous goods which his father had sent down to the quays already, such haste as he had made. Walter thanked his father's love in his heart, but otherwise took little heed to his affairs, but wore away the time about the haven, gazing listlessly on the ships that were making them ready outward, or unlading,[6] and the mariners and aliens coming and going: and all these were to him as the curious images woven on a tapestry.[7]

---

1 Know.

2 Official in charge of loading ships.

3 Trading.

4 Protection. The ship is named after St. Katherine, a virgin martyred in the fourth century in the city of Alexandria in Egypt.

5 Part of a church near the altar. As a young man Morris trained to be an architect for a firm specializing in neo-gothic churches.

6 Unloading.

7 Morris's decorating firm sold tapestries, many designed by himself in collaboration with Edward Burne-Jones, the artist who designed the frontispiece for the Kelmscott Press edition of *The Wood Beyond the World*.

Walter on the quay

At last when he had well-nigh[1] come back again to the Katherine, he saw there a tall ship, which he had scarce noted before, a ship all-boun,[2] which had her boats out, and men sitting to the oars thereof ready to tow her outwards when the hawser[3] should be cast off, and by seeming her mariners were but abiding for some one or other to come aboard.

Of those Three

So Walter stood idly watching the said ship, and as he looked, lo! folk passing him toward the gangway. These were three; first came a dwarf, dark-brown of hue and hideous, with long arms and ears exceeding great and dog-teeth that stuck out like the fangs of a wild beast. He was clad in a rich coat of yellow silk, and bare in his hand a crooked bow, and was girt with a broad sax.[4]

After him came a maiden, young by seeming, of scarce twenty summers; fair of face as a flower; grey-eyed, brown-haired, with lips full and red, slim and gentle of body. Simple was her array, of a short and strait[5] green gown, so that on her right ankle was clear to see an iron ring.

Last of the three was a lady, tall and stately, so radiant of visage[6] and glorious of raiment,[7] that it were hard to say what like she was; for scarce might the eye gaze steady upon her exceeding beauty; yet must every son of Adam who found himself anigh her, lift up his eyes again after he had dropped them, and look again on her, and yet again and yet again. Even so did Walter, and as the three passed by him, it seemed to him as if all the other folk there about had vanished and were nought; nor had he any vision before his eyes of any looking on them, save himself alone. They went over the gangway into the ship, and he saw them go along the deck till they came to the house on the poop,[8] and entered it, and were gone from his sight.

The strange ship departs

There he stood staring, till little by little the thronging people of the quays came into his eye-shot again; then he saw how the hawser was cast off and the boats fell to tugging the big ship

---

1 CW: wellnigh.
2 Prepared, loaded.
3 Large rope.
4 Short, single-edged sword.
5 Tight.
6 Face.
7 Clothing.
8 Stern, back end of a ship.

toward the harbour-mouth with hale and how[1] of men. Then the sail fell down from the yard[2] and was sheeted home[3] and filled with the fair wind as the ship's bows ran up on the first green wave outside the haven. Even therewith the shipmen[4] cast abroad a banner, whereon was done in a green field a grim wolf ramping[5] up against a maiden, and so went the ship upon her way.

Those Three again

Walter stood awhile staring at her empty place where the waves ran into the haven-mouth, and then turned aside and toward the Katherine; and at first he was minded to go ask shipmaster Geoffrey of what he knew concerning the said ship and her alien way-farers;[6] but then it came into his mind, that all this was but an imagination or dream of the day, and that he were best to leave it untold to any. So therewith he went his way from the water-side, and through the streets unto his father's house; but when he was but a little way thence, and the door was before him, him-seemed[7] for a moment of time that he beheld those three coming out down the steps of stone and into the street; to wit the dwarf, the maiden, and the stately lady: but when he stood still to abide their coming, and looked toward them, lo! there was nothing before him save the goodly house of Bartholomew Golden, and three children and a cur[8] dog playing about the steps thereof, and about him were four or five passers-by going about their business. Then was he all confused in his mind, and knew not what to make of it, whether those whom he had seemed to see pass aboard ship were but images of a dream, or children of Adam in very flesh.

The images abide with him

Howsoever, he entered the house, and found his father in the chamber, and fell to speech with him about their matters; but for all that he loved his father, and worshipped him as a wise and valiant man, yet at that hour he might not hearken the words of his mouth, so much was his mind entangled in the thought of those three, and they were ever before his eyes, as if they had been

---

1 Shout and pull.

2 Cross-beam.

3 Tied secure.

4 LB: ship-men.

5 Threatening.

6 CW: wayfarers.

7 It seemed to him.

8 Stray.

painted on a table by the best of limners.[1] And of the two women he thought exceeding much, and cast no wyte[2] upon himself for running after the desire of strange women. For he said to himself that he desired not either of the twain; nay, he might not tell which of the twain, the maiden or the stately queen, were clearest to his eyes; but sore he desired to see both of them again, and to know what they were.

Walter sails away

So wore the hours till the Wednesday morning, and it was time that he should bid farewell to his father and get aboard ship; but his father led him down to the quays and on to the Katherine, and there Walter embraced him, not without tears and forebodings; for his heart was full. Then presently the old man went aland; the gangway was unshipped, the hawsers cast off; the oars of the towing boats[3] splashed in the dark water, the sail fell down from the yard, and was sheeted home, and out plunged the Katherine into the misty sea and rolled up the grey slopes, casting abroad her ancient[4] withal, whereon was beaten the token of Bartholomew Golden, to wit a B and a G to the right and the left, and thereabove a cross and a triangle rising from the midst.

Walter stood on the stern and beheld, yet more with the mind of him than with his eyes; for it all seemed but the double of what the other ship had done; and he thought of it as if the twain were as beads strung on one string and led away by it into the same place, and thence to go in the like order, and so on again and again, and never to draw nigher to each other.

Chapter III.
Walter Heareth Tidings of the Death of His Father

Fast sailed the Katherine over the seas, and nought befell to tell of, either to herself or her crew. She came to one cheaping-town[5] and then to another, and so on to a third and a fourth; and at each was buying and selling after the manner of chapmen;[6] and

---

1 Decorators. Morris, himself a decorator, had experience painting pictures on furniture.

2 Blame.

3 LB, CW: towing-boats.

4 Banner.

5 Merchant town.

6 Merchants.

Walter not only looked on the doings of his father's folk, but lent a hand, what he might, to help them in all matters, whether it were in seaman's craft, or in chaffer.[1] And the further he went and the longer the time wore, the more he was eased of his old trouble wherein his wife and her treason had to do.

But as for the other trouble, to wit his desire and longing to come up with those three, it yet flickered before him; and though he had not seen them again as one sees people in the streets, and as if he might touch them if he would, yet were their images often before his mind's eye; and yet, as time wore, not so often, nor so troublously; and forsooth both to those about him and to himself, he seemed as a man well healed of his melancholy mood.

The last of the cheaping steads

Now they left that fourth stead,[2] and sailed over the seas,[3] and came to a fifth, a very great and fair city, which they had made more than seven months from Langton on Holm; and by this time was Walter taking heed and joyance[4] in such things as were toward in that fair city, so far from his kindred, and especially he looked on the fair women there, and desired them, and loved them; but lightly, as befalleth young men.

Now this was the last country whereto the Katherine was boun;[5] so there they abode some ten months in daily chaffer, and in pleasuring them in beholding all that there was of rare and goodly, and making merry with the merchants and the towns-folk, and the country-folk beyond the gates, and Walter was grown as busy and gay as a strong young man is like to be, and was as one who would fain[6] be of some account amongst his own folk.

A messenger of evil

But at the end of this while, it befell[7] on a day, as he was leaving his hostel for his booth in the market, and had the door in his hand, there stood before him three mariners in the guise of his own country, and with them was one of clerkly aspect, whom he knew at once for his father's scrivener,[8] Arnold Pen-strong by name; and when Walter saw him his heart failed him

1 Trade.
2 Place.
3 CW: *omit comma.*
4 Pleasure.
5 Prepared [to go].
6 Gladly.
7 K: befel.
8 Scribe, copier.

and he cried out: "Arnold, what tidings? Is all well with the folk at Langton?"

Said Arnold: "Evil tidings are come with me; matters are ill with thy folk; for I may not hide that thy father, Bartholomew Golden, is dead, God rest his soul."

At that word it was to Walter as if all that trouble which but now had sat so light upon him, was once again fresh and heavy, and that his past life of the last few months had never been; and it was to him as if he saw his father lying dead on his bed, and heard the folk lamenting about the house. He held his peace a while,[1] and then he said in a voice as of an angry man: "What, Arnold! and did he die in his bed, or how? for he was neither old nor ailing when we parted."

A tale of strife

Said Arnold: "Yea, in his bed he died: but first he was somewhat sword-bitten."

"Yea, and how?" quoth Walter.

Said Arnold: "When thou wert gone, in a few days' wearing, thy father sent thy wife out of his house back to her kindred of the Reddings with no honour, and yet with no such shame as might have been, without blame to us of those who knew the tale of thee and her; which, God-a-mercy,[2] will be pretty much the whole of the city.

"Nevertheless, the Reddings took it amiss, and would have a mote[3] with us Goldings to talk of booting.[4] By ill-luck we yea-said[5] that for the saving of the city's peace. But what betid?[6] We met in our Gild-hall,[7] and there befell the talk between us; and in that talk certain words could not be hidden, though they were none too seemly nor too meek. And the said words once spoken drew forth the whetted[8] steel; and there then was the hewing and thrusting! Two of ours were slain outright on the floor, and four of theirs, and many were hurt on either side. Of these was thy father, for as thou mayst well deem, he was nought backward in the fray; but despite his hurts, two in the side and one on the arm, he went home on his own feet, and we deemed that we had come

1 CW: awhile.
2 God have mercy.
3 Meeting.
4 Remedy, recompense.
5 Agreed to.
6 Happened.
7 Meeting hall for a trade guild.
8 Sharpened.

to our above.[1] But well-a-way![2] it was an evil victory, whereas in ten days he died of his hurts. God have his soul! But now[3] my master, thou mayst well wot that I am not come to tell thee this only, but moreover to bear the word of the kindred, to wit that thou come back with me straightway in the swift cutter[4] which hath borne me and the tidings; and thou mayst look to it, that though she be swift and light, she is a keel full weatherly."[5]

A bidding to return

Then said Walter: "This is a bidding of war. Come back will I, and the Reddings shall wot of my coming. Are ye all-boun?"[6]

"Yea," said Arnold, "we may up anchor this very day, or to-morrow morn at latest. But what aileth thee, master, that thou starest so wild over my shoulder? I pray thee take it not so much to heart! Ever it is the wont[7] of fathers to depart this world before their sons."

But Walter's visage[8] from wrathful red had become pale, and he pointed up street, and cried out: "Look! dost thou see?"

Here come the Three again

"See what, master?" quoth Arnold:[9] "What! here cometh an ape in gay raiment; belike the beast of some jongleur.[10] Nay, by God's wounds! 'tis a man, though he be exceeding mis-shapen like a very devil. Yea and now there cometh a pretty maid going as if she were of his meney;[11] and lo! here, a most goodly and noble lady! Yea, I see; and doubtless she owneth both the two, and is of the greatest of the folk of this fair city; for on the maiden's ankle I saw an iron ring, which betokeneth thralldom[12] amongst these aliens. But this is strange! for notest thou not how the folk in the street heed not this quaint[13] show; nay not even the stately lady, though she be as lovely as a goddess of the gentiles, and beareth on her gems that would buy Langton twice over; surely

1 Had come out on top.
2 Alas.
3 LB, CW: *add comma.*
4 Small ship, sloop.
5 A ship prepared for all weather.
6 Completely prepared.
7 Custom.
8 Face.
9 K, LB: *add paragraph marker.*
10 Entertainer.
11 Company.
12 Slavery.
13 Odd.

they must be over-wont[1] to strange and gallant sights. But now, master, but now!"

"Yea, what is it?" said Walter.

They are gone suddenly

"Why, master, they should not yet be gone out of eye-shot, yet gone they are.[2] What is become of them, are they sunk into the earth?"[3]

"Tush, man!" said Walter, looking not on Arnold, but still staring down the street; "they have gone into some house while thine eyes were turned from them a moment."

"Nay,[4] master, nay," said Arnold, "mine eyes were not off them one instant of time."[5]

"Well," said Walter, somewhat snappishly, "they are gone now, and what have we to do to heed such toys,[6] we with all this grief and strife on our hands? Now would I be alone to turn the matter of thine errand over in my mind.[7] Meantime do thou tell the shipmaster Geoffrey and our other folk of these tidings, and thereafter get thee all ready; and come hither to me before sunrise to-morrow, and I shall be ready for my part; and so sail we back to Langton."

Walter pondereth the matter

Therewith he turned him back into the house, and the others went their ways; but Walter sat alone in his chamber a long while, and pondered these things in his mind. And whiles[8] he made up his mind that he would think no more of the vision of those three, but would fare back to Langton, and enter into the strife with the Reddings and quell[9] them, or die else. But lo, when he was quite steady in this doom,[10] and his heart was lightened thereby, he found that he thought no more of the Reddings and their strife, but as matters that were passed and done with, and that now he was thinking and devising if by any means he might find out in what land dwelt those three. And then again he strove to put that from him, saying that what he had seen was but meet[11] for one

---

1 Overly accustomed; LB: overwont.

2 K, LB: *add paragraph marker.*

3 CW: *omit paragraph marker.*

4 CW: *omit comma.*

5 K, LB: *omit paragraph marker.*

6 Trifles.

7 K: *add paragraph marker.*

8 Sometimes.

9 Kill.

10 Decision.

11 Appropriate.

brainsick, and a dreamer of dreams. But furthermore he thought, Yea, and was Arnold, who this last time had seen the images of those three, a dreamer of waking dreams? for he was nought wonted in such wise;[1] then thought he: At least I am well content that he spake to me of their likeness, not I to him; for so I may tell that there was at least something before my eyes which grew not out of mine own brain. And yet again, why should I follow them; and what should I get by it; and indeed how shall I set about it?

Thus he turned the matter over and over; and at last, seeing that if he grew no foolisher over it, he grew no wiser, he became weary thereof, and bestirred him,[2] and saw to the trussing[3] up of his goods, and made all ready for his departure, and so wore the day and slept at nightfall; and at daybreak comes Arnold to lead him to their keel, which hight[4] the Bartholomew. He tarried nought, and with few farewells went aboard ship, and an hour after they were in the open sea with the ship's head turned toward Langton on Holm.

Chapter IV.
Storm Befalls the Bartholomew, and She is Driven Off Her Course

A calm

Now swift sailed the Bartholomew for four weeks toward the north-west with a fair wind, and all was well with ship and crew. Then the wind died out on even of a day, so that the ship scarce made way at all, though she rolled in a great swell of the sea, so great, that it seemed to ridge all the main athwart.[5] Moreover down in the west was a great bank of cloud huddled up in haze, whereas for twenty days past the sky had been clear, save for a few bright white clouds flying before the wind. Now the shipmaster, a man right cunning[6] in his craft, looked long on sea and sky, and then turned and bade[7] the mariners take in sail and be right

1 Accustomed in such a way.
2 Stirred himself [to action].
3 Packing.
4 Was named.
5 To furrow all the [waves of] the sea sidewards.
6 Skillful.
7 Commanded.

heedful. And when Walter asked him what he looked for, and wherefore he spake not to him thereof, he said surlily: "Why should I tell thee what any fool can see without telling, to wit that there is weather to hand?"

A gale

So they abode what should befall, and Walter went to his room to sleep away the uneasy while, for the night was now fallen; and he knew no more till he was waked up by great hubbub and clamour of the shipmen, and the whipping of ropes, and thunder of flapping sails, and the tossing and weltering[1] of the ship withal. But, being a very stout-hearted young man, he lay still in his room, partly because he was a landsman, and had no mind to tumble about amongst the shipmen and hinder them; and withal he said to himself: What matter whether I go down to the bottom of the sea, or come back to Langton, since either way my life or my death will take away from me the fulfillment of desire? Yet soothly[2] if there hath been a shift of wind, that is not so ill; for then shall we be driven to other lands, and so at the least our homecoming shall be delayed, and other tidings may hap[3] amidst of our tarrying. So let all be as it will.

A foul wind

So in a little while, in spite of the ship's wallowing and the tumult of the wind and waves, he fell asleep again, and woke no more till it was full daylight, and there was the shipmaster standing in the door of his room, the sea-water all streaming from his wet-weather raiment. He said to Walter: "Young master, the sele[4] of the day to thee! For by good hap[5] we have gotten into another day. Now I shall tell thee that we have striven to beat, so as not to be driven off our course, but all would not avail, wherefore for these three hours we have been running before the wind; but, fair sir, so big hath been the sea that but for our ship being of the stoutest, and our men all yare,[6] we had all grown exceeding wise concerning the ground of the mid-main.[7] Praise be to St. Nicholas[8] and all

1 Rolling about.

2 Truly.

3 Arrive.

4 Good wishes.

5 Luck.

6 Ready, prepared.

7 Middle sea.

8 St. Nicholas, a fourth-century bishop of the city of Myra in Asia Minor (modern Turkey), was patron saint of sailors and children (the latter occasioning his association with Christmas).

Hallows![1] for though ye shall presently look upon a new sea, and maybe a new land to boot,[2] yet is that better than looking on the ugly things down below."

"Is all well with ship and crew then?" said Walter.

"Yea forsooth," said the shipmaster; "verily the Bartholomew is the darling of Oak Woods; come up and look at it, how she is dealing with wind and waves all free from fear."

So Walter did on his foul-weather raiment, and went up on to the quarter-deck, and there indeed was a change of days; for the sea was dark and tumbling mountain-high, and the white-horses[3] were running down the valleys thereof, and the clouds drave[4] low over all, and bore a scud[5] of rain along with them; and though there was but a rag of sail on her, the ship flew before the wind, rolling a great wash of water from bulwark[6] to bulwark.

The stern towards Langton

Walter stood looking on it all awhile, holding on by a stay-rope, and saying to himself that it was well that they were driving so fast toward new things.

Then the shipmaster came up to him and clapped him on the shoulder and said: "Well, shipmate, cheer up! and now come below again and eat some meat,[7] and drink a cup with me."

So Walter went down and ate and drank, and his heart was lighter than it had been since he had heard of his father's death, and the feud awaiting him at home, which forsooth he had deemed would stay his wanderings a weary while, and therewithal his hopes. But now it seemed as if he needs must wander, would he, would he not; and so it was that even this fed his hope; so sore his heart clung to that desire of his to seek home to those three that seemed to call him unto them.

Chapter V. Now They Come to a New Land

Three days they drave[8] before the wind, and on the fourth the clouds lifted, the sun shone out and the offing was clear; the wind

1 All the saints.

2 In addition.

3 *That is*, the white-caps.

4 Drove, hovered.

5 Squall, shower.

6 Side of a ship.

7 Food.

8 Drove.

had much abated, though it still blew a breeze, and was a head wind for sailing toward the country of Langton. So then the master said that, since they were bewildered, and the wind so ill to deal with, it were best to go still before the wind that they might make some land and get knowledge of their whereabouts from the folk thereof. Withal he said that he deemed the land not to be very far distant.

So did they, and sailed on pleasantly enough, for the weather kept on mending, and the wind fell till it was but a light breeze, yet still foul for Langton.

So wore three days, and on the eve of the third, the man from the topmast cried out that he saw land ahead; and so did they all before the sun was quite set, though it were but a cloud no bigger than a man's hand.

A new land of mountains

When night fell they struck not sail, but went forth toward the land fair and softly; for it was early summer, so that the nights were neither long nor dark.

But when it was broad daylight, they opened[1] a land, a long shore of rocks and mountains, and nought else that they could see at first. Nevertheless as day wore and they drew nigher, first they saw how the mountains fell away from the sea, and were behind a long wall of sheer cliff; and coming nigher yet, they beheld a green plain going up after a little in green bents and slopes to the feet of the said cliff-wall.[2] No city nor haven did they see there, not even when they were far nigher to the land; nevertheless,[3] whereas they hankered for the peace of the green earth after all the tossing and unrest of the sea, and whereas also they doubted not to find at the least good and fresh water, and belike[4] other bait in the plain under the mountains, they still sailed on not unmerrily; so that by nightfall they cast anchor in five-fathom[5] water hard[6] by the shore.

A river and a homestead thereby

Next morning they found that they were lying a little way off the mouth of a river not right great; so they put out their boats and towed the ship up into the said river, and when they had

---

1 Saw clearly.

2 LB, CW: *add paragraph break.*

3 K: *omit comma.*

4 Perhaps.

5 The length of the arms outstretched, approximately six feet.

6 Close.

gone up it for a mile or thereabouts they found the sea water failed, for little was the ebb and flow of the tide on that coast. Then was the river deep and clear, running between smooth grassy land like to meadows. Also on their left board they saw presently three head of neat[1] cattle going, as if in a meadow of a homestead in their own land, and a few sheep; and thereafter, about a bow-draught[2] from the river, they saw a little house of wood and straw-thatch under a wooded mound, and with orchard trees about it. They wondered little thereat, for they know no cause why that land should not be builded, though it were in the far outlands. However, they drew their ship up to the bank, thinking that they would at least abide awhile and ask tidings and have some refreshing of the green plain, which was so lovely and pleasant.

A new comer

But while they were busied herein they saw a man come out of the house, and down to the river to meet them; and they soon saw that he was tall and old, long-hoary of hair[3] and beard, and clad mostly in the skins of beasts.

He drew nigh without any fear or mistrust, and coming close to them gave them the sele[4] of the day in a kindly and pleasant voice. The shipmaster greeted him in his turn, and said withal: "Old man, art thou the king of this country?"

The elder laughed; "It hath had none other a long while," said he; "and at least there is no other son of Adam here to gainsay."[5]

"Thou art alone here then?" said the master.

"Yea," said the old man; "save for the beasts of the field and the wood, and the creeping things, and fowl. Wherefore it is sweet to me to hear your voices."

Said the master: "Where be the other houses of the town?"

Of the Bears

The old man laughed. Said he: "When I said that I was alone, I meant that I was alone in the land and not only alone in this stead.[6] There is no house save this betwixt the sea and the dwellings of the Bears, over the cliff-wall yonder, yea and a long way over it."

---

1 Tame.
2 The distance one can shoot an arrow from a bow.
3 With long gray hair.
4 Good wishes.
5 To deny it.
6 Place.

"Yea," quoth the shipmaster grinning, "and be the bears of thy country so manlike, that they dwell in builded houses?"

The old man shook his head. "Sir," said he, "as to their bodily fashion, it is altogether manlike, save that they be one and all higher and bigger than most. For they be bears only in name; they be a nation of half wild men; for I have been told by them that there be many more than that tribe whose folk I have seen, and that they spread wide about behind these mountains from east to west. Now[1] sir, as to their souls and understandings I warrant them not; for miscreants[2] they be, trowing[3] neither in God nor his hallows."[4]

Said the master: "Trow they in Mahound[5] then?"

"Nay," said the elder, "I wot not for sure that they have so much as a false God; though I have it from them that they worship a certain woman with mickle[6] worship."

Fresh victual for the mariners

Then spake Walter: "Yea, good sir, and how knowest thou that? dost thou deal with them at all?"

Said the old man: "Whiles some of that folk come hither and have of me what I can spare; a calf or two, or a half-dozen of lambs or hoggets;[7] or a skin of wine or cyder[8] of mine own making: and they give me in return such things as I can use, as skins of hart[9] and bear and other peltries;[10] for now I am old, I can but little of the hunting hereabout. Whiles, also, they bring little lumps of pure copper, and would give me gold also, but it is of little use in this lonely land. Sooth[11] to say, to me they are not masterful or rough-handed; but glad am I that they have been here but of late, and are not like to come again this while; for terrible they are of aspect,[12] and whereas ye be aliens, belike they would not hold their hands from off you; and moreover ye have weapons and other matters which they would covet sorely."

---

1 LB, CW: *add comma.*

2 Villains, heretics.

3 Believing.

4 Saints.

5 Muhammad.

6 Much.

7 Piglets.

8 Cider.

9 Deer.

10 Pelts, skins.

11 Truth.

12 In appearance.

A bounteous Carle

Quoth[1] the master: "Since thou dealest with these wild men, will ye not deal with us in chaffer?[2] For whereas we are come from long travel, we hanker after fresh victual,[3] and here aboard are many things which were for thine avail."

Of the wild-deer

Said the old man: "All that I have is yours, so that ye do but leave me enough till my next ingathering:[4] of wine and cyder, such as it is, I have plenty for your service; ye may drink it till it is all gone, if ye will: a little corn[5] and meal I have, but not much; yet are ye welcome thereto, since the standing corn in my garth[6] is done blossoming, and I have other meat.[7] Cheeses have I and dried fish; take what ye will thereof. But as to my neat[8] and sheep, if ye have sore need of any, and will have them, I may not say you nay: but I pray you if ye may do without them, not to take my milch-beasts[9] or their engenderers;[10] for, as ye have heard me say, the Bear-folk have been here but of late, and they have had of me all I might spare: but now let me tell you, if ye long after flesh-meat, that there is venison of hart and hind, yea, and of buck and doe, to be had on this plain, and about the little woods at the feet of the rock-wall yonder: neither are they exceeding wild; for since I may not take them, I scare them not, and no other man do they see to hurt them; for the Bear-folk come straight to my house, and fare straight home thence. But I will lead you the nighest way to where the venison is easiest to be gotten. As to the wares in your ship, if ye will give me aught I will take it with a good will; and chiefly if ye have a fair knife or two and a roll of linen cloth, that were a good refreshment to me. But in any case what I have to give is free to you and welcome."

The shipmaster laughed: "Friend," said he, "we can thee mickle thanks[11] for all that thou biddest us. And wot well that we be no lifters or sea-thieves to take thy livelihood from thee. So to-

---

1 Said.
2 Trade.
3 Food.
4 Harvest.
5 Grain.
6 Enclosure, garden.
7 Food.
8 Tame beasts, in this instance cattle.
9 Animals capable of being milked.
10 Impregnators.
11 Owe you many thanks.

morrow, if thou wilt, we will go with thee and upraise the hunt, and meanwhile we will come aland, and walk on the green grass, and water our ship with thy good fresh water."[1]

They feast on the meadow

So the old carle[2] went back to his house to make them ready what cheer[3] he might, and the shipmen, who were twenty and one, all told, what with the mariners and Arnold and Walter's servants, went ashore, all but two who watched the ship and abode their turn. They went well-weaponed, for both the master and Walter deemed wariness wisdom, lest all might not be so good as it seemed. They took of their sail-cloths ashore, and tilted them in on the meadow betwixt the house and the ship, and the carle brought them what he had for their avail, of fresh fruits, and cheeses, and milk, and wine, and cyder, and honey, and there they feasted nowise ill, and were right fain.[4]

Chapter VI.
The Old Man Tells Walter of Himself. Walter Sees a Shard[5] in the Cliff-wall

Walter talks alone with the carle

But when they had done their meat[6] and drink the master and the shipmen went about the watering of the ship, and the others strayed off along the meadow, so that presently Walter was left alone with the carle, and fell to speech with him and said: "Father, meseemeth[7] thou shouldest have some strange tale to tell, and as yet we have asked thee of nought save meat for our bellies: now if I ask thee concerning thy life, and how thou camest hither, and abided here, wilt thou tell me aught?"

The old man smiled on him and said: "Son, my tale were long to tell; and mayhappen[8] concerning much thereof my memory should fail me; and withal there is grief therein, which I were

---

1 K: *no paragraph break.*
2 Fellow.
3 Welcome.
4 Glad.
5 *Here,* gap; a shard normally is a broken piece of something.
6 Finished their food.
7 It seems to me.
8 Perhaps.

loth[1] to awaken: nevertheless if thou ask, I will answer as I may, and in any case will tell thee nought save the truth."

Said Walter: "Well then, hast thou been long here?"

"Yea," said the carle, "since I was a young man, and a stalwart knight."

Said Walter: "This house, didst thou build it, and raise these garths, and plant orchard and vineyard, and gather together the neat and the sheep, or did some other do all this for thee?"

Of him who was before the carle

Said the carle: "I did none of all this; there was one here before me, and I entered into his inheritance, as though this were a lordly manor, with a fair castle thereon, and all well stocked and plenished."[2]

Said Walter: "Didst thou find thy foregoer alive here?'

"Yea," said the elder, "yet he lived but for a little while after I came to him."

He was silent a while, and then he said: "I slew him: even so would he have it, though I bade him a better lot."

Said Walter: "Didst thou come hither of thine own will?"

"Mayhappen," said the carle; "who knoweth? Now have I no will to do either this or that. It is wont that maketh me do, or refrain."

Said Walter: "Tell me this; why didst thou slay the man? did he any scathe[3] to thee?"

Said the elder: "When I slew him, I deemed that he was doing me all scathe: but now I know that it was not so. Thus it was:[4] I would needs go where he had been before, and he stood in the path against me; and I overthrew him, and went on the way I would."

"What came thereof?" said Walter.

A downright nay-say

"Evil came of it," said the carle.

Then was Walter silent a while, and the old man spake nothing; but there came a smile in his face that was both sly and somewhat sad. Walter looked on him and said: "Was it from hence that thou wouldst go that road?"

"Yea," said the carle.

Said Walter: "And now wilt thou tell me what that road was;

---

1 Reluctant.

2 Supplied.

3 Harm.

4 K, LB: *semi-colon.*

whither it went and whereto it led, that thou must needs wend[1] it, though thy first stride were over a dead man?"

"I will not tell thee," said the carle.

Then they held their peace, both of them, and thereafter got on to other talk of no import.

So wore the day till night came; and they slept safely, and on the morrow after they had broken their fast, the more part of them set off with the carle to the hunting, and they went, all of them, a three hours' faring towards the foot of the cliffs, which was all grown over with coppice,[2] hazel and thorn, with here and there a big oak or ash-tree; there it was, said the old man, where the venison was most and best.

Of the hunting and how Walter abode behind with the carle

Of their hunting need nought be said, saving that when the carle had put them on the track of the deer and shown them what to do, he came back again with Walter, who had no great lust for the hunting, and sorely longed to have some more talk with the said carle. He for his part seemed nought loth thereto, and so led Walter to a mound or hillock amidst the clear of the plain, whence all was to be seen save where the wood covered it; but just before where they now lay down there was no wood, save low bushes, betwixt them and the rock-wall; and Walter noted that whereas otherwhere, save in one place whereto their eyes were turned, the cliffs seemed well-nigh[3] or quite sheer, or indeed in some places beetling over,[4] in that said place they fell away from each other on either side; and before this sinking was a slope or scree,[5] that went gently up toward the sinking of the wall. Walter looked long and earnestly at this place, and spake nought, till the carle said: "What! thou hast found something before thee to look on. What is it then?"

Of the shard in the cliff-wall

Quoth Walter: "Some would say that where yonder slopes run together up towards that sinking in the cliff-wall there will be a pass into the country beyond."

The carle smiled and said: "Yea, son; nor, so saying, would they err; for that is the pass into the Bear-country, whereby those huge men come down to chaffer[6] with me."

---

1 Travel.

2 Scrub trees.

3 CW: wellnigh.

4 Hanging over.

5 Broken rocks.

6 Trade.

"Yea," said Walter; and therewith he turned him a little, and scanned the rock-wall, and saw how a few miles from that pass it turned somewhat sharply toward the sea, narrowing the plain much there, till it made a bight,[1] the face whereof looked well-nigh[2] north, instead of west, as did the more part of the wall. And in the midst of that northern-looking bight was a dark place which seemed to Walter like a downright shard[3] in the cliff. For the face of the wall was of[4] bleak grey, and it was but little furrowed.

Walter has a deeming concerning that shard

So then Walter spake: "Lo, old friend, there yonder is again a place that meseemeth is a pass; whereunto doth that one lead?" And he pointed to it: but the old man did not follow the pointing of his finger, but, looking down on the ground, answered confusedly, and said:

"Maybe: I wot not. I deem that it also leadeth into the Bear-country by a round-about[5] road. It leadeth into the far land."

Walter answered nought: for a strange thought had come uppermost in his mind, that the carle knew far more than he would say of that pass, and that he himself might be led thereby to find the wondrous three. He caught his breath hardly, and his heart knocked against his ribs; but he refrained from speaking for a long while; but at last he spake in a sharp hard voice, which he scarce knew for his own: "Father, tell me, I adjure thee by God and All-hallows,[6] was it through yonder shard that the road lay, when thou must needs make thy first stride over a dead man?"

A lie downright

The old man spake not a while, then he raised his head, and looked Walter full in the eyes, and said in a steady voice: "NO, IT WAS NOT." Thereafter they sat looking at each other a while; but at last Walter turned his eyes away, but knew not what they beheld nor where he was, but he was as one in a swoon. For he knew full well that the carle had lied to him, and that he might as well have said aye[7] as no, and told him, that it verily was by that same shard that he had stridden over a dead man. Nevertheless he made as little semblance thereof as he might, and presently

---

1 Angle.

2 K, LB, and CW: *all omit the hyphen of* well-nigh.

3 *Here* gap.

4 LB: *has a gap in the text, omitting* of.

5 CW: roundabout.

6 All the saints.

7 Yes.

came to himself, and fell to talking of other matters, that had nought to do with the adventures of the land. But after a while he spake suddenly, and said: "My master, I was thinking of a thing."

"Yea, of what?" said the carle.

"Of this," said Walter; "that here in this land be strange adventures toward, and that if we, and I in especial, were to turn our backs on them, and go home with nothing done, it were pity of our lives: for all will be dull and deedless there. I was deeming it were good if we tried the adventure."

The carle tells of the Bear-folk and their ways

"What adventure?" said the old man, rising up on his elbow and staring sternly on him.

Said Walter: "The wending yonder pass to the eastward, whereby the huge men come to thee from out of the Bear-country; that we might see what should come thereof."

The carle leaned back again, and smiled and shook his head, and spake: "That adventure were speedily proven: death would come of it, my son."

"Yea, and how?" said Walter.

The carle said: "The big men would take thee, and offer thee up as a blood-offering to that woman, who is their Mawmet.[1] And if ye go all, then shall they do the like with all of you."

Said Walter: "Is that sure?"

"Dead sure," said the carle.

"How knowest thou this?" said Walter.

"I have been there myself," said the carle.

"Yea," said Walter, "but thou camest away whole."

"Art thou sure thereof?" said the carle.

"Thou art alive yet, old man," said Walter, "for I have seen thee eat thy meat,[2] which ghosts use not to do." And he laughed.

The carle warneth Walter of the adventure

But the old man answered soberly: "If I escaped, it was by this, that another woman saved me, and not often shall that befall. Nor wholly was I saved; my body escaped forsooth. But where is my soul? Where is my heart, and my life? Young man, I rede[3] thee, try no such adventure; but go home to thy kindred if thou canst. Moreover, wouldst thou fare alone? The others shall hinder thee."

Said Walter: "I am the master; they shall do as I bid them: besides, they will be well pleased to share my goods amongst

---

1 God.

2 Food.

3 Advise.

them if I give them a writing to clear them of all charges which might be brought against them."

"My son! my son!" said the carle, "I pray thee go not to thy death!"

Walter heard him silently, but as if he were persuaded to refrain; and then the old man fell to, and told him much concerning this Bear-folk and their customs, speaking very freely of them; but Walter's ears were scarce open to this talk: whereas he deemed that he should have nought to do with those wild men; and he durst not ask again concerning the country whereto led the pass on the northward.

Chapter VII.
Walter Comes to the Shard[1] in the Rock-wall

Walter's folk are coming back from the hunting

As they were in converse thus, they heard the hunters blowing on their horns all together; whereon the old man arose, and said: "I deem by the blowing that the hunt will be over and done, and that they be blowing on their fellows who have gone scatter-meal[2] about the wood. It is now some five hours after noon, and thy men will be getting back with their venison, and will be fainest[3] of the victuals they have caught; therefore will I hasten on before, and get ready fire and water and other matters for the cooking. Wilt thou come with me, young master, or abide thy men here?"

Walter said lightly: "I will rest and abide them here; since I cannot fail to see them hence as they go on their ways to thine house. And it may be well that I be at hand to command them and forbid, and put some order amongst them, for rough playmates they be, some of them, and now all heated with the hunting and the joy of the green earth." Thus he spoke, as if nought were toward save[4] supper and bed; but inwardly hope and fear were contending in him, and again his heart beat so hard, that he deemed that the carle must surely hear it. But the old man took him but according to his outward seeming, and nodded his head, and went away quietly toward his house.

---

1 Gap.

2 Here and there.

3 Most eager [to eat].

4 Were going to happen except.

Walter maketh him ready

When he had been gone a little, Walter rose up heedfully; he had with him a scrip[1] wherein was some cheese and hard-fish, and a little flasket[2] of wine; a short bow he had with him, and a quiver of arrows; and he was girt with a strong and good sword, and a wood-knife withal. He looked to all this gear that it was nought amiss, and then speedily went down off the mound, and when he was come down, he found that it covered him[3] from men coming out of the wood, if he went straight thence to that shard of the rock-wall where was the pass that led southward.

He sundereth him from his folk

Now it is no nay[4] that thitherward he turned, and went wisely, lest the carle should make a backward cast, and see him, or lest any straggler of his own folk might happen upon him.

For to say sooth, he deemed that did they wind him,[5] they would be like to let[6] him of his journey. He had noted the bearings of the cliffs nigh the shard, and whereas he could see their heads everywhere except from the depths of the thicket, he was not like to go astray.

He had made no great way ere he heard the horns blowing all together again in one place, and looking thitherward through the leafy boughs (for he was now amidst of a thicket) he saw his men thronging the mound, and had no doubt therefore that they were blowing on him;[7] but being well under cover he heeded it nought, and lying still a little, saw them go down off the mound and go all of them toward the carle's house, still blowing as they went, but not faring scatter-meal. Wherefore it was clear that they were nought troubled about him.

He entereth the Pass

So he went on his way to the shard; and there is nothing to say of his journey till he got before it with the last of the clear day, and entered it straightway. It was in sooth a downright breach or cleft in the rock-wall, and there was no hill or bent[8] leading up to it, nothing but a tumble of stones before it, which was somewhat uneasy going, yet needed nought but labour to overcome it, and

---

1 Bag.

2 Small bottle.

3 Blocked him from view.

4 It cannot be denied.

5 Get wind of him; i.e., discover his doings.

6 Hinder.

7 Blowing horns to catch his attention.

8 Grassy slope.

when he had got over this, and was in the very pass itself, he found it no ill going: forsooth at first it was little worse than a rough road betwixt two great stony slopes, though a little trickle of water ran down amidst of it. So, though it was so nigh nightfall, yet Walter pressed on, yea, and long after the very night was come. For the moon rose wide and bright a little after nightfall. But at last he had gone so long, and was so wearied, that he deemed it nought but wisdom to rest him, and so lay down on a piece of green-sward[1] betwixt the stones, when he had eaten a morsel out of his satchel, and drunk of the water out of the stream. There as he lay, if he had any doubt of peril, his weariness soon made it all one to him, for presently he was sleeping as soundly as any man in Langton on Holm.

Chapter VIII. Walter Wends the Waste

The first morning in the Waste

Day was yet young when he awoke: he leapt to his feet, and went down to the stream and drank of its waters, and washed the night off him in a pool thereof, and then set forth on his way again. When he had gone some three hours, the road, which had been going up all the way, but somewhat gently, grew steeper, and the bent on either side lowered, and lowered, till it sank at last altogether, and then was he on a rough mountain-neck with little grass, and no water; save that now and again was a soft place with a flow amidst of it, and such places he must needs fetch a compass about,[2] lest he be mired.[3] He gave himself but little rest, eating what he needs must as he went. The day was bright and calm, so that the sun was never hidden, and he steered by it due south. All that day he went, and found no more change in that huge neck,[4] save that whiles it was more and whiles less steep. A little before nightfall he happened on a shallow pool some twenty yards over; and he deemed it good to rest there, since there was water for his avail,[5] though he might have made somewhat more out of the tail end of the day.

---

1 Grassy ground; CW: greensward.

2 Walk around.

3 Caught in the swampy ground.

4 Ridge.

5 Use.

The wending of the Waste

When dawn came again he awoke and arose, nor spent much time over his breakfast; but pressed on all he might; and now he said to himself, that whatsoever other peril were athwart[1] his way, he was out of the danger of the chase of his own folk.

All this while he had seen no four-footed beast, save now and again a hill-fox, and once some outlandish kind of hare; and of fowl but very few: a crow or two, a long-winged hawk, and twice an eagle high up aloft.

The wending of the Waste

Again, the third night, he slept in the stony wilderness, which still led him up and up. Only toward the end of the day, him-seemed[2] that it had been less steep for a long while: otherwise nought was changed, on all sides it was nought but the endless neck, wherefrom nought could be seen, but some other part of itself. This fourth night withal he found no water whereby he might rest, so that he awoke parched, and longing to drink just when the dawn was at its coldest.

But on the fifth morrow the ground rose but little, and at last, when he had been going wearily a long while, and now, hard on noon-tide,[3] his thirst grieved him sorely, he came on a spring welling out from under a high rock, the water wherefrom trickled feebly away. So eager was he to drink, that at first he heeded nought else; but when his thirst was fully quenched his eyes caught sight of the stream which flowed from the well, and he gave a shout, for lo! it was running south.[4] Wherefore it was with a merry heart that he went on, and as he went, came on more streams, all running south or thereabouts. He hastened on all he might, but in despite of all the speed he made, and that he felt the land now going down southward, night overtook him in that same wilderness. Yet when he stayed at last for sheer weariness, he lay down in what he deemed by the moonlight to be a shallow valley, with a ridge at the southern end thereof.

The wending of the Waste

He slept long, and when he awoke the sun was high in the heavens, and never was brighter or clearer morning on the earth than was that. He arose and ate of what little was yet left him, and

1 Were lying across.

2 It seemed to him.

3 CW: noontide.

4 Walter has discovered that he has reached the top of the ridge and is now descending to the other side.

drank of the water of a stream which he had followed the evening before, and beside which he had laid him down; and then set forth again with no great hope to come on new tidings that day. But yet when he was fairly afoot,[1] himseemed that there was something new in the air which he breathed, that was soft and bore sweet scents home to him; whereas heretofore, and that especially for the last three or four days, it had been harsh and void, like the face of the desert itself.

A fair land in the offing

So on he went, and presently was mounting the ridge aforesaid, and, as oft happens when one climbs a steep place, he kept his eyes on the ground, till he felt he was on the top of the ridge. Then he stopped to take breath, and raised his head and looked, and lo! he was verily on the brow of the great mountain-neck, and down below him was the hanging of the great hill-slopes, which fell down, not slowly, as those he had been those days a-mounting, but speedily enough, though with little of broken places or sheer cliffs. But beyond this last of the desert[2] there was before him a lovely land of wooded hills, green plains, and little valleys, stretching out far and wide, till it ended at last in great blue mountains and white snowy peaks beyond them.

Then for very surprise of joy his spirit wavered, and he felt faint and dizzy, so that he was fain[3] to sit down a while and cover his face with his hands. Presently he came to his sober mind again, and stood up and looked forth keenly, and saw no sign of any dwelling of man. But he said to himself that that might well be because the good and well-grassed land was still so far off, and that he might yet look to find men and their dwellings when he had left the mountain wilderness quite behind him. So therewith he fell to going his ways down the mountain, and lost little time therein, whereas he now had his livelihood[4] to look to.

Chapter IX.
Walter Happeneth on the First of Those Three Creatures

What with one thing, what with another, as his having to turn out of his way for sheer rocks, or for slopes so steep that he might not

1 Walking.
2 Wilderness.
3 Eager.
4 Survival.

try the peril of them, and again for bogs impassable, he was fully three days more before he had quite come out of the stony waste, and by that time, though he had never lacked water, his scanty victual was quite done, for all his careful husbandry[1] thereof. But this troubled him little, whereas he looked to find wild fruits here and there, and to shoot some small deer,[2] as hare or coney,[3] and make a shift to cook the same, since he had with him flint and fire-steel. Moreover the further he went, the surer he was that he should soon come across a dwelling, so smooth and fair as everything looked before him. And he had scant fear, save that he might happen on men who should enthrall[4] him.

A sweet sleep

But when he was come down past the first green slopes, he was so worn, that he said to himself that rest was better than meat,[5] so little as he had slept for the last three days; so he laid him down under an ash-tree by a stream-side, nor asked what was o'clock, but had his fill of sleep, and even when he awoke in the fresh morning was little fain of rising,[6] but lay betwixt sleeping and waking for some three hours more; then he arose, and went further down the next green bent, yet somewhat slowly because of his hunger-weakness. And the scent of that fair land came up to him like the odour of one great nosegay.[7]

So he came to where the land was level, and there were many trees, as oak and ash, and sweet-chestnut and wych-elm, and hornbeam and quicken-tree,[8] not growing in a close wood or tangled thicket, but set as though in order on the flowery greensward, even as it might be in a great king's park.

A strange and terrible noise

So came he to a big bird-cherry, whereof many boughs hung low down laden with fruit: his belly rejoiced at the sight, and he caught hold of a bough, and fell to plucking and eating. But

---

1 Saving.

2 In Old English, "deer" meant any species of wild animal.

3 Rabbit.

4 Enslave.

5 Food.

6 Eager to rise.

7 Bunch of flowers, bouquet.

8 The wych-elm is a broad leafed elm; found in Britain, the hornbeam is a tree with very hard wood; the quicken-tree is the rowan or mountain-ash. When Morris was a child, his family's property was on the border of Epping Forest, noted for its hornbeam trees. Queen Elizabeth I had a hunting lodge in this forest.

whiles he was amidst of this, he heard suddenly, close anigh him, a strange noise of roaring and braying,[1] not very great, but exceeding fierce and terrible, and not like to the voice of any beast that he knew. As has been aforesaid, Walter was no faint-heart; but what with the weakness of his travail and hunger, what with the strangeness of his adventure and his loneliness, his spirit failed him; he turned round towards the noise, his knees shook and he trembled: this way and that he looked, and then gave a great cry and tumbled down in a swoon; for close before him, at his very feet, was the dwarf whose image he had seen before, clad in his yellow coat, and grinning up at him from his hideous hairy countenance.

An evil creature

How long he lay there as one dead, he knew not, but when he woke again there was the dwarf sitting on his hams[2] close by him. And when he lifted up his head, the dwarf sent out that fearful harsh voice again; but this time Walter could make out words therein, and knew that the creature spoke and said:

"How now! What art thou? Whence comest? What wantest?"

Walter sat up and said: "I am a man; I hight[3] Golden Walter; I come from Langton; I want victual."

Said the dwarf, writhing[4] his face grievously, and laughing forsooth:[5] "I know it all: I asked thee to see what wise thou wouldst lie. I was sent forth to look for thee; and I have brought thee loathsome bread with me, such as ye aliens must needs eat: take it!"

Therewith he drew a loaf from a satchel which he bore, and thrust it towards Walter, who took it somewhat doubtfully for all his hunger.

The passion of the Evil Thing

The dwarf yelled at him: "Art thou dainty,[6] alien? Wouldst thou have flesh? Well, give me thy bow and an arrow or two, since thou art lazy-sick, and I will get thee a coney[7] or a hare, or a quail maybe. Ah, I forgot; thou art dainty, and wilt not eat flesh as I do, blood and all together, but must needs half burn it in the fire, or

1 Crying [like a donkey].

2 Knees.

3 Am named.

4 Twisting.

5 In truth, indeed.

6 A picky eater.

7 Rabbit.

mar it with hot water; as they say my Lady does: or as the Wretch, the Thing does; I know that, for I have seen It eating."

"Nay," said Walter, "this sufficeth;" and he fell to eating the bread, which was sweet between his teeth. Then when he had eaten a while, for hunger compelled him, he said to the dwarf: "But what meanest thou by the Wretch and the Thing? And what Lady is thy Lady?"

The passion of the Evil Thing

The creature let out another wordless roar as of furious anger; and then the words came: "It hath a face white and red, like to thine; and hands white as thine, yea, but whiter; and the like it is underneath its raiment, only whiter still: for I have seen It ...[1] yes, I have seen It; ah yes and yes and yes."

And therewith his words ran into gibber[2] and yelling, and he rolled about and smote at the grass: but in a while he grew quiet again and sat still, and then fell to laughing horribly again, and then said: "But thou, fool, wilt think It fair if thou fallest into Its[3] hands, and wilt repent it thereafter, as I did. Oh, the mocking and gibes[4] of It, and the tears and shrieks of It; and the knife! What! sayest thou of my Lady? ...[5] What Lady? O alien, what other Lady is there? And what shall I tell thee of her? it is like that she made me, as she made the Bear men. But she made not the Wretch, the Thing; and she hateth It sorely, as I do. And some day to come ..."[6]

Thereat he brake off and fell to wordless yelling a long while, and thereafter spake all panting: "Now I have told thee overmuch, and O if my Lady come to hear thereof. Now I will go."

Bread to eat and fear to brood over

And therewith he took out two more loaves from his wallet, and tossed them to Walter, and so turned and went his ways; whiles walking upright, as Walter had seen his image on the quay of Langton; whiles bounding and rolling like a ball thrown by a lad; whiles scuttling along on all-fours like an evil beast, and ever and anon giving forth that harsh and evil cry.

Walter sat a while after he was out of sight, so stricken with horror and loathing and a fear of he knew not what, that he might

1 CW: *dash.*

2 Inarticulate sounds.

3 K, LB: It's.

4 Scornful remarks.

5 CW: *dash.*

6 CW: *dash.*

not move. Then he plucked up a heart, and looked to his weapons and put the other loaves into his scrip.[1]

Then he arose and went his ways wondering, yea and dreading, what kind of creature he should next fall in with. For soothly it seemed to him that it would be worse than death if they were all such as this one; and that if it were so, he must needs slay and be slain.

Chapter X.
Walter Happeneth on Another Creature in the Strange Land

Walter goeth forward

But as he went on through the fair and sweet land so bright and sun-litten,[2] and he now rested and fed, the horror and fear ran off from him, and he wandered on merrily, neither did aught befall[3] him save the coming of night, when he laid him down under a great spreading oak with his drawn sword ready to hand, and fell asleep at once, and woke not till the sun was high.

Then he arose and went on his way again; and the land was no worser than yesterday; but even better, it might be; the greensward more flowery, the oaks and chestnuts greater. Deer[4] of diverse kinds he saw, and might easily have got his meat thereof; but he meddled not with them since he had his bread, and was timorous of lighting a fire. Withal he doubted little of having some entertainment; and that, might be, nought evil; since even that fearful dwarf had been courteous to him after his kind, and had done him good and not harm. But of the happening on the Wretch and the Thing, whereof the dwarf spake, he was yet somewhat afeard.

A shamefast[5] maiden

After he had gone a while and whenas the summer morn was at its brightest, he saw a little way ahead a grey rock rising up from amidst of a ring of oak-trees; so he turned thither straightway; for in this plain land[6] he had seen no rocks heretofore; and as he went he saw that there was a fountain gushing out from

---

1 Bag.
2 Sunshiny; K: sunlitten.
3 Anything happen.
4 Wild animals.
5 Bashful.
6 CW: plain-land.

under the rock, which ran thence in a fair little stream. And when he had the rock and the fountain and the stream clear before him, lo! a child of Adam sitting beside the fountain under the shadow of the rock. He drew a little nigher, and then saw that it was a woman, clad in green like the sward[1] whereon she lay. She was playing with the welling out of the water, and she had trussed[2] up her sleeves to the shoulder that she might thrust her bare arms therein. Her shoes of black leather lay on the grass beside her, and her feet and legs yet shone with the brook.

Belike amidst the splashing and clatter of the water she did not hear him drawing nigh, so that he was close to her before she lifted up her face and saw him, and he beheld her, that it was the maiden of the thrice-seen pageant. She reddened when she saw him, and hastily covered up her legs with her gown-skirt, and drew down the sleeves over her arms, but otherwise stirred not. As for him, he stood still, striving to speak to her; but no word might he bring out, and his heart beat sorely.

They talk together

But the maiden spake to him in a clear sweet voice, wherein was now no trouble: "Thou art an alien, art thou not? For I have not seen thee before."

"Yea," he said, "I am an alien; wilt thou be good to me?"

She said: "And why not? I was afraid at first, for I thought it had been the King's Son. I looked to see none other; for of goodly men he has been the only one here in the land this long while, till thy coming."

He said: "Didst thou look for my coming at about this time?"

"O nay," she said; "how might I?"

Said Walter: "I wot not; but the other man seemed to be looking for me, and knew of me, and he brought me bread to eat."

She looked on him anxiously, and grew somewhat pale, as she said: "What other one?"

Now Walter did not know what the dwarf might be to her, fellow-servant or what not, so he would not show his loathing of him; but answered wisely: "The little man in the yellow raiment."

But when she heard that word, she went suddenly very pale, and leaned her head aback, and beat the air with her hands; but said presently in a faint voice: "I pray thee talk not of that one while I am by, nor even think of him, if thou mayest forbear."[3]

---

1 Meadow.

2 Rolled.

3 Restrain yourself.

The Maid must have time for pondering

He spake not, and she was a little while before she came to herself again; then she opened her eyes, and looked upon Walter and smiled kindly on him, as though to ask his pardon for having scared him. Then she rose up in her place, and stood before him; and they were nigh together, for the stream betwixt them was little.

But he still looked anxiously upon her and said: "Have I hurt thee? I pray thy pardon."

She looked on him more sweetly still, and said: "O nay; thou wouldst not hurt me, thou!"

Then she blushed very red, and he in like wise;[1] but afterwards she turned pale, and laid a hand on her breast, and Walter cried out hastily: "O me! I have hurt thee again. Wherein have I done amiss?"

"In nought, in nought," she said; "but I am troubled, I wot not wherefore; some thought hath taken hold of me, and I know it not. Mayhappen[2] in a little while I shall know what troubles me. Now I bid thee depart from me a little, and I will abide here; and when thou comest back, it will either be that I have found it out or not; and in either case I will tell thee."

She spoke earnestly to him; but he said: "How long shall I abide away?"[3]

Her face was troubled as she answered him: "For no long while."

Walter comes back

He smiled on her and turned away, and went a space to the other side of the oak-trees, whence she was still within eye-shot. There he abode until the time seemed long to him; but he schooled himself and forbore;[4] for he said: Lest she send me away again. So he abided until again the time seemed long to him, and she called not to him: but once again he forbore to go; then at last he arose, and his heart beat and he trembled, and he walked back again speedily, and came to the maiden, who was still standing by the rock of the spring, her arms hanging down, her eyes downcast. She looked up at him as he drew nigh, and her face changed with eagerness as she said: "I am glad thou art come back, though it be no long while since thy departure" (sooth[5] to say it was

---

1 In a similar manner.

2 Perhaps.

3 K, LB: *no paragraph break.*

4 Restrained himself.

5 Truth.

scarce half an hour in all). "Nevertheless I have been thinking many things, and thereof will I now tell thee."

He said: "Maiden, there is a river betwixt us, though it be no big one. Shall I not stride over, and come to thee, that we may sit down together side by side on the green grass?"

The Maid telleth her finding

"Nay," she said, "not yet; tarry a while till I have told thee of matters. I must now tell thee of my thoughts in order."

Her colour went and came now, and she plaited[1] the folds of her gown with restless fingers. At last she said: "Now the first thing is this; that though thou hast seen me first only within this hour, thou hast set thine heart upon me to have me for thy speech-friend[2] and thy darling. And if this be not so, then is all my speech, yea and all my hope, come to an end at once."

"O yea!" said Walter, "even so it is: but how thou hast found this out I wot not; since now for the first time I say it, that thou art indeed my love, and my dear and my darling."

"Hush," she said, "hush! lest the wood have ears, and thy speech is loud: abide, and I shall tell thee how I know it. Whether this thy love shall outlast the first time that thou holdest my body in thine arms, I wot not, nor dost thou. But sore is my hope that it may be so; for I also, though it be but scarce an hour since I set eyes on thee, have cast mine eyes on thee to have thee for my love and my darling, and my speech-friend. And this is how I wot that thou lovest me, my friend. Now is all this dear and joyful, and overflows my heart with sweetness. But now must I tell thee of the fear and the evil which lieth behind it."

She will not be touched

Then Walter stretched out his hands to her, and cried out: "Yea, yea! But whatever evil entangle us, now we both know these two things, to wit, that thou lovest me, and I thee, wilt thou not come hither, that I may cast mine arms about thee, and kiss thee, if not thy kind lips or thy friendly face at all, yet at least thy dear hand: yea, that I may touch thy body in some wise?"

She looked on him steadily, and said softly: "Nay, this above all things must not be; and that it may not be is a part of the evil which entangles us. But hearken, friend, once again I tell thee that thy voice is over loud in this wilderness fruitful of evil. Now I have told thee, indeed, of two things whereof we both wot; but next I must needs tell thee of things whereof I wot, and thou

---

1 Twisted.

2 Confidant.

wottest not. Yet this were better, that thou pledge thy word not to touch so much as one of my hands, and that we go together a little way hence away from these tumbled stones, and sit down upon the open greensward; whereas here is cover if there be spying abroad."

They depart from the fountain that they may talk safely

Again, as she spoke, she turned very pale; but Walter said: "Since it must be so, I pledge thee my word to thee as I love thee."

And therewith she knelt down, and did on her foot-gear, and then sprang lightly over the rivulet; and then the twain of them went side by side some half a furlong[1] thence, and sat down, shadowed by the boughs of a slim quicken-tree[2] growing up out of the greensward, whereon for a good space around was neither bush nor brake.[3]

The Maid telleth of the Mistress
And of the King's Son

There began the maiden to talk soberly, and said: "This is what I must needs say to thee now, that thou art come into a land perilous for any one that loveth aught of good; from which, forsooth, I were fain[4] that thou wert gotten away safely, even though I should die of longing for thee. As for myself, my peril is, in a measure, less than thine; I mean the peril of death. But lo, thou, this iron on my foot is token that I am a thrall,[5] and thou knowest in what wise thralls must pay for transgressions. Furthermore, of what I am, and how I came hither, time would fail me to tell; but somewhile, maybe, I shall tell thee. I serve an evil mistress, of whom I may say that scarce I wot if she be a woman or not; but by some creatures is she accounted for a god, and as a god is heried;[6] and surely never god was crueller nor colder than she. Me she hateth sorely; yet if she hated me little or nought, small were the gain to me if it were her pleasure to deal hardly by me. But as things now are, and are like to be, it would not be for her pleasure, but for her pain and loss, to make an end of me, therefore, as I said e'en[7] now, my mere

---

1 "Furlong" originally meant the length of a plowed furrow. It is a measurement standardized as 220 yards, which is one-eighth of a mile.

2 Rowan, mountain-ash.

3 Thicket.

4 Eager.

5 Slave.

6 Worshipped.

7 Even.

life is not in peril with her; unless, perchance, some sudden passion get the better of her, and she slay me, and repent of it thereafter. For so it is, that if it be the least evil of her conditions that she is wanton,[1] at least wanton she is to the letter. Many a time hath she cast the net for the catching of some goodly young man; and her latest prey (save it be thou) is the young man whom I named, when first I saw thee, by the name of the King's Son. He is with us yet, and I fear him; for of late hath he wearied of her, though it is but plain truth to say of her, that she is the wonder of all Beauties of the World. He hath wearied of her, I say, and hath cast his eyes upon me, and if I were heedless, he would betray me to the uttermost of the wrath of my mistress. For needs must I say of him, though he be a goodly man, and now fallen into thralldom,[2] that he hath no bowels of compassion;[3] but is a dastard, who for an hour's pleasure would undo me, and thereafter stand[4] by smiling and taking my mistress's pardon with good cheer, while for me would be no pardon. Seest thou, therefore, how it is with me between these two cruel fools? And moreover there are others of whom I will not even speak to thee."

The grief of the Maid

And therewith she put her hands before her face, and wept, and murmured: "Who shall deliver me from this death in life?"

But Walter cried out: "For what else am I come hither, I, I?"

And it was a near thing that he did not take her in his arms, but he remembered his pledged word, and drew aback from her in terror, whereas he had an inkling of why she would not suffer it; and he wept with her.

But suddenly the Maid left weeping, and said in a changed voice: "Friend, whereas thou speakest of delivering me, it is more like that I shall deliver thee. And now I pray thy pardon for thus grieving thee with my grief, and that more especially because thou mayst not solace thy grief with kisses and caresses; but so it was, that for once I was smitten by the thought of the anguish of this land, and the joy of all the world besides."

Therewith she caught her breath in a half-sob, but refrained her and went on: "Now dear friend and darling, take good heed to all that I shall say to thee, whereas thou must do after the

---

1 Sexually immoral.

2 Slavery.

3 According to pre-modern anatomy, the organ that governs compassion is the bowels.

4 CW: would stand.

teaching of my words. And first, I deem by the monster having met thee at the gates of the land, and refreshed thee, that the Mistress hath looked for thy coming; nay, by thy coming hither at all, that she hath cast her net and caught thee. Hast thou noted aught that might seem to make this more like?"

Walter tells of his vision

Said Walter: "Three times in full daylight have I seen go past me the images of the monster and thee and a glorious lady, even as if ye were alive."

And therewith he told her in few words how it had gone with him since that day on the quay at Langton.

She said: "Then it is no longer perhaps, but certain, that thou art her latest catch; and even so I deemed from the first: and, dear friend, this is why I have not suffered thee to kiss or caress me, so sore as I longed for thee. For the Mistress will have thee for her only, and hath lured thee hither for nought else; and she is wise in wizardry (even as some deal[1] am I), and wert thou to touch me with hand or mouth on my naked flesh, yea, or were it even my raiment, then would she scent the savour of thy love upon me, and then, though it may be she would spare thee, she would not spare me."

The Maid pondereth

Then was she silent a little, and seemed very downcast, and Walter held his peace from grief and confusion and helplessness; for of wizardry he knew nought.

At last the Maid spake again, and said: "Nevertheless we will not die redeless.[2] Now thou must look to this, that from henceforward it is thee, and not the King's Son, whom she desireth, and that so much the more that she hath not set eyes on thee. Remember this, whatsoever her seeming may be to thee. Now, therefore, shall the King's Son be free, though he know it not, to cast his love on whomso he will; and, in a way, I also shall be free to yeasay him.[3] Though, forsooth, so fulfilled is she with malice and spite, that even then she may turn round on me to punish me for doing that which she would have me do. Now let me think of it."

She hath a hidden rede

Then was she silent a good while, and spoke at last: "Yea, all things are perilous, and a perilous rede[4] I have thought of,

---

1 In some way.

2 Without advice.

3 Agree to him.

4 Advice, plan.

whereof I will not tell thee as yet; so waste not the short while by asking me. At least the worst will be no worse than what shall come if we strive not against it. And now, my friend, amongst perils it is growing more and more perilous that we twain should be longer together. But I would say one thing yet; and maybe another thereafter. Thou hast cast thy love upon one who will be true to thee, whatsoever may befall; yet is she a guileful[1] creature, and might not help it her life long, and now for thy very sake must needs be more guileful now than ever before. And as for me, the guileful, my love have I cast upon a lovely man, and one true and simple, and a stout-heart; but at such a pinch is he, that if he withstand all temptation, his withstanding may belike undo both him and me. Therefore swear we both of us, that by both of us shall all guile and all falling away be forgiven on the day when we shall be free to love each the other as our hearts will."

They swear leal[2] love together

Walter cried out: "O love, I swear it indeed! thou art my Hallow,[3] and I will swear it as on the relics of a Hallow; on thy hands and thy feet I swear it."

The words seemed to her a dear caress; and she laughed, and blushed, and looked full kindly on him; and then her face grew solemn, and she said: "On thy life I swear it!"

Then she said: "Now is there nought for thee to do but to go hence straight to the Golden House, which is my Mistress's house, and the only house in this land (save one which I may not see), and lieth southward no long way. How she will deal with thee, I wot not; but all I have said of her and thee and the King's Son is true. Therefore I say to thee, be wary[4] and cold at heart, whatsoever outward semblance thou mayst make. If thou have to yield thee to her, then yield rather late than early, so as to gain time. Yet not so late as to seem shamed in yielding for fear's sake. Hold fast to thy life, my friend, for in warding[5] that, thou wardest me from grief without remedy. Thou wilt see me ere long; it may be to-morrow, it may be some days hence. But forget not, that what I may do, that I am doing. Take heed also that thou pay no more heed to me, or rather less, than if thou wert meeting a maiden of no account in the streets of thine own town. O my

---

1 Tricky.

2 Loyal.

3 Saint.

4 Careful.

5 Guarding.

love! barren is this first farewell, as was our first meeting; but surely shall there be another meeting better than the first, and the last farewell may be long and long yet."

Now they part for a while

Therewith she stood up, and he knelt before her a little while without any word, and then arose and went his ways; but when he had gone a space he turned about, and saw her still standing in the same place; she stayed a moment when she saw him turn, and then herself turned about.

So he departed through the fair land, and his heart was full with hope and fear as he went.

Chapter XI. Walter Happeneth on the Mistress

It was but a little after noon when Walter left the Maid behind: he steered south by the sun, as the Maid had bidden him, and went swiftly; for, as a good knight wending to battle, the time seemed long to him till he should meet the foe.

So an hour before sunset he saw something white and gay gleaming through the boles[1] of the oak-trees, and presently there was clear before him a most goodly house builded of white marble, carved all about with knots and imagery,[2] and the carven folk were all painted of their lively colours, whether it were their raiment or their flesh, and the housings wherein they stood all done with gold and fair hues. Gay were the windows of the house; and there was a pillared porch before the great door, with images betwixt the pillars both of men and beasts: and when Walter looked up to the roof of the house, he saw that it gleamed and shone; for all the tiles were of yellow metal, which he deemed to be of very gold.

Walter cometh into the Hall

All this he saw as he went, and tarried not to gaze upon it; for he said, belike[3] there will be time for me to look on all this before I die. But he said also, that, though the house was not of

1 Trunks.

2 Morris here describes relief carving—decorative designs and human figures carved into stone—but the statues are not free-standing, only partially emerging from the stone walls. Not only was Morris trained in architecture, but he published a tale while an undergraduate, "The Story of the Unknown Church," set in the Middle Ages, which involves a brother and sister who carve such decorations for the construction of a church.

3 CW: Belike.

the greatest,[1] it was beyond compare of all houses of the world.

There sit two on the high-seat

Now he entered it by the porch, and came into a hall many-pillared, and vaulted over,[2] the walls painted with gold and ultramarine,[3] the floor dark, and spangled with many colours, and the windows[4] glazed with knots and pictures. Midmost thereof was a fountain of gold, whence the water ran two ways in gold-lined runnels,[5] spanned twice with little bridges of silver. Long was that hall, and now not very light, so that Walter was come past the fountain before he saw any folk therein: then he looked up toward the high-seat, and him-seemed[6] that a great light shone thence, and dazzled his eyes; and he went on a little way, and then fell on his knees; for there before him on the high-seat sat that wondrous Lady, whose lively image had been shown to him thrice before; and she was clad in gold and jewels, as he had erst[7] seen her. But now she was not alone; for by her side sat a young man, goodly enough, so far as Walter might see him, and most richly clad, with a jewelled sword by his side, and a chaplet[8] of gems on his head. They held each other by the hand, and seemed to be in dear converse together; but they spake softly, so that Walter might not hear what they said, till at last the man spake aloud to the Lady: "Seest thou not that there is a man in the hall?"

"Yea," she said, "I see him yonder, kneeling on his knees; let him come nigher and give some account of himself."

So Walter stood up and drew nigh, and stood there, all shamefaced and confused, looking on those twain, and wondering at the beauty of the Lady. As for the man, who was slim, and black-haired, and straight-featured, for all his goodliness Walter accounted him little, and nowise deemed him to look chieftain-like.

---

1 Largest.

2 The vaults referred to here are the arches that typically support the roofs of large medieval buildings.

3 Blue.

4 Morris and Company sold a well-respected line of stained glass windows.

5 Small streams.

6 It seemed to him; CW: himseemed.

7 Earlier.

8 Wreath.

Walter is shamed

Now the Lady spake not to Walter any more than erst; but at last the man said: "Why doest thou not kneel as thou didst erewhile?"[1]

Walter was on the point of giving him back a fierce answer; but the Lady spake and said: "Nay, friend, it matters not whether he kneel or stand; but he may say, if he will, what he would have of me, and wherefore he is come hither."

Then spake Walter, for as wroth[2] and ashamed as he was: "Lady, I have strayed into this land, and have come to thine house as I suppose, and if I be not welcome, I may well depart straightway, and seek a way out of thy land, if thou wouldst drive me thence, as well as out of thine house."

The Disdain of the Lady

Thereat the Lady turned and looked on him, and when her eyes met his, he felt a pang of fear and desire mingled shoot through his heart. This time she spoke to him; but coldly, without either wrath or any thought of him: "New-comer,"[3] she said, "I have not bidden thee hither; but here mayst thou abide a while if thou wilt; nevertheless, take heed that here is no King's Court. There is, forsooth, a folk that serveth me (or, it may be, more than one), of whom thou wert best to know nought. Of others I have but two servants, whom thou wilt see; and the one is a strange creature, who should scare thee or scathe[4] thee with a good will, but of a good will shall serve nought save me; the other is a woman, a thrall, of little avail,[5] save that, being compelled, she will work woman's service for me, but whom none else shall compel ... Yea, but what is all this to thee; or to me that I should tell it to thee? I will not drive thee away; but if thine entertainment please thee not, make no plaint thereof to me, but depart at thy will. Now is this talk betwixt us overlong, since, as thou seest, I and this King's Son are in converse together. Art thou a King's Son?"

"Nay, Lady," said Walter, "I am but of the sons of the merchants."

"It matters not," she said; "go thy ways into one of the chambers."

---

1 Before.

2 Angry.

3 CW: Newcomer.

4 Harm.

5 Account.

And straightway she fell a-talking to the man who sat beside her concerning the singing of the birds beneath her window in the morning; and of how she had bathed her that day in a pool of the woodlands, when she had been heated with hunting, and so forth; and all as if there had been none there save her and the King's Son.

But Walter departed all ashamed, as though he had been a poor man thrust away from a rich kinsman's door; and he said to himself that this woman was hateful, and nought love-worthy, and that she was little like to tempt him, despite all the fairness of her body.

No one else he saw in the house that even:[1] he found meat and drink duly served on a fair table, and thereafter he came on a goodly bed, and all things needful, but no child of Adam to do him service, or bid him welcome or warning. Nevertheless he ate, and drank, and slept, and put off thought of all these things till the morrow, all the more as he hoped to see the kind maiden some time betwixt sunrise and sunset on that new day.

Chapter XII.

The Wearing of Four Days in the Wood Beyond the World

He arose betimes, but found no one to greet him, neither was there any sound of folk moving within the fair house; so he but broke his fast, and then went forth and wandered amongst the trees, till he found him a stream to bathe in, and after he had washed the night off him he lay down under a tree thereby for a while, but soon turned back toward the house, lest perchance the Maid should come thither and he should miss her.

It should be said that half a bow-shot from the house on that side (i.e.[2] due north thereof) was a little hazel-brake,[3] and round about it the trees were smaller of kind than the oaks and chestnuts he had passed through before, being mostly of birch and quicken-beam[4] and young ash, with small wood betwixt them; so now he passed through the thicket, and, coming to the edge thereof, beheld the Lady and the King's Son walking together hand in hand, full lovingly by seeming.

---

1 Evening; CW: *semi-colon.*

2 LB: *add italics for* i.e.

3 Thicket of hazel trees.

4 Rowan, mountain-ash.

Walter sees the Evil Thing again, or one like him

He deemed[1] it unmeet[2] to draw back and hide him, so he went forth past them toward the house. The King's Son scowled on him as he passed, but the Lady, over whose beauteous face flickered the joyous morning smiles, took no more heed of him than if he had been one of the trees of the wood. But she had been so high and disdainful with him the evening before, that he thought little of that. The twain went on, skirting the hazel-copse,[3] and he could not choose but turn his eyes on them, so sorely did the Lady's beauty draw them. Then befell another thing; for behind them the boughs of the hazels parted, and there stood that little evil thing, he or another of his kind; for he was quite unclad,[4] save by his fell of yellowy-brown hair, and that he was girt with a leathern girdle,[5] wherein was stuck an ugly two-edged knife: he stood upright a moment, and cast his eyes at Walter and grinned, but not as if he knew him; and scarce could Walter say whether it were the one he had seen, or another: then he cast himself down on his belly, and fell to creeping through the long grass like a serpent, following the footsteps of the Lady and her lover; and now, as he crept, Walter deemed, in his loathing, that the creature was liker to a ferret than aught else. He crept on marvelously swiftly, and was soon clean out of sight. But Walter stood staring after him for a while, and then lay down by the copse-side, that he might watch the house and the entry thereof; for he thought, now perchance presently[6] will the kind maiden come hither to comfort me with a word or two. But hour passed by hour, and still she came not; and still he lay there, and thought of the Maid, and longed for her kindness and wisdom, till he could not refrain his tears, and wept for the lack of her. Then he arose, and went and sat in the porch, and was very downcast of mood.

Walter longeth for the Maid

But as he sat there, back comes the Lady again, the King's Son leading her by the hand; they entered the porch, and she passed by him so close that the odour of her raiment filled all the air about him, and the sleekness of her side nigh touched him, so that he could not fail to note that her garments were somewhat disarrayed, and that she kept her right hand (for her left the

---

1 Judged.

2 Inappropriate.

3 Thicket of hazel trees.

4 Naked.

5 Belt.

6 Perhaps soon.

King's Son held) to her bosom to hold the cloth together there, whereas the rich raiment had been torn off from her right shoulder. As they passed by him, the King's Son once more scowled on him, wordless, but even more fiercely than before; and again the Lady heeded him nought.

Those two pass him disdainfully

After they had gone on a while, he entered the hall, and found it empty from end to end, and no sound in it save the tinkling of the fountain; but there was victual set on the board. He ate and drank thereof to keep life lusty[1] within him, and then went out again to the wood-side to watch and to long; and the time hung heavy on his hands because of the lack of the fair Maiden.

The King's Son drives him in

He was of mind not to go into the house to his rest that night, but to sleep under the boughs of the forest. But a little after sunset he saw a bright-clad image moving amidst the carven images of the porch, and the King's Son came forth and went straight to him, and said: "Thou art to enter the house, and go into thy chamber forthwith, and by no means to go forth of it betwixt sunset and sunrise. My Lady will not away with[2] thy prowling round the house in the night-tide."

Therewith he turned away, and went into the house again; and Walter followed him soberly, remembering how the Maid had bidden[3] him forbear. So he went to his chamber, and slept.

A fair sight but perilous

But amidst of the night he awoke and deemed that he heard a voice not far off, so he crept out of his bed and peered around, lest, perchance, the Maid had come to speak with him; but his chamber was dusk and empty: then he went to the window and looked out, and saw the moon shining bright and white upon the greensward. And lo! the Lady walking with the King's Son, and he clad in thin and wonton[4] raiment, but she in nought else save what God had given her of long, crispy[5] yellow hair. Then was Walter ashamed to look on her, seeing that there was a man with her, and gat him back[6] to his bed; but yet a long while ere he slept

---

1 Healthy.

2 Put up with.

3 Commanded.

4 Lascivious.

5 Curled.

6 Went back.

again he had the image before his eyes of the fair woman on the dewy moonlit grass.

The next day matters went much the same way, and the next also, save that his sorrow was increased, and he sickened sorely of hope deferred. On the fourth day also the forenoon wore as erst;[1] but in the heat of the afternoon Walter sought to the hazel-copse, and laid him down there hard by a little clearing thereof, and slept from very weariness of grief. There, after a while, he woke with words still hanging in his ears, and he knew at once that it was they twain talking together.

The Lady mocks the King's Son

The King's Son had just done his say, and now it was the Lady beginning in her honey-sweet voice, low but strong, wherein even was a little of huskiness; she said: "Otto, belike it were well to have a little patience, till we find out what the man is, and whence he cometh; it will always be easy to rid us of him; it is but a word to our Dwarf-king, and it will be done in a few minutes."

"Patience!" said the King's Son, angrily; "I wot not how to have patience with him; for I can see of him that he is rude and violent and headstrong, and a low-born wily one. Forsooth, he had patience enough with me the other even,[2] when I rated[3] him in, like the dog that he is, and he had no manhood to say one word to me. Soothly, as he followed after me, I had a mind to turn about and deal him a buffet[4] on the face, to see if I could but draw one angry word from him."

The Lady laughed, and said: "Well, Otto, I know not; that which thou deemest dastardy[5] in him may be but prudence and wisdom, and he an alien, far from his friends and nigh to his foes. Perchance we shall yet try him what he is. Meanwhile, I rede[6] thee try him not with buffets, save[7] he be weaponless and with bounden[8] hands; or else I deem that but a little while shalt thou be fain of[9] thy blow."

---

1 Earlier.

2 Evening.

3 Insulted.

4 Blow.

5 Cowardice.

6 Advise.

7 Unless.

8 Tied.

9 Regret.

The Lady seems more friendly

Now when Walter heard her words and the voice wherein they were said, he might not forbear[1] being stirred by them, and to him, all lonely there, they seemed friendly.

But he lay still, and the King's Son answered the Lady and said: "I know not what is in thine heart concerning this runagate,[2] that thou shouldst bemock[3] me with his valiancy, whereof thou knowest nought. If thou deem me unworthy of thee, send me back safe to my father's country; I may look to have worship there; yea, and the love of fair women belike."

Therewith it seemed as if he had put forth his hand to the Lady to caress her, for she said: "Nay, lay not thine hand on my shoulder, for to-day and now it is not the hand of love, but of pride and folly, and would-be mastery. Nay, neither shalt thou rise up and leave me until thy mood is softer and kinder to me."

And yet again

Then was there silence betwixt them a while, and thereafter the King's Son spake in a wheedling[4] voice: "My goddess, I pray thee pardon me! But canst thou wonder that I fear thy wearying of me, and am therefore peevish and jealous? thou so far above the Queens of the World, and I a poor youth that without thee were nothing!"

She answered nought, and he went on again: "Was it not so, O goddess, that this man of the sons of the merchants was little heedful of thee, and thy loveliness and thy majesty?"

She laughed and said: "Maybe he deemed not that he had much to gain of us, seeing thee sitting by our side, and whereas we spake to him coldly and sternly and disdainfully. Withal, the poor youth was dazzled and shamefaced before us; that we could see in the eyes and the mien[5] of him."

The King's Son would draw wrath on the Maid

Now this she spoke so kindly and sweetly, that again was Walter all stirred thereat; and it came into his mind that it might be she knew he was anigh and hearing her, and that she spake as much for him as for the King's Son: but that one answered: "Lady, didst thou not see somewhat else in his eyes, to wit, that they had but of late looked on some fair woman other than thee?

---

1 Avoid.

2 Runaway.

3 Mock.

4 Coaxing.

5 Manner, bearing.

As for me, I deem it not so unlike that on the way to thine hall he may have fallen in with thy Maid."

He spoke in a faltering voice, as if shrinking from some storm that might come. And forsooth the Lady's voice was changed as she answered, though there was no outward heat in it; rather it was sharp and eager and cold at once. She said: "Yea, that is not ill thought of; but we may not always keep our thrall in mind. If it be so as thou deemest, we shall come to know it most like when we next fall in with her; or if she hath been shy this time, then shall she pay the heavier for it; for we will question her by the Fountain in the Hall as to what betid[1] by the Fountain of the Rock."

Spake the King's Son, faltering yet more: "Lady, were it not better to question the man himself? the Maid is stout-hearted, and will not be speedily quelled[2] into a true tale; whereas the man I deem of no account."

The Lady threatens the Maid

"No, no," said the Lady sharply, "it shall not be."

Then was she silent a while; and then she said: "How if the man should prove to be our master?"

"Nay, our Lady," said the King's Son, "thou art jesting with me; thou and thy might and thy wisdom, and all that thy wisdom may command, to be over-mastered by a gangrel churl!"[3]

"But how if I will not have it command, King's Son?" said the Lady. "I tell thee I know thine heart, but thou knowest not mine. But be at peace! For since thou hast prayed for this woman ...[4] nay, not with thy words, I wot, but with thy trembling hands, and thine anxious eyes, and knitted brow ...[5] I say, since thou hast prayed for her so earnestly, she shall escape this time. But whether it will be to her gain in the long run, I misdoubt me. See thou to that, Otto! Thou who hast held me in thine arms so oft. And now thou mayest depart if thou wilt."

The next day

It seemed to Walter as if the King's Son were dumbfoundered at her words: he answered nought, and presently he rose from the ground, and went his ways slowly toward the house. The Lady lay there a little while, and then went her ways also; but turned away

---

1 Happened.

2 Subdued.

3 Wandering beggar.

4 CW: *dash.*

5 CW: *dash.*

from the house toward the wood at the other end thereof, whereby Walter had first come thither.

As for Walter, he was confused in mind and shaken in sprit; and withal he seemed to see guile and cruel deeds under the talk of those two, and waxed wrathful thereat.[1] Yet he said to himself, that nought might he do, but was as one bound hand and foot, till he had seen the Maid again.

Chapter XIII. Now is the Hunt Up

The Lady is grown gracious to Walter

Next morning was he up betimes,[2] but he was cast down and heavy of heart, not looking for aught else to betide[3] than had betid those last four days. But otherwise it fell out; for when he came down into the hall, there was the Lady sitting on the high-seat all alone, clad but in a coat of white linen; and she turned her head when she heard his footsteps, and looked on him, and greeted him, and said: "Come hither, guest."

So yet he went and stood before her, and she said: "Though as yet thou hast had no welcome here, and no honour, it hath not entered into thine heart to flee from us; and to say sooth, that is well for thee, for flee away from our hand thou mightest not, nor mightest thou depart without our furtherance.[4] But for this we can thee thank, that thou hast abided here our bidding, and eaten thine heart through the heavy wearing of four days, and made no plaint.[5] Yet I cannot deem thee a dastard; thou so well knit and shapely of body, so clear-eyed and bold of visage. Wherefore now I ask thee, art thou willing to do me service, thereby to earn thy guesting?"[6]

She biddeth him service

Walter answered her, somewhat faltering at first, for he was astonished at the change which had come over her; for now she spoke to him in friendly wise,[7] though indeed as a great lady would speak to a young man ready to serve her in all honour.

---

1 Grew angry at it.

2 Early.

3 Happen.

4 Help.

5 Complaint.

6 Earn your keep.

7 Manner.

Said he: "Lady, I can thank thee humbly and heartily in that thou biddest me do thee service; for these days past I have loathed the emptiness of the hours, and nought better could I ask for than to serve so glorious a Mistress in all honour."

She frowned somewhat, and said: "Thou shalt not call me Mistress; there is but one who so calleth me, that is my thrall; and thou art none such. Thou shalt call me Lady, and I shall be well pleased that thou be my squire, and for this present thou shalt serve me in the hunting. So get thy gear; take thy bow and arrows, and gird thee to thy sword. For in this fair land may one find beasts more perilous than be buck or hart. I go now to array[1] me; we will depart while the day is yet young; for so make we the summer day the fairest."

Now cometh the Maid again

He made obeisance[2] to her, and she arose and went to her chamber, and Walter dight[3] himself, and then abode her in the porch; and in less than an hour she came out of the hall, and Walter's heart beat when he saw that the Maid followed her hard at heel, and scarce might he school his eyes not to gaze over-eagerly at his dear friend. She was clad even as she was before, and was changed in no wise,[4] save that love troubled her face when she first beheld him, and she had much ado to master it: howbeit the Mistress heeded not the trouble of her, or made no semblance[5] of heeding it, till the Maiden's face was all according to its wont.[6]

The Lady is kind

But this Walter found strange, that after all that disdain of the Maid's thralldom which he had heard of the Mistress, and after all the threats against her, now was the Mistress become mild and debonair[7] to her, as a good lady to her good maiden. When Walter bowed the knee to her, she turned unto the Maid, and said: "Look thou, my Maid, at this fair new Squire that I have gotten! Will not he be valiant in the greenwood?[8] And see whether he be well shapen or not. Doth he not touch thine heart, when thou thinkest of all the woe, and fear, and trouble of the World beyond

1 Clothe [with decorative clothing].
2 Bowed.
3 Dressed, prepared.
4 Way.
5 Appearance.
6 Custom.
7 Courteous.
8 Woods.

the Wood,[1] which he hath escaped, to dwell in this little land peaceably, and well-beloved both by the Mistress and the Maid? And thou, my Squire, look a little at this fair slim Maiden, and say if she pleaseth thee not: didst thou deem that we had any thing so fair in this lonely place?"

Frank and kind was the smile on her radiant visage, nor did she seem to note any whit[2] the trouble on Walter's face, nor how he strove to keep his eyes from the Maid. As for her, she had so wholly mastered her countenance, that belike she used her face guilefully,[3] for she stood as one humble but happy, with a smile on her face, blushing, and with her head hung down as if shamefaced before a goodly young man, a stranger.

But the Lady looked upon her kindly and said: "Come hither, child, and fear not this frank and free young man, who belike feareth thee a little, and full certainly feareth me; and yet only after the manner of men."

A lovely thing in the land

And therewith she took the Maid by the hand and drew her to her, and pressed her to her bosom, and kissed her cheeks and her lips, and undid the lacing of her gown and bared a shoulder of her, and swept away her skirt from her feet; and then turned to Walter and said: "Lo thou, Squire, is not this a lovely thing to have grown up amongst our rough oak-boles?[4] What! art thou looking at the iron ring there? It is nought, save a token that she is mine, and that I may not be without her."

Then she took the Maid by the shoulders and turned her about as in sport, and said: "Go thou now, and bring hither the good grey ones;[5] for needs must we bring home some venison to-day, whereas this stout warrior may not feed on nought save manchets[6] and honey."

So the Maid went her way, taking care, as Walter deemed, to give no side glance to him. But he stood there shamefaced, so confused with all this open-hearted kindness of the great Lady and with the fresh sight of the darling beauty of the Maid, that he went nigh to thinking that all he had heard since he had come to the porch of the house that first time was but a dream of evil.

---

1 LB: Wood beyond the World.

2 Bit.

3 Deceitfully.

4 Oak trunks.

5 That is, her hunting dogs.

6 Fine loaves of wheat bread.

The Lady jests bitter-sweet

But while he stood pondering these matters, and staring before him as one mazed,[1] the Lady laughed out in his face, and touched him on the arm and said: "Ah, our Squire, is it so that now thou hast seen my Maid thou wouldst with a good will abide behind to talk with her? But call to mind thy word pledged to me e'en now! And moreover I tell thee this for thy behoof[2] now she is out of ear-shot, that I will above all things take thee away to-day: for there be other eyes, and they nought uncomely, that look at whiles on my fair-ankled thrall; and who knows but the swords might be out if I take not the better heed, and give thee not every whit of thy will."

Walter meets guile with guile

As she spoke and moved forward, he turned a little, so that now the edge of that hazel coppice was within his eye-shot, and he deemed that once more he saw the yellow-brown evil thing crawling forth from the thicket; then, turning suddenly on the Lady, he met her eyes, and seemed in one moment of time to find a far other look in them than that of frankness and kindness; though in a flash they changed back again, and she said merrily and sweetly: "So, so,[3] Sir Squire, now art thou awake again, and mayest for a little while look on me."

Now it came into his head, with that look of hers, all that might befall[4] him and the Maid if he mastered not his passion, nor did what he might to dissemble;[5] so he bent the knee to her, and spoke boldly to her in her own vein,[6] and said: "Nay, most gracious of ladies, never would I abide behind to-day since thou farest afield. But if my speech be hampered, or mine eyes stray, is it not because my mind is confused by thy beauty, and the honey of kind words which floweth from thy mouth?"

Of the Lady's array

She laughed outright at his word, but not disdainfully, and said: "This is well spoken, Squire, and even what a squire should say to his liege[7] lady, when the sun is up on a fair morning, and she and he and all the world are glad."

---

1 Amazed.

2 Advantage.

3 K, LB: So so.

4 Happen to.

5 Pretend.

6 Manner.

7 One owed service under the medieval social system of feudalism.

She stood quite near him as she spoke, her hand was on his shoulder, and her eyes shone and sparkled. Sooth to say, that excusing of his confusion was like enough in seeming to the truth; for sure never creature was fashioned fairer than she: clad she was for the greenwood as the hunting-goddess of the Gentiles,[1] with her green gown gathered unto her girdle, and sandals on her feet; a bow in her hand and a quiver at her back: she was taller and bigger of fashion than the dear Maiden, whiter of flesh, and more glorious, and brighter of hair; as a flower of flowers for fairness and fragrance.

She said: "Thou art verily a fair squire before the hunt is up, and if thou be as good in the hunting, all will be better than well, and the guest will be welcome. But lo! here cometh our Maid with the good grey ones.[2] Go meet her, and we will tarry no longer than for thy taking the leash in hand."

The Lady lies somewhat

So Walter looked, and saw the Maid coming with two couple of great hounds in the leash straining against her as she came along. He ran lightly to meet her, wondering if he should have a look, or a half-whisper from her; but she let him take the white thongs[3] from her hand, with the same half-smile of shamefacedness still set on her face, and, going past him, came softly up to the Lady, swaying like a willow-branch in the wind, and stood before her, with her arms hanging down by her side. Then the Lady turned to her, and said: "Look to thyself, our Maid, while we are away. This fair young man thou needest not to fear indeed, for he is good and leal;[4] but what thou shalt do with the King's Son I wot not. He is a hot lover forsooth, but a hard man; and whiles[5] evil is his mood, and perilous both to thee and me. And if thou do his will, it shall be ill for thee; and if thou do it not, take heed of him, and let me, and me only, come between his wrath and thee. I may do somewhat for thee. Even yesterday he was instant[6] with me to have thee chastised[7] after the manner of thralls; but I bade[8] him keep silence of such words, and jeered

1 The reference here is to the Roman goddess Diana, who, among other things, was goddess of the hunt.

2 That is, the hunting dogs.

3 Leashes.

4 Loyal.

5 Sometimes.

6 Insistent.

7 Punished.

8 Commanded.

him and mocked him, till he went away from me peevish and in anger. So look to it that thou fall not into any trap. of his contrivance."

Now is the Maid left behind

Then the Maid cast herself at the Mistress's feet, and kissed and embraced them; and as she rose up, the Lady laid her hand lightly on her head, and then, turning to Walter, cried out: "Now, Squire, let us leave all these troubles and wiles[1] and desires behind us, and flit through the merry greenwood like the Gentiles[2] of old days."

And therewith she drew up the laps of her gown till the whiteness of her knees was seen, and set off swiftly toward the wood that lay south of the house, and Walter followed, marvelling at her goodliness; nor durst he cast a look backward to the Maiden, for he knew that she desired him, and it was her only that he looked to for his deliverance from this house of guile and lies.

Chapter XIV. The Hunting of the Hart[3]

As they went, they found a change in the land, which grew emptier of big and wide-spreading trees, and more beset[4] with thickets. From one of these they roused a hart, and Walter let slip his hounds thereafter, and he and the Lady followed running. Exceeding swift was she, and well-breathed withal, so that Walter wondered at her; and eager she was in the chase as the very hounds, heeding nothing the scratching of briars or the whipping of stiff twigs as she sped on. But for all their eager hunting, the quarry outran both dogs and folk, and gat him[5] into a great thicket, amidmost whereof was a wide plash[6] of water. Into the thicket they followed him, but he took to the water under their eyes and made land on the other side; and because of the tangle of underwood, he swam across much faster than they might have any hope to come round on him; and so were the hunters left undone for that time.

---

1 Tricks.
2 Pagans.
3 Deer.
4 Covered.
5 Got itself.
6 Shallow pool.

The Lady is peevish

So the Lady cast herself down on the green grass anigh[1] the water, while Walter blew the hounds in[2] and coupled[3] them up; then he turned round to her, and lo! she was weeping for despite that they had lost the quarry; and again did Walter wonder that so little a matter should raise a passion of tears in her. He durst not ask what ailed her, or proffer her solace,[4] but was not ill apaid[5] by beholding her loveliness as she lay.

Presently she raised up her head and turned to Walter, and spake to him angrily and said: "Squire, why dost thou stand staring at me like a fool?"

"Yea, Lady," he said; "but the sight of thee maketh me foolish to do aught else but to look on thee."

She said, in a peevish[6] voice: "Tush, Squire, the day is too far spent for soft and courtly speeches; what was good there is nought so good here. Withal, I know more of thine heart than thou deemest."

The Lady will bathe

Walter hung down his head and reddened, and she looked on him, and her face changed, and she smiled and said, kindly this time: "Look ye, Squire, I am hot and weary, and ill-content; but presently it will be better with me; for my knees have been telling my shoulders that the cold water of this little lake will be sweet and pleasant this summer noonday, and that I shall forget my foil[7] when I have taken my pleasure therein. Wherefore, go thou with thine hounds without the thicket and there abide my coming. And I bid thee look not aback as thou goest, for therein were peril to thee:[8] I shall not keep thee tarrying long alone."

He bowed his head to her, and turned and went his ways. And now, when he was a little space away from her, he deemed her indeed a marvel of women, and well-nigh[9] forgat all his doubts and fears concerning her, whether she were a fair image fash-

---

1 Near.

2 Gathered the dogs with a hunting horn.

3 Tied them two by two.

4 Offer her comfort.

5 Rewarded.

6 Irritated.

7 Defeat.

8 According to the ancient legend, the goddess Diana turned Acteon into a stag and had her hounds kill him after he saw her bathing naked. In the Middle Ages, Diana was associated with witchcraft as well as the hunt.

9 CW: wellnigh.

ioned out of lies and guile, or it might be but an evil thing in the shape of a goodly woman. Forsooth, when he saw her caressing the dear and friendly Maid, his heart all turned against her, despite what his eyes and his ears told his mind, and she seemed like as it were a serpent enfolding the simplicity of the body which he loved.

Now is she kind again

But now it was all changed, and he lay on the grass and longed for her coming; which was delayed for somewhat more than an hour. Then she came back to him, smiling and fresh and cheerful, her green gown let down to her heels.

He sprang up to meet her, and she came close to him, and spake from a laughing face: "Squire, has thou no meat in thy wallet? For, meseemeth, I fed thee when thou wert hungry the other day; do thou now the same by me."

He smiled, and louted[1] to her, and took his wallet and brought out thence bread and flesh and wine, and spread them all out before her on the green grass, and then stood by humbly before her. But she said: "Nay, my Squire, sit down by me and eat with me, for to-day are we both hunters together."

So he sat down by her trembling, but neither for awe of her greatness, nor for fear and horror of her guile and sorcery.

She asks Walter of Langton and its folk

A while they sat there together after they had done their meat, and the Lady fell a-talking with Walter concerning the parts of the earth, and the manners of men, and of his journeyings to and fro.

At last she said: "Thou hast told me much and answered all my questions wisely, and as my good Squire should, and that pleaseth me. But now tell me of the city wherein thou wert born and bred; a city whereof thou hast hitherto told me nought."

"Lady," he said, "it is a fair and a great city, and to many it seemeth lovely. But I have left it, and now it is nothing to me."

"Hast thou not kindred there?" said she.

"Yea," said he, "and foemen withal; and a false woman waylayeth my life there."

"And what was she?" said the Lady.

Said Walter: "She was but my wife."

"Was she fair?" said the Lady.

---

1 Bowed.

Walter telleth her of his vision

Walter looked on her a while, and then said: "I was going to say that she was well-nigh[1] as fair as thou; but that may scarce be. Yet was she very fair. But now, kind and gracious Lady, I will say this word to thee: I marvel that thou askest so many things concerning the city of Langton on Holm, where I was born, and where are my kindred yet; for meseemeth that thou knowest it thyself."

"I know it, I?" said the Lady,

"What, then! thou knowest it not?" said Walter.

Spake the Lady, and some of her old disdain was in her words: "Dost thou deem that I wander about the world and its cheaping-steads[2] like one of the chapmen?[3] Nay, I dwell in the Wood beyond the World, and nowhere else. What hath put this word into thy mouth?"

He said: "Pardon me, Lady, if I have misdone; but thus it was: Mine own eyes beheld thee going down the quays of our city, and thence a ship-board, and the ship sailed out of the haven. And first of all went a strange dwarf, whom I have seen here, and then thy Maid; and then went thy gracious and lovely body."

The Lady is wroth

The Lady's face changed as he spoke, and she turned red and then pale, and set her teeth; but she refrained her, and said: "Squire, I see of thee that thou art no liar, nor light of wit, therefore I suppose that thou hast verily seen some appearance of me; but never have I been in Langton, nor thought thereof, nor known that such a stead[4] there was until thou namedst it e'en now. Wherefore, I deem that an enemy hath cast the shadow of me on the air of that land."

"Yea, my Lady," said Walter; "and what enemy mightest thou have to have done this?"

She was slow of answer, but spake at last from a quivering mouth of anger: "Knowest thou not the saw,[5] that a man's foes are they of his own house? If I find out for a truth who hath done this, the said enemy shall have an evil hour with me."

Now is she kind again

Again she was silent, and she clenched her hands and strained her limbs in the heat of her anger; so that Walter was afraid of her,

---

1 CW: wellnigh.

2 Merchant cities.

3 Merchants.

4 Place.

5 Saying, aphorism.

and all his misgivings came back to his heart again, and he repented that he had told her so much. But in a little while all that trouble and wrath seemed to flow off her, and again was she of good cheer, and kind and sweet to him; and she said: "But in sooth, however it may be, I thank thee, my Squire and friend, for telling me hereof. And surely no wyte[1] do I lay on thee. And, moreover, is it not this vision which hath brought thee hither?"

"So it is, Lady," said he.

"Then have we to thank it," said the Lady, "And thou art welcome to our land."

And therewith she held out her hand to him, and he took it on his knees and kissed it; and then it was as if a red-hot iron had run through his heart, and he felt faint, and bowed down his head. But he held her hand yet, and kissed it many times, and the wrist and the arm, and knew not where he was.

But she drew a little away from him, and arose and said: "Now is the day wearing, and if we are to bear back any venison we must buckle to the work. So arise, Squire, and take the hounds and come with me; for not far off is a little thicket which mostly harbours foison[2] of deer, great and small. Let us come our ways."

Chapter XV. The Slaying of the Quarry

So they walked on quietly thence some half a mile, and ever the Lady would have Walter to walk by her side, and not follow a little behind her, as was meet for a servant to do; and she touched his hand at whiles[3] as she showed him beast and fowl and tree, and the sweetness of her body overcame him, so that for a while he thought of nothing save her.

Now when they were come to the thicket-side, she turned to him and said: "Squire, I am no ill woodman, so that thou mayst trust me that we shall not be brought to shame the second time; and I shall do sagely:[4] so nock an arrow to thy bow, and abide me here, and stir not hence; for I shall enter this thicket without the hounds, and arouse the quarry for thee; and see that thou be brisk and clean-shooting, and then shalt thou have a reward of me."

---

1 Blame.

2 Abundance.

3 Sometimes.

4 Wisely.

New tidings

Therewith she drew up her skirts through her girdle again, took her bent bow in her hand, and drew an arrow out of the quiver, and stepped lightly into the thicket, leaving him longing for the sight of her, as he hearkened to the tread of her feet on the dry leaves, and the rustling of the brake[1] as she thrust through it.

Thus he stood for a few minutes, and then he heard a kind of gibbering[2] cry without words, yet as of a woman, coming from the thicket, and while his heart was yet gathering the thought that something had gone amiss, he glided swiftly, but with little stir, into the brake.

He had gone but a little way ere he saw the Lady standing there in a narrow clearing, her face pale as death, her knees cleaving[3] together, her body swaying and tottering, her hands hanging down, and the bow and arrow fallen to the ground; and ten yards before her a great-headed yellow creature[4] crouching flat to the earth and slowly drawing nigher.

The lion slain

He stopped short; one arrow was already notched to the string, and another hung loose to the lesser fingers of his string-hand. He raised his right hand, and drew and loosed in a twinkling; the shaft flew close to the Lady's side, and straightway all the wood rung with a huge roar, as the yellow lion turned about to bite at the shaft which had sunk deep into him behind the shoulder, as if a bolt out of the heavens had smitten him. But straightway had Walter loosed again, and then, throwing down his bow, he ran forward with his drawn sword gleaming in his hand, while the lion weltered[5] and rolled, but had no might to move forward. Then Walter went up to him warily[6] and thrust him through to the heart, and leapt aback, lest the beast might yet have life in him to smite; but he left his struggling, his huge voice died out, and he lay there moveless before the hunter.

The Lady fleeth the field of deed

Walter abode a little, facing him, and then turned about to the Lady, and she had fallen down in a heap whereas she stood, and lay there all huddled up and voiceless. So he knelt down by her,

---

1 Thicket.

2 Inarticulate.

3 Holding.

4 That is, a lion.

5 Tumbled.

6 Cautiously.

and lifted up her head, and bade[1] her arise, for the foe was slain. And after a little she stretched out her limbs, and turned about on the grass, and seemed to sleep, and the colour came into her face again, and it grew soft and a little smiling. Thus she lay awhile, and Walter sat by her watching her, till at last she opened her eyes and sat up, and knew him, and smiling on him said: "What hath befallen, Squire, that I have slept and dreamed?"

He answered nothing, till her memory came back to her, and then she arose, trembling and pale, and said: "Let us leave this wood, for the Enemy is therein."

And she hastened away before him till they came out at the thicket-side whereas the hounds had been left, and they were standing there uneasy and whining; so Walter coupled[2] them, while the Lady stayed not, but went away swiftly homeward, and Walter followed.

At last she stayed her swift feet, and turned round on Walter, and said: "Squire, come hither."

So did he, and she said: "I am weary again; let us sit under this quicken-tree,[3] and rest us."

Now she cometh to herself

So they sat down, and she sat looking between her knees a while; and at last she said: "Why didst thou not bring the lion's hide?"

He said: "Lady, I will go back and flay[4] the beast, and bring on the hide."

And he arose therewith, but she caught him by the skirts and drew him down, and said: "Nay, thou shalt not go; abide with me. Sit down again."

He did so, and she said: "Thou shalt not go from me; for I am afraid: I am not used to looking on the face of death."

She grew pale as she spoke, and set a hand to her breast, and sat so a while without speaking. At last she turned to him smiling, and said: "How was it with the aspect of me when I stood before the peril of the Enemy?" And she laid a hand upon his.

"O gracious one," quoth he, "thou wert, as ever, full lovely, but I feared for thee."

She moved not her hand from his, and she said: "Good and true Squire, I said ere I entered the thicket e'en now that I would

---

1 Asked.

2 Tied them two by two.

3 Rowan, mountain-ash.

4 Skin.

reward thee if thou slewest the quarry. He is dead, though thou hast left the skin behind upon the carcase. Ask now thy reward, but take time to think what it shall be."

A reward of valiancy

He felt her hand warm upon his, and drew in the sweet odour of her mingled with the woodland scents under the hot sun of the afternoon, and his heart was clouded with manlike desire of her. And it was a near thing but he had spoken, and craved of her the reward of the freedom of her Maid, and that he might depart with her into other lands; but as his mind wavered betwixt this and that, the Lady, who had been eyeing him keenly, drew her hand away from him; and therewith doubt and fear flowed into his mind, and he refrained him of speech.

Then she laughed merrily and said: "The good Squire is shamefaced; he feareth a lady more than a lion. Will it be a reward to thee if I bid thee to kiss my cheek?"

Therewith she leaned her face toward him, and he kissed her well-favouredly, and then sat gazing on her, wondering what should betide[1] to him on the morrow.

Then she arose and said: "Come, Squire, and let us home; be not abashed, there shall be other rewards hereafter."

So they went their ways quietly; and it was nigh sunset against[2] they entered the house again. Walter looked round for the Maid, but beheld her not; and the Lady said to him: "I go to my chamber, and now is thy service over for this day."

Then she nodded to him friendly and went her ways.

Chapter XVI. Of the King's Son and the Maid

But as for Walter, he went out of the house again, and fared slowly over the woodlawns till he came to another close thicket or brake; he entered from mere wantonness,[3] or that he might be the more apart and hidden, so as to think over his case. There he lay down under the thick boughs, but could not so herd his thoughts that they would dwell steady in looking into what might come to him within the next days; rather visions of those two women and the monster did but float before him, and fear and desire and the hope of life ran to and fro in his mind.

---

1 Happen.

2 As.

3 Caprice.

The Maid and the King's Son

As he lay thus he heard footsteps drawing near, and he looked between the boughs, and though the sun had just set, he could see close by him a man and a woman going slowly, and they hand in hand; at first he deemed it would be the King's Son and the Lady, but presently he saw that it was the King's Son indeed, but that it was the Maid whom he was holding by the hand. And now he saw of him that his eyes were bright with desire, and of her that she was very pale. Yet when he heard her begin to speak, it was in a steady voice that she said:

"King's Son, thou hast threatened me oft and unkindly, and now thou threatenest me again, and no less unkindly. But whatever were thy need herein before, now is there no more need; for my Mistress, of whom thou wert weary, is now grown weary of thee, and belike will not now reward me for drawing thy love to me, as once she would have done; to wit, before the coming of this stranger. Therefore I say, since I am but a thrall, poor and helpless, betwixt you two mighty ones, I have no choice but to do thy will."

Walter noteth the spy

As she spoke she looked all round about her, as one distraught by the anguish of fear. Walter, amidst of his wrath and grief, had well-nigh[1] drawn his sword and rushed out of his lair[2] upon the King's Son. But he deemed it sure that, so doing, he should undo the Maid altogether, and himself also belike, so he refrained him, though it were a hard matter.

The Maid had stayed her feet now close to where Walter lay, some five yards from him only, and he doubted whether she saw him not from where she stood. As to the King's Son, he was so intent upon the Maid, and so greedy of her beauty, that it was not like that he saw anything.

Now moreover Walter looked, and deemed that he beheld something through the grass and bracken[3] on the other side of those two, an ugly brown and yellow body, which, if it were not some beast of the foumart[4] kind, must needs be the monstrous dwarf, or one of his kin; and the flesh crept upon Walter's bones with the horror of him.

---

1 CW: wellnigh.

2 Hiding place.

3 Ferns.

4 Polecat.

An unkind lover

But the King's Son spoke unto the Maid: "Sweetling, I shall take the gift thou givest me, neither shall I threaten thee any more, howbeit thou givest it not very gladly or graciously."

She smiled on him with her lips alone, for her eyes were wandering and haggard. "My lord," she said, "is not this the manner of women?"

"Well," he said, "I say that I will take thy love even so given. Yet let me hear again that thou lovest not that vile newcomer, and that thou hast not seen him, save this morning along with my Lady. Nay now, thou shalt swear it."

"What shall I swear by?" she said.

Quoth[1] he, "Thou shalt swear by my body;" and therewith he thrust himself close up against her; but she drew her hand from his, and laid it on his breast, and said: "I swear it by thy body."

He smiled on her licorously,[2] and took her by the shoulders, and kissed her face many times, and then stood aloof from her, and said: "Now have I had hansel:[3] but tell me, when shall I come to thee?"

She spoke out clearly: "Within three days at furthest; I will do thee to wit of the day and the hour to-morrow, or the day after."

He kissed her once more, and said: "Forget it not, or the threat holds good."

And therewith he turned about and went his ways toward the house; and Walter saw the yellow-brown thing creeping after him in the gathering dusk.

Walter and the Maid

As for the Maid, she stood for a while without moving, and looking after the King's Son and the creature that followed him. Then she turned about to where Walter lay and lightly put aside the boughs, and Walter leapt up, and they stood face to face. She said softly but eagerly: "Friend, touch me not yet!"

He spake not, but looked on her sternly. She said: "Thou art angry with me?"

Her sweetness and her valiancy

Still he spake not; but she said: "Friend, this at least I will pray thee; not to play with life and death; with happiness and misery. Dost thou not remember the oath which we swore each to each but a little while ago? And dost thou deem that I have changed in

---

1 Said.

2 Lecherously.

3 Down payment.

these few days? Is thy mind concerning thee and me the same as it was? If it be not so, now tell me. For now have I the mind to do as if neither thou nor I are changed to each other, whoever may have kissed mine unwilling lips, or whomsoever thy lips may have kissed. But if thou hast changed, and wilt no longer give me thy love, nor crave mine, then shall this steel" (and she drew a sharp knife from her girdle) "be for the fool and the dastard who hath made thee wroth with me, my friend, and my friend that I deemed I had won. And then let come what will come! But if thou be nought changed, and the oath yet holds, then, when a little while hath passed, may we thrust all evil and guile and grief behind us, and long joy shall lie before us, and long life, and all honour in death: if only thou wilt do as I bid thee, O my dear, and my friend, and my first friend!"

Walter overcome by love

He looked on her, and his breast heaved up as all the sweetness of her kind love took hold on him, and his face changed, and the tears filled his eyes and ran over, and rained down before her, and he stretched out his hand toward her.

She pleads with Walter

Then she said exceeding sweetly: "Now indeed I see that it is well with me, yea, and with thee also. A sore pain it is to me, that not even now may I take thine hand, and cast mine arms about thee, and kiss the lips that love me. But so it has to be. My dear, even so I were fain[1] to stand here long before thee, even if we spake no more word to each other; but abiding here is perilous; for there is ever an evil spy upon my doings, who has now as I deem followed the King's Son to the house, but who will return when he has tracked him home thither: so we must sunder.[2] But belike there is yet time for a word or two: first, the rede[3] which I had thought on for our deliverance is now afoot,[4] though I durst[5] not tell thee thereof, nor have time thereto. But this much shall I tell thee, that whereas great is the craft of my Mistress in wizardry,[6] yet I also have some little craft therein, and this, which she hath not, to change the aspect of folk so utterly that they seem other than they verily are; yea, so that one may have the aspect of

---

1 Eager.

2 Part from each other.

3 Advice.

4 On the move.

5 Dare.

6 Magic.

another. Now the next thing is this: whatsoever my Mistress may bid thee, do her will therein with no more nay-saying[1] than thou deemest may please her. And the next thing: wheresoever thou mayst meet me, speak not to me, make no sign to me, even when I seem to be all alone, till I stoop down and touch the ring on my ankle with my right hand; but if I do so, then stay[2] thee, without fail, till I speak. The last thing I will say to thee, dear friend, ere we both go our ways, this it is. When we are free, and thou knowest all that I have done, I pray thee deem me not evil and wicked, and be not wroth with me for my deed; whereas thou wottest well that I am not in like plight[3] with other women. I have heard tell that when the knight goeth to the war, and hath overcome his foes by the shearing of swords and guileful tricks, and hath come back home to his own folk, they praise him and bless him, and crown him with flowers, and boast of him before God in the minster[4] for his deliverance of friend and folk and city. Why shouldst thou be worse to me than this? Now is all said, my dear and my friend; farewell, farewell!"

Therewith she turned and went her ways toward the house in all speed, but making somewhat of a compass.[5] And when she was gone, Walter knelt down and kissed the place where her feet had been, and arose thereafter, and made his way toward the house, he also, but slowly, and staying oft on his way.

Chapter XVII.
Of the House and the Pleasance[6] in the Wood

On the morrow morning Walter loitered a while about the house till the morn was grown old, and then about noon he took his bow and arrows and went into the woods to the northward, to get him some venison. He went somewhat far ere he shot him a fawn, and then he sat him down to rest under the shade of a great chestnut tree,[7] for it was not far past the hottest of the day. He looked around thence and saw below him

1 Disagreement.
2 Delay.
3 Distress.
4 Monastery, church.
5 Roundabout way.
6 Pleasure.
7 CW: chestnut-tree.

a little dale[1] with a pleasant stream running through it, and he bethought[2] him of bathing therein, so he went down and had his pleasure of the water and the willowy banks; for he lay naked a while on the grass by the lip of the water, for joy of the flickering shade, and the little breeze that ran over the downlong ripples of the stream.

The Lady is here

Then he did on his raiment, and began to come his ways up the bent, but had scarce gone three steps ere he saw a woman coming towards him from down-stream. His heart came into his mouth when he saw her, for she stooped and reached down her arm, as if she would lay her hand on her ankle, so that at first he deemed it had been the Maid, but at the second eye-shot he saw that it was the Mistress. She stood still and looked on him, so that he deemed she would have him come to her. So he went to meet her, and grew somewhat shamefaced as he drew nigher, and wondered at her, for now was she clad but in one garment of some dark grey silky stuff, embroidered[3] with, as it were, a garland of flowers about the middle, but which was so thin that, as the wind drifted it from side and limb, it hid her no more, but for the said garland, than if water were running over her: her face was full of smiling joy and content as she spake to him in a kind, caressing voice, and said: "I give thee good day, good Squire, and well art thou met." And she held out her hand to him. He knelt down before her and kissed it, and abode still upon his knees, and hanging down his head.

Walter is abashed

But she laughed outright, and stooped down to him, and put her hand to his arms, and raised him up, and said to him: "What is this, my Squire, that thou kneelest to me as to an idol?"

He said faltering: "I wot not; but perchance[4] thou art an idol; and I fear thee."

"What!" she said, "more than yesterday, whenas thou sawest me afraid?"

Said he: "Yea, for that now I see thee unhidden, and meseemeth there hath been none such since the old days of the Gentiles."[5]

---

1 Valley.

2 Considered.

3 Early in his career as a designer, Morris experimented with medieval-style embroidery.

4 Perhaps.

5 Pagans (Greeks and Romans).

She said: "Hast thou not yet bethought thee of a gift to crave of me, a reward for the slaying of mine enemy, and the saving of me from death?"

The Lady is wrath with Walter

"O my Lady," he said, "even so much would I have done for any other lady, or, forsooth, for any poor man; for so my manhood would have bidden me. Speak not of gifts to me then. Moreover" (and he reddened therewith, and his voice faltered), "didst thou not give me my sweet reward yesterday? What more durst I ask?"

She held her peace awhile, and looked on him keenly; and he reddened under her gaze. Then wrath came into her face, and she reddened and knit her brows, and spake to him in a voice of anger, and said: "Nay, what is this? It is growing in my mind that thou deemest the gift of me unworthy! Thou, an alien, an outcast; one endowed with the little wisdom of the World without the Wood! And here I stand before thee, all glorious in my nakedness, and so fulfilled of wisdom, that I can make this wilderness to any whom I love more full of joy than the kingdoms and cities of the world ...[1] and thou! ...[2] Ah, but it is the Enemy that hath done this, and made the guileless guileful![3] Yet will I have the upper hand at least, though thou suffer for it, and I suffer for thee."

Walter is careful of his speech

Walter stood before her with hanging head, and he put forth his hands as if praying off her anger, and pondered what answer he should make; for now he feared for himself and the Maid; so at last he looked up to her, and said boldly: "Nay, Lady, I know what thy words mean, whereas I remember thy first welcome of me. I wot, forsooth, that thou wouldst call me base-born, and of no account, and unworthy to touch the hem of thy raiment; and that I have been overbold, and guilty towards thee; and doubtless this is sooth, and I have deserved thine anger: but I will not ask thee to pardon me, for I have done but what I must needs."[4] She looked on him calmly now, and without any wrath, but rather as if she would read what was written in his inmost heart. Then her face changed into joyousness again, and she smote her palms together, and cried out: "This is but foolish talk; for yesterday did I see thy valiancy, and to-day I have seen thy goodliness; and I

---

1 CW: *dash.*

2 CW: *dash.*

3 Makes one who doesn't use tricks into a trickster.

4 CW: *add paragraph break.*

say, that though thou mightest not be good enough for a fool woman of the earthly baronage,[1] yet art thou good enough for me, the wise and the mighty, and the lovely. And whereas thou sayest that I gave thee but disdain when first thou camest to us, grudge not against me therefor, because it was done but to prove thee; and now thou art proven."

The Lady would be friends with him

Then again he knelt down before her, and embraced her knees, and against she raised him up, and let her arm hang down over his shoulder, and her cheek brush his cheek; and she kissed his mouth and said: "Hereby is all forgiven, both thine offence and mine; and now cometh joy and merry days."

A garden in the Wood

Therewith her smiling face grew grave, and she stood before him looking stately and gracious and kind at once, and she took his hand and said: "Thou mightest deem my chamber in the Golden House of the Wood over-queenly,[2] since thou art no masterful man. So now hast thou chosen well the place wherein to meet me to-day, for hard by on the other side of the stream is a bower[3] of pleasance,[4] which, forsooth, not every one who cometh to this land may find; there shall I be to thee as one of the up-country damsels of thine own land, and thou shalt not be abashed."[5]

She sidled up to him as she spoke, and would he, would he not, her sweet voice tickled his very soul with pleasure, and she looked aside on him happy and well-content.

So they crossed the stream by the shallow below the pool wherein Walter had bathed, and within a little they came upon a tall fence of flake-hurdles,[6] and a simple gate therein. The Lady opened the same, and they entered thereby into a close[7] all planted as a most fair garden, with hedges of rose and woodbine,[8] and with linden-trees[9] a-blossom, and long ways of green grass betwixt borders of lilies and clove-gilliflowers,[10] and other sweet garland-flowers. And a branch of the stream which they had

---

1 Nobility.

2 K, LB: over queenly.

3 A shady place.

4 Pleasure.

5 Confused.

6 Sections of a wicker fence.

7 Enclosure.

8 Climbing vines.

9 Lime trees.

10 Species of dianthus that smells like cloves.

crossed erewhile[1] wandered through that garden; and in the midst was a little house built of post and pan,[2] and thatched with yellow straw, as if it were new done.

A house of pleasance

Then Walter looked this way and that, and wondered at first, and tried to think in his mind what should come next, and how matters would go with him; but his thought would not dwell steady on any other matter than the beauty of the Lady amidst the beauty of the garden; and withal she was now grown so sweet and kind, and even somewhat timid and shy with him, that scarce did he know whose hand he held, or whose fragrant bosom and sleek side went so close to him.

So they wandered here and there through the waning of the day, and when they entered at last into the cool dusk house, then they loved and played together, as if they were a pair of lovers guileless,[3] with no fear for the morrow, and no seeds of enmity and death sown betwixt them.

Chapter XVIII. The Maid Gives Walter Tryst[4]

Now[5] on the morrow, when Walter was awake, he found there was no one lying beside him, and the day was no longer very young; so he arose, and went through the garden from end to end, and all about, and there was none there; and albeit that he dreaded to meet the Lady there, yet was he sad at heart and fearful of what might betide. Howsoever, he found the gate whereby they had entered yesterday, and he went out into the little dale; but when he had gone a step or two he turned about, and could see neither garden nor fence, nor any sign of what he had seen thereof but lately. He knit his brow and stood still to think of it, and his heart grew the heavier thereby; but presently he went his ways and crossed the stream, but had scarce come up on to the grass on the further side, ere he saw a woman coming to meet him, and at first, full as he was of the tide[6] of yesterday and the wondrous garden, deemed that it would be the Lady; but

---

1 A while ago.

2 Timber framework.

3 Innocent.

4 Meeting.

5 CW: *add comma.*

6 Tidings, news.

the woman stayed her feet, and, stooping, laid a hand on her right ankle, and he saw that it was the Maid. He drew anigh to her, and saw that she was nought so sad of countenance as the last time she had met him, but flushed of cheek and bright-eyed.

The Maid cometh again

As he came up to her she made a step or two to meet him, holding out her two hands, and then refrained her, and said smiling: "Ah, friend, belike this shall be the last time that I shall say to thee, touch me not, nay, not so much as my hand, or if it were but the hem of my raiment."

The joy grew up in his heart, and he gazed on her fondly, and said: "Why, what then[1] hath befallen[2] of late?"

"O friend," she began, "this hath befallen."

She giveth Walter tryst in strange wise

But as he looked on her, the smile died from her face, and she became deadly pale to the very lips; she looked askance[3] to her left side, whereas ran the stream; and Walter followed her eyes, and deemed for one instant that he saw the misshapen yellow visage[4] of the dwarf peering round from a grey rock, but the next there was nothing. Then the Maid, though she were as pale as death, went on in a clear, steady, hard voice, wherein was no joy or kindness, keeping her face to Walter and her back to the stream: "This hath befallen, friend, that there is no longer any need to refrain thy love nor mine; therefore I say to thee, come to my chamber (and it is the red chamber over against thine, though thou knewest it not) an hour before this next midnight, and then thy sorrow and mine shall be at an end: and now I must needs depart. Follow me not, but remember!"

And therewith she turned about and fled like the wind down the stream.

But Walter stood wondering, and knew not what to make of it, whether it were for good or ill: for he knew now that she had paled and been seized with terror because of the upheaving[5] of the ugly head; and yet she had seemed to speak out the very thing she had to say. Howsoever it were, he spake aloud to himself: Whatever comes, I will keep tryst with her.

---

1 CW: *omit* then.

2 Happened.

3 Sideways.

4 Face.

5 Raising up.

Then he drew his sword, and turned this way and that, looking all about if he might see any sign of the Evil Thing; but nought might his eyes behold, save the grass, and the stream, and the bushes of the dale. So then, still holding his naked sword in his hand, he clomb the bent out of the dale; for that was the only way he knew to the Golden House; and when he came to the top, and the summer breeze blew in his face, and he looked down a fair green slope beset with goodly oaks and chestnuts, he was refreshed with the life of the earth, and he felt the good sword in his fist, and knew that there was might and longing in him, and the world seemed open unto him.

So he smiled, if it were somewhat grimly, and sheathed his sword and went on toward the house.

Chapter XIX.
Walter Goes to Fetch Home the Lion's Hide

He entered the cool dusk through the porch, and, looking down the pillared hall, saw beyond the fountain a gleam of gold, and when he came past the said fountain he looked up to the high-seat, and lo! the Lady sitting there clad in her queenly raiment. She called to him, and he came; and she hailed[1] him, and spake graciously and calmly, yet as if she knew nought of him save as the leal[2] servant of her, a high Lady. "Squire," she said, "we have deemed it meet[3] to have the hide of the servant of the Enemy, the lion to wit, whom thou slewest yesterday, for a carpet to our feet; wherefore go now, take thy wood-knife, and flay[4] the beast, and bring me home his skin. This shall be all thy service for this day, so mayst thou do it at thine own leisure, and not weary thyself. May good go with thee."

He bent the knee before her, and she smiled on him graciously, but reached out no hand for him to kiss, and heeded him but little. Wherefore, in spite of himself, and though he knew somewhat of her guile,[5] he could not help marvelling that this should be she who had lain in his arms night-long but of late.

---

1 Greeted.

2 Loyal.

3 Judged it fitting.

4 Skin.

5 Trickery.

Where then is the carcase of the Lion?

Howso that might be, he took his way toward the thicket where he had slain the lion, and came thither by then[1] it was afternoon, at the hottest of the day. So he entered therein, and came to the very place whereas the Lady had lain, when she fell down before the terror of the lion; and there was the mark of her body on the grass where she had lain that while, like as it were the form of[2] a hare. But when Walter went on to where he had slain that great beast, lo! he was gone, and there was no sign of him; but there were Walter's own footprints, and the two shafts which he had shot, one feathered red, and one blue. He said at first: Belike someone hath been here, and hath had the carcase away. Then he laughed in very despite, and said: How may that be, since there are no signs of dragging away of so huge a body, and no blood or fur on the grass if they had cut him up, and moreover no trampling of feet, as if there had been many men at the deed[?][3] Then was he all abashed,[4] and again laughed in scorn of himself, and said: Forsooth I deemed[5] I had done manly; but now forsooth I shot nought, and nought there was before the sword of my father's son. And what may I deem now, but that this is a land of mere lies, and that there is nought real and alive therein save me. Yea, belike even these trees and the green grass will presently depart from me, and leave me falling down through the clouds.

Walter is abashed

Therewith he turned away, and gat him to[6] the road that led to the Golden House, wondering what next should befall him, and going slowly as he pondered his case. So came he to that first thicket where they had lost their quarry by water; so he entered the same, musing, and bathed him in the pool that was therein, after he had wandered about it awhile, and found nothing new.

So again he set him to the homeward road, when the day was now waning, and it was near sunset that he was come nigh unto the house, though it was hidden from him as then by a low bent that rose before him; and there he abode and looked about him.

---

1 [The time] when.

2 LB: for mof.

3 K, LB, CW: *omit question mark, add period.*

4 Confused.

5 Truly I thought.

6 Got on to.

Now comes the Maid

Now as he looked, over the said bent came the figure of a woman, who stayed on the brow thereof and looked all about her, and then ran swiftly down to meet Walter, who saw at once that it was the Maid.

She made no stay then till she was but three paces from him, and then she stooped down and made the sign to him, and then spake to him breathlessly, and said: "Hearken! but speak not till I have done: I bade[1] thee to-night's meeting because I saw that there was one anigh whom I must needs beguile.[2] But by thine oath, and thy love, and all that thou art, I adjure thee come not unto me this night as I bade thee! but be hidden in the hazel-copse[3] outside the house, as it draws toward midnight, and abide me there. Dost thou hearken, and wilt thou? Say yes or no in haste, for I may not tarry a moment of time. Who knoweth what is behind me?"

A change of tryst

"Yes," said Walter hastily; "but friend and love ..."[4]

"No more," she said; "hope the best;" and turning from him she ran away swiftly, not by the way she had come, but sideways, as though to reach the house by fetching a compass.[5]

But Walter went slowly on his way, thinking within himself that now at that present moment there was nought for it but to refrain him from doing, and to let others do; yet deemed he that it was little manly to be as the pawn upon the board, pushed about by the will of others.

Then, as he went, he bethought[6] him of the Maiden's face and aspect,[7] as she came running to him, and stood before him for that minute; and all eagerness he saw in her, and sore love of him, and distress of soul, all blent together.

The King's Son is glad

So came he to the brow of the bent, whence he could see lying before him, scarce more than a bow-shot away, the Golden House, now gilded again and reddened by the setting sun. And even therewith came a gay image toward him, flashing back the

---

1 Commanded.

2 Trick.

3 Hazel thicket.

4 CW: *dash*.

5 By a roundabout way.

6 Remembered.

7 Appearance.

level rays from gold and steel and silver; and lo! there was come the King's Son. They met presently, and the King's Son turned to go beside him, and said merrily: "I give thee good even,[1] my Lady's Squire! I owe thee something of courtesy, whereas it is by thy means that I shall be made happy, both to-night, and to-morrow, and many to-morrows; and sooth it is, that but little courtesy have I done thee hitherto."

His face was full of joy, and the eyes of him shone with gladness. He was a goodly man, but to Walter he seemed an ill one; and he hated him so much, that he found it no easy matter to answer him; but he refrained himself, and said: "I can thee thank, King's Son; and good it is that someone is happy in this strange land."

"Art thou not happy then, Squire of my Lady?" said the other.

He doubteth Walter

Walter had no mind to show this man his heart, nay, nor even a corner thereof; for he deemed[2] him an enemy. So he smiled sweetly and somewhat foolishly, as a man luckily in love, and said: "O yea, yea, why should I not be so? How might I be otherwise?"

"Yea then," said the King's Son, "why didst thou say that thou wert glad someone is happy? Who is unhappy,[3] deemest thou?" and he looked on him keenly.

Walter answered slowly: "Said I so? I suppose then that I was thinking of thee; for when first I saw thee, yea, and afterwards, thou didst seem heavy-hearted and ill-content."

The face of the King's Son cleared at this word, and he said: "Yea, so it was; for look you, both ways it was: I was unfree, and I had sown the true desire of my heart whereas it waxed not.[4] But now I am on the brink and verge of freedom, and presently shall my desire be blossomed. Nay now, Squire, I deem thee a good fellow, though it may be somewhat of a fool; so I will no more speak riddles to thee. Thus it is: the Maid hath promised me all mine asking, and is mine; and in two or three days, by her helping also, I shall see the world again."

Quoth Walter, smiling askance[5] on him: "And the Lady? what shall she say to this matter?"

---

1 Good [wishes for the] evening.

2 Considered.

3 K, LB: *omit comma.*

4 Where it did not grow.

5 Sideways.

The King's Son fears nought in his joy

The King's Son reddened, but smiled falsely enough, and said: "Sir Squire, thou knowest enough not to need to ask this. Why should I tell thee that she accounteth more of thy little finger than of my whole body? Now I tell thee hereof freely; first, because this my fruition of love, and my freeing from thralldom, is, in a way, of thy doing. For thou art become my supplanter, and hast taken thy place with yonder lovely tyrant. Fear not for me! she will let me go. As for thyself, see thou to it! But again I tell thee hereof because my heart is light and full of joy, and telling thee will pleasure me, and cannot do me any harm. For if thou say: How if I carry the tale to my Lady? I answer, thou wilt not. For I know that thine heart hath been somewhat set on the jewel that my hand holdeth; and thou knowest well on whose head the Lady's wrath would fall, and that would be neither thine nor mine."

"Thou sayest sooth," said Walter; "neither is treason my wont."

So they walked on silently a while, and then Walter said: "But how if the Maiden had nay-said[1] thee; what hadst thou done then?"

He looks to come back happy to his own land

"By the heavens!" said the King's Son fiercely, "she should have paid for her nay-say; then would I ..."[2] But he broke off, and said quietly, yet somewhat doggedly: "Why talk of what might have been? She gave me her yea-say pleasantly and sweetly."

Now Walter knew that the man lied, so he held his peace thereon; but presently he said: "When thou are free wilt thou go to thine own land again?"

"Yea," said the King's Son; "she will lead me thither."

"And wilt thou make her thy lady and queen when thou comest to thy father's land?" said Walter.

The King's Son knit his brow, and said: "When I am in mine own land I may do with her what I will; but I look for it that I shall do no otherwise with her than that she shall be well-content."

Then the talk between them dropped, and the King's Son turned off toward the wood, singing and joyous; but Walter went soberly toward the house. Forsooth he was not greatly cast down, for besides that he knew that the King's Son was false, he deemed that under this double tryst lay something which was a-doing in

---

1 Refused.

2 CW: *dash.*

his own behalf. Yet was he eager and troubled, if not down-hearted, and his soul was cast about betwixt hope and fear.

Chapter XX. Walter is Bidden[1] to Another Tryst

The Lady asks Walter of his service

So came he into the pillared hall, and there he found the Lady walking to and fro by the high-seat; and when he drew nigh she turned on him, and said in a voice rather eager than angry: "What hast thou done, Squire? Why art thou come before me?"

He was abashed,[2] and bowed before her and said: "O gracious Lady, thou badest me service,[3] and I have been about it."

She said: "Tell me then, tell me, what hath betided?"

"Lady," said he, "when I entered the thicket of thy swooning I found there no carcase of the lion, nor any sign of the dragging away of him."

The wrath of her

She looked full in his face for a little, and then went to her chair, and sat down therein; and in a little while spake to him in a softer voice, and said: "Did I not tell thee that some enemy had done that unto me? and lo! now thou seest that so it is."

Then was she silent again, and knit her brows and set her teeth; and thereafter she spake harshly and fiercely: "But I will overcome her, and make her days evil, but keep death away from her, that she may die many times over; and know all the sickness of the heart, when foes be nigh, and friends afar, and there is none to deliver!"

Walter new clad

Her eyes flashed, and her face was dark with anger; but she turned and caught Walter's eyes, and the sternness of his face, and she softened at once, and said: "But thou! this hath little to do with thee; and now to thee I speak: Now cometh even[4] and night. Go thou to thy chamber, and there shalt thou find raiment worthy of thee, what thou now art, and what thou shalt be; do on[5] the same, and make thyself most goodly,[6] and then come

---

1 Commanded.

2 Confused.

3 Commanded me to do a service [the recovery of the lion's skin].

4 Evening.

5 Put on.

6 Handsome.

thou hither and eat and drink with me, and afterwards depart whither thou wilt, till the night has worn to its midmost; and then come thou to my chamber, to wit, through the ivory door in the gallery above; and then and there shall I tell thee a thing, and it shall be for the weal[1] both of thee and of me, but for the grief and woe of the Enemy."

Therewith she reached her hand to him, and he kissed it, and departed and came to his chamber, and found raiment therebefore rich beyond measure; and he wondered if any new snare lay therein; yet if there were, he saw no way whereby he might escape it, so he did it on, and became as the most glorious of kings, and yet lovelier than any king of the world.

Sithence[2] he went his way into the pillared hall, when it was now night, and without[3] the moon was up, and the trees of the wood as still as images. But within[4] the hall shone bright with many candles, and the fountain glittered in the light of them, as it ran tinkling sweetly into the little stream; and the silvern[5] bridges gleamed, and the pillars shone all round about.

A banquet in the Golden House

And there on the dais[6] was a table dight[7] most royally, and the Lady sitting thereat, clad in her most glorious array, and behind her the Maid standing humbly, yet clad in precious web of shimmering gold, but with feet unshod,[8] and the iron ring upon her ankle.

Walter is made much of

So Walter came his ways to the high-seat, and the Lady rose and greeted him, and took him by the hands, and kissed him on either cheek, and sat him down beside her. So they fell to their meat, and the Maid served them; but the Lady took no more heed of her than if she were one of the pillars of the hall; but Walter she caressed oft with sweet words, and the touch of her hand, making him drink out of her cup and eat out of her dish. As to him, he was bashful by seeming, but verily fearful; he took the Lady's caresses with what grace he might, and durst not so

---

1 Benefit.
2 Afterwards.
3 Outside.
4 Inside.
5 Silver.
6 Main table [as in a banquet].
7 Set, arrayed.
8 Bare feet.

much as glance at her Maid. Long indeed seemed that banquet to him, and longer yet endured the weariness of his abiding there, kind to his foe and unkind to his friend; for after the banquet they still sat a while, and the Lady talked much to Walter about many things of the ways of the world, and he answered what he might, distraught as he was with the thought of those two trysts which he had to deal with.

At last spake the Lady and said: "Now must I leave thee for a little, and thou wottest[1] where and how we shall meet next; and meanwhile disport[2] thee as thou wilt, so that thou weary not thyself, for I love to see thee joyous."

Then she arose stately and grand; but she kissed Walter on the mouth ere she turned to go out of the hall. The Maid followed her; but or[3] ever she was quite gone, she stopped and made that sign, and looked over her shoulder at Walter, as if in entreaty to him, and there was fear and anguish in her face; but he nodded his head to her in yea-say of the tryst in the hazel-copse,[4] and in a trice[5] she was gone.

The King's Son is still joyous

Walter went down the hall, and forth into the early night; but in the jaws of the porch he came up against the King's Son, who, gazing at his attire glittering with all its gems in the moonlight, laughed out, and said: "Now may it be seen how thou art risen in degree above me, whereas I am but a king's son, and that a king of a far country; whereas thou art a king of kings, or shalt be this night, yea, and of this very country wherein we both are."

Now Walter saw the mock which lay under his words; but he kept back his wrath, and answered: "Fair sir, art thou as well contented with thy lot as when the sun went down? Hast thou no doubt or fear? Will the Maid verily keep tryst with thee, or hath she given thee yea-say but to escape thee this time? Or, again, may she not turn to the Lady and appeal to her against thee?"

They sunder

Now when he had spoken these words, he repented thereof, and feared for himself and the Maid, lest he had stirred some misgiving in that young man's foolish heart. But the King's son did but laugh, and answered nought but to Walter's last words,

---

1 Know.

2 Divert, play.

3 Before.

4 Hazel-thicket.

5 Right away.

and said: "Yea, yea! this word of thine showeth how little thou wottest[1] of that which lieth betwixt my darling and thine. Doth the lamb appeal from the shepherd to the wolf? Even so shall the Maid appeal from me to thy Lady. What! ask thy Lady at thy leisure what her wont[2] hath been with her thrall; she shall think it a fair tale to tell thee thereof. But thereof is my Maid all whole now by reason of her wisdom in leechcraft,[3] or somewhat more. And now I tell thee again, that the beforesaid Maid must needs do my will; for if I be the deep sea, and I deem not so ill of myself, that other one is the devil;[4] as belike thou shalt find out for thyself later on. Yea, all is well with me, and more than well."

And therewith he swung merrily into the litten[5] hall. But Walter went out into the moonlit night, and wandered about for an hour or more, and stole warily[6] into the hall and thence into his own chamber. There he did off that royal array, and did his own raiment upon him; he girt him with sword and knife,[7] took his bow and quiver, and stole down and out again, even as he had come in. Then he fetched a compass,[8] and came down into the hazel coppice from the north, and lay hidden there while the night wore, till he deemed it would lack but little of midnight.

Chapter XXI.
Walter and the Maid Flee from the Golden House

There he abode[9] amidst the hazels, hearkening[10] every littlest sound; and the sounds were nought but the night voices of the wood, till suddenly there burst forth from the house a great wailing cry. Walter's heart came up into his mouth, but he had no time to do aught,[11] for following hard on the cry came the sound of light feet close to him, the boughs were thrust aside, and there

---

1 Know.
2 Preference.
3 Healing.
4 The reference here is to the proverbial expression of distress, "between the devil and the deep blue sea."
5 Lighted.
6 Sneaked.
7 Put on his belt with sword and knife.
8 Went a roundabout way.
9 Waited.
10 Listening to.
11 Anything.

was come the Maid, and she but in her white coat, and barefoot. And then first he felt the sweetness of her flesh on his, for she caught him by the hand and said breathlessly: "Now, now! there may yet be time, or even too much, it may be. For the saving of breath ask me no questions, but come!"

On the way of flight

He dallied not, but went as she led, and they were light-foot, both of them.

They went the same way, due south to wit, whereby he had gone a-hunting with the Lady; and whiles they ran and whiles they walked; but so fast they went, that by grey of the dawn they were come as far as that coppice or thicket of the Lion; and still they hastened onward, and but little had the Maid spoken, save here and there a word to hearten up Walter, and here and there a shy word of endearment. At last the dawn grew into early day, and as they came over the brow of a bent, they looked down over a plain land[1] whereas the trees grew scatter-meal,[2] and beyond the plain rose up the land into long green hills, and over those again were blue mountains great and far away.

Then spake the Maid: "Over yonder lie the outlying mountains of the Bears, and through them we needs must pass, to our great peril.

They must needs rest

"Nay, friend," she said, as he handled his sword-hilt, "it must be patience and wisdom to bring us through, and not the fallow[3] blade of one man, though he be a good one. But look! below there runs a stream through the first of the plain, and I see nought for it but we must now rest our bodies. Moreover I have a tale to tell thee which is burning my heart; for maybe there will be a pardon to ask of thee moreover; wherefore I fear thee."

Quoth Walter: "How may that be?"

She answered him not, but took his hand and led him down the bent. But he said: "Thou sayest, rest; but are we now out of all peril of the chase?"

She said: "I cannot tell till I know what hath befallen[4] her. If she be not to hand[5] to set on her trackers, they will scarce happen on us now; if it be not for that one."

---

1 CW: plain-land.

2 Here and there.

3 Pale brown.

4 Happened to.

5 Able.

And she shuddered, and he felt her hand change as he held it.

Then she said: "But peril or no peril, needs must we rest; for I tell thee again, what I have to say to thee burneth my bosom for fear of thee, so that I can go no further until I have told thee."

Then he said: "I wot[1] not of this Queen and her mightiness and her servants. I will ask thereof later. But besides the others, is there not the King's Son, he who loves thee so unworthily?"

A bath withal

She paled somewhat, and said: "As for him, there had been nought for thee to fear in him, save his treason: but now shall he neither love nor hate any more; he died last midnight."

"Yea, and how?" said Walter.

"Nay," she said, "let me tell my tale altogether once for all, lest thou blame me overmuch. But first we will wash us and comfort us as best we may, and then amidst our resting shall the word be said."

By then were they come down to the stream-side, which ran fair in pools and stickles[2] amidst rocks and sandy banks. She said: "There behind the great grey rock is my bath, friend; and here is thine; and lo! the uprising of the sun!"

So she went her ways to the said rock, and he bathed him, and washed the night off him, and by then he was clad again she came back fresh and sweet from the water, and with her lap full of cherries from a wilding[3] which overhung her bath. So they sat down together on the green grass above the sand, and ate the breakfast of the wilderness: and Walter was full of content as he watched her, and beheld her sweetness and her loveliness; yet were they, either of them, somewhat shy and shamefaced each with the other; so that he did but kiss her hands once again, and though she shrank not from him, yet had she no boldness to cast herself into his arms.

Chapter XXII. Of the Dwarf and the Pardon

Now she began to say: "My friend, now shall I tell thee what I have done for thee and me; and if thou have a mind to blame me, and

---

1 Know.

2 Thorn bushes. This word is possibly derived from Old English *sticel*, meaning "thorn."

3 Fruit tree. The word properly refers to a crab-apple tree, not a cherry tree.

punish me, yet remember first, that what I have done has been for thee and our hope of happy life. Well, I shall tell thee ..."[1]

But therewithal her speech failed her; and, springing up, she faced the bent and pointed with her finger, and she all deadly pale, and shaking so that she might scarce stand, and might speak no word, though a feeble gibbering[2] came from her mouth.

Two shafts shot

Walter leapt up and put his arm about her, and looked witherward[3] she pointed, and at first saw nought; and then nought but a brown and yellow rock rolling down the bent: and then at last he saw that it was the Evil Thing which had met him when first he came into that land; and now it stood upright, and he could see that it was clad in a coat of yellow samite.[4]

Then Walter stooped down and gat[5] his bow into his hand, and stood before the Maid, while he nocked an arrow. But the monster made ready his tackle while Walter was stooping down, and or ever[6] he could loose, his bow-string twanged, and an arrow flew forth and grazed the Maid's arm above the elbow, so that the blood ran, and the Dwarf gave forth a harsh and horrible cry. Then flew Walter's shaft, and true was it aimed, so that it smote the monster full on the breast, but fell down from him as if he were made of stone. Then the creature set up his horrible cry again, and loosed withal, and Walter deemed that he had smitten the Maid, for she fell down in a heap behind him. Then waxed Walter wood-wroth,[7] and cast down his bow and drew his sword, and strode forward towards the bent against the Dwarf. But he roared out again, and there were words in his roar, and he said: "Fool! thou shalt go free if thou wilt give up the Enemy."

Two wraths

"And who," said Walter, "is the Enemy?"

Yelled the Dwarf: "She, the pink and white thing lying there; she is not dead yet; she is but dying for fear of me. Yea, she hath reason! I could have set the shaft in her heart as easily as scratching her arm; but I need her body alive, that I may wreak me[8] on her."

---

1 CW: *dash.*

2 Inarticulate sound.

3 Towards where.

4 Silk.

5 Got.

6 Before.

7 Then Walter grew insanely angry.

8 Avenge myself.

"What wilt thou do with her?" said Walter; for now he had heard that the Maid was not slain he had waxed wary[1] again, and stood watching his chance.

The Dwarf yelled so at his last word, that no word came from the noise a while, and then he said: "What will I with her? Let me at her, and stand by and look on, and then shalt thou have a strange tale to carry off with thee. For I will let thee go this while."

Said Walter: "But what need to wreak thee? What hath she done to thee?"

The cleaving of a head

"What need! what need!" roared the Dwarf; "have I not told thee that she is the Enemy? And thou askest of what she hath done! of what! Fool, she is the murderer! she hath slain the Lady that was our Lady, and that made us; she whom all we worshipped and adored. O impudent fool!"

Therewith he nocked and loosed another arrow, which would have smitten Walter in the face, but that he lowered his head in the very nick of time; then with a great shout he rushed up the bent, and was on the Dwarf before he could get his sword out, and leaping aloft dealt the creature a stroke amidmost of the crown; and so mightily he smote, that he drave[2] the heavy sword right through to the teeth, so that he fell dead straightway.

The Maid is sore afeared

Walter stood over him a minute, and when he saw that he moved not, he went slowly down to the stream, whereby the Maid yet lay cowering down and quivering all over, and covering her face with her hands. Then he took her by the wrist and said: "Up, Maiden, up! and tell me this tale of the slaying!"

But she shrunk away from him, and looked at him with wild eyes, and said: "What hast thou done with him? Is he gone?"

"He is dead," said Walter; "I have slain him; there lies he with cloven[3] skull on the bent-side:[4] unless, forsooth, he vanish away like the lion I slew! or else, perchance, he will come to life again! And art thou a lie like to the rest of them? let me hear of this slaying."

She rose up, and stood before him trembling, and said: "O, thou art angry with me, and thine anger I cannot bear. Ah, what

---

1 Grown cautious.

2 Drove.

3 Cut in two.

4 Side of the slope.

have I done? Thou has slain one, and I, maybe, the other; and never had we escaped till both these twain were dead. Ah! thou doest not know! thou dost not know! O me! what shall I do to appease thy wrath!"

Friends at one again

He looked on her, and his heart rose to his mouth at the thought of sundering[1] from her. Still he looked on her, and her piteous friendly face melted all his heart; he threw down his sword, and took her by the shoulders, and kissed her face over and over, and strained her to him, so that he felt the sweetness of her bosom. Then he lifted her up like a child, and set her down on the green grass, and went down to the water, and filled his hat therefrom, and came back to her; then he gave her to drink, and bathed her face and her hands, so that the colour came aback to the cheeks and lips of her; and she smiled on him and kissed his hands, and said: "O now thou art kind to me."

"Yea," said he, "and true it is that if thou hast slain, I have done no less, and if thou hast lied, even so have I; and if thou hast played the wanton,[2] as I deem not that thou hast,[3] I full surely have so done. So now thou shalt pardon me, and when thy spirit has come back to thee, thou shalt tell me thy tale in all friendship, and in all loving-kindness will I hearken[4] the same."

She thinketh of the burial

Therewith he knelt before her and kissed her feet. But she said: "Yea, yea; what thou willest, that will I do. But first tell me one thing. Hast thou buried this horror and hidden him in the earth?"

He deemed that fear had bewildered her, and that she scarcely yet knew how things had gone. But he said: "Fair sweet friend, I have not done it as yet; but now will I go and do it, if it seem good to thee."

"Yea," she said, "but first must thou smite off his head, and lie it by his buttocks when he is in the earth; or evil things will happen else. This of the burying is no idle matter, I bid thee believe."

"I doubt it not," said he; "surely such malice as was in this one will be hard to slay." And he picked up his sword, and turned to go to the field of deed.

---

1 Parting.

2 Sexually immoral person.

3 As I suppose you have not.

4 Listen to.

She said: "I must needs go with thee; terror hath so filled my soul, that I durst not abide here[1] without thee."

They leave the place

So they went both together to where the creature lay. The Maid durst not look on the dead monster, but Walter noted that he was girt with a big ungainly sax;[2] so he drew it from the sheath, and there smote off the hideous head of the fiend with his own weapon. Then they twain together laboured the earth, she with Walter's sword, he with the ugly sax, till they had made a grave deep and wide enough; and therein they thrust the creature, and covered him up, weapons and all together.

Chapter XXIII. Of the Peaceful Ending of that Wild Day

Thereafter Walter led the Maid down again, and said to her: "Now, sweetling, shall the story be told."

"Nay[3] friend," she said, "not here. This place hath been polluted by my craven[4] fear, and the horror of the vile wretch, of whom no words may tell his vileness. Let us hence and onward. Thou seest I have once more come to life again."

"But," said he, "thou hast been hurt by the Dwarf's arrow."

The Maid is eager to go

She laughed, and said: "Had I never had greater hurt from them than that, little had been the tale thereof: yet whereas thou lookest dolorous[5] about it, we will speedily heal it."

Therewith she sought about, and found nigh the stream-side certain herbs; and she spake words over them, and bade Walter lay them on the wound, which, forsooth, was of the least, and he did so, and bound a strip of his shirt about her arm; and then would she set forth. But he said: "Thou art all unshod; and but if that be seen to, our journey shall be stayed[6] by thy foot-soreness: I may make a shift to fashion thee brogues."[7]

She said: "I may well go barefoot. And in any case, I entreat thee that we tarry here no longer, but go away hence, if it be but for a mile."

---

1 Dare not wait here.

2 Had a large, ugly short sword on his belt.

3 LB, CW: *add comma.*

4 Cowardly.

5 Sad.

6 Delayed.

7 Rustic shoes.

And she looked piteously on him, so that he might not gainsay[1] her.

So then they crossed the stream, and set forward, when amidst all these haps[2] the day was worn to mid-morning. But after they had gone a mile, they sat them down on a knoll under the shadow of a big thorn-tree, within sight of the mountains. Then said Walter: "Now will I cut thee the brogues from the skirt of my buff-coat, which shall be well meet[3] for such work; and meanwhile shalt thou tell me thy tale."

Of the dwarf-kin

"Thou art kind," she said; "but be kinder yet, and abide my tale till we have done our day's work. For we were best to make no long delay here; because, though thou hast slain the King-dwarf, yet there be others of his kindred, who swarm in some parts of the wood as the rabbits in a warren.[4] Now true it is that they have but little understanding, less, it may be, than the very brute beasts; and that, as I said afore, unless they be set on our slot[5] like to hounds, they shall have no inkling of where to seek us, yet might they happen upon us by mere misadventure. And moreover, friend," quoth she, blushing, "I would beg of thee some little respite;[6] for though I scarce fear thy wrath any more, since thou hast been so kind to me, yet is there shame in that which I have to tell thee. Wherefore[7] since the fairest of the day is before us, let us use it all we may, and, when thou hast done[8] me my new foot-gear, get us gone forward again."

Walter maketh the Maid shoes

He kissed her kindly and yea-said[9] her asking: he had already fallen to work on the leather, and in a while had fashioned her the brogues; so she tied them to her feet, and arose with a smile and said: "Now am I hale[10] and strong again, what with the rest, and what with thy loving-kindness, and thou shalt see how nimble I shall be to leave this land, for as fair as it is. Since forsooth a land of lies it is, and of grief to the children of Adam."

---

1 Resist.

2 Happenings.

3 Very appropriate.

4 Rabbit den.

5 Track.

6 Reprieve, delay.

7 LB, CW: *add comma.*

8 Made.

9 Agreed to.

10 Healthy.

Now they rest for the even

So they went their ways thence, and fared nimbly indeed, and made no stay till some three hours after noon, when they rested by a thicket-side, where the strawberries grew plenty; they ate thereof what they would: and from a great oak hard by Walter shot him first one culver,[1] and then another, and hung them to his girdle to be for their evening's meat; sithence they went forward again, and nought befell them to tell of, till they were come, whenas it lacked scarce an hour of sunset, to the banks of another river, not right great, but bigger than the last one. There the Maid cast herself down and said: "Friend, no further will thy friend go this even;[2] nay, to say sooth, she cannot. So now we will eat of thy venison, and then shall my tale be, since I may no longer delay it; and thereafter shall our slumber be sweet and safe as I deem."

She spake merrily now, and as one who feared nothing, and Walter was much heartened by her words and her voice, and he fell to and made a fire, and a woodland oven in the earth, and sithence dighted[3] his fowl, and baked them after the manner of woodmen. And they ate, both of them, in all love, and in good-liking of life, and were much strengthened by their supper. And when they were done, Walter eked[4] his fire, both against the chill of the midnight and dawning, and for a guard against wild beasts, and by that time night was come, and the moon arisen. Then the Maiden drew up to the fire, and turned to Walter and spake.

Chapter XXIV.
The Maid Tells of What Had Befallen Her

A teacher

"Now, friend, by the clear of the moon and this firelight will I tell what I may and can of my tale. Thus it is: If I be wholly of the race of Adam I wot not; nor can I tell thee how many years old I may be. For there are, as it were, shards or gaps in my life, wherein are but a few things dimly remembered, and doubtless many things forgotten. I remember well when I was a little child, and right happy, and there were people about me whom I loved,

---

1 Dove, wood-pigeon.

2 Evening.

3 Afterwards prepared.

4 Built up.

and who loved me. It was not in this land; but all things were lovely there; the year's beginning, the happy mid-year, the year's waning, the year's ending, and then again its beginning. That passed away, and then for a while is more than dimness, for nought I remember save that I was. Thereafter I remember again, and am a young maiden, and I know some things, and long to know more. I am nowise happy; I am amongst people who bid[1] me go, and I go; and do this, and I do it: none loveth me, none tormenteth me; but I wear my heart in a longing for I scarce know what. Neither then am I in this land, but in a land that I love not, and a house that is big and stately, but nought lovely. Then is a dim time again, and sithence a time not right clear; an evil time, wherein I am older, well-nigh grown to womanhood. There are a many folk about me, and they foul, and greedy, and hard; and my spirit is fierce, but my body feeble; and I am set to tasks that I would not do, by them that are unwiser than I; and smitten[2] I am by them that are less valiant than I; and I know lack, and stripes and divers[3] misery. But all that is now become but a dim picture to me, save that amongst all these unfriends is a friend to me; an old woman, who telleth me sweet tales of other life, wherein all is high and goodly, or at the least valiant and doughty,[4] and she setteth hope in my heart and learneth[5] me, and maketh me to know much ... O much ... so that at last I am grown wise, and wise to be mighty if I durst. Yet am I nought in this land all this while, but, as meseemeth, in a great and a foul city.

She is marked for a thrall

"And then, as it were, I fall asleep; and in my sleep is nought, save here and there a wild dream, somedeal[6] lovely, somedeal hideous: but of this dream is my Mistress a part, and the monster, withal, whose head thou didst cleave[7] to-day. But when I am awaken from it, then am I verily in this land, and myself, as thou seest me to-day. And the first part of my life here is this, that I am in the pillared hall yonder, half-clad and with bound hands; and the Dwarf leadeth me to the Lady, and I hear his horrible croak

---

1 Command.
2 Beaten.
3 Various kinds of.
4 Courageous.
5 Teaches.
6 Somewhat.
7 Cut in two.

as he sayeth: 'Lady, will this one do?' and then the sweet voice of the Lady saying: 'This one will do; thou shalt have thy reward: now, set thou the token upon her.' Then I remember the Dwarf dragging me away, and my heart sinking for fear of him; but for that time he did me no more harm than the rivetting upon my leg this iron ring which here thou seest.

The Mistress notes the Maid's wisdom
The Dwarf is threatened

"So from that time forward I have lived in this land, and been the thrall of the Lady; and I remember my life here day by day, and no part of it has fallen into the dimness of dreams. Thereof will I tell thee but little: but this I will tell thee, that in spite of my past dreams, or it may be because of them, I had not lost the wisdom which the old woman had erst learned me,[1] and for more wisdom I longed. Maybe this longing shall now make both thee and me happy, but for the passing time it brought me grief. For at first my Mistress was indeed wayward[2] with me, but as any great lady might be with her bought thrall, whiles caressing me, and whiles chastising me, as her mood went; but she seemed not to be cruel of malice, or with any set purpose. But so it was (rather little by little than by any great sudden uncovering of my intent), that she came to know that I also had some of the wisdom whereby she lived her queenly life. That was about two years after I was first her thrall, and three weary years have gone by since she began to see in me the enemy of her days. Now why or wherefore I know not, but it seemeth that it would not avail[3] her to slay me outright, or suffer me to die; but nought withheld her from piling up griefs and miseries on my head. At last she set her servant, the Dwarf, upon me, even he whose head thou clavest[4] to-day. Many things I bore from him whereof it were unseemly for my tongue to tell before thee; but the time came when he exceeded, and I could bear no more; and then I showed him this sharp knife (wherewith I would have thrust me through to the heart if thou hadst not pardoned me e'en now), and I told him that if he forbore[5] me not, I would slay, not him, but myself; and this he might not away with because of the commandment of the Lady, who had given him the word that in any case I must be

---

1 Earlier taught to me.

2 Erratic.

3 Benefit.

4 Split.

5 Spared.

kept living. And her hand, withal, fear held somewhat hereafter. Yet was there need to me of all my wisdom; for with all this her hatred grew, and whiles raged within her so furiously that it over-mastered her fear, and at such times she would have put me to death if I had not escaped her by some turn of my lore.

Of the Coming of the King's Son

"Now further, I shall tell thee that somewhat more than a year ago hither to this land came the King's Son, the second goodly man, as thou art the third, whom her sorceries have drawn hither since I have dwelt here. Forsooth, when he first came, he seemed to us, to me, and yet more to my Lady, to be as beautiful as an angel, and sorely she loved him; and he her, after his fashion: but he was light-minded, and cold-hearted, and in a while he must needs turn his eyes upon me, and offer me his love, which was but foul and unkind as it turned out; for when I nay-said[1] him, as maybe I had not done save for fear of my Mistress, he had no pity upon me, but spared not to lead me into the trap of her wrath, and leave me without help, or a good word. But, O friend, in spite of all grief and anguish, I learned still, and waxed[2] wise, and wiser, abiding the day of my deliverance, which has come, and thou art come."

Of the vision at Langton

Therewith she took Walter's hands and kissed them; but he kissed her face, and her tears wet her lips. Then she went on: "But sithence, months ago, the Lady began to weary of this dastard, despite of his beauty; and then it was thy turn to be swept into her net; I partly guess how. For on a day in broad daylight, as I was serving my Mistress in the hall, and the Evil Thing, whose head is now cloven, was lying across the threshold of the door, as it were a dream fell upon me, though I strove to cast it off for fear of chastisement; for the pillared hall wavered, and vanished from my sight, and my feet were treading a rough stone pavement instead of the marble wonder of the hall, and there was the scent of the salt sea and of the tackle of ships, and behind me were tall houses, and before me the ships indeed, with their ropes beating and their sails flapping and their masts wavering; and in mine ears was the hale and how[3] of mariners; things that I had seen and heard in the dimness of my life gone by.

1 Denied.

2 Grew.

3 Pull and shout.

The blazon of the ancient

"And there was I, and the Dwarf before me, and the Lady after me, going over the gangway aboard of a tall ship, and she gathered way and was gotten out of the haven, and straightway I saw the mariners cast abroad their ancient."[1]

Quoth[2] Walter: "What then! Sawest thou the blazon[3] thereon, of a wolf-like beast ramping[4] up against a maiden? And that might well have been thou."

She said: "Yea, so it was; but refrain thee, that I may tell on my tale! The ship and the sea vanished away, but I was not back in the hall of the Golden House; and again were we three in the street of the self-same town which we had but just left; but somewhat dim was my vision thereof, and I saw little save the door of a goodly house before me, and speedily it died out, and we were again in the pillared hall, wherein my thralldom was made manifest."[5]

"Maiden," said Walter, "one question I would ask thee; to wit, didst thou see me on the quay by the ships?"

They are in a new city

"Nay," she said, "there were many folk about, but they were all as images of the aliens to me. Now hearken further: three months thereafter came the dream upon me again, and when we were all three together in the Pillared Hall; and again was the vision somewhat dim. Once more we were in the street of a busy town, but all unlike to that other one, and there were men standing together on our right hands by the door of a house."

"Yea, yea," quoth Walter; "and, forsooth, one of them was who but I."

Forebodings of evil

"Refrain thee, beloved!" she said; "for my tale draweth to its ending, and I would have thee hearken heedfully:[6] for maybe thou shalt once again deem my deed past pardon. Some twenty days after this last dream, I had some leisure from my Mistress's service, so I went to disport[7] me by the Well of the Oak-tree (or forsooth she might have set in my mind the thought of going

---

1 Banner.

2 Said.

3 Heraldic banner.

4 Threatening.

5 Slavery was revealed.

6 Attentively.

7 Pass time pleasantly.

there, that I might meet thee and give her some occasion against me); and I sat thereby, nowise[1] loving the earth, but sick at heart, because of late the King's Son had been more than ever instant[2] with me to yield him my body, threatening me else with casting me into all that the worst could do to me of torments and shames day by day. I say my heart failed me, and I was well-nigh[3] brought to the point of yea-saying his desires, that I might take the chance of something befalling me that were less bad than the worst. But here must I tell thee a thing, and pray thee to take it to heart. This, more than aught else, had given me strength to nay-say that dastard, that my wisdom both hath been, and now is, the wisdom of a wise maid, and not of a woman, and all the might thereof shall I lose with my maidenhead. Evil wilt thou think of me then, for all I was tried so sore, that I was at point to cast it all away, so wretchedly as I shrank from the horror of the Lady's wrath.

The Maid feareth again

"But there as I sat pondering these things, I saw a man coming, and thought no otherwise thereof but that it was the King's Son, till I saw the stranger drawing near, and his golden hair, and his grey eyes; and then I heard his voice, and his kindness pierced my heart, and I knew that my friend had come to see me; and O, friend, these tears are for the sweetness of that past hour!"

Said Walter: "I came to see my friend, I also. Now have I noted what thou badest me; and I will forbear all as thou commandest me, till we be safe out of the desert[4] and far away from all evil things; but wilt thou ban me from all caresses?"

She laughed amidst of her tears, and said: "O, nay, poor lad, if thou wilt be but wise."

Then she leaned toward him, and took his face betwixt her hands and kissed him oft, and the tears started in his eyes for love and pity of her.

Then she said: "Alas, friend! even yet mayst thou doom[5] me guilty, and all thy love may turn away from me, when I have told thee all that I have done for the sake of thee and me. O, if then there might be some chastisement for the guilty woman, and not mere sundering!"[6]

---

1 In no way.

2 Insistent.

3 CW: wellnigh.

4 Wilderness.

5 Judge.

6 Parting.

"Fear nothing, sweetling," said he; "for indeed I deem that already I know partly what thou hast done."

How the Maid took rede from the first
Concerning that tryst
Concerning that lion

She sighed, and said: "I will tell thee next, that I banned thy kissing and caressing of me till to-day because I knew that my Mistress would surely know if a man, if thou, hadst so much as touched a finger of mine in love. It was to try me herein that on the morning of the hunting she kissed and embraced me, till I almost died thereof, and showed thee my shoulder and my limbs; and to try thee withal, if thine eye should glister[1] or thy cheek flush[2] thereat; for indeed she was raging in jealousy of thee. Next, my friend, even whiles we were talking together at the Well of the Rock, I was pondering on what we should do to escape from this land of lies. Maybe thou wilt say: Why didst thou not take my hand and flee with me as we fled to-day? Friend, it is most true, that were she not dead we had not escaped thus far. For her trackers would have followed us, set on by her, and brought us back to an evil fate. Therefore I tell thee that from the first I did plot the death of those two, the Dwarf and the Mistress. For no otherwise mightest thou live, or I escape from death in life. But as to the dastard who threatened me with a thrall's pains, I heeded him nought to live or die, for well I knew that thy valiant sword, yea, or thy bare hands, would speedily tame him. Now first I knew that I must make a show of yielding to the King's Son; and somewhat how I did therein, thou knowest. But no night and no time did I give him to bed me, till after I had met thee as thou wentest to the Golden House, before the adventure of fetching the lion's skin; and up to that time I had scarce known what to do, save ever to bid thee, with sore grief and pain, to yield thee to the wicked woman's desire. But as we spake together there by the stream, and I saw that the Evil Thing (whose head thou clavest e'en now) was spying on us, then amidst the sickness of terror which ever came over me whensoever I thought of him, and much more when I saw him (ah! he is dead now!), it came flashing into my mind how I might destroy my enemy. Therefore I made the Dwarf my messenger to her, by bidding thee to my bed in such wise[3] that he might hear it. And wot thou well, that

1 Shine.

2 Blush.

3 In such a way.

he speedily carried her the tidings. Meanwhile I hastened to lie to the King's Son, and all privily bade him[1] come to me and not thee. And thereafter, by dint[2] of waiting and watching, and taking the only chance that there was, I met thee as thou camest back from fetching the skin of the lion that never was, and gave thee that warning, or else had we been undone indeed."

Said Walter: "Was the lion of her making or of thine then?"

She said: "Of hers: why should I deal with such a matter?"

"Yea," said Walter, "but she verily swooned,[3] and she was verily wroth with the Enemy."

The Maid smiled, and said: "If her lie was not like very sooth, then had she not been the crafts-master that I knew her: one may lie otherwise than with the tongue alone: yet indeed her wrath against the Enemy was nought feigned;[4] for the Enemy was even I, and in these latter days never did her wrath leave me. But to go on with my tale.

What befell while Walter lay in the hazel-copse

"Now doubt thou not, that, when thou camest into the hall yester eve,[5] the Mistress knew of thy counterfeit tryst with me, and meant nought but death for thee; yet first would she have thee in her arms again, therefore did she make much of thee at table (and that was partly for my torment also), and therefore did she make that tryst with thee, and deemed doubtless that thou wouldst not dare to forgo it, even if thou shouldst go to me thereafter.

"Now I had trained that dastard to me as I have told thee, but I gave him a sleepy draught,[6] so that when I came to the bed he might not move toward me nor open his eyes: but I lay down beside him, so that the Lady might know that my body had been there; for well had she wotted if it had not. Then as there I lay I cast over him thy shape, so that none might have known but that thou wert lying by my side, and there, trembling, I abode what should befall. Thus I passed through the hour whenas thou shouldest have been at her chamber, and the time of my tryst with thee was come as the Mistress would be deeming; so that I

---

1 Secretly told him.

2 By means of.

3 Truly fainted.

4 Pretended.

5 Last night.

6 Sleeping potion.

looked for her speedily, and my heart well-nigh[1] failed me for fear of her cruelty.

Further tidings in that same while
Yet further

"Presently then I heard a stirring in her chamber, and I slipped from out the bed, and hid me behind the hangings,[2] and was like to die for fear of her; and lo, presently she came stealing in softly, holding a lamp in one hand and a knife in the other. And I tell thee of a sooth that I also had a sharp knife in my hand to defend my life if need were. She held the lamp up above her head before she drew near to the bed-side, and I heard her mutter: 'She is not there then! but she shall be taken.' Then she went up to the bed and stooped over it, and laid her hand on the place where I had lain; and therewith her eyes turned to that false image of thee lying there, and she fell a-trembling and shaking, and the lamp fell to the ground and was quenched[3] (but there was bright moonlight in the room, and still I could see what betid[4]). But she uttered a noise like the low roar of a wild beast, and I saw her arm and hand rise up, and the flashing of the steel beneath the hand, and then down came the hand and the steel, and I went nigh to swooning[5] lest perchance I had wrought over well, and thine image were thy very self. The dastard died without a groan: why should I lament him? I cannot. But the Lady drew him toward her, and snatched the clothes from off his shoulders and breast, and fell a-gibbering sounds[6] mostly without meaning, but broken here and there with words. Then I heard her say: 'I shall forget; I shall forget; and the new days shall come.' Then was there silence of her a little, and thereafter she cried out in a terrible voice: 'O no, no, no! I cannot forget; I cannot forget;' and she raised a great wailing cry that filled all the night with horror (didst thou not hear it?), and caught up the knife from the bed and thrust it into her breast, and fell down a dead heap over the bed and on to the man whom she had slain. And then I thought of thee, and joy smote[7] across my terror; how shall I gainsay[8] it? And I fled away

1 CW: wellnigh.
2 Decorative curtains. Morris and Company produced a line of decorative textiles that its customers could use for "hangings."
3 Extinguished.
4 Happened.
5 Fainting.
6 Uttering inarticulate noises.
7 Struck.
8 Deny.

to thee, and I took thine hands in mine, thy dear hands, and we fled away together. Shall we be still together?"

Walter answereth the Maid's tale

He spoke slowly, and touched her not, and she, forbearing[1] all sobbing and weeping, sat looking wistfully on him. He said: "I think thou hast told me all; and whether thy guile slew her, or her own evil heart, she was slain last night who lay in mine arms the night before. It was ill, and ill done of me, for I loved not her, but thee, and I wished for her death that I might be with thee. Thou wottest this, and still thou lovest me, it may be overweeningly.[2] What have I to say then? If there be any guilt of guile, I also was in the guile; and if there be any guilt of murder, I also was in the murder. Thus we say to each other; and to God and his Hallows[3] we say: 'We two have conspired and slain[4] the woman who tormented one of us, and would have slain the other; and if we have done amiss therein, then shall we two together pay the penalty; for in this have we done as one body and one soul.'"

Therewith he put his arms about her and kissed her, but soberly and friendly, as if he would comfort her. And thereafter he said to her: "Maybe to-morrow, in the sunlight, I will ask thee of this woman, what she verily was; but now let her be. And thou, thou art over-wearied, and I bid thee sleep."[5]

So he went about and gathered of bracken[6] a great heap for her bed, and did his coat thereover,[7] and led her thereto, and she lay down meekly, and smiled and crossed her arms over her bosom, and presently fell asleep. But as for him, he watched by the fire-side till dawn began to glimmer, and then he also laid him down and slept.

Chapter XXV.
Of the Triumphant Summer Array[8] of the Maid

When the day was bright Walter arose, and met the Maid coming from the river-bank, fresh and rosy from the water. She paled a

1 Avoiding.
2 With too high an opinion.
3 Saints.
4 CW: to slay.
5 Ask you to sleep.
6 Ferns, undergrowth.
7 Put his coat over it.
8 Clothing.

little when they met face to face, and she shrank from him shyly. But he took her hand and kissed her frankly; and the two were glad, and had no need to tell each other of their joy, though much else they deemed they had to say, could they have found words thereto.

Concerning the Bear-folk

So they came to their fire and sat down, and fell to breakfast; and ere they were done, the Maid said: "My Master, thou seest we be come nigh unto the hill-country, and to-day about sunset, belike, we shall come into the Land of the Bear-folk; and both it is, that there is peril if we fall into their hands, and that we may scarce escape them. Yet I deem that we may deal with the peril by wisdom."

"What is the peril?" said Walter; "I mean, what is the worst of it?"

Said the Maid: "To be offered up in sacrifice to their God."

"But if we escape death at their hands, what then?" said Walter.

"One of two things," said she; "the first,[1] that they shall take us into their tribe."

"And will they sunder[2] us in that case?" said Walter.

"Nay," said she.

Walter laughed and said: "Therein is little harm then. But what is the other chance?"

Said she: "That we leave them with their good-will, and come back to one of the lands of Christendom."

Of the God of the Bears

Said Walter: "I am not all so sure that this is the better of the two choices, though, forsooth, thou seemest to think so. But tell me now, what like[3] is their God, that they should offer up new-comers to him?"

"Their God is a woman," she said, "and the Mother of their nation and tribes (or so they deem) before the days when they had chieftains and Lords of Battle."

"That will be long ago," said he; "how then may she be living now?"

Said the Maid: "Doubtless that woman of yore agone[4] is dead this many and many a year; but they take to them still a new

---

1 CW: *omit comma.*

2 Part.

3 Kind, type.

4 Long ago.

woman, one after other, as they may happen on them, to be in the stead[1] of the Ancient Mother. And to tell thee the very truth right out, she that lieth dead in the Pillared Hall was even the last of these; and now, if they knew it, they lack a God. This shall we tell them."

"Yea, yea!" said Walter, "a goodly welcome shall we have of them then, if we come amongst them with our hands red with the blood of their God!"

Who shall be their God now?

She smiled on him and said: "If I come amongst them with the tidings that I have slain her, and they trow therein,[2] without doubt they shall make me Lady and Goddess in her stead."

"This is a strange word," said Walter; "but if so they do, how shall that further us in reaching the kindreds of the world, and the folk of Holy Church?"

She laughed outright, so joyous was she grown, now that she knew that his life was yet to be a part of hers. "Sweetheart," she said, "now I see that thou desirest wholly what I desire; yet in any case, abiding[3] with them would be living and not dying, even as thou hadst it e'en now. But, forsooth, they will not hinder our departure if they deem me their God; they do not look for it, nor desire it, that their God should dwell with them daily. Have no fear." Then she laughed again, and said: "What! thou lookest on me and deemest me to be but a sorry image of a goddess; and me with my scanty coat and bare arms and naked feet! But wait! I know well how to array me when the time cometh. Thou shalt see it! And now, my Master, were it not meet[4] that we took to the road?"

A fair place

So they arose, and found a ford of the river that took the Maid but to the knee, and so set forth up the greensward of the slopes whereas there were but few trees; so went they faring toward the hill-country.

At the last they were come to the feet of the very hills, and in the hollows[5] betwixt the buttresses of them grew nut and berry trees, and the greensward round about them was both thick and much[6] flowery. There they stayed them and dined, whereas Walter had shot a hare by the way, and they had found a bubbling

---

1 Place.

2 Believe in it.

3 Staying.

4 Appropriate.

5 Vallies.

6 Very.

spring under a grey stone in a bight of the coppice, wherein now the birds were singing their best.

When they had eaten and had rested somewhat, the Maid arose and said: "Now shall the Queen array herself, and seem like a very goddess."

Then she fell to work, while Walter looked on; and she made a garland for her head of eglantine[1] where the roses were the fairest; and with mingled flowers of the summer she wreathed her middle about, and let the garland of them hang down to below her knees; and knots of the flowers she made fast to the skirts of her coat, and did them for arm-rings about her arms, and for anklets and sandals for her feet. Then she set a garland about Walter's head, and then stood a little off from him and set her feet together, and lifted up her arms, and said: "Lo now! am I not as like to the Mother of Summer as if I were clad in silk and gold? and even so shall I be deemed by the folk of the Bear. Come now, thou shalt see how all shall be well."

The flowers fade? or come alive again?

She laughed joyously; but he might scarce laugh for pity of his love. Then they set forth again, and began to climb the hills, and the hours wore as they went in sweet converse;[2] till at last Walter looked on the Maid, and smiled on her; and said: "One thing I would say to thee, lovely friend, to wit: wert thou[3] clad in silk and gold, thy stately raiment might well suffer a few stains, or here and there a rent[4] maybe; but stately would it be still when the folk of the Bear should come up against thee. But as to this flowery array of thine, in a few hours it shall be all faded and nought. Nay, even now, as I look on thee, the meadow-sweet[5] that

---

1 Briar-rose, sweetbriar. Eglantine is the earliest known species of rose; even its leaves, when crushed, are fragrant. Chaucer named the Prioress in *The Canterbury Tales* after it, and it is used as an allegory for the lady who is the poet's would-be lover in the thirteenth-century poem *The Romance of the Rose*. Morris's colleague Edward Burne-Jones produced a famous series of paintings, collectively known as *The Briar Rose Series*, in which the eglantine branches figure prominently and which is now displayed at Buscot Park in North Berkshire.

2 Conversation.

3 If you were.

4 Tear.

5 This is the species of flower *Spiraea Ulmaria*, characterized by its dense heads of white and very fragrant flowers. Morris frequently depicted species of flowers in his designs and designed a wallpaper, *Meadowsweet*, with this flower in a repeating pattern.

hangeth from thy girdle-stead[1] has waxen dull, and welted;[2] and the blossoming eyebright[3] that is for a hem to the little white coat of thee is already forgetting how to be bright and blue. What sayest thou then?"

She laughed at his word, and stood still, and looked back over her shoulder, while with her fingers she dealt with the flowers about her side like to a bird preening his feathers. Then she said: "Is it verily so as thou sayest? Look again!"

So he looked, and wondered; for lo! beneath his eyes the spires of the meadow-sweet grew crisp and clear again, the eyebright blossoms shone once more over the whiteness of her legs; the eglantine roses opened, and all was as fresh and bright as if it were still growing on its own roots.

On the downs

He wondered, and was even somedeal aghast;[4] but she said: "Dear friend, be not troubled! did I not tell thee that I am wise in hidden lore?[5] But in my wisdom shall be no longer any scathe[6] to any man. And again, this my wisdom, as I told thee erst,[7] shall end on the day whereon I am made all happy.[8] And it is thou that shall wield it all, my Master. Yet must my wisdom needs endure for a little season yet. Let us on then,[9] boldly and happily."

Chapter XXVI. They come to the Folk of the Bears

A dale of the downs

On they went, and before long they were come up on to the down-country,[10] where was scarce a tree, save gnarled and knotty thorn-bushes here and there, but nought else higher than the

---

1 The place where a belt should be.

2 Grown dull and wilted.

3 This is the species of flower *Euphrasia Officinalis*, which is characterized by small, white, or purple flowers variegated with yellow. In 1883 Morris designed a printed textile, *Eyebright*, that depicts this flower in a repeating pattern.

4 Somewhat afraid or amazed.

5 Magic.

6 Harm.

7 Earlier.

8 That is, the day she loses her virginity.

9 Let us [go] on then.

10 Elevated meadowland.

whin.[1] And here on these upper lands they saw that the pastures were much burnt with the drought, albeit summer was not worn old. Now they went making due south toward the mountains, whose heads they saw from time to time rising deep blue over the bleak greyness of the downland ridges. And so they went, till at last, hard on[2] sunset, after they had climbed long over a high bent, they came to the brow thereof, and, looking down, beheld new tidings.

There was a wide valley below them, greener than the downs which they had come over, and greener yet amidmost, from the watering of a stream which, all beset with willows, wound about the bottom. Sheep and neat were pasturing about the dale, and moreover a long line of smoke was going up straight into the windless heavens from the midst of a ring of little round houses built of turfs, and thatched with reed.[3] And beyond that, toward an eastward-lying bight[4] of the dale, they could see what looked like to a doom-ring of big stones,[5] though there were no rocky places in that land. About the cooking-fire amidst of the houses, and here and there otherwise, they saw, standing or going to and fro, huge figures of men and women, with children playing about betwixt them.

The down-dwellers

They stood and gazed down at it for a minute or two, and though all were at peace there, yet to Walter, at least, it seemed strange and awful. He spake softly, as though he would not have his voice reach those men, though they were, forsooth, out of ear-shot of anything save a shout: "Are these then the children of the Bear? What shall we do now?"

She said: "Yea, of the Bear they be, though there be other folks of them far and far away to the northward and eastward, near to the borders of the sea. And as to what we shall do, let us go down at once, and peacefully. Indeed, by now there will be no escape from them; for lo you! they have seen us."

---

1 Thorny shrubs [like furze or gorse].

2 Close to.

3 These houses, like some rustic houses in the British Isles, are built of sods with reeds used as roofing.

4 Angle.

5 There are a number of prehistoric circles of standing stones in the vicinity of Marlborough School, where Morris as a child was educated, the most famous being those of Avebury and Stonehenge.

The like of them

Forsooth, some three or four of the big men had turned them toward the bent whereon stood the twain, and were hailing[1] them in huge, rough voices, wherein, howsoever, seemed to be no anger or threat. So the Maid took Walter by the hand, and thus they went down quietly, and the Bear-folk, seeing them, stood all together, facing them, to abide their coming. Walter saw of them, that though they were very tall and bigly made, they were not so far above the stature of men as to be marvels. The carles were long-haired, and shaggy of beard, and their hair all red or tawny; their skins, where their naked flesh showed, were burned brown with sun and weather, but to a fair and pleasant brown, nought like to blackamoors.[2] The queans[3] were comely and well-eyed; nor was there anything of fierce or evil-looking about either the carles or the queans, but somewhat grave and solemn of aspect[4] were they. Clad were they all, saving the young men-children, but somewhat scantily, and in nought save sheep-skins or deer-skins.

For weapons they saw amongst them clubs, and spears headed with bone or flint, and ugly axes of big flints set in wooden handles; nor was there, as far as they could see, either now or afterward, any bow amongst them.[5] But some of the young men seemed to have slings done about their shoulders.

Gods or mere aliens?

Now when they were come but three fathom[6] from them, the Maid lifted up her voice, and spake clearly and sweetly: "Hail, ye folk of the Bears! we have come amongst you, and that for your good and not for your hurt: wherefore we would know if we be welcome."

There was an old man who stood foremost in the midst, clad in a mantle of deer-skins worked very goodly, and with a gold ring on his arm, and a chaplet[7] of blue stones on his head, and he spake: "Little are ye, but so goodly, that if ye were but bigger, we should deem that ye were come from the Gods' House. Yet have I heard, that how mighty soever may the Gods be, and chiefly our God, they be at whiles nought so bigly made as we of the Bears.

---

1 Calling to.

2 Inhabitants of Morocco.

3 Women.

4 Appearance.

5 In other words, the Bear-folk used prehistoric weapons and tools.

6 A fathom is the length of the outstretched arms, about six feet.

7 Circle, wreath.

How this may be, I wot not. But if ye be not of the Gods or their kindred, then are ye mere aliens; and we know not what to do with aliens, save[1] we meet them in battle, or give them to the God,[2] or save we make them children of the Bear. But yet again, ye may be messengers of some folk who would bind friendship and alliance with us: in which case ye shall at the least depart in peace, and whiles ye are with us shall be our guests in all good cheer. Now, therefore, we bid you declare the matter unto us."

The Maid will answer at the Mote

Then spake the Maid: "Father, it were easy for us to declare what we be unto you here present. But, meseemeth, ye who be gathered round the fire here this evening are less than the whole tale of the children of the Bear."

"So it is, Maiden," said the elder, "that many more children hath the Bear."

"This then we bid you," said the Maid, "that ye send the tokens round and gather your people to you, and when they be assembled in the Doom-ring,[3] then shall we put our errand before you; and according to that, shall ye deal with us."

"Thou hast spoken well," said the elder; "and even so had we bidden[4] you ourselves. To-morrow, before noon, shall ye stand in the Doom-ring in this Dale, and speak with the children of the Bear."

Supper amidst of the Bears

Therewith he turned to his own folk and called out something, whereof those twain knew not the meaning; and there came to him, one after another, six young men, unto each of whom he gave a thing from out his pouch, but what it was Walter might not see, save that it was little and of small account: to each, also, he spake a word or two, and straight[5] they set off running, one after the other, turning toward the bent which was over against that whereby the twain had come into the Dale, and were soon out of sight in the gathering dusk.

Then the elder turned him again to Walter and the Maid, and spake: "Man and woman, whatsoever ye may be, or whatsoever may abide you to-morrow, to-night, ye are welcome guests to us; so we bid you come eat and drink at our fire."

---

1 Unless.

2 Sacrifice them.

3 Ring of judgment.

4 Commanded.

5 Right away.

The Bears are shy of the aliens

So they sat all together upon the grass round about the embers of the fire, and ate curds[1] and cheese, and drank milk in abundance; and as the night grew on them they quickened[2] the fire, that they might have light. This wild folk talked merrily amongst themselves, with laughter enough and friendly jests, but to the new-comers they were few-spoken,[3] though, as the twain deemed, for no enmity[4] that they bore them. But this found Walter, that the younger ones, both men and women, seemed to find it a hard matter to keep their eyes off them; and seemed, withal, to gaze on them with somewhat of doubt, or, it might be, of fear.

So when the night was wearing a little, the elder arose and bade the twain to come with him, and led them to a small house or booth, which was amidmost of all, and somewhat bigger than the others, and he did them to wit[5] that they should rest there that night, and bade them sleep in peace and without fear till the morrow. So they entered, and found beds thereon of heather and ling,[6] and they laid them down sweetly, like brother and sister, when they had kissed each other. But they noted that four brisk men lay without the booth, and across the door, with their weapons beside them, so that they must needs look upon themselves as captives.

Walter bids farewell

Then Walter might not refrain him, but spake: "Sweet and dear friend, I have come a long way from the quay at Langton, and the vision of the Dwarf, the Maid, and the Lady; and for this kiss wherewith I have kissed thee e'en now, and the kindness of thine eyes, it was worth the time and the travail. But to-morrow, meseemeth, I shall go no further in this world, though my journey be far longer than from Langton hither. And now may God and All Hallows[7] keep thee amongst this wild folk, whenas I shall be gone from thee."

She laughed low and sweetly, and said: "Dear friend, dost thou speak to me thus mournfully to move me to love thee better?

---

1 Coagulated milk that can be made into cheese or eaten as is.

2 Lighted.

3 Taciturn.

4 Hostility.

5 Explained to them.

6 A species of heather [likely *Calluna Vulgaris*].

7 All the saints.

Then is thy labour lost; for no better may I love thee than now I do; and that is with mine whole heart. But keep a good courage, I bid thee; for we be not sundered[1] yet, nor shall we be. Nor do I deem that we shall die here, or to-morrow; but many years hence, after we have known all the sweetness of life. Meanwhile, I bid thee good night, fair friend!"

Chapter XXVII. Morning Amongst the Bears

So Walter laid him down and fell asleep, and knew no more till he awoke in bright daylight with the Maid standing over him. She was fresh from the water, for she had been to the river to bathe her, and the sun through the open door fell streaming on her feet close to Walter's pillow. He turned about and cast his arm about them, and caressed them, while she stood smiling upon him; then he arose and looked on her, and said: "How thou art fair and bright this morning! And yet ... and yet ... were it not well that thou do off thee all this faded and drooping bravery of leaves and blossoms, that maketh thee look like to a jongleur's damsel[2] on a morrow of Mayday?"[3]

And he gazed ruefully[4] on her.

She laughed on him merrily and said: "Yea, and belike these others think no better of my attire, or not much better; for yonder they are gathering small wood for the burnt-offering; which, forsooth, shall be thou and I, unless I better it all by means of the wisdom I learned of the old woman, and perfected betwixt the stripes of my Mistress, whom a little while ago thou lovedst somewhat."

Walter doubteth

And as she spake her eyes sparkled, her cheek flushed, and her limbs and her feet seemed as if they could scarce refrain from dancing for joy. Then Walter knit his brow, and for a moment a thought half-framed was in his mind: Is it so, that she will bewray[5] me and live without me? and he cast his eyes on to the

1 Parted.

2 An entertainer's girlfriend.

3 May 1st was traditionally the time to celebrate the arrival of Spring and was thus associated with fertility rites, such as dancing around the maypole. Socialists use May 1st as a day to celebrate the contribution of workers to society.

4 With sorrow or regret.

5 Betray.

ground. But she said: "Look up, and into mine eyes, friend, and see if there be in them any falseness toward thee! For I know thy thought; I know thy thought. Dost thou not see that my joy and gladness is for the love of thee, and the thought of the rest from trouble that is at hand?"

She hearteneth him

He looked up, and his eyes met the eyes of her love, and he would have cast his arms about her; but she drew aback and said: "Nay, thou must refrain thee awhile, dear friend, lest these folk cast eyes on us, and deem us over lover-like for what I am to bid them deem me. Abide a while, and then shall all be in me according to thy will. But now I must tell thee that it is not very far from noon, and that the Bears are streaming into the Dale, and already there is an host of men at the Doom-ring, and, as I said, the bale[1] for the burnt-offering is well-nigh[2] dight,[3] whether it be for us, or for some other creature. And now I have to bid thee this, and it will be a thing easy for thee to do, to wit, that thou look as if thou wert of the race of the Gods, and not to blench,[4] or show sign of blenching, whatever betide: to yea-say both my yea-say and my nay-say: and lastly this, which is the only hard thing for thee (but thou hast already done it before somewhat), to look upon me with no masterful eyes of love, nor as if thou wert at once praying me and commanding me; rather thou shalt so demean thee[5] as if thou wert my man[6] all simply, and nowise[7] my master."

"O friend beloved," said Walter, "here at least art thou the master, and I will do all thy bidding, in certain hope of[8] this, that either we shall live together or die together."

Here cometh breakfast

But as they spoke, in came the elder, and with him a young maiden, bearing with them their breakfast of curds and cream and strawberries, and he bade them eat. So they ate, and were not unmerry; and the while of their eating the elder talked with them soberly, but not hardly, or with any seeming enmity: and ever his

---

1 Fire.
2 CW: wellnigh.
3 Prepared.
4 Grow pale.
5 Humble yourself.
6 Servant.
7 In no way.
8 CW: or.

talk gat on to[1] the drought, which was now burning up the down-pastures;[2] and how the grass in the watered dales, which was no wide spread of land, would not hold out much longer unless the God sent them rain. And Walter noted that those two, the elder and the Maid, eyed each other curiously amidst of this talk; the elder intent on what she might say, and if she gave heed to his words; while on her side the Maid answered his speech graciously and pleasantly, but said little that was of any import:[3] nor would she have him fix her eyes, which wandered lightly from this thing to that; nor would her lips grow stern and stable, but ever smiled in answer to the light of her eyes, as she sat there with her face as the very face of the gladness of the summer day.

Chapter XXVIII. Of the New God of the Bears

At last the old man said: "My children, ye shall now come with me unto the Doom-ring of our folk, the Bears of the Southern Dales, and deliver to them your errand; and I beseech[4] you to have pity upon your own bodies, as I have pity on them; on thine especially, Maiden, so fair and bright a creature as thou art; for so it is, that if ye deal us out light and lying words after the manner of dastards, ye shall miss the worship and glory of wending away amidst of the flames, a gift to the God and a hope to the people, and shall be passed by the rods[5] of the folk, until ye faint and fail amongst them, and then shall ye be thrust down into the flow[6] at the Dale's End, and a stone-laden hurdle[7] cast upon you, that we may thenceforth forget your folly."

The Man-mote

The Maid now looked full into his eyes, and Walter deemed that the old man shrank before her; but she said: "Thou art old and wise, O great man of the Bears, yet nought I need to learn of thee. Now lead us on our way to the Stead[8] of the Errands."

So the elder brought them along to the Doom-ring at the eastern end of the Dale; and it was now all peopled with those

1 Focused upon.
2 Elevated meadowland.
3 Significance.
4 Request.
5 Clubs.
6 Thrown down into the river.
7 A gate weighted down with stones.
8 Place.

huge men, weaponed after their fashion, and standing up, so that the grey stones thereof but showed a little over their heads. But amidmost of the said Ring was a big stone, fashioned as a chair, whereon sat a very old man, long-hoary[1] and white-bearded, and on either side of him stood a great-limbed woman clad in war-gear,[2] holding, each of them, a long spear, and with a flint-bladed knife in the girdle; and there were no other women in all the Mote.[3]

They stand before the folk

Then the elder led those twain into the midst of the Mote, and there bade[4] them go up on to a wide, flat-topped stone, six feet above the ground, just over against the ancient chieftain; and they mounted it by a rough stair, and stood there before that folk; Walter in his array of the outward world, which had been fair enough, of crimson cloth and silk, and white linen, but was now travel-stained and worn; and the Maid with nought upon her, save the smock[5] wherein she had fled from the Golden House of the Wood beyond the World, decked with the faded flowers which she had wreathed about her yesterday. Nevertheless, so it was, that those big men eyed her intently, and with somewhat of worship.

Now did Walter, according to her bidding, sink down on his knees beside her, and drawing his sword, hold it before him, as if to keep all interlopers[6] aloof from[7] the Maid. And there was silence in the Mote, and all eyes were fixed on those twain.

The Maid is bidden to speak

At last the old chief arose and spake: "Ye men, here are come a man and a woman, we know not whence; whereas they have given word to our folk who first met them, that they would tell their errand to none save the Mote of the People; which it was their due to do, if they were minded to risk it. For either they be aliens without an errand hither, save,[8] it may be, to beguile us, in which case they shall presently die an evil death; or they have come amongst us that we may give them to the God with flint-

---

1 With long gray hair.

2 Armor.

3 Meeting, assembly.

4 Commanded.

5 Plain dress used as an undergarment.

6 All those who would interfere.

7 Away from.

8 Unless.

edge and fire; or they have a message to us from some folk or other, on the issue of which lieth life or death. Now shall ye hear what they have to say concerning themselves and their faring hither. But, meseemeth, it shall be the woman who is the chief and hath the word in her mouth; for, lo you! the man kneeleth at her feet, as one who would serve and worship her. Speak out then, woman, and let our warriors hear thee."

She declareth her Godhead

Then the Maid lifted up her voice, and spake out clear and shrilling, like to a flute of the best of the minstrels: "Ye men of the Children of the Bear, I would ask you a question, and let the chieftain who sitteth before me answer it."

The old man nodded his head, and she went on: "Tell me, Children of the Bear, how long a time is worn[1] since ye saw the God of your worship made manifest in the body of a woman!"

Said the elder: "Many winters have worn since my father's father was a child, and saw the very God in the bodily form of a woman."

Then she said again: "Did ye rejoice at her coming, and would ye rejoice if once more she came amongst you?"

"Yea," said the old chieftain, "for she gave us gifts, and learned us lore,[2] and came to us in no terrible shape, but as a young woman as goodly as thou."

Then said the Maid: "Now, then, is the day of your gladness come; for the old body is dead, and I am the new body of your God, come amongst you for your welfare."

The Bears crave a token of her

Then fell a great silence on the Mote, till the old man spake and said: "What shall I say and live? For if thou be verily the God, and I threaten thee, wilt thou not destroy me? But thou hast spoken a great word with a sweet mouth, and hast taken the burden of blood on thy lily hands; and if the Children of the Bear be befooled of[3] light liars, how shall they put the shame off them? Therefore I say, show to us a token; and if thou be the God, this shall be easy to thee;[4] and if thou show it not, then is thy falsehood manifest, and thou shalt dree the weird.[5] For we shall deliver thee into the hands of these women here, who shall thrust

---

1 Has passed.

2 Taught us [traditional] knowledge.

3 Are fooled by.

4 LB: *question mark.*

5 Endure the fate.

thee down into the flow which is hereby, after they have wearied themselves with whipping thee. But thy man that kneeleth at thy feet shall we give to the true God, and he shall go to her by the road of the flint and the fire. Hast thou heard? Then give to us the sign and the token."

She answereth

She changed countenance no whit[1] at his word; but her eyes were the brighter, and her cheek the fresher; and her feet moved a little, as if they were growing glad before the dance; and she looked out over the Mote, and spake in her clear voice: "Old man, thou needest not to fear for thy words. Forsooth it is not me whom thou threatenest with stripes and a foul death, but some light fool and liar, who is not here. Now hearken! I wot well that ye would have somewhat of me, to wit, that I should send you rain to end this drought, which otherwise seemeth like to lie long upon you: but this rain, I must go into the mountains of the south to fetch it you; therefore shall certain of your warriors bring me on my way, with this my man, up to the great pass of the said mountains, and we shall set out thitherward this very day."

She was silent a while, and all looked on her, but none spake or moved, so that they seemed as images of stone amongst the stones.

Now is the token made manifest

Then she spake again and said: "Some would say, men of the Bear, that this were a sign and a token great enough;[2] but I know you, and how stubborn and perverse of heart ye be; and how that the gift not yet within your hand is not gift to you; and the wonder ye see not, your hearts trow[3] not. Therefore look ye upon me as here I stand, I who have come from the fairer country and the greenwood of the lands, and see if I bear not the summer with me, and the heart that maketh increase and the hand that giveth."

Lo then! as she spake, the faded flowers that hung about her gathered life and grew fresh again; the woodbine[4] round her neck and her sleek[5] shoulders knit itself together and embraced her freshly, and cast its scent about her face. The lilies that girded her loins lifted up their heads, and the gold of their tassels fell upon her; the eyebright grew clean blue again upon her smock; the

1 Not at all.

2 LB: *question mark.*

3 Believe.

4 Climbing vine.

5 Smooth.

eglantine found its blooms again, and then began to shed the leaves thereof upon her feet; the meadow-sweet wreathed amongst it made clear the sweetness of her legs, and the mouse-ear[1] studded her raiment as with gems. There she stood amidst of the blossoms, like a great orient pearl against the fretwork[2] of the goldsmiths, and the breeze that came up the valley from behind bore the sweetness of her fragrance all over the Man-mote.

Glad are the Bears

Then, indeed, the Bears stood up, and shouted and cried, and smote[3] on their shields, and tossed their spears aloft. Then the elder rose from his seat, and came up humbly to where she stood, and prayed her to say what she would have done; while the others drew about in knots, but durst not come very nigh to her. She answered the ancient chief, and said, that she would depart presently toward the mountains, whereby she might send them the rain which they lacked, and that thence she would away[4] to the southward for a while; but that they should hear of her, or, it might be, see her, before they who were now of middle age should be gone to their fathers.

They give the God to eat

Then the old man besought[5] her that they might make her a litter[6] of fragrant green boughs, and so bear her away toward the mountain pass amidst a triumph of the whole folk. But she leapt lightly down from the stone, and walked to and fro on the greensward, while it seemed of her that her feet scarce touched the grass; and she spake to the ancient chief where he still kneeled in worship of her, and said: "Nay; deemest thou of me that I need bearing by men's hands, or that I shall tire at all when I am doing my will, and I, the very heart of the year's increase? So it is, that the going of my feet over your pastures shall make them to thrive, both this year and the coming years: surely will I go afoot."

So they worshipped her the more, and blessed her; and then first of all they brought meat, the dainties they might, both for her and for Walter. But they would not look on the Maid whiles she ate, or suffer Walter to behold her the while. Afterwards, when

---

1 This is a common name for a number of small flowers with soft, hairy leaves, such as hawkweed, chickweed, forget-me-not, and cress.

2 Decorative work consisting largely of intersecting lines.

3 Beat.

4 Would [go] away.

5 Begged.

6 Carrying-chair.

they had eaten, some twenty men, weaponed after their fashion, made them ready to wend with the Maiden up into the mountains, and anon[1] they set out thitherward all together. Howbeit, the huge men held them ever somewhat aloof[2] from the Maid; and when they came to the resting-place for that night, where was no house, for it was up amongst the foot-hills before the mountains, then it was a wonder to see how carefully they built up a sleeping-place for her, and tilted it over with their skin-cloaks, and how they watched nightlong[3] about her. But Walter they let sleep peacefully on the grass, a little way aloof from the watchers round the Maid.

Chapter XXIX.

Walter Strays in the Pass and is Sundered from the Maid

The Maid commandeth and forbiddeth

Morning came, and they arose and went on their ways, and went all day till the sun was nigh set, and they were come up into the very pass; and in the jaws thereof was an earthen howe.[4] There the Maid bade them stay, and she went up on to the howe, and stood there and spake to them, and said: "O men of the Bear, I give you thanks for your following, and I bless you, and promise you the increase of the earth. But now ye shall turn aback, and leave me to go my ways; and my man with the iron sword shall follow me. Now, maybe, I shall come amongst the Bear-folk again before long, and yet again, and learn them wisdom; but for this time it is enough. And I shall tell you that ye were best to hasten home straightway[5] to your houses in the downland dales, for the weather which I have bidden[6] for you is even now coming forth from the forge of storms in the heart of the mountains. Now this last word I give you, that times are changed since I wore the last shape of God that ye have seen, wherefore a change I command you. If so be aliens come amongst you, I will not that ye send them to me by the flint and the fire; rather unless they be baleful[7] unto you, and worthy of an evil death, ye shall suffer them to

1 Immediately.

2 Apart.

3 All the night.

4 Mound [especially used for burial].

5 You had better return home quickly.

6 Commanded, requested.

7 Harmful.

abide with you; ye shall make them become children of the Bears, if they be goodly enough and worthy, and they shall be my children as ye be; otherwise, if they be ill-favoured and weakling,[1] let them live and be thralls to you, but not join with you, man to woman. Now depart ye with my blessing."

Walter and the Maid are sundered

Therewith she came down from the mound, and went her ways up to the pass so lightly,[2] that it was to Walter, standing amongst the Bears, as if she had vanished away. But the men of that folk abode standing and worshipping their God for a little while, and that while he durst not sunder[3] him from their company. But when they had blessed him and gone on their way backward, he betook him[4] in haste to following the Maid, thinking to find her abiding him in some nook[5] of the pass.

Howsoever, it was now twilight or more, and, for all his haste, dark night overtook him, so that perforce[6] he was stayed amidst the tangle of the mountain ways. And, moreover, ere the night was grown old, the weather came upon him on the back of a great south wind, so that the mountain nooks rattled and roared, and there was the rain and the hail, with thunder and lightning, monstrous and terrible, and all the huge array[7] of a summer storm. So he was driven at last to crouch under a big rock and abide the day.

Walter is troubled

But not so were his troubles at an end. For under the said rock he fell asleep, and when he awoke it was day indeed; but as to the pass, the way thereby was blind with the driving rain and the lowering lift;[8] so that, though he struggled as well as he might against the storm and the tangle, he made but little way.

And now once more the thought came on him, that the Maid was of the fays,[9] or of some race even mightier; and it came on him now not as erst,[10] with half fear and whole desire, but with a bitter oppression of dread, of loss and misery; so that he began

1 Ugly and weak.
2 Quickly.
3 Dared not part.
4 Roused himself.
5 Corner.
6 By necessity.
7 All the assembled characteristics.
8 That is, fog and rain have hidden the pass from him.
9 Elves.
10 Before.

to fear that she had but won his love to leave him and forget him for a new-comer, after the wont of fay-women,[1] as old tales tell.

He finds rest

Morning in the dale

Two days he battled thus with storm and blindness, and wanhope[2] of his life; for he was growing weak and fordone.[3] But the third morning the storm abated, though the rain yet fell heavily, and he could see his way somewhat as well as feel it: withal he found that now his path was leading him downwards. As it grew dusk, he came down into a grassy valley with a stream running through it to the southward, and the rain was now but little, coming down but in dashes from time to time. So he crept down to the stream-side, and lay amongst the bushes there; and said to himself, that on the morrow he would get him victual, so that he might live to seek his Maiden through the wide world. He was of somewhat better heart: but now that he was laid quiet, and had no more for that present to trouble him about the way, the anguish of his loss fell upon him the keener, and he might not refrain him from lamenting his dear Maiden aloud, as one who deemed himself in the empty wilderness: and thus he lamented for her sweetness and her loveliness, and the kindness of her voice and her speech, and her mirth. Then he fell to crying out concerning the beauty of her shaping, praising the parts of her body, as her face, and her hands, and her shoulders, and her feet, and cursing the evil fate which had sundered him from the friendliness of her, and the peerless fashion[4] of her.

Chapter XXX. Now They Meet Again

Complaining thus-wise,[5] he fell asleep from sheer weariness, and when he awoke it was broad day, calm and bright and cloudless, with the scent of the earth refreshed going up into the heavens, and the birds singing sweetly in the bushes about him: for the dale whereunto he was now come was a fair and lovely place amidst the shelving[6] slopes of the mountains, a paradise of the

---

1 According to the custom of women of the race of elves.

2 Despair.

3 Worn out.

4 Matchless shape.

5 In this way.

6 Projecting.

wilderness, and nought but pleasant and sweet things were to be seen there, now that the morn was so clear and sunny.

Now they meet again

He arose and looked about him, and saw where, a hundred yards aloof,[1] was a thicket of small wood, as thorn and elder and whitebeam, all wreathed about with the bines[2] of wayfaring tree;[3] it hid a bight[4] of the stream, which turned round about it, and betwixt it and Walter was the grass short and thick, and sweet, and all beset with flowers; and he said to himself that it was even such a place as wherein the angels were leading the Blessed in the great painted paradise in the choir of the big church at Langton on Holm.[5] But lo! as he looked he cried aloud for joy, for forth from the thicket on to the flowery grass came one like to an angel from out of the said picture, white-clad and bare-foot, sweet of flesh, with bright eyes and ruddy cheeks; for it was the Maid herself. So he ran to her, and she abode him,[6] holding forth kind hands to him, and smiling, while she wept for joy of the meeting. He threw himself upon her, and spared not to kiss her, her cheeks and her mouth, and her arms and her shoulders, and wheresoever she would suffer it. Till at last she drew aback a little, laughing on him for love, and said: "Forbear[7] now, friend, for it is enough for this time, and tell me how thou hast sped."

Here is breakfast

"Ill, ill," said he.

"What ails thee?" she said.

"Hunger," he said, "and longing for thee."

"Well," she said, "me thou hast; there is one ill quenched; take my hand, and we will see to the other one."

So he took her hand, and to hold it seemed to him sweet beyond measure. But he looked up, and saw a little blue smoke going up into the air from beyond the thicket; and he laughed, for he was weak with hunger, and he said: "Who is at the cooking yonder?"

"Thou shalt see," she said; and led him therewith into the said thicket and through it, and lo! a fair little grassy place, full of

---

1 Away.

2 Stems.

3 This is the tall shrub *Viburnum Lantana*.

4 Angle.

5 The reference here is to a wall painting in a church. Morris and Company did much work early on in the decoration of churches.

6 Waited for him.

7 Restrain yourself.

flowers, betwixt the bushes and the bight of the stream; and on the little sandy ere,[1] just off the greensward, was a fire of sticks, and beside it two trouts lying, fat and red-flecked.

She heard him last night

"Here is the breakfast," said she; "when it was time to wash the night off me e'en now, I went down the strand[2] here into the rippling shallow, and saw the bank below it, where the water draws together yonder, and deepens, that it seemed like to hold fish; and whereas I looked to meet thee presently, I groped the bank for them, going softly; and lo thou! Help me now, that we cook them."

So they roasted them on the red embers, and fell to and ate well, both of them, and drank of the water of the stream out of each other's hollow hands; and that feast seemed glorious to them, such gladness went with it.

But when they were done with their meat, Walter said to the Maid:[3] "And how didst thou know that thou shouldst see me presently?"

She said, looking on him wistfully: "This needed no wizardry. I lay not so far from thee last night, but that I heard thy voice and knew it."

Said he, "Why didst thou not come to me then, since thou heardest me bemoaning thee?"

She tells of her fear

She cast her eyes down, and plucked at the flowers and grass, and said: "It was dear to hear thee praising me; I knew not before that I was so sore desired, or that thou hadst taken such note of my body, and found it so dear."

Then she reddened sorely, and said: "I knew not that aught of me had such beauty as thou didst bewail."

And she wept for joy. Then she looked on him and smiled, and said: "Wilt thou have the very truth of it? I went close up to thee, and stood there hidden by the bushes and the night. And amidst thy bewailing, I knew that thou wouldst soon fall asleep, and in sooth I out-waked thee."

Then was she silent again; and he spake not, but looked on her shyly; and she said, reddening yet more: "Furthermore, I must needs tell thee that I feared to go to thee in the dark night, and my heart so yearning towards thee."

---

1 Field.

2 Beach [of a river].

3 K, LB: *add paragraph break.*

And she hung her head adown; but he said: "Is it so indeed, that thou fearest me? Then doth that make me afraid ...[1] afraid of thy nay-say. For I was going to entreat thee, and say to thee: Beloved, we have now gone through many troubles; let us now take a good reward at once, and wed together, here amidst this sweet and pleasant house of the mountains, ere we go further on our way; if indeed we go further at all. For where shall we find any place sweeter or happier than this?"

She would live amidst folk

But she sprang up to her feet, and stood there trembling before him, because of her love; and she said: "Beloved, I have deemed that it were good for us to go seek mankind as they live in the world, and to live amongst them. And as for me, I will tell thee the sooth, to wit, that I long for this sorely. For I feel afraid in the wilderness, and as if I needed help and protection against my Mistress, though she be dead; and I need the comfort of many people, and the throngs of the cities. I cannot forget her: it was but last night that I dreamed (I suppose as the dawn grew a-cold) that I was yet under her hand, and she was stripping me for the torment;[2] so that I woke up panting and crying out. I pray thee be not angry with me for telling thee of my desires; for if thou wouldst not have it so, then here will I abide with thee as thy mate, and strive to gather courage."

He feareth the city

He rose up and kissed her face, and said: "Nay, I had in sooth no mind to abide here for ever; I meant but that we should feast a while here, and then depart: sooth it is, that if thou dreadest the wilderness, somewhat I dread the city."

She turned pale, and said: "Thou shalt have thy will, my friend, if it must be so. But bethink thee! we be not yet at our journey's end, and may have many things and much strife to endure, before we be at peace and in welfare. Now shall I tell thee ...[3] did I not before? ...[4] that while I am a maid untouched, my wisdom, and somedeal[5] of might, abideth with me, and only so long. Therefore I entreat thee, let us go now, side by side, out of this fair valley, even as we are, so that my wisdom and might may help thee at need. For, my friend, I would not that our lives be short, so much of joy as hath now come into them."

---

1 CW: *dash.*

2 That is, for whipping.

3 CW: *dash.*

4 CW: *dash.*

5 Some portion.

"Yea, beloved," he said, "let us on straightway then, and shorten the while that sundereth us."

They leave that dale

"Love," she said, "thou shalt pardon me one time for all. But this is to be said, that I know somewhat of the haps[1] that lie a little way ahead of us; partly by my lore, and partly by what I learned of this land of the wild folk whiles thou wert lying asleep that morning."

So they left that pleasant place by the water, and came into the open valley, and went their ways through the pass; and it soon became stony again, as they mounted the bent which went up from out the dale. And when they came to the brow of the said bent, they had a sight of the open country lying fair and joyous in the sunshine, and amidst of it, against the blue hills, the walls and towers of a great city.

Then said the Maid: "O, dear friend, lo you! is not that our abode that lieth yonder, and is so beauteous? Dwell not our friends there, and our protection against uncouth wights,[2] and mere evil things in guileful shapes? O city, I bid thee hail!"

Of the city which they see aloof

But Walter looked on her, and smiled somewhat; and said: "I rejoice in thy joy. But there be evil things in yonder city also, though they be not fays nor devils, or it is like to no city that I wot of. And in every city shall foes grow up to us without rhyme or reason, and life therein shall be tangled[3] unto us."

"Yea," she said; "but in the wilderness amongst the devils, what was to be done by manly might or valiancy? There hadst thou to fall back upon the guile and wizardry which I had filched[4] from my very foes. But when we come down yonder, then shall thy valiancy prevail to cleave[5] the tangle for us. Or at the least, it shall leave a tale of thee behind, and I shall worship thee."

He laughed, and his face grew brighter: "Mastery mows the meadow," quoth he, "and one man is of little might against many. But I promise thee I shall not be slothful[6] before thee."

---

1 Chances, what will happen.

2 Unknown creatures.

3 Complicated.

4 Stolen.

5 Cut through.

6 Lazy.

Chapter XXXI. They Come upon New Folk

With that they went down from the bent again, and came to where the pass narrowed so much, that they went betwixt a steep wall of rock on either side; but after an hour's going, the said wall gave back suddenly, and, or they were ware almost,[1] they came on another dale like to that which they had left, but not so fair, though it was grassy and well watered, and not so big either. But there indeed befell a change to them; for lo! tents and pavilions pitched in the said valley, and amidst of it a throng of men, mostly weaponed, and with horses ready saddled at hand. So they stayed their feet, and Walter's heart failed him, for he said to himself: Who wotteth what these men may be, save[2] that they be aliens? It is most like that we shall be taken as thralls; and then, at the best, we shall be sundered; and that is all one with the worst.

They come amongst those men

But the Maid, when she saw the horses, and the gay tents, and the pennons[3] fluttering, and the glitter of spears, and gleaming of white armour, smote her palms[4] together for joy, and cried out: "Here now are come the folk of the city for our welcoming, and fair and lovely are they, and of many things shall they be thinking, and a many things shall they do, and we shall be partakers thereof. Come then, and let us meet them, fair friend!"

But Walter said: "Alas! thou knowest not: would that we might flee! But now is it over late; so put we a good face on it, and go to them quietly, as erewhile[5] we did in the Bear-country."

They are borne away

So did they; and there sundered six from the men-at-arms and came to those twain, and made humble obeisance[6] to Walter, but spake no word. Then they made as they would lead them to the others, and the twain went with them wondering, and came into the ring of men-at-arms, and stood before an old hoar[7] knight, armed all, save his head, with most goodly armour, and he also bowed before Walter, but spake no word. Then they took them to the master pavilion, and made signs to them to sit, and they

---

1 Almost before they were aware.

2 Except.

3 Banners.

4 Clapped her hands.

5 Earlier.

6 Bowed low.

7 Gray.

brought them dainty meat and good wine. And the while of their eating[1] arose up a stir about them; and when they were done with their meat, the ancient knight came to them, still bowing in courteous wise,[2] and did them to wit by signs that they should depart: and when they were without,[3] they saw all the other tents struck, and men beginning to busy them with striking the pavilion,[4] and the others mounted and ranked in good order for the road; and there were two horse-litters[5] before them, wherein they were bidden to mount, Walter in one, and the Maid in the other, and no otherwise might they do. Then presently was a horn blown, and all took to the road together; and Walter saw betwixt the curtains of the litter that men-at-arms rode on either side of him, albeit they had left him his sword by his side.

The Gate of a City
A palace

So they went down the mountain-passes, and before sunset were gotten into the plain; but they made no stay for nightfall, save to eat a morsel and drink a draught, going through the night as men who knew their way well. As they went, Walter wondered what would betide, and if peradventure[6] they also would be for offering them up to their Gods; whereas they were aliens for certain, and belike also Saracens.[7] Moreover there was a cold fear at his heart that he should be sundered from the Maid, whereas their masters now were mighty men of war, holding in their hands that which all men desire, to wit, the manifest beauty of a woman. Yet he strove to think the best of it that he might. And so at last, when the night was far spent, and dawn was at hand, they stayed at a great and mighty gate in a huge wall. There they blew loudly on the horn thrice, and thereafter the gates were opened, and they all passed through into a street, which seemed to Walter in the glimmer to be both great and goodly amongst the abodes of men. Then it was but a little ere they came into a square, widespreading, one side whereof Walter took to be the front of a most goodly house. There the doors of the court opened to them or[8] ever the horn might blow, though, forsooth, blow it did loudly

1 While they were eating.
2 Manner.
3 Outside.
4 Taking down the large tent.
5 Covered chairs drawn by horses.
6 Perhaps.
7 Muslims.
8 Before.

three times; all they entered therein, and men came to Walter and signed to him to alight. So did he, and would have tarried to look about for the Maid, but they suffered it not, but led him up a huge stair into a chamber, very great, and but dimly lighted because of its greatness. Then they brought him to a bed dight[1] as fair as might be, and made signs to him to strip and lie therein. Perforce[2] he did so, and then they bore away his raiment, and left him lying there. So he lay there quietly, deeming it no avail for him,[3] a mother-naked[4] man, to seek escape thence; but it was long ere he might sleep, because of his trouble of mind. At last, pure weariness got the better of his hopes and fears, and he fell into slumber just as the dawn was passing into day.

Chapter XXXII.
Of the New King of the City and Land of Stark-wall

When he awoke again the sun was shining brightly into that chamber, and he looked, and beheld that it was peerless of beauty and riches, amongst all that he had ever seen: the ceiling done with gold and over-sea blue;[5] the walls hung with arras[6] of the fairest, though he might not tell what was the history done therein. The chairs and stools were of carven work well be-painted,[7] and amidmost was a great ivory chair under a cloth of estate, of bawdekin[8] of gold and green, much be-pearled;[9] and all the floor was of fine work alexandrine.[10]

---

1 Prepared.
2 By necessity.
3 Deciding that it would not help him.
4 Completely naked.
5 Ultramarine. The name for this blue color literally means "over-sea."
6 Tapestries. True to his career as a designer, Morris gives loving details to the interior decoration of this room. Morris and Company produced a distinguished line of tapestries. Often medieval tapestries depicted narratives from various stories, including the Bible; thus, the tapestries mentioned here relate an unknown "history." The sixteenth-century tapestries at Kelmscott Manor depict the story of Sampson from the Book of Judges.
7 Decorated with painted illumination.
8 Rich brocade cloth.
9 Woven with pearls.
10 Work like that done in [the Egyptian city of] Alexandria. Craftspeople from that city were famous for decorative work, particularly in embroidery.

Walter is taken to the bath

He looked on all this, wondering what had befallen him, when lo! there came folk into the chamber, to wit, two serving-men well-bedight,[1] and three old men clad in rich gowns of silk. These came to him and (still by signs, without speech) bade him arise and come with them; and when he bade them look to it that he was naked, and laughed doubtfully, they neither laughed in answer, or offered him any raiment, but still would have him arise, and he did so perforce.[2] They brought him with them out of the chamber, and through certain passages pillared and goodly, till they came to a bath as fair as any might be; and there the serving-men washed him carefully and tenderly, the old men looking on the while. When it was done, still they offered not to clothe him, but led him out, and through the passages again, back to the chamber. Only this time he must pass between a double hedge of men, some weaponed, some in peaceful array, but all clad gloriously, and full chieftain-like of aspect,[3] either for valiancy[4] or wisdom.

In the chamber itself was now a concourse of men, of great estate by deeming of their array;[5] but all these were standing orderly in a ring about the ivory chair aforesaid. Now said Walter to himself: Surely all this looks toward the knife and the altar for me;[6] but he kept a stout countenance despite of all.

The two raiments

So they led him up to the ivory chair, and he beheld on either side thereof a bench, and on each was laid a set of raiment from the shirt upwards; but there was much diversity betwixt these arrays. For one was all of robes of peace, glorious and be-gemmed, unmeet[7] for any save a great king; while on the other was war-weed,[8] seemly, well-fashioned, but little adorned;[9] nay rather, worn and bestained with weather, and the pelting of the spear-storm.

Now those old men signed to Walter to take which of those raiments he would, and do it on. He looked to the right and the left,

---

1 Well dressed.

2 By necessity.

3 Appearance.

4 Courage.

5 An assembly of men of high social position, judging from their clothing.

6 That is, he expects to be sacrificed to their gods.

7 Unfit.

8 Armor.

9 Decorated.

and when he had looked on the war-gear, the heart arose in him, and he called to mind the array of the Goldings in the forefront of battle, and he made one step toward the weapons, and laid his hand thereon. Then ran a glad murmur through that concourse, and the old men drew up to him smiling and joyous, and helped him to do them on; and as he took up the helm, he noted that over its broad brown iron sat a golden crown.

Walter taketh the war-gear

So when he was clad and weaponed, girt with a sword,[1] and a steel axe in his hand, the elders showed him to the ivory throne, and he laid the axe on the arm of the chair, and drew forth the sword from the scabbard, and sat him down, and laid the ancient blade across his knees; then he looked about on those great men, and spake: "How long shall we speak no word to each other, or is it so that God hath stricken you dumb?"

Then all they cried out with one voice: "All hail to the King, the King of Battle!"

Spake Walter: "If I be king, will ye do my will as I bid you?"

Answered the elder: "Nought have we will to do, lord, save as thou biddest."

Said Walter: "Thou then, wilt thou answer a question in all truth?"

"Yea, lord," said the elder, "if I may live afterward."

Then said Walter: "The woman that came with me into your Camp of the Mountain, what hath befallen her?"

The elder answered: "Nought hath befallen her, either of good or evil, save that she hath slept and eaten and bathed her. What, then, is the King's pleasure concerning her?"

The King commandeth concerning the Maid

"That ye bring her hither to me straightway,"[2] said Walter.

"Yea," said the elder; "and in what guise shall we bring her hither? shall she be arrayed as a servant, or a great lady?"

Then Walter pondered a while, and spake at last: "Ask her what is her will herein, and as she will have it, so let it be. But set ye another chair beside mine, and lead her thereto. Thou wise old man, send one or two to bring her in hither, but abide thou, for I have a question or two to ask of thee yet. And ye, lords, abide here the coming of my she-fellow, if it weary you not."

So the elder spake to three of the most honourable of the lords, and they went their ways to bring in the Maid.

---

1 With a sword on his belt.

2 Immediately.

Chapter[1] XXXIII.

Concerning the Fashion of King-making in Stark-wall

Meanwhile the King spake to the elder, and said: "Now tell me whereof I am become king, and what is the fashion and cause of the king-making; for wondrous it is to me, whereas I am but an alien amidst of mighty men."

The proof of a true king-sending

The proof again

"Lord," said the old man, "thou art become king of a mighty city, which hath under it many other cities and wide lands, and havens by the sea-side, and which lacketh no wealth which men desire. Many wise men dwell therein, and of fools not more than in other lands. A valiant host shall follow thee to battle when needs must thou wend afield; an host not to be withstood, save by the ancient God-folk,[2] if any of them were left upon the earth, as belike none are. And as to the name of our said city, it hight[3] the City of the Stark-wall,[4] or more shortly, Stark-wall. Now as to the fashion of our king-making: If our king dieth and leaveth an heir male, begotten of his body, then is he king after him; but if he die and leave no heir, then send we out a great lord, with knights and sergeants, to that pass of the mountain whereto ye came yesterday; and the first man that cometh unto them, they take and lead to the city, as they did with thee, lord. For we believe and trow[5] that of old time our forefathers came down from the mountains by that same pass, poor and rude,[6] but full of valiancy, before they conquered these lands, and builded the Stark-wall. But now furthermore, when we have gotten the said wanderer, and brought him home to our city, we behold him mother-naked, all the great men of us, both sages[7] and warriors; then if we find him ill-fashioned and counterfeit[8] of his body, we roll him in a great carpet till he dies; or whiles, if he be but a simple man, and without guile, we deliver him for thrall to some

---

1 CW: CHAP.

2 The reference is to pagan deities, such as those of ancient Greece and Rome.

3 Named.

4 That is, the city with the strong wall.

5 Trust.

6 Rustic.

7 People of wisdom.

8 False.

artificer[1] amongst us, as a shoemaker, a wright,[2] or what not, and so forget him. But in either case we make as if no such man had come to us, and we send again the lord and his knights to watch the pass; for we say that such an one the Fathers of old time have not sent us. But again, when we have seen to the new-comer that he is well-fashioned of his body, all is not done; for we deem that never would the Fathers send us a dolt[3] or a craven to be our king. Therefore we bid the naked one take to him which he will of these raiments, either the ancient armour, which now thou bearest, lord, or this golden raiment here; and if he take the war-gear, as thou takedst it, King, it is well; but if he take the raiment of peace, then hath he the choice either to be thrall of some goodman[4] of the city, or to be proven how wise he may be, and so fare the narrow edge betwixt death and kingship; for if he fall short of his wisdom, then shall he die the death. Thus is thy question answered, King, and praise be to the Fathers that they have sent us one whom none may doubt, either for wisdom or valiancy."

Chapter XXXIV. Now Cometh the Maid to the King

Then all they bowed before the King, and he spake again: "What is that noise that I hear without, as if it were the rising of the sea on a sandy shore, when the south-west wind is blowing?"[5]

She is set in the Queen's seat

Then the elder opened his mouth to answer; but before he might get out the word, there was a stir without the chamber door, and the throng parted, and lo! amidst of them came the Maid, and she yet clad in nought save the white coat wherewith she had won through the wilderness, save that on her head was a garland of red roses, and her middle was wreathed with the same. Fresh and fair she was as the dawn of June; her face bright, red-lipped, and clear-eyed, and her cheeks flushed with hope and love. She went straight to Walter where he sat, and lightly put away with her hand the elder who would lead her to the ivory throne beside the King; but she knelt down before him, and laid her hand on his steel-clad knee, and said: "O my lord, now I see that thou has beguiled me, and that thou wert all along a king-

1 Craftsperson.

2 Carpenter.

3 Stupid person.

4 Citizen, merchant.

5 LB, CW: *period.*

born man coming home to thy realm. But so dear thou hast been to me; and so fair and clear, and so kind withal do thine eyes shine on me from under the grey war-helm, that I will beseech thee not to cast me out utterly, but suffer me to be thy servant and handmaid for a while. Wilt thou not?"

But the King stooped down to her and raised her up, and stood on his feet, and took her hands and kissed them, and set her down beside him, and said to her: "Sweetheart, this is now thy place till the night cometh,[1] even by my side."

So she sat down there meek and valiant, her hands laid in her lap, and her feet one over the other; while the King said: "Lords, this is my beloved, and my spouse. Now, therefore, if ye will have me for King, ye must worship this one for Queen and Lady; or else suffer[2] us both to go our ways in peace."

All those love the Maid

Then all they that were in the chamber cried out aloud: "The Queen, the Lady! The beloved of our lord!"

And this cry came from their hearts, and not their lips only; for as they looked on her, and the brightness of her beauty, they saw also the meekness of her demeanour,[3] and the high heart of her, and they all fell to loving her. But the young men of them, their cheeks flushed as they beheld her, and their hearts went out to her, and they drew their swords and brandished them aloft, and cried out for her as men made suddenly drunk with love: "The Queen, the Lady, the lovely one!"

Chapter XXXV.
Of the King of Stark-wall and his Queen

But while this betid,[4] that murmur without, which is aforesaid, grew louder; and it smote on[5] the King's ear, and he said again to the elder: "Tell us now of that noise withoutward, what is it?"

Now they look on the throng of the folk

Said the elder: "If thou, King, and the Queen, wilt but arise and stand in the window, and go forth into the hanging[6] gallery

1 That is, until they die.
2 Allow.
3 Facial expression, behavior.
4 Happened.
5 Forcefully reached.
6 Tapestry. Morris and Company often decorated rooms of wealthy clients with tapestries.

thereof, then shall ye know at once what is this rumour, and therewithal shall ye see a sight meet[1] to rejoice the heart of a king new come into kingship."

So the King arose and took the Maid by the hand, and went to the window and looked forth; and lo! the great square of the place all thronged with folk as thick as they could stand, and the more part of the carles with a weapon in hand, and many armed right gallantly. Then he went out into the gallery with his Queen, still holding her hand, and his lords and wise men stood behind him. Straightway then arose a cry, and a shout of joy and welcome that rent the very heavens, and the great place was all glittering and strange with the tossing up of spears and the brandishing of swords, and the stretching forth of hands.

But the Maid spake softly to King Walter and said: "Here then is the wilderness left behind a long way, and here is warding[2] and protection against the foes of our life and soul. O blessed be thou and thy valiant heart!"

The talk of two neighbours

But Walter spake nothing, but stood as one in a dream; and yet, if that might be, his longing toward her increased manifold.[3]

But down below, amidst of the throng, stood two neighbours somewhat anigh to the window; and quoth one to the other: "See thou! the new man in the ancient armour of the Battle of the Waters, bearing the sword that slew the foeman king on the Day of the Doubtful Onset![4] Surely this is a sign of good-luck to us all."

"Yea," said the second, "he beareth his armour well, and the eyes are bright in the head of him;[5] but hast thou beheld well his she-fellow, and what the like of her is?"

"I see her," said the other, "that she is a fair woman; yet somewhat worse clad than simply. She is in her smock, man, and were it not for the balusters[6] I deem ye should see her barefoot. What is amiss[7] with her?"

The King and Queen arrayed anew

"Dost thou not see her," said the second neighbour, "that she is not only a fair woman, but yet more, one of those lovely ones

---

1 Fitting.

2 Guarding.

3 Many times.

4 The day of the battle that could have been lost.

5 CW: *colon.*

6 Railings.

7 Wrong.

that draw the heart out of a man's body, one may scarce say for why? Surely Stark-wall hath cast a lucky net this time. And as to her raiment, I see of her that she is clad in white and wreathed with rose, but that the flesh of her is so wholly pure and sweet that it maketh all her attire but a part of her body, and halloweth it,[1] so that it hath the semblance[2] of gems. Alas, my friend! let us hope that this Queen will fare abroad unseldom[3] amongst the people."

They ride to the church
The Anointing of the King

Thus, then, they spake; but after a while the King and his mate went back into the chamber, and he gave command that the women of the Queen should come and fetch her away, to attire her in royal array. And thither came the fairest of the honourable damsels, and were fain of being[4] her waiting-women.[5] Therewithal the King was unarmed, and dight most gloriously, but still he bore the Sword of the King's Slaying: and sithence were the King and the Queen brought into the great hall of the palace, and they met on the dais,[6] and kissed before the lords and other folk that thronged the hall. There they ate a morsel and drank a cup together, while all beheld them; and then they were brought forth, and a white horse of the goodliest, well bedight, brought for each of them, and thereon they mounted, and went their ways together, by the lane which the huge throng made for them, to the great church, for the hallowing[7] and the crowning; and they were led by one squire alone, and he unarmed; for such was the custom of Stark-wall when a new king should be hallowed: so came they to the great church (for that folk was not miscreant,[8] so to say), and they entered it, they two alone, and went into the choir: and when they had stood there a little while wondering at their lot, they heard how the bells fell a-ringing tunefully over their heads; and then drew near the sound of many trumpets blowing together, and thereafter the voices of many folk singing; and then were the great doors thrown open, and the bishop and his priest came into the church with singing and minstrelsy, and

---

1 Sanctifies it.
2 Appearance.
3 Often.
4 Happy to be.
5 Ladies in waiting.
6 High table.
7 Anointing.
8 Heathen.

thereafter came the whole throng of the folk, and presently the nave of the church was filled by it, as when the water follows the cutting of the dam, and fills up the dyke. Thereafter came the bishop and his mates into the choir, and came up to the King, and gave him and the Queen the kiss of peace. Then was mass sung gloriously;[1] and thereafter was the King anointed and crowned, and great joy was made throughout the church. Afterwards they went back afoot to the palace, they two alone together, with none but the esquire going before to show them the way. And as they went, they passed close beside those two neighbours, whose talk has been told of afore, and the first one, he who had praised the King's war-array, spake and said: "Truly, neighbour, thou art in the right of it; and now the Queen has been dight duly,[2] and hath a crown on her head, and is clad in white samite[3] done all over with pearls, I see her to be of exceeding goodliness; as goodly, maybe, as the Lord King."

Those two neighbours again

Quoth the other: "Unto me she seemeth as she did e'en now; she is clad in white, as then she was, and it is by reason of the pure and sweet flesh of her that the pearls shine out and glow, and by the holiness of her body is her rich attire hallowed; but, forsooth, it seemed to me as she went past as though paradise had come anigh to our city, and that all the air breathed of it. So I say, praise be to God and His Hallows who hath suffered her to dwell amongst us!"

Said the first man: "Forsooth, it is well; but knowest thou at all whence she cometh, and of what lineage she may be?"

"Nay," said the other, "I wot not whence she is; but this I wot full surely, that when she goeth away, they whom she leadeth with her shall be well bestead. Again, of her lineage nought know I; but this I know, that they that come of her, to the twentieth generation, shall bless and praise the memory of her, and hallow her name[4] little less than they hallow the name of the Mother of God."

So spake those two; but the King and Queen came back to the palace, and sat among the lords and at the banquet which was held thereafter, and long was the time of their glory, till the night was far spent and all men must seek to their beds.

---

1 Medieval church services were typically sung rather than spoken.

2 Fittingly clothed.

3 Silk.

4 Bless.

Chapter XXXVI.
Of Walter and the Maid in the Days of the Kingship

Long it was, indeed, till the women, by the King's command, had brought the Maid to the King's chamber; and he met her, and took her by the shoulders and kissed her, and said: "Art thou not weary, sweetheart? Doth not the city, and the thronging folk, and the watching eyes of the great ones ... doth it not all lie heavy on thee, as it doth upon me?"

She said: "And where is the city now? is not this the wilderness again, and thou and I alone together therein?"

He gazed at her eagerly, and she reddened, so that her eyes shone light amidst the darkness of the flush of her cheeks.

He spake trembling and softly, and said: "Is it not in one matter better than the wilderness? is not the fear gone, yea, every whit[1] thereof?"

The Maid ungirdeth herself

The dark flush had left her face, and she looked on him exceeding sweetly, and spoke steadily and clearly: "Evenso it is, beloved." Therewith she set her hand to the girdle that girt her loins,[2] and did it off, and held it out toward him, and said: "Here is the token; this is a maid's girdle, and the woman is ungirt."[3]

So he took the girdle and her hand withal, and cast his arms about her: and amidst the sweetness of their love and their safety, and assured hope of many days of joy, they spake together of the hours when they fared the razor-edge betwixt guile and misery and death, and the sweeter yet it grew to them because of it; and many things she told him ere the dawn, of the evil days bygone, and the dealings of the Mistress with her, till the grey day stole into the chamber to make manifest her loveliness; which, forsooth, was better even than the deeming of that man amidst the throng whose heart had been so drawn towards her. So they rejoiced together in the new day.

The King dealeth with his councillors

But when the full day was, and Walter arose, he called his thanes[4] and wise men to the council; and first he bade open the prison-doors, and feed the needy and clothe them, and make good cheer to all men, high and low, rich and unrich; and there-

---

1 Bit.

2 The belt that secured [the clothing on] her hips.

3 Unclothed.

4 Band of warriors.

after he took counsel with them on many matters, and they marvelled at his wisdom and the keenness of his wit; and so it was, that some were but half pleased thereat, whereas they saw that their will was like to give way before his in all matters. But the wiser of them rejoiced in him, and looked for good days while his life lasted.

Now of the deeds that he did, and his joys and his griefs, the tale shall tell no more; nor of how he saw Langton again, and his dealings there.

Of the King's good ending

In Stark-wall he dwelt, and reigned a King, well beloved of his folk, sorely feared of their foemen. Strife he had to deal with, at home and abroad; but therein he was not quelled,[1] till he fell asleep[2] fair and softly, when this world had no more of deeds for him to do. Nor may it be said that the needy lamented[3] him; for no needy had he left in his own land. And few foes he left behind to hate him.

As to the Maid, she so waxed in loveliness and kindness, that it was a year's joy for any to have cast eyes upon her in street or in field. All wizardry left her since the day of her wedding; yet of wit and wisdom she had enough left, and to spare; for she needed no going about, and no guile, any more than hard commands, to have her will done. So loved she was by all folk, forsooth, that it was a mere joy for any to go about her errands. To be short, she was the land's increase, and the city's safeguard, and the bliss of the folk.

Somewhat, as the days passed, it misgave her[4] that she had beguiled the Bear-folk to deem her their God; and she considered and thought how she might atone[5] it.

The Queen goes to visit the Bears

So the second year after they had come to Stark-wall, she went with certain folk to the head of the pass that led down to the Bears; and there she stayed[6] the men-at-arms, and went on further with a two score of husbandmen[7] whom she had redeemed from thralldom in Stark-wall; and when they were hard

1 Defeated.

2 Died.

3 Mourned for.

4 She regretted.

5 Make amends for.

6 Halted.

7 Farmers.

on[1] the dales of the Bears, she left them there in a certain little dale, with their wains[2] and horses, and seed-corn,[3] and iron tools, and went down all bird-alone[4] to the dwelling of those huge men, unguarded now by sorcery, and trusting in nought but her loveliness and kindness. Clad she was now, as when she fled from the Wood beyond the World, in a short white coat alone, with bare feet and naked arms; but the said coat was now embroidered with the imagery of blossoms in silk and gold, and gems, whereas now her wizardry had departed from her.

Her gift to them

So she came to the Bears, and they knew her at once, and worshipped and blessed her, and feared her. But she told them that she had a gift for them, and was come to give it; and therewith she told them of the art of tillage,[5] and bade them learn it; and when they asked her how they should do so, she told them of the men who were abiding[6] them in the mountain dale, and bade the Bears take them for their brothers and sons of the ancient Fathers, and then they should be taught of them. This they behight[7] her to do, and so she led them to where her freedmen lay, whom the Bears received with all joy and loving-kindness, and took them into their folk.

So they went back to their dales together; but the Maid went her ways back to her men-at-arms and the city of Stark-wall.

Thereafter she sent more gifts and messages to the Bears, but never again went herself to see them; for as good a face as she put on it that last time, yet her heart waxed cold with fear, and it almost seemed to her that her Mistress was alive again, and that she was escaping from her and plotting against her once more.

What betid the Bears sithence

As for the Bears, they throve and multiplied; till at last strife arose great and grim[8] betwixt them and other peoples; for they had become mighty in battle: yea, once and again they met the host of Stark-wall in fight, and overthrew and were overthrown. But that was a long while after the Maid had passed away.

---

1 Close to.

2 Wagons.

3 Seeds of grain.

4 Completely alone. The main character of Morris's prose romance *The Water of the Wondrous Isles* (1897) is named Birdalone.

5 Farming.

6 Waiting for.

7 Promised.

8 Savage.

Now of Walter and the Maid is no more to be told, saving that they begat between them goodly sons and fair daughters; whereof came a great lineage in Stark-wall; which lineage was so strong, and endured so long a while, that by then[1] it had died out, folk had clean forgotten their ancient custom of king-making, so that after Walter of Langton there was never another king that came down to them poor and lonely from out of the Mountains of the Bears.

HERE ends the tale of the Wood beyond the World, made by William Morris, and printed by him at the Kelmscott Press, Upper Mall, Hammersmith. Finished the 30th day of May, 1894.

Sold by William Morris, at the Kelmscott Press.

Colophon of *The Wood Beyond the World* (Hammersmith: Kelmscott Press, 1894); editor's collection.

1 By the time that.

Appendix A: Morris and Medieval Narrative

1. From Morris's and A.J. Wyatt's Translation of *Beowulf* (1895)

[Morris issued the Kelmscott Press *Beowulf* in 1895. The main story of that famous Old English poem recounts Beowulf's fight against the trolls Grendel and Grendel's Mother and, after many years, a dragon. The following excerpt is a narrative sung by a *scop*, or poet, that celebrates Beowulf's initial victory over Grendel. Like *The Wood Beyond the World*, the story of Finn and Hengest involves betrayal and conflicted loyalties. Wyatt was a Cambridge Anglo-Saxonist who gave Morris lessons in Old English and prepared a prose translation of the poem which Morris worked into poetry. Because of his new enthusiasm for Old English, which convinced him to keep as many of the original words in his translation as possible, Morris's use of archaic language is even more pronounced in his *Beowulf* than in *The Wood Beyond the World*. My literal translation from the Old English of this section of the poem follows Morris's and Wyatt's original translation.]

XVII. They Feast in Hart. The Gleeman Sings of Finn and Hengest

Then the lord of the earl-folk to every and each one 1050
Of them who with Beowulf the sea-ways had worn
Then and there on the mead-bench did handsel them treasure,
An heir-loom to wit; for him also he bade it
That a were-gild be paid, whom Grendel aforetime
By wickedness quell'd, as far more of them would he,
Save from them God all-witting the Weird away wended,
And that man's mood withal. But the Maker all wielded
Of the kindred of mankind, as yet now he doeth.
Therefore through-witting will be the best everywhere
And the forethought of mind. Many things must abide 1060
Of lief and of loth, he who here a long while
In these days of the strife with the world shall be dealing.

There song was and sound all gather'd together
Of that Healfdene's warrior and wielder of battle,
The wood of glee greeted, the lay wreaked often,

Whenas the hall-game the minstrel of Hrothgar
All down by the mead-bench tale must be making:

"By Finn's sons aforetime, when the fear gat them,
The hero of Half-Danes, Hnæf of the Scyldings,
On the slaughter-field Frisian needs must he fall. 1070
Forsooth never Hildeburh needed to hery
The troth of the Eotens; she all unsinning
Was lorne of her lief ones in that play of the linden,
Her bairns and her brethren, by fate there they fell
Spear-wounded. That was the all-woeful of women.
Not unduly without cause the daughter of Hoc
Mourn'd the Maker's own shaping, sithence came the morn
When she under the heavens that tide came to see
Murder-bale of her kinsmen, where most had she erewhile 1080
Of world's bliss. The war-tide took all men away
Of Finn's thanes that were, save only a few;
E'en so that he might not on the field of the meeting
Hold Hengest a war-tide, or fight any whit,
Nor yet snatch away thence by war the woe-leavings
From the thane of the King; but terms now they bade him
That for them other stead all for all should make room,
A hall and high settle, whereof the half-wielding
They with the Eotens' bairns henceforth might hold,
And with fee-gifts moreover the son of Folkwalda 1090
Each day of the days the Danes should be worthy;
The war-heap of Hengest with rings should he honour
Even so greatly with treasure of treasures,
Of gold all beplated, as he the kin Frisian
Down in the beer-hall duly should dight.
Troth then they struck there each of the two halves,
A peace-troth full fast. There Finn unto Hengest
Strongly, unstrifeful, with oath-swearing swore,
That he the woe-leaving by the doom of the wise ones
Should hold in all honour, that never man henceforth 1100
With word or with work the troth should be breaking,
Nor through craft of the guileful should undo it ever,
Though their ring-giver's bane they must follow in rank
All lordless, e'en so need is it to be:
But if any of Frisians by over-bold speaking
The murderful hatred should call unto mind,
Then naught but the edge of the sword should avenge it.
Then done was the oath there, and gold of the golden

Peace made between Finn and Hengest

Of this matter of Finn and Hengest

Heav'd up from the hoard. Of the bold Here-Scyldings
All yare on the bale was the best battle-warrior; 1110
On the death-howe beholden was easily there
The sark stain'd with war-sweat, the all-golden swine,
The iron-hard boar; there was many an atheling
With wounds all outworn; some on slaughter-field welter'd.
But Hildeburh therewith on Hnæf's bale she bade them
The own son of herself to set fast in the flame,
His bone-vats to burn up and lay on the bale there:
On his shoulder all woeful the woman lamented,
Sang songs of bewailing, as the warrior strode upward,
Wound up to the welkin that most of death-fires, 1120
Before the howe howled; there molten the heads were,
The wound-gates burst open, there blood was out-springing
From foe-bites of the body; the flame swallow'd all,
The greediest of ghosts, of them that war gat him
Of either of folks; shaken off was their life-breath.

XVIII. The Ending of the Tale of Finn

Departed the warriors their wicks to visit
All forlorn of their friends now, Friesland to look on,
Their homes and their high burg. Hengest a while yet
Through the slaughter-dyed winter bode dwelling with Finn
And all without strife: he remember'd his homeland,
Though never he might o'er the mere be a-driving 1130
The high prow be-ringed: with storm the holm welter'd,
Won war 'gainst the winds; winter locked the waves
With bondage of ice, till again came another
Of years into the garth, as yet it is ever,
And the days which the season to watch never cease,
The glory-bright weather; then gone was the winter,
And fair was the earth's barm. Now hasten'd the exile,
The guest from the garths; he on getting of vengeance
Of harms thought more greatly than of the sea's highway,
If he but a wrath-mote might yet be a-wending 1140
Where the bairns of the Eotens might he still remember. — The son of Hunlaf slays Hengest
The ways of the world forwent he in nowise
Then, whenas Hunlafing the light of the battle,
The best of all bills, did into his breast,
Whereof mid the Eotens were the edges well knowen.
"Withal to the bold-hearted Finn befell after
Sword-bales the deadly at his very own dwelling,
When the grim grip of war Guthlaf and Oslaf

After the sea-fare lamented with sorrow
And wyted him deal of their woes; nor then might he 1150
In his breast hold his wavering heart. Was the hall dight
With the lives of slain foemen, and slain eke was Finn
The King midst of his court-men; and there the Queen, taken,
The shooters of the Scyldings ferry'd down to the sea-ships,
And the house-wares and chattels the earth-king had had,
E'en such as at Finn's home there might they find,
Of collars and cunning gems. They on the sea-path
The all-lordly wife to the Danes straightly wended,
Led her home to their people."

The slaying of Finn

Here ends the Lay of Finn

Translation of Beowulf, *Lines 1050-1159 into Modern English*

XVII

Yet again the lord of earls 1050
gave gifts at the mead benches
to all who took the sea-trip with Beowulf,
old heirlooms. And then he ordered
gold be given over for the one whom earlier
Grendel had wickedly killed—as he wanted with more.
But the wise God and one warrior's heart
would not give him that fate. The Measurer governs
all the kin of man, as he continually does.
Therefore understanding is everywhere best,
forethought of mind. Much of good and ill 1060
will he have, he who here long
enjoys the world in these times of trouble.

There was song and sound all together
before the war-warden of the Half-Danes,
the joy-wood touched, a tale often told,
when Hrothgar's bard had to provide
a hall-game, after the mead-bench was gone,
about Finn's sons, when disaster fell on them.

The hero of the Half-Danes, Hnæf of the Scyldings,
had to fall in Frisian slaughter! 1070
Nor indeed did Hildeburh have reason to revel
in the good faith of the giants. Without guilt she was
deprived of her loved ones in the play of linden shields,
son and brother. They fell in succession,
wounded by a spear. That was a woeful lady!

Hardly in vain did Hoc's daughter
mourn the Measurer's decree after morning came,
when she might see under the sky
the murder of her kin, where she most held
worldly joy. War seized all 1080
of Finn's thanes, except only a few,
so that he might not at all manage
his fight with Hengest in that field of battle
nor crush in war the woe-survivors,
their princes' thanes. So they proffered a truce—
that they would find them room on another floor,
a hall and a high throne, so that they would have half,
might secure it against the sons of giants,
and Folcwalda's offspring would honor
the Danes every day with precious gifts, 1090
treat Hengest's retainers well with rings,
ever as much as he would encourage
the Frisian kin with fine treasures,
give plated gold in the beer hall.
Then on both sides they sealed
a fast pact of peace. Finn swore
to Hengest by oaths all uncontested
that he would hold the woe-survivors in honor
according to the judgment of the wise, that no one would
destroy the pact by words or deeds 1100
or ever complain about it in cunning malice,
though they would serve the slayer of their ring-giver
without a prince, as need pushed them.
If one of the Frisians should with foolish speech
remind them of the murderous hate,
then afterwards the edge of the sword would arise!
An oath was agreed to and splendid gold
brought from the hoard. The best warrior
of the Battle-Scyldings was brought to the fire.
On the pyre in plain sight was 1110
the blood-stained shirt, gilded over with boar-figures,
iron-hard animals, many an atheling
slain by wounds. Some fell in the slaughter.
Then Hildeburh ordered her own son
be proffered to the flames of Hnæf's pyre,
the bone-vessel be burned and placed on the fire.
At his side the lady sorrowed,
grieved with songs of mourning. The soldier ascended.
The great killing-fire wound up to the clouds;

it roared before the mound. Heads melted, 1120
wounds burst. Then blood sprang out,
hateful bites on the body. Flame ate it all,
greediest of ghosts, all whom battle took
of both nations. Their glory had gone!

XVIII

Then the warriors went to visit their dwellings,
deprived of friends, to see Frisia,
homes and high castle. Then Hengest yet
stayed with Finn a slaughter-stained winter,
all without choice. He held his home in his memory.
Nevertheless he could set out to sea 1130
in a ring-prowed ship. The sea surged with storm,
fought against the wind. Winter locked up the waves
in ice-bonds until another year
came to their dwellings, as it still does
for those who always await the occasion,
the wondrously bright weather. Then winter was gone,
the earth's bosom fair. The exile was anxious,
the guest to get out of the dwellings. He meditated more
on vengeance for wrong than on a voyage at sea—
if he might bring about an angry meeting, 1140
so that he might remember inside the offspring of giants.
So he did not withstand worldly counsel,
when Hunlafing placed on his heart
a battle-light, best of swords.
Its edges were known among the giants.
Thus harsh sword-death happened
in his own home to bold-hearted Finn,
when Guthlaf and Oslaf with a grim grip
complained in sorrow for the sea-journey,
lamented their share of woes. He could not keep 1150
his restless spirit in his breast. Then was the hall reddened
by the corpses of enemies, also Finn killed,
a king in his troop, and the queen taken.
The soldiers of the Scyldings carried to their ships
all the household goods of the earthly king,
whatever they could find in Finn's home—
jewels, skillfully-wrought gems. They carried
the lordly lady on a voyage to the Danes,
led her to her people.

2. From Morris's and Eírikr Magnússon's Translation of *The Story of the Volsungs and Niblungs* (1870)

[In the late 1860s and early 1870s Morris collaborated with the Icelander Eírikr Magnússon on a series of translations from the medieval Old Norse sagas. The complicated love-and-betrayal story of Sigurd, Brynhild, Gudrun, and Gunnar so appealed to Morris that in 1876 he published his own poetic version of the story, providing the characters with much to say about those complexities—a departure from the understated original.]

Chapter XXIII. Sigurd Comes to Hlymdale

Forth Sigurd rides till he comes to a great and goodly dwelling, the lord whereof was a mighty chief called Heimir; he had to wife a sister of Brynhild, who was hight[1] Bekkhild, because she had bidden[2] at home, and learned handicraft, whereas Brynhild fared with helm and byrny[3] unto the wars, wherefore was she called Brynhild.

Heimir and Bekkhild had a son called Alswid, the most courteous of men.

Now at this stead[4] were men disporting them abroad, but when they see the man riding thereto, they leave their play to wonder at him, for none such had they ever seen erst;[5] so they went to meet him, and gave him good welcome: Alswid bade him abide[6] and have such things at his hands as he would; and he takes his bidding blithesomely;[7] due service withal[8] was established for him; four men bore the treasure of gold from off the horse, and the fifth took it to him to guard the same; therein were many things to behold, things of great price, and seldom seen; and great game and joy men had to look on byrnies and helms, and mighty rings, and wondrous great golden stoups,[9] and all kinds of war weapons.

So there dwelt Sigurd long in great honour holden;[10] and tidings of that deed of fame spread wide through all lands, of how he had slain

1 Named.
2 Remained.
3 Coat of mail [armor].
4 Place.
5 Before.
6 Asked him to stay.
7 Happily.
8 In addition.
9 Buckets.
10 Held in great honor.

that hideous and fearful dragon.[1] So good joyance[2] had they there together, and each was leal[3] to other; and their sport was in the arraying[4] of their weapons, and the shafting of their arrows,[5] and the flying of their falcons.

Chapter XXIV. Sigurd Sees Brynhild at Hlymdale

In those days came home to Heimir, Brynhild, his foster-daughter, and she sat in her bower[6] with her maidens, and could[7] more skill in handycraft than other women; she sat, overlaying cloth with gold, and sewing therein the great deeds which Sigurd had wrought, the slaying of the Worm,[8] and the taking of the wealth of him, and the death of Regin[9] withal.

Now tells the tale, that on a day Sigurd rode into the wood with hawk, and hound, and men thronging;[10] and whenas he came home his hawk flew up to a high tower, and sat him down on a certain window. Then fared Sigurd after his hawk, and he saw where sat a fair woman, and knew that it was Brynhild, and he deems[11] all things he sees there to be worthy together, both her fairness, and the fair things she wrought: and therewith he goes into the hall, but has no more joyance[12] in the games of the men folk.

Then spake Alswid, "Why art thou so bare of bliss? this manner of thine grieveth us thy friends; why then wilt thou not hold to thy gleesome[13] ways? Lo, thy hawks pine now, and thy horse Grani droops; and long will it be ere[14] we are booted thereof?"[15]

---

1 The dragon, named Fafnir, was stabbed by Sigurd in its underbelly. Morris had a hedge at Kelmscott Manor that he kept clipped to resemble a dragon, naming it Fafnir.

2 Pleasure.

3 Loyal.

4 Polishing and sharpening.

5 Affixing points to arrow shafts.

6 Bedroom.

7 Knew, possessed.

8 Dragon.

9 Regin is Sigurd's evil foster father. After Sigurd eats the heart of the dragon Fafnir, he can understand the language of birds, who inform him that Regin is plotting his death. In consequence, Sigurd kills Regin.

10 Gathering in a crowd.

11 Judges.

12 Pleasure.

13 Happy.

14 Before.

15 Compensated by it.

Sigurd answered, "Good friend, hearken to what lies on my mind; for my hawk flew up into a certain tower; and when I came thereto and took him, lo there I saw a fair woman, and she sat by a needlework of gold, and did thereon[1] my deeds that are passed, and my deeds that are to come."

Then said Alswid, "Thou hast seen Brynhild, Budli's daughter, the greatest of great women."

"Yea, verily," said Sigurd; "but how came she hither?"

Alswid answered, "Short space there was betwixt the coming hither of the twain of you."

Says Sigurd, "Yea, but a few days agone I knew her for the best of the world's women."

Alswid said, "Give not all thine heed to one woman, being such a man as thou art; ill life to sit lamenting for what we may not have."

"I shall go meet her," says Sigurd, "and get from her love like my love, and give her a gold ring in token thereof."

Alswid answered, "None has ever yet been known whom she would let sit beside her, or to whom she would give drink; for ever will she hold to warfare and to the winning of all kinds of fame."

Sigurd said, "We know not for sure whether she will give us answer or not, or grant us a seat beside her."

So the next day after, Sigurd went to the bower, but Alswid stood outside the bower door, fitting shafts to his arrows.

Now Sigurd spake, "Abide, fair and hale lady,—how farest thou?"[2]

She answered, "Well it fares; my kin and my friends live yet: but who shall say what goodhap[3] folk may bear to their life's end?"

He sat him down by her, and there came in four damsels with great golden beakers,[4] and the best of wine therein; and these stood before the twain.

Then said Brynhild, "This seat is for few, but and if my father come."

He answered, "Yet is it granted to one that likes me well."

Now that chamber was hung with the best and fairest of hangings,[5] and the floor thereof was all covered with cloth.

Sigurd spake, "Now has it come to pass even as thou didst promise."

"O be thou welcome here!" said she, and arose therewith, and the four damsels with her, and bore the golden beaker to him, and bade

1 Embroidered on it.

2 How are you?

3 Good luck.

4 Jars.

5 Tapestries.

him drink; he stretched out his hand to the beaker, and took it, and her hand withal,[1] and drew her down beside him; and cast his arms round about her neck and kissed her, and said:

"Thou art the fairest that was ever born!"

But Brynhild said, "Ah, wiser is it not to cast faith and troth[2] into a woman's power, for ever shall they break that[3] they have promised."

He said, "That day would dawn the best of days over our heads whereon each of each should be made happy."

Brynhild answered, "It is not fated that we should abide[4] together; I am a shield-may,[5] and wear helm on head even as the kings of war, and them full oft I help, neither is the battle become loathsome[6] to me."

Sigurd answered, "What fruit shall be of our life if we live not together: harder to bear this pain that lies hereunder, than the stroke of sharp sword."

Brynhild answers, "I shall gaze on the hosts of the war-kings, but thou shalt wed Gudrun, the daughter of Giuki."

Sigurd answered, "What king's daughter lives to beguile me? neither am I double-hearted herein; and now I swear by the Gods that thee shall I have for mine own, or no woman else."

And even suchlike wise[7] spake she.

Sigurd thanked her for her speech, and gave her a gold ring, and now they swore oath anew, and so he went his ways to his men, and is with them awhile in great bliss.

Chapter XXV. Of the Dream of Gudrun, Giuki's Daughter

There was a king hight[8] Giuki, who ruled a realm south of the Rhine;[9] three sons he had, thus named: Gunnar, Hogni, and Guttorm, and Gudrun was the name of his daughter, the fairest of maidens; and all these children were far before all other kings' children in all prowess, and in goodliness and growth withal;[10] ever were his sons at the wars

---

1 In addition.

2 Promise.

3 What.

4 Remain.

5 Female warrior, amazon.

6 Hateful.

7 In a similar way.

8 Named.

9 The famous Rhine River flows through Germany and the Netherlands, emptying into the North Sea.

10 In addition.

and wrought many a deed of fame. But Giuki had wedded Grimhild the Wise-wife.

Now Budli was the name of a king, mightier than Giuki, mighty though they both were: and Atli was the brother of Brynhild; Atli was a fierce man and a grim, great and black to look on, yet noble of mien[1] withal, and the greatest of warriors. Grimhild was a fierce-hearted woman.

Now the days of the Giukings bloomed fair, chiefly because of those children, so far before the sons of men.

On a day Gudrun says to her mays[2] that she may have no joy of heart; then a certain woman asked her wherefore her joy was departed.

She answered, "Grief came to me in my dreams, therefore is there sorrow in my heart, since thou must needs ask thereof."

"Tell it me, then, thy dream," said the woman, "for dreams oft forecast but the weather."

Gudrun answers, "Nay, nay, no weather is this; I dreamed that I had a fair hawk on my wrist, feathered with feathers of gold."

Says the woman, "Many have heard tell of thy beauty, thy wisdom, and thy courtesy; some king's son abides thee, then."

Gudrun answers, "I dreamed that naught was so dear to me as this hawk, and all my wealth had I cast aside rather than him."

The woman said, "Well, then, the man thou shalt have will be of the goodliest, and well shalt thou love him."

Gudrun answered, "It grieves me that I know not who he shall be; let us go seek Brynhild, for she belike will wot thereof."[3]

So they arrayed them[4] in gold and many a fair thing, and she went with her damsels till they came to the hall of Brynhild, and that hall was dight[5] with gold, and stood on a high hill; and whenas their goings were seen, it was told Brynhild, that a company of women drove toward the burg[6] in gilded[7] waggons.

"That shall be Gudrun, Giuki's daughter," says she: "I dreamed of her last night; let us go meet her; no fairer woman may come to our house."

So they went abroad to meet them, and gave them good greeting, and they went into the goodly hall together; fairly painted it was

---

1 Manner, expression.

2 Maidens, ladies-in-waiting.

3 Likely will know about it [since she has the gift of prophesy].

4 Clothed themselves.

5 Decorated.

6 City, castle.

7 Plated with gold.

within, and well adorned with silver vessel;[1] cloths were spread under the feet of them, and all folk served them, and in many wise[2] they sported.

But Gudrun was somewhat silent.

Then said Brynhild, "Ill to abash[3] folk of their mirth; prithee[4] do not so; let us talk together for our disport[5] of mighty kings and their great deeds."

"Good talk," says Gudrun, "let us do even so; what kings deemest[6] thou to have been the first of all men?"

Brynhild says, "The sons of Haki, and Hagbard withal; they brought to pass many a deed of fame in their warfare."

Gudrun answers, "Great men certes,[7] and of noble fame! Yet Sigar took their one sister, and burned the other, house and all; and they may be called slow to revenge the deed; why didst thou not name my brethren,[8] who are held to be the first of men as at this time?"

Brynhild says, "Men of good hope are they surely, though but little proven hitherto; but one I know far before them, Sigurd, the son of Sigmund the King; a youngling[9] was he in the days when he slew the sons of Handing, and revenged his father, and Eylimi, his mothers' father."

Said Gudrun, "By what token tellest thou that?"

Brynhild answered, "His mother went amid the dead, and found Sigmund the King sore wounded, and would bind up his hurts; but he said he grew over old for war, and bade[10] her lay this comfort to her heart, that she should bear the most famed of sons; and wise was the wise man's word therein: for after the death of King Sigmund, she went to King Alf, and there was Sigurd nourished in great honour, and day by day he wrought[11] some deed of fame, and is the man most renowned of all the wide world."

Gudrun says, "From love hast thou gained these tidings of him; but for this cause came I here, to tell thee dreams of mine which have brought me great grief."

---

1 Plates.

2 Ways.

3 Disturb, disconcert.

4 I ask you.

5 Enjoyment.

6 Judge.

7 Certainly.

8 Brothers.

9 Youth.

10 Commanded.

11 Did.

Says Brynhild, "Let not such matters sadden thee; abide with thy friends who wish thee blithesome,[1] all of them!"

"This I dreamed," said Gudrun, "that we went, a many of us in company, from the bower, and we saw an exceeding great hart,[2] that far excelled all other deer ever seen, and the hair of him was golden; and this deer we were all fain[3] to take, but I alone got him; and he seemed to me better than all things else; but sithence[4] thou, Brynhild, didst shoot and slay my deer even at my very knees, and such grief was that to me that scarce might I bear it; and then afterwards thou gavest me a wolf-cub, which besprinkled[5] me with the blood of my brethren."

Brynhild answers, "I will arede[6] thy dream, even as things shall come to pass hereafter; for Sigurd shall come to thee, even he whom I have chosen for my well-beloved; and Grimhild shall give him mead[7] mingled with hurtful things, which shall cast us all into mighty strife. Him shalt thou have, and him shalt thou quickly miss; and Atli the King shalt thou wed; and thy brethren shalt thou lose, and slay Atli withal in the end."

Gudrun answers, "Grief and woe to know that such things shall be!"

And therewith she and hers get them gone home to King Giuki.

Chapter XXVI. Sigurd Comes to the Giukings and is Wedded to Gudrun

Now Sigurd goes his ways with all that great treasure, and in friendly wise[8] he departs from them; and on Grani he rides with all his war-gear and the burden withal;[9] and thus he rides until he comes to the hall of King Giuki; there he rides into the burg,[10] and that sees one of the king's men, and he spake withal:

"Sure it may be deemed[11] that here is come one of the Gods, for his array[12] is all done with gold, and his horse is far mightier than

1 Happy.

2 Deer.

3 Eager.

4 Afterwards.

5 Splattered.

6 Interpret.

7 Fermented honey. Mead, along with ale, was the main drink of Germanic tribes, giving the name "meadhall" to the halls of Germanic kings.

8 Manner.

9 In addition.

10 Fortification.

11 Judged.

12 Clothing, equipment.

other horses, and the manner of his weapons is most exceeding goodly, and most of all the man himself far excels all other men ever seen."

So the king goes out with his court and greets the man, and asks, "Who art thou who thus ridest into my burg, as none has durst[1] hitherto without the leave of my sons?"

He answered, "I am called Sigurd, son of King Sigmund."

Then said King Giuki, "Be thou welcome here, then, and take at our hands whatso thou willest."[2]

So he went into the king's hall, and all men seemed little beside him, and all men served him, and there he abode[3] in great joyance.[4]

Now oft they all ride abroad together, Sigurd and Gunnar and Hogni, and ever is Sigurd far the foremost of them, mighty men of their hands though they were.

But Grimhild finds how heartily Sigurd loved Brynhild, and how oft he talks of her; and she falls to thinking how well it were, if he might abide there and wed the daughter of King Giuki, for she saw that none might come anigh[5] to his goodliness, and what faith and goodhap[6] there was in him, and how that he had more wealth withal than folk might tell of any man; and the king did to him even as unto his own sons, and they for their parts held him of more worth than themselves.

So on a night as they sat at the drink, the Queen arose, and went before Sigurd, and said:

"Great joy we have in thine abiding here, and all good things will we put before thee to take of us; lo now, take this horn[7] and drink thereof."

So he took it and drank, and therewithal she said, "Thy father shall be Giuki the King, and I shall be thy mother, and Gunnar and Hogni shall be thy brethren, and all this shall be sworn with oaths each to each; and then surely shall the like of you never be found on earth."

Sigurd took her speech well, for with the drinking of that drink all memory of Brynhild departed from him. So there he abode awhile.

And on a day went Grimhild to Giuki the King, and cast her arms about his neck, and spake:

"Behold, there has now come to us the greatest of great hearts that

---

1 Dared.

2 Whatever you want.

3 Remained.

4 Pleasure.

5 Near.

6 Good luck.

7 Drinking horn.

the world holds; and needs must he be trusty and of great avail;[1] give him thy daughter then, with plenteous[2] wealth, and as much of rule as he will; perchance thereby[3] he will be well content to abide here ever."

The king answered, "Seldom does it befall that kings offer their daughters to any; yet in higher wise[4] will it be done to offer her to this man, than to take lowly prayer for her from others."

On a night Gudrun pours out the drink, and Sigurd holds[5] her how fair she is and how full of all courtesy.

Five seasons Sigurd abode there, and ever they passed their days together in good honour and friendship.

And so it befell[6] that the kings held talk together, and Giuki said,

"Great good thou givest us, Sigurd, and with exceeding strength thou strengthenest our realm."

Then Gunnar said, "All things that may be will we do for thee, so thou abidest here long; both dominion shalt thou have, and our sister freely and unprayed[7] for, whom another man would not get for all his prayers."[8]

Sigurd says, "Thanks have ye for this wherewith ye honour me, and gladly will I take the same."

Therewith they swore brotherhood together, and to be even as if they were children of one father and one mother; and a noble feast was holden,[9] and endured[10] many days, and Sigurd drank at the wedding of him and Gudrun; and there might men behold all manner of game and glee,[11] and each day they feast better and better.

Now fare these folk wide over the world, and do many great deeds, and slay many kings' sons, and no man has ever done such works of prowess[12] as did they; then home they come again with much wealth won in war.

Sigurd gave of the serpent's heart to Gudrun, and she ate thereof, and became greater-hearted, and wiser than e'er[13] before: and the son of these twain was called Sigmund.

---

1 Advantage.

2 Plentiful.

3 Perhaps with it.

4 Manner.

5 Beholds, sees.

6 Happened.

7 Unasked.

8 Requests.

9 Held.

10 Lasted.

11 Song.

12 Might.

13 Ever.

Now on a time went Grimhild to Gunnar her son, and spake:

"Fair blooms the life and fortune of thee, but for one thing only, and namely whereas thou art unwedded; go woo Brynhild; good rede[1] is this, and Sigurd will ride with thee.

Gunnar answered, "Fair is she certes,[2] and I am fain enow[3] to win her;" and therewith he tells his father, and his brethren,[4] and Sigurd, and they all prick[5] him on to that wooing.

3. From Malory's *Morte D'Arthur* (1471)

[The following passage from Caxton's Malory recounts the complicated love triangle involving the famous knight Gawain, Sir Pelleas, who suffers from unrequited love, and the Lady Ettard. It is a good example of the emotionally complex, morally ambiguous medieval narratives that Morris evokes in *The Wood Beyond the World*. The use of u/v and i/j, interchangeable in late Middle English, has been modernized.]

Book IV, Chapter 21

How a knyght and a dwarf stroof[6] for a lady

And thewith he passed unto the one syde of the launde.[7] And on the other syde sawe Syr Gawayne x[8] knyghtes that hoved styll[9] and made hem redy[10] with her sheldes and speres ageynst that one knyght that cam by Syr Gawayn. Thenne this one knyght aventryd[11] a grete spere, and one of the x[12] knyghtes encountred with hym, but this woful knyght smote hym so hard that he fell over his hors taylle.[13] So this same dolorous[14] knyght served hem al, that at the lest way he smote

1 Advice.
2 Certainly.
3 Eager enough.
4 Brothers.
5 Urge.
6 Fought.
7 Land.
8 Ten.
9 Remained still on their horses.
10 Made themselves ready.
11 Attacked with.
12 The number 10 in roman numerals.
13 Over his horse's tail.
14 Sad.

doune[1] hors and man, and alle he dyd with one spere. And soo whan they were all x on fote they wente to that one knyght, and he stode stone styll and suffred hem[2] to pulle hym doune of his hors, and bound hym hande and foote and tayed hym under the hors bely,[3] and so ledde hym with hem. O Ihesu,[4] sayd Syr Gawayne, this is a dooleful syghte,[5] to see the yonder knyghte so to be entreted;[6] and it semeth by the knyght that he suffreth hem to bynde hym soo, for he maketh no resystence. Noo, said his hoost, that is trouthe, for and he wold,[7] they al were to weyke[8] soo to doo hym. Syr, said the damoysel unto Syr Gawayn, me semeth[9] hit were youre worship[10] to helpe that dolorous knyghte, for me thynketh he is one of the best knyghtes that ever I sawe. I wold doo for hym, sayd Syre Gawayn, but hit semeth he wyll have no helpe. Thenne, sayd the damoysel, me thynketh ye have no luste[11] to helpe hym.

Thus as they talked they sawe a knyghte on the other syde of the launde, al armed sauf the hede.[12] And on the other syde ther cam a dwerf[13] on horsbak, all armed sauf the hede, with a grete mouthe and a shorte nose. And whan the dwerf came nyghe he said, Where is the lady shold mete us here? And therwithall she came forth out of the wood. And thenne they began to stryve[14] for the lady, for the knyghte sayd he wold have her, and the dwerf said he wold have her. Wylle we doo wel? sayd the dwerf. Yonder is a knyght at the crosse; let us put it bothe upon hym, and as he demeth,[15] so shall it be. I wylle wel, said the knyght. And so they wente all thre unto Syre Gawayn and told hym wherfor they strofe.[16] Wel, syrs, said he, wylle ye put the mater in my hand? Ye, they sayd both. Now damoysel, sayd Syr Gawayn, ye shal stande betwixe them both, and whether ye lyst[17] better to go to he shal

1 Struck down.
2 Allowed them.
3 Tied him under his horse's belly.
4 Jesus.
5 Sad sight.
6 Treated.
7 If he would.
8 Weak.
9 It seems to me.
10 It is honorable for you.
11 Desire.
12 Except his head.
13 Dwarf.
14 Fight.
15 Judges.
16 Why they fought.
17 Desire.

have yow. And whan she was sette bitwene them both she left the knyghte and wente to the dwerf, and the dwerf took her and wente his waye syngynge, and the knyghte wente his wey with grete mornyng.[1]

Thenne came ther two knyghtes all armed and cryed on hyghe,[2] Syre Gawayn, knyghte of Kynge Arthurs, make the redy in al hast and juste with me.[3] Soo they ranne togyders that eyther felle doune, and thenne on foote they drewe their swerdes and dyd ful actually.[4] The mene whyle the other knyghte wente to the damoysel and asked her why she abode[5] with that knyghte: and yf ye wold abyde with me, I wylle be your feythful knyghte. And with yow wylle I be, said the damoysel, for with Syr Gawayn, I may not fynde in myn herte to be with hym. For now here was one knyght scomfyte x knyghtes,[6] and at the laste he was cowardly led awey, and therfore let us two goo whylest they fyghte. And Syre Gawayn fought with that other knyght longe, but at the last they accorded[7] both. And thenne the knyght prayd Syr Gawayn to lodge with hym that nyghte.

Soo as Syre Gawayn wente with this knyghte he asked hym, what knyghte is he in this countrey that smote doune the ten knyghtes? For whan he had done so manfully he suffred hem to bynde hym hand and foote, and soo ledde hym awey. A,[8] sayd the knyghte, that is the best knyghte I trowe in the world, and the moost man of prowesse,[9] and he hath be served soo as he was e*ven* more than x tymes; and his name hyghte Syr Pelleas, and he loveth a grete lady in this countrey, and her name is Ettard. And so when he loved her, there was cryed in this countrey a grete justes[10] thre dayes, and alle the knyghtes of this countrey were there and gentylwymmen. And who that preved hym[11] the best knyght shold have a passyng good swerd and a serklet of gold,[12] and the serklet the knyght shold gyve hit to the fayrest lady that was at the justes. And this knyghte Syre Pelleas was the best knyghte that was there, and there were fyve hondred knyghtes, but there was never man that ever Syre Pelleas met withal but he stroke hym doune, or els[13]

---

1 Mourning.
2 Cried out loudly.
3 Make yourself ready quickly and fight with me.
4 Very bravely.
5 Stayed.
6 Defeated ten knights.
7 Made peace between them.
8 Ah.
9 The man of most strength.
10 Joust.
11 Proved himself.
12 A surpassingly good sword and wreath of gold for his head.
13 Else.

from his hors. And every day of thre dayes he strake[1] doune twenty knyghtes; therfore they gaf hym the pryse.[2] And forthwithall he went thereas the Lady Ettard was and gaf her the serklet, and said openly she was the fayrest lady that there was, and that wold he preve[3] upon any knyghte that wold say nay.

Chapter 22

How Kyng Pelleas suffred[4] hymself to be taken prysoner bycause he wold have a syght of his lady, and how Syr Gawayn promysed hym for to get to hym the love of his lady

And so he chose her for his soverayne lady, and never to love other but her, but she was so proude that she had scorne of hym and sayd that she wold never love hym, though he wold dye for her. Wherfor al ladyes and gentylwymmen hadde scorne of her that she was so proude, for there were fayre[5] than she, and there was none that was ther but an Sir Pelleas wold have profered hem[6] love, they would have loved hym for his noble prowesse.[7] And so this knyght promysed the Lady Ettard to folowe her into the countrey, and never to leve her tyl she loved hym. And thus he is here the moost party[8] nyghe her, and lodged by a pryory,[9] and every weke[10] she sendeth knyghtes to fyghte with hym. And whan he hath put hem to the wers,[11] than wylle he suffre hem[12] wylfully to take hym prysoner bycause he wold have a syghte of this lady. And alweyes she doth hym grete despyte,[13] for sometyme she maketh her knyghtes to taye hym to his hors taylle,[14] and some to bynd hym under the hors bely.

Thus in the moost shamefullest wyse[15] that she can thynke he is broughte to her, and alle she doth hyt for to cause hym to leve this

1 Struck.
2 Gave him the prize.
3 Prove [in battle] with.
4 Allowed.
5 Fairer [ones].
6 Offered them.
7 Strength in arms.
8 For the most part.
9 Priory [religious house].
10 Week.
11 Worse.
12 Allow them.
13 Insult.
14 Tie him to his horse's tail.
15 Way.

countreye and to leve his lovynge. But all this can not make hym to leve, for and[1] he wold have foughte on foote he myghte have had the better of the ten knyghtes as wel on foote as on horsbak. Allas, sayd Syr Gawayn, it is grete pyte of hym,[2] and after this nyghte I wylle seke[3] hym tomorowe in the forest to doo hym all the help I can.

So on the morne Syr Gawayne tooke his leve of his hoost, Syre Carados, and rode into the forest. And at the last he mette with Syr Pelleas makyng grete moone[4] oute of mesure; so eche of hem salewed other,[5]and asked hym why he made suche sorowe. And as it is above reherced, Syre Pelleas told Syre Gawayne: but alweys I suffre her knyghtes to fare soo with me as ye sawe yesterdaye, in truste at the last to wynne her love, for she knoweth wel alle her knyghtes should not lyghtely wynne me and me lyste[6] to fyghte with them to the uttermest.[7] Wherfore and[8] I loved her not so sore, I hadde lever dye[9] an honderd tymes and I myght dye soo ofte rather than I wold suffre that despyte,[10] but I truste she wylle have pyte[11] upon me at the laste; for love causeth many a good knyght to suffre to have his entent,[12] but allas, I am unfortunate. And therwith he made soo grete dole[13] and sorowe that unnethe[14] he myghte holde hym[15] on horsback.

Now, sayd Syre Gawayne, leve your mornynge[16] and I shall promyse yow, by the feythe[17] of my body, to doo alle that lyeth in my power to gete yow the love of your lady, and therto I wylle plyte yow my trouthe.[18] A, sayd Syr Pelleas, of what courte are ye? Telle me, I praye yow, my good frend. And thenne Syr Gawayne sayd, I am of the courte of Kynge Arthur, and his susters sone,[19] and Kynge Lott of Orkeney was my fader, and my name is Syre Gawayne.

---

1 If.
2 A great pity for him.
3 Seek.
4 Lamentation.
5 Each of them greeted the other.
6 If I wanted.
7 To the death.
8 If.
9 Rather die.
10 Insult.
11 Pity.
12 Intent.
13 Sorrow.
14 Scarcely.
15 Keep himself.
16 Mourning.
17 Faith.
18 Give you my promise.
19 His nephew.

And thenne he sayd, my name is Syre Pelleas, borne in the Iles,[1] and of many iles I am lord, and never have I loved lady nor damoysel tyl now in an unhappy[2] tyme. And sir knyghte, syn[3] ye are soo nyghe cosyn[4] unto Kynge Arthur and a kynges sone, therfor bytraye me not, but helpe me; for I may never come by her but by somme good knyghte, for she is in a stronge castel here fast by[5] within this four myle,[6] and over all this countrey she is lady of. And so I may never come to her presence, but as I suffre her knyghtes to take me, and but yf I dyd so, that I myghte have a syghte of her, I had ben dede long or[7] this tyme; and yet fayre[8] word had I never of her, but whan I am brought tofore[9] her, she rebuketh me in the fowlest maner. And thenne they take my hors and harneis[10] and putten me oute of the yates,[11] and she wylle not suffre me to ete[12] nor drynke; and alweyes I offre me to be her prysoner, but that she wylle not suffre me. For I wold desyre no more, what paynes soever I had, soo that I myghte have a syghte of her dayly.[13]

Wel, sayd Syr Gawayne, al this shalle I amende and[14] ye wylle do as I shal devyse.[15] I wylle have[16] your hors and your armour, and so wylle I ryde unto her castel and telle her that I have slayne yow, and soo shal I come withynne her[17] to cause her to cherysshe[18] me, and thenne shalle I doo my true parte, that ye shalle not faylle to have the love of her.

Chapter 23

How Syr Gawayn came to the Lady Ettard and laye[19] by hyr, and how Syr Pelleas fonde them slepyng

---

1 Islands.
2 Unlucky.
3 Since.
4 Relative.
5 Close by.
6 Miles.
7 Before.
8 Fair.
9 Before.
10 Harness.
11 Gates.
12 Eat.
13 Daily.
14 If.
15 Plan.
16 Take.
17 Within her [castle].
18 Cherish.
19 Lay.

And therewith Syr Gawayne plyghte his trouthe[1] unto Syr Pelleas to be true and feythful unto hym. Soo eche one plyghte their trouthe to other, and soo they chaunged horses and harneis, and Sire Gawayn departed and came to the castel whereas stoode the pavelions[2] of this lady withoute the yate.[3] And as soone as Ettard had aspyed Syr Gawayn she fledde in toward the castel. Syre Gawayn spak on hyghe[4] and badde her abyde,[5] for he was not Syre Pelleas: I am another knyghte that have slayne Syr Pelleas. Doo of your helme,[6] said the Lady Ettard, that I maye see your vysage.[7] And soo whan she sawe that it was not Syr Pelleas, she made hym alyghte[8] and ledde hym unto her castel and asked hym feythfully whether he had slayne Syr Pelleas. And he sayd her ye[9] and told her his name was Syre Gawayne of the courte of Kynge Arthur and his syster sone.[10] Truly sayd she, that is grete pyte,[11] for he was a passynge[12] good knyghte of his body, but of al men on lyve[13] I hated hym moost, for I coude never be quyte[14] of hym. And for ye have slayne hym I shalle be your woman, and to doo onythynge[15] that myghte please yow. Soo she made Syr Gawayne good chere.[16]

Thenne Syr Gawayn sayd that he loved a lady, and by no meane she wold love him. She is to blame, sayd Ettard, and[17] she wylle not love yow, for ye that be soo wel borne a man and suche a man of prowesse, there is no lady in the world to[18] good for yow. Wylle ye, sayd Syre Gawayne, promyse me to doo alle that ye maye, by the feythe of youre body, to gete me the love of my lady? Ye, syre, sayd she, and that I promyse yow by the feythe of my body. Now, sayd Syre Gawayne, it is yourself that I love so wel; thefore I praye yow hold your promyse. I

1 Gave his promise.
2 Large tents.
3 Outside the gate.
4 Spoke loudly.
5 Asked her to delay.
6 Take off your helmet.
7 Face.
8 Get down.
9 Told her so.
10 Nephew.
11 Pity.
12 Surpassingly.
13 Alive.
14 Rid.
15 Anything.
16 Fair welcome.
17 If.
18 Too.

maye not chese,[1] sayd the Lady Ettard, but yf I shold be forsworne.[2] And soo she graunted hym to fulfylle alle his desyre.

Soo it was thenne in the moneth of May that she and Syre Gawayn wente oute of the castel and souped in a pavelione, and there was made a bedde, and there Syre Gawayne and the Lady Ettard wente to bedde togyders; and in another pavelione she layd her damoysels, and in the thyrd pavelione she leyd parte of her knyghtes, for thenne she had no drede[3] of Syr Pelleas. And there Syre Gawayn lay with her in that pavelione two dayes and two nyghtes. And on the thyrd day in the mornyng erly[4] Syr Pelleas armed hym, for he hadde never slepte syn[5] Syr Gawayn departed from hym. For Syr Gawayne had promysed hym, by the feythe[6] of hys body, to come to hym unto his pavelione by that pryory[7] within the space of a daye and an nyghte.

Thenne Syre Pelleas mounted upon horsbak and cam to the pavelions that stode without the castel, and fonde in the fyrst pavelione thre knyghtes in thre beddes, and thre squyers lyggynge at their feet. Thenne wente he to the seconde pavelione and fond four gentylwymmen lyenge in four beddes. And thenne he yede[8] to the thyrd pavelion and fond Syr Gawayn lyggyng in bedde with his Lady Ettard, and eyther clyppyng other[9] in armes. And whan he sawe that his herte wel nyghe brast for sorou[10] and said, allas, that ever a knyght shold be founde so fals.[11] And thenne he took his hors and myght not abyde[12] no lenger for pure sorowe. And whanne he hadde ryden nyghe half a myle, he torned ageyne and thoughte to slee[13] hem bothe. And whanne he sawe hem bothe soo lye slypynge faste,[14] unnethe[15] he myght holde hym on horsbak for sorowe, and sayd thus to hymself: though this knyght be never soo fals, I wyl never slee hym slepynge, for I wylle never destroye the hygh ordre of knyghthode. And thewith he departed ageyne.

---

1 Choose.
2 Perjured.
3 Fear.
4 Early.
5 Since.
6 Faith.
7 Priory.
8 Went.
9 Either embracing the other.
10 His heart very nearly broke for sorrow.
11 False.
12 Remain [there].
13 Kill.
14 Sleeping soundly.
15 Scarcely.

And or[1] he hadde ryden half a myle, he retorned ageyne and thoughte thenne to slee hem bothe, makynge the grettest sorou that ever man made. And whanne he came to the pavelions he tayed[2] his hors unto a tree, and pulled oute his swerd naked in his hand, and wente to them thereas they lay; and yet he thought it were shame to slee them slepynge and layd the naked swerd[3] overthwart bothe their throtes,[4] and soo tooke his hors and rode his waye.

And whanne Syre Pelleas came to his pavelions, he told his knyghtes and his squyers how he had sped and sayd thus to them: for your true and good servyse ye have done me I shall gyve[5] yow alle my goodes,[6] for I wylle goo unto my bedde and never aryse untyl I am dede.[7] And whan that I am dede, I charge yow that ye take the herte oute of my body and bere it her betwyxe two sylver dysshes,[8] and telle her how I sawe her lye with the fals knyght Syr Gawayne. Ryght soo Syr Pelleas unarmed hymself and wente unto his bedde, makynge merveyllous dole[9] and sorowe.

Thenne Syre Gawayne and Ettard awoke of her slepe and fonde the naked swerd overthwart[10] their throtes. Thenne she knewe wel it was Syr Pelleas swerd. Allas, sayd she to Syr Gawayne, ye have bitrayed me and Syr Pelleas bothe, for ye told me ye had slayne hym, and now I knowe wel it is not soo; he is on lyve.[11] And yf Syre Pelleas had ben as uncurteis[12] to yow as ye have ben to hym, ye hadde ben a dede knyghte. But ye have deceyved me and bytrayd me falsly, that al ladyes and damoysels may beware of yow and me. And therwith Syr Gawayn made hym redy and wente into the forest.

Soo it happed thenne that the Damoysel of the Lake, Nymue, mette with a knyghte of Syr Pelleas that wente on his foote in the forest makyng grete dole, and she asked hym the cause. And soo the woful knyghte told her how his mayster and lorde was bitrayed thurgh[13] a knyghte and a lady, and how he wyll never aryse oute of his bed tyl he

---

1 Before.

2 Tied.

3 Unsheathed sword.

4 Across both of their throats.

5 Give.

6 Possessions.

7 Dead.

8 Silver platters.

9 Great lamentation.

10 Across.

11 Alive.

12 Discourteous.

13 Through.

be dede. Brynge me to hym, sayd she anone,[1] and I wyl waraunt[2] his lyf; he shal not dye for love. And she that hath caused hym so to love, she shalle be in as evyl plyte[3] as he is or[4] it be long to, for it is no joy of suche a prowde[5] lady that wylle have no mercy of suche a valyaunt knyght. Anone that knyghte broughte her unto hym. And whan she sawe hym lye in his bedde she thoughte she saw never so lykely[6] a knyght. And therwith she threwe an enchauntement[7] upon hym and he felle on slepe;[8] and the whyle she rode unto the Lady Ettard and charged no man to awake hym tyl she came ageyne.

Soo within two houres she broughte the Lady Ettard thydder, and both ladyes fonde hym on slepe. Loo, sayd the Damoysel of the Lake, ye oughte to be ashamed for to murdre[9] suche a knyght. And therwith she threwe such an enchauntement upon her that she loved hym sore, that wel nyghe[10] she was oute of her mynde. O Lord Ihesu, saide the Lady Ettard, how is it befallen[11] unto me that I love now hym that I have moost hated of ony man alyve? That is the ryghtwys jugement[12] of God, sayd the damoysel. And thenne anone Syr Pelleas awaked and loked upon Ettard. And whan he sawe her he knewe her, and thenne he hated her more than ony woman alyve and said, Awey, traitresse, come never in my syght. And whan she herd hym say so she wepte and made grete sorou oute of mesure.[13]

Chapter 24

How Syr Pelleas loved nomore Ettard by the moyan[14] of the Damoysel of the Lake, whome he loved ever after

Syr knyghte Pelleas, sayd the Damoysel of the Lake, take your hors and come furthe[15] with me oute of this countrey, and ye shal love a

---

1 Immediately.
2 Save.
3 Evil a plight.
4 Before.
5 Proud.
6 Handsome.
7 Spell.
8 Asleep.
9 Murder.
10 Almost.
11 Has it happened.
12 Righteous judgment.
13 Excessively.
14 Doings.
15 Away.

lady that shal love yow. I wylle wel, said Syr Pelleas, for this Lady Ettard hath done me grete despyte[1] and shame. And there he told her the begynnynge and endynge, and how he had purposed[2] never to have arysen tyll that he hadde ben dede: and now such grace God hath sente me that I hate her as moche[3] as ever I loved her, thanked be our Lord Ihesus. Thank me, sayde the Damoysel of the Lake. Anone Syre Pellas armed hym, and tooke his hors and commaunded his men to brynge his pavelions[4] and his stuffe where the Damoysel of the Lake wold assigne.[5] Soo the Lady Ettard dyed for sorowe, and the Damoysel of the Lake rejoysed Syr Pellas, and loved togeders durynge their lyf dayes.[6]

* * * * *

[The fresco Morris painted in 1857 for the Oxford Union was based on this passage from Malory's monumental cycle of Arthurian stories, first published by William Caxton in 1485.]

Chapter 14

How Kyng Marke and Syr Dynadan herde Syr Palomydes makyng greet sorowe and mornyng for La Bele Isoude

... And soo Syre Dynadan rode after this knyghte, and so dyd Kyng Marke, that sought hym thurgh[7] the forest. Soo as Kynge Mark rode after Sir Palomydes, he herd a noyse of a man that made grete dole.[8] Thanne Kyng Mark rode as nyghe that noyse as he myght and as he durst.[9] Thenne was he ware[10] of a knyght that was descended of his hors, and hadde putte of his helme, and there he made a pyteous complaynte, and a dolorous,[11] of love.

---

1 Insult.

2 Intended.

3 Much.

4 Large tents.

5 Wherever the Damsel of the Lake would direct.

6 For the rest of their lives.

7 Through.

8 Lamentation.

9 Dared.

10 Aware.

11 Sorrowful.

Now leve[1] we that, and talke we of Sire Dynadan that rode to seke Syr Palomydes. And as he came within a foreste, he mette with a knyght, a chacer of dere.[2] Syr, said Sire Dynadan, mette ye with a knyghte with a shelde of sylver and lyons hedes?[3] Ye, fayr knyghte, sayd the other, with suche a knyght mette I with but a whyle agone, and strayte yonder waye he yede.[4] Gramercy,[5] said Sir Dynadann, for myght I fynde the trak of his hors, I shold not fayle to fynde that knyghte. Ryghte so, as Sir Dynadan rode in toward that noyse, and whanne he came nyghe that noyse, he alyghte[6] of his hors and wente nere hym on foote. Thenne was he ware[7] of a knyght that stood under a tree, and his hors teyed[8] by hym, and the helme of his hede, and ever that knyght made a doleful complaynte as ever made knyghte. And alweyes he made his complaynte of La Bele Isoud, the Quene of Cornewaile, and said, A, fayr lady, why love I the? For thou art fayrest of all other, and yet shewest thou never love to me nor bounte.[9] Allas, yet must I love thee, and I may not blame the,[10] fayre lady, for myn eyen been cause of this sorowe. And yet to love the I am but a foole, for the best knyghte of the world loveth the, and ye hym ageyne, that is Sir Tristram de Lyones. And the falsest kynge and knyghte is youre husband, and the moost coward and ful of treason is your lord Kyng Marke. Allas, that ever so fayre a lady and pyerles[11] of alle other shold be matched with the moost vylaynous knyght of the world.

Alle this langage herd Kynge Marke, what Sir Palomydes said by hym. Wherfore he was adradde,[12] whanne he sawe Sir Dynadan, lest and[13] he aspyed hym, that he wold telle Syre Palomydes that he was Kynge Marke. And therefor he withdrew hym and took his hors and rode to his men, where he commaunded hem to abyde....

1 Leave.
2 A pursuer of deer.
3 A silver shield with a heraldic device involving lions' heads.
4 Went.
5 Thank you.
6 Dismounted.
7 Aware.
8 Tied.
9 Generosity.
10 You.
11 Peerless.
12 Afraid.
13 If.

Appendix B: Morris and Socialism

1. "The Socialist Ideal: Art" (1891)

[Morris published this article in *The New Review* in January 1891 as one of a series of three articles explaining the socialist point of view about important topics. George Bernard Shaw contributed a piece on "The Socialist Ideal: Politics," and H.S. Salt discussed "The Socialist Ideal: Literature." They were simultaneously issued together as a pamphlet under the title *The Socialist Ideal.*]

Some people will perhaps not be prepared to hear that Socialism has any ideal of art, for in the first place it is so obviously founded on the necessity for dealing with the bare economy of life that many, and even some Socialists, can see nothing save that economic basis; and moreover, many who might be disposed to admit the necessity of an economic change in the direction of Socialism believe quite sincerely that art is fostered by the inequalities of condition which it is the first business of Socialism to do away with, and indeed that it cannot exist without them. Nevertheless, in the teeth of these opinions I assert first that Socialism is an all-embracing theory of life, and that as it has an ethic and a religion of its own, so also it has an aesthetic: so that to every one who wishes to study Socialism duly it is necessary to look on it from the aesthetic point of view. And, secondly, I assert that inequality of condition, whatever may have been the case in former ages of the world, has now become incompatible with the existence of a healthy art.

But before I go further I must explain that I use the word *art* in a wider sense than is commonly used amongst us to-day; for convenience sake, indeed, I will exclude all appeals to the intellect and emotions that are not addressed to the eyesight, though properly speaking, music and all literature that deals with style should be considered as portions of art; but I can exclude from consideration as a possible vehicle of art no production of man which can be looked at. And here at once becomes obvious the sundering[1] of the ways between the Socialist and the commercial view of art. To the Socialist a house, a knife, a cup, a steam engine, or what not, anything, I repeat, that is made by man and has form, must either be a work of art or destructive to art. The Commercialist, on the other hand, divides "manufac-

1 Parting.

tured articles" into those which are prepensely[1] works of art, and are offered for sale in the market as such, and those which have no pretence and could have no pretence to artistic qualities. The one side asserts indifference, the other denies it. The Commercialist sees that in the great mass of civilized human labour there is no pretence to art, and thinks that this is natural, inevitable, and on the whole desirable. The Socialist, on the contrary, sees in this obvious lack of art a *disease* peculiar to modern civilization and hurtful to humanity; and furthermore believes it to be a disease which can be remedied.

This disease and injury to humanity, also, he thinks is no trifling matter, but a grievous deduction from the happiness of man; for he knows that the all-pervading art of which I have been speaking, and to the possibility of which the Commercialist is blind, is *the expression of pleasure in the labour of production*; and that, since all persons who are not mere burdens on the community must produce, in some form or another, it follows that under our present system most *honest* men must lead unhappy lives, since their work, which is the most important part of their lives, is devoid of pleasure.

Or, to put it very bluntly and shortly, under the present state of society happiness is only possible to artists and thieves.

It will at once be seen from this statement how necessary it is for Socialists to consider the due relation of art to society; for it is their aim to realize a reasonable, logical, and stable society; and of the two groups above-named it must be said that the artists (using the word in its present narrow meaning) are few, and are too busy over their special work (small blame to them) to pay much heed to public matters; and that the thieves (of all classes) form a disturbing element in society.

Now, the Socialist not only sees this disease in the body politic, but also thinks that he knows the cause of it, and consequently can conceive of a remedy; and that all the more because the disease is in the main peculiar, as above-said, to modern civilization. Art was once the common possession of the whole people; it was the rule in the Middle Ages that the produce of handicraft was beautiful.[2] Doubtless, there were eyesores in the palmy days of mediaeval art, but these were caused by destruction of wares, not as now by the making of them: it was the act of war and devastation that grieved the eye of the artist then; the sacked town, the burned village, the deserted fields. Ruin

1 Premeditated; here, intended.

2 Unlike Karl Marx, who sees the Middle Ages as economically oppressive, as is evident in the selection from his *Das Kapital* (Appendix C1), Morris depicts the Middle Ages as an economic garden that has been lost.

bore on its face the tokens of its essential hideousness; to-day, it is prosperity that is externally ugly.

The story of the Lancashire manufacturer who, coming back from Italy, that sad museum of the nations, rejoiced to see the smoke, with which he was poisoning the beauty of the earth, pouring out of his chimneys, gives us a genuine type of the active rich man of the Commercial Period, degraded into incapacity of even wishing for decent surroundings. In those past days the wounds of war were grievous indeed, but peace would bring back pleasure to men, and the hope of peace was at least conceivable; but now, peace can no longer help us and has no hope for us; the prosperity of the country, by whatever "leaps and bounds" it may advance, will but make everything more and more ugly about us; it will become more a definitely established axiom that the longing for beauty, the interest in history, the intelligence of the whole nation, shall be of no power to stop one rich man from injuring the whole nation to the full extent of his riches, that is, of his privilege of taxing other people; it will be proved to demonstration, at least to all lovers of beauty and a decent life, that private property is public robbery.

Nor, however much we may suffer from this if we happen to be artists, should we Socialists at least complain of it. For, in fact, the "peace" of Commercialism is not peace, but bitter war, and the ghastly waste of Lancashire[1] and the ever-spreading squalor of London are at least object-lessons to teach us that this is so, that there is war in the land which quells all our efforts to live wholesomely and happily. The *necessity* of the time, I say, is to feed the commercial war which we are all of us waging in some way or another; if, while we are doing this, we can manage, some of us, to adorn our lives with some little pleasure of the eyes, it is well, but it is no *necessity*, it is a luxury, the lack of which we must endure.

Thus, in this matter also does the artificial famine of inequality, felt in so many other ways, impoverish us despite of our riches; and we sit starving amidst our gold, the Midas[2] of the ages.

Let me state bluntly a few facts about the present condition of the arts before I try to lay before my readers the definite Socialist ideal which I have been asked to state. It is necessary to do this because no

1 Some regions of nineteenth-century Lancashire, the South Lancashire cities of Manchester and Liverpool foremost among them, were heavily industrialized, as were some parts of London.

2 According to the well-known myth, Midas was given by the god Dionysius the gift of turning all things he touched into gold. The gift in reality turned out to be a curse, because everything he wished to eat or drink turned to gold before he could consume it.

ideal for the future can be conceived of unless we proceed by way of contrast; it is the desire to escape from the present failure which forces us into what are called "ideals"; in fact, they are mostly attempts by persons of strong hope to embody their discontent with the present.

It will scarcely be denied, I suppose, that at present art is only enjoyed, or indeed thought of, by comparatively a few persons, broadly speaking, by the rich and the parasites that minister to them directly. The poor can only afford to have what art is given to them in charity; which is of the inferior quality inherent in all such gifts—not worth picking up except by starving people.

Now, having eliminated the poor (that is, almost the whole mass of those that make anything that has *form*, which, as before-said, must either be helpful to life or destructive of it) as not sharing in art from any side, let us see how the rich, who do share in it to a certain extent, get on with it. But poorly, I think, although they are rich. By abstracting themselves from the general life of man that surrounds them, they can get some pleasure from a few works of art; whether they be part of the wreckage of times past, or produced by the individual labour, intelligence, and patience of a few men of genius to-day fighting desperately against all the tendencies of the age. But they can do no more than surround themselves with a little circle of hot-house atmosphere of art hopelessly at odds with the common air of day. A rich man may have a house full of pictures, and beautiful books, and furniture and so forth; but as soon as he steps out into the streets he is again in the midst of ugliness to which he must blunt his senses, or be miserable if he really cares about art. Even when he is in the country, amidst the beauty of trees and fields, he cannot prevent some neighbouring landowner making the landscape hideous with utilitarian agriculture; nay, it is almost certain that his own steward or agent will force him into doing the like on his own lands; he cannot even rescue his parish church from the hands of the restoring parson.[1] He can go where he likes and do what he likes outside the realm of art, but there he is helpless. Why is this? Simply because the great mass of effective art, that which pervades all life, *must* be the result of the harmonious cooperation of neighbours. And a rich man has no neighbours—nothing but rivals and parasites.

Now the outcome of this is that though the educated classes (as we call them) have theoretically some share in art, or might have, as a matter of fact they have very little. Outside the circle of the artists

1 In 1877, Morris founded the Society for the Protection of Ancient Buildings, a group still operating today, which lobbies against the destruction of old buildings, including restoration that damages their original fabric and artistic integrity.

themselves there are very few even of the educated classes who care about art. Art is kept alive by a small group of artists working in a spirit quite antagonistic to the spirit of the time; and they also suffer from the lack of co-operation which is an essential lack in the art of our epoch. They are limited, therefore, to the production of a few individualistic works, which are looked upon by almost everybody as curiosities to be examined, and not as pieces of beauty to be enjoyed. Nor have they any position or power of helping the public in general matters of taste (to use a somewhat ugly word). For example, in laying out all the parks and pleasure grounds which have lately been acquired for the public, as far as I know, no artist has been consulted; whereas they ought to have been laid out by a committee of artists; and I will venture to say that even a badly chosen committee (and it might easily be well chosen) would have saved the public from most of the disasters which have resulted from handing them over to the tender mercies of the landscape gardener.

This, then, is the position of art in this epoch. It is helpless and crippled amidst the sea of utilitarian brutality. It cannot perform the most necessary functions: it cannot build a decent house, or ornament a book, or lay out a garden, or prevent the ladies of the time from dressing in a way that caricatures the body and degrades it.[1] On the one hand it is cut off from the traditions of the past, on the other from the life of the present. It is the art of a clique and not of the people. The people are too poor to have any share of it.

As an artist I *know* this, because I can *see* it. As a Socialist I know that it can never be bettered as long as we are living in that special condition of inequality which is produced by the direct and intimate exploitation of the makers of wares, the workmen, at the hands of those who are not producers in any, even the widest, acceptation of the word.

The first point, therefore, in the Socialist ideal of art is that it should be common to the whole people; and this can only be the case if it comes to be recognized that art should be an integral part of all manufactured wares that have definite form and are intended for any endurance. In other words, instead of looking upon art as a luxury incidental to a certain privileged position, the Socialist claims art as a necessity of human life which society has no right to withhold from any one of the citizens; and he claims also that in order that this claim may be established people shall have every opportunity of taking to the work which each is best fitted for; not only that there may be the least possible waste of human effort, but also that that effort may be exercised pleasurably. For I must here repeat what I have often had to say,

1 Girdles and bustles were in fashion among Victorian women.

that the pleasurable exercise of our energies is at once the source of all art and the cause of all happiness: that is to say, it is the end of life. So that once again the society which does not give a due opportunity to all its members to exercise their energies pleasurably has forgotten the end of life, is not fulfilling its functions, and therefore is a mere tyranny to be resisted at all points.

Furthermore, in the making of wares there should be some of the spirit of the handicraftsman, whether the goods be made by hand, or by a machine that helps the hand, or by one that supersedes it. Now the essential part of the spirit of the handicraftsman is the instinct for looking at the wares in themselves and their essential use as the object of his work. Their secondary uses, the exigencies of the market, are nothing to him; it does not matter to him whether the goods he makes are for the use of a slave or a king, his business is to make them as excellent as may be; if he does otherwise he is making wares for rogues to sell to fools, and he is himself a rogue by reason of his complicity. All this means that he is making the goods for *himself*; for his own pleasure in making them and using them. But to do this he requires reciprocity, or else he will be ill-found, except in the goods that he himself makes. His neighbours must make goods in the same spirit that he does; and each, being a good workman after his kind, will be ready to recognize excellence in the others, or to note defects; because the primary purpose of the goods, their *use* in fact, will never be lost sight of. Thus the market of neighbours, the interchange of mutual good services, will be established, and will take the place of the present gambling-market, and its bond-slave the modern factory system. But the working in this fashion, which the unforced and instinctive reciprocity of service, clearly implies the existence of something more than a mere gregarious collection of workmen. It implies a consciousness of the existence of a society of neighbours, that is of equals; of men who do indeed expect to be made use of by others, but only so far as the services they give are pleasing to themselves; so far as they are services the performance of which is necessary to their own well-being and happiness.

Now, as on the one hand I *know* that no worthy popular art can grow out of any other soil than this of freedom and mutual respect, so on the other I feel sure both that this opportunity will be given to art and also that it will avail itself of it, and that, once again, nothing which is made by man will be ugly, but will have its due form, and its due ornament, will tell the tale of its making and the tale of its use, even where it tells no other tale. And this because when people once more take pleasure in their work, when the pleasure rises to a certain point, the expression of it will become irresistible, and that expression of pleasure is art, whatever form it may take. As to that form, do not let us trouble ourselves about it; remembering that after all the earliest art which we have record of is still art to us; that Homer[1] is no more out of date than Browning;[2] that the most scientifically-minded of people (I had almost said the most utilitarian), the ancient Greeks, are still thought to have produced good artists; that the most superstitious epoch of the world, the early Middle Ages, produced the freest art; though there is reason enough for that if I had time to go into it.

For in fact, considering the relation of the modern world to art, our business is now, and for long will be, not so much attempting to produce definite art, as rather clearing the ground to give art its opportunity. We have been such slaves to the modern practice of the unlimited manufacture of makeshifts for real wares, that we run a serious risk of destroying the very material of art; of making it necessary that men, in order to have any artistic perception, should be born blind, and should get their ideas of beauty from the hearsay of books. This degradation is surely the first thing which we should deal with; and certainly Socialists must deal with it at the first opportunity; *they* at least must see, however much others may shut their eyes: for they cannot help reflecting that to condemn a vast population to live in South Lancashire while art and education are being furthered in decent places, is like feasting within earshot of a patient on the rack.

Anyhow, the first step toward the fresh new-birth of art *must* interfere with the privilege of private persons to destroy the beauty of the earth for their private advantage, and thereby to rob the community. The day when some company of enemies of the community are forbidden, for example, to turn the fields of Kent into another collection of cinder heaps in order that they may extract wealth, unearned by them, from a mass of half-paid labourers; the day when some hitherto all powerful "pig-skin stuffed with money" is told that he shall not pull down some ancient building in order that he may force his fellow citizens to pay him additional rack-rent for land which is not his (save as the newly acquired watch of the highwayman[3] is)—that day will be the beginning of the fresh new-birth of art in modern times.

But that day will also be one of the memorable days of Socialism; for this very privilege, which is but the privilege of the robber by force of arms, is just the thing which it is the aim and end of our present

1 Homer is the ninth-century BCE epic poet who is the purported author of *The Iliad* and *The Odyssey*.

2 This is the great Victorian poet Robert Browning (1812-89). Among his many works, *The Ring and the Book* (1868-69) is arguably the best known. His distinctive style of writing dramatic monologues influenced the young Morris, and several poems in Morris's first book, *The Defence of Guenevere and Other Poems* (1858), exhibit Browning's influence over him.

3 Roadside thief.

organization to uphold; and all the formidable executive at the back of it, army, police, law courts, presided over by the judge as representing the executive, is directed towards this one end—to take care that the richest shall rule, and shall have full license to injure the commonwealth to the full extent of his riches.

2. "How I Became a Socialist" (1894)

[Morris wrote the following essay for the British periodical *Justice*. It appeared in the issue for 16 June 1894, 17 days after Morris dated the colophon at the end of *The Wood Beyond the World* (though the book did not appear until 16 October 1894). His essay was reprinted twice in *Justice* for the May Day issues in 1895 and 1896.]

I am asked by the Editor to give some sort of a history of the above conversion, and I feel that it may be of some use to do so, if my readers will look upon me as a type of a certain group of people, but not so easy to do clearly, briefly and truly. Let me, however, try. But first, I will say what I mean by being a Socialist, since I am told that the word no longer expresses definitely and with certainty what it did ten years ago. Well, what I mean by Socialism is a condition of society in which there should be neither rich nor poor, neither master nor master's man, neither idle nor overworked, neither brain-sick brain workers, nor heart-sick hand workers, in a word, in which all men would be living in equality of condition, and would manage their affairs unwastefully, and with the full consciousness that harm to one would mean harm to all—the realization at last of the meaning of the word COMMONWEALTH.[1]

Now this view of Socialism which I hold to-day, and hope to die holding, is what I began with; I had no transitional period, unless you may call such a brief period of political radicalism during which I saw my ideal clear enough, but had no hope of any realization of it. That came to an end some months before I joined the (then) Democratic Federation,[2] and the meaning of my joining that body was that I had conceived a hope of the realization of my ideal. If you ask me how much of a hope, or what I thought we Socialists then living and working would accomplish towards it, or when there would be effected any change in

1 By Morris's time, this term primarily meant, as it does today, "nation-state," as in "the British Commonwealth." Morris reminds his reader here of its etymology—wealth held for the common good.

2 In January 1883, Morris joined the Democratic Federation, which had been founded by H.M. Hyndman (1842-1921) and was soon to declare itself for Socialism. He resigned from this group in December of the next year, because of its factionalism and differences in ideology, particularly over the use of violence in achieving socialist goals.

the face of society, I must say, I do not know. I can only say that I did not measure my hope, nor the joy that it brought me at the time. For the rest, when I took that step I was blankly ignorant of economics; I had never so much as opened Adam Smith,[1] or heard of Ricardo,[2] or of Karl Marx.[3] Oddly enough, I *had* read some of Mill,[4] to wit, those posthumous papers of his (published, was it in the *Westminster Review* or the *Fortnightly*?)[5] in which he attacks Socialism in its Fourierist[6] guise. In those papers he put the arguments, as far as they go, clearly and honestly, and the result, so far as I was concerned, was to convince me that Socialism was a necessary change, and that it was possible to bring it about in our own days. Those papers put the finishing touch to my conversion to Socialism. Well, having joined a Socialist body (for the Federation soon became definitely Socialist), I put some conscience into trying to learn the economical side of Socialism, and even tackled Marx, though I must confess that, whereas I thoroughly enjoyed the historical part of "Capital," I suffered agonies of confusion of the brain over reading the pure economics of that great work. Anyhow, I read what I could, and will hope that some information stuck to me from my reading; but more, I must think, from continuous conversation with such friends as Bax and Hyndman and Scheu,[7] and the brisk course of

---

1 Adam Smith (1723-90) was a pioneer of political economics whose most famous work is *The Wealth of Nations* (1776).

2 David Ricardo (1772-1823) was a Member of Parliament and a theoretical political economist, a proponent of free trade. His most famous work is *Principals of Political Economy and Taxation* (1817).

3 Karl Marx (1818-83), the famous pioneering Socialist, published his *The Communist Manifesto* in 1848 and *Capital* [*Das Kapital*] in 1867. He emigrated to Britain in 1849 and died there in 1883. Morris was a socialist colleague of Marx's daughter, Eleanor.

4 John Stuart Mill (1806-73) was a British philosopher and political economist, a proponent of utilitarianism, which holds that actions should be governed by the principle of the greatest amount of happiness for the most people. His most famous work is *On Liberty* (1859).

5 These were Victorian periodicals.

6 This is the social theory proposed by Charles Fourier (1772-1837), which maintained that society should comprise small communal groups capable of sustaining themselves.

7 For Hyndman, see the note above (p. 213, note 2) on the Democratic Federation. E. Belford Bax (1854-1926) was a British socialist who in 1886 collaborated with Morris and Victor Dave on *A Short Account of the Paris Commune of 1871* and whose most famous work is *Religion of Socialism* (1886). Andreas Scheu (1844-1927) was an Austrian anarchist and furniture designer who emigrated to Britain.

propaganda meetings which were going on at the time, and in which I took my share. Such finish to what of education in practical Socialism as I am capable of I received afterwards from some of my Anarchist friends, from whom I learned, quite against their intention, that anarchism was impossible, much as I learned from Mill against *his* intention that Socialism was necessary.

But in this telling how I fell into *practical* Socialism I have begun, as I perceive, in the middle, for in my position of a well-to-do man, not suffering from the disabilities which oppress a working-man at every step, I feel that I might never have been drawn into the practical side of the question if an ideal had not forced me to seek towards it. For politics as politics, *i.e.*, not regarded as a necessary if cumbersome and disgustful means to an end, would never have attracted me, nor when I had become conscious of the wrongs of society as it now is, and the oppression of poor people, could I have ever believed in the possibility of a *partial* setting right of those wrongs. In other words, I could never have been such a fool as to believe in the happy and "respectable" poor.

If, therefore, my ideal forced me to look for practical Socialism, what was it that forced me to conceive of an ideal? Now, here comes in what I said (in this paper) of my being a type of a certain group of mind.

Before the uprising of *modern* Socialism almost all intelligent people either were, or professed themselves to be, quite contented with the civilization of this century. Again, almost all of these really were thus contented, and saw nothing to do but to perfect the said civilization by getting rid of a few ridiculous survivals of the barbarous ages. To be short, this was the *Whig*[1] frame of mind, natural to the modern prosperous middle-class men, who, in fact, as far as mechanical progress is concerned, have nothing to ask for, if only Socialism would leave them alone to enjoy their plentiful style.

But besides these contented ones there were others who were not really contented, but had a vague sentiment of repulsion to the triumph of civilization, but were coerced into silence by the measureless power of Whiggery. Lastly, there were a few who were in open rebellion against the said Whiggery—a few, say two, Carlyle[2] and

---

1 This was an influential political party in Britain from the seventeenth to nineteenth centuries. Whigs were liberal opponents of the conservative Tories.

2 Thomas Carlyle (1795-1881) was a Scottish essayist whose most famous work is *Sartor Resartus* (1833-34), which, among other things, attacks utilitarianism and British commercialism.

Ruskin.[1] The latter, before my days of practical Socialism, was my master towards the ideal aforesaid, and, looking backward, I cannot help saying, by the way, how deadly dull the world would have been twenty years ago but for Ruskin! It was through him that I learned to give form to my discontent, which I must say was not by any means vague. Apart from the desire to produce beautiful things, the leading passion of my life has been and is hatred of modern civilization. What shall I say of it now, when the words are put into my mouth, my hope of its destruction—what shall I say of its supplanting by Socialism?

What shall I say concerning its mastery of and its waste of mechanical power, its commonwealth so poor, its enemies of the commonwealth so rich, its stupendous organization—for the misery of life! Its contempt of simple pleasures which everyone could enjoy but for its folly? Its eyeless vulgarity which has destroyed art, the one certain solace of labour? All this I felt then as now, but I did not know why it was so. The hope of the past times was gone, the struggles of mankind for many ages had produced nothing but this sordid, aimless, ugly confusion; the immediate future seemed to me likely to intensify all the present evils by sweeping away the last survivals of the days before the dull squalor of civilization had settled down on the world. This was a bad look-out indeed, and, if I may mention myself as a personality and not as a mere type, especially so to a man of my disposition, careless of metaphysics and religion, as well as of scientific analysis, but with a deep love of the earth and the life on it, and a passion for the history of the past of mankind. Think of it! Was it all to end in a counting-house on the top of a cinder-heap, with Podsnap's[2] drawing-room in the offing, and a Whig committee dealing out champagne to the rich and margarine to the poor in such convenient proportions as would make all men contented together, though the pleasure of the eyes was gone from the world, and the place of Homer was to be taken by Huxley?[3] Yet, believe me, in my heart, when I really forced myself to

---

1 John Ruskin (1819-1900) was a British art critic and essayist whose writings greatly influenced Morris. His most famous work was the multi-volume *Modern Painters*, whose first volume appeared in 1843. Ruskin often used his art criticism to mount an attack on his contemporary British society. Morris eventually became his friend, publishing Ruskin's *The Nature of Gothic* (a chapter of his *The Stones of Venice*, one of the volumes of *Modern Painters*) at the Kelmscott Press in 1892; in that work, among other things, Ruskin attacked the economic theories of Adam Smith.

2 John Podsnap is a pompous character in Charles Dickens's novel *Our Mutual Friend* (1865).

3 The British biologist Thomas Henry Huxley (1825-95) was a proponent of Darwin's theories.

look towards the future, that is what I saw in it, and, as far as I could tell, scarce anyone seemed to think it worth while to struggle against such a consummation of civilization. So there I was in for a fine pessimistic end of life, if it had not somehow dawned on me that amidst all this filth of civilization the seeds of a great chance, what we others call Social-Revolution, were beginning to germinate. The whole face of things was changed to me by that discovery, and all I had to do then in order to become a Socialist was to hook myself on to the practical movement, which, as before said, I have tried to do as well as I could.

To sum up, then, the study of history and the love and practice of art forced me into a hatred of the civilization which, if things were to stop as they are, would turn history into inconsequent nonsense, and make art a collection of the curiosities of the past which would have no serious relation to the life of the present.

But the consciousness of revolution stirring amidst our hateful modern society prevented me, luckier than many others of artistic perceptions, from crystallizing into a mere railer against "progress" on the one hand, and on the other from wasting time and energy in any of the numerous schemes by which the quasi-artistic of the middle classes hope to make art grow when it has no longer any root, and thus I became a practical Socialist.

A last word or two. Perhaps some of our friends will say, what have we to do with these matters of history and art? We want by means of Social-Democracy to win a decent livelihood, we want in some sort to live, and that at once. Surely any one who professes to think that the question of art and cultivation must go before that of the knife and fork (and there are some who do propose that) does not understand what art means, or how that its roots must have a soil of a thriving and unanxious life. Yet it must be remembered that civilization has reduced the workman to such a skinny and pitiful existence, that he scarcely knows how to frame a desire for any life much better than that which he now endures perforce. It is the province of art to set the true ideal of a full and reasonable life before him, a life to which the perception and creation of beauty, the enjoyment of real pleasure that is, shall be felt to be as necessary to man as his daily bread, and that no man, and no set of men, can be deprived of this except by mere opposition, which should be resisted to the utmost.

Appendix C: Works by Morris's Contemporaries

1. From Karl Marx, *Das Kapital* (1867), translated by Samuel Moore and Edward Aveling (1887)

[Morris first read Karl Marx's *Das Kapital* in a French translation, admitting he had trouble understanding the theoretical sections but expressing his enjoyment of the historical parts. Some of Marx's attitudes about the Middle Ages are to be found in the twenty-sixth chapter; unlike Morris, he was not enamored of it. Samuel Moore and Edward Aveling published the first English translation seven years before the publication of *The Wood Beyond the World*. Aveling had married Marx's daughter Eleanor, and both were socialist colleagues of Morris.]

Chapter XXVI. The Secret of Primitive Accumulation

We have seen how money is changed into capital; how through capital surplus-value is made, and from surplus-value more capital. But the accumulation of capital presupposes surplus-value; surplus-value presupposes capitalistic production; capitalistic production presupposes the pre-existence of considerable masses of capital and of labour-power in the hands of producers of commodities. The whole movement, therefore, seems to turn in a vicious circle, out of which we can only get by supposing primitive accumulation (previous accumulation of Adam Smith[1]) preceding capitalistic accumulation; an accumulation not the result of the capitalist mode of production, but its starting point.

This primitive accumulation plays in Political Economy about the same part as original sin in theology. Adam bit the apple, and thereupon sin fell on the human race. Its origin is supposed to be explained when it is told as an anecdote of the past. In times long gone by there were two sorts of people; one, the diligent, intelligent; and above all, frugal elite; the other, lazy rascals, spending their substance, and more, in riotous living. The legend of theological original sin tells us certainly how man came to be condemned to eat his bread in the sweat of his brow; but the history of economic original sin reveals to us that there

1 Adam Smith (1723-90) was a pioneer of political economics whose most famous work is *The Wealth of Nations* (1776).

are people to whom this is by no means essential. Never mind! Thus it came to pass that the former sort accumulated wealth, and the latter sort had at last nothing to sell except their own skins. And from this original sin dates the poverty of the great majority that, despite all its labour, has up to now nothing to sell but itself, and the wealth of the few that increases constantly although they have long ceased to work. Such insipid childishness is every day preached to us in the defence of property. M. Thiers,[1] *e.g.*, had the assurance to repeat it with all the solemnity of a statesman, to the French people, once so spiritual. But as soon as the question of property crops up, it becomes a sacred duty to proclaim the intellectual food of the infant as the one thing fit for all ages and for all stages of development in actual history. It is notorious that conquest, enslavement, robbery, murder, briefly force, play the great part in the tender annals of Political Economy, the idyllic reigns from time immemorial. Right and "labour" were from all time the sole means of enrichment, the present year of course always excepted. As a matter of fact, the methods of primitive accumulation are anything but idyllic.

In themselves, money and commodities are no more capital than are the means of production and of subsistence. They want transforming into capital. But this transformation itself can only take place under certain circumstances that centre on this, *viz.*, that two very different kinds of commodity-possessors must come face to face and into contact; on the one hand, the owners of money, means of production, means of subsistence, who are eager to increase the sum of values they possess, by buying other people's labour-power; on the other hand, free labourers, the sellers of their own labour-power, and therefore the sellers of labour. Free labourers, in the double sense that neither they themselves form part and parcel of the means of production, as in the case of slaves, bondsmen, &c., nor do the means of production belong to them, as in the case of peasant-proprietors; they are, therefore, free from, unencumbered by, any means of production of their own. With this polarisation of the market for commodities, the fundamental conditions of capitalist production are given. The capitalist system presupposes the complete separation of the labourers from all property in the means by which they can realize their labour. As soon as capitalist production is once on its own legs, it not only maintains this separation, but reproduces it on a continually extending scale. The process, therefore, that clears the way for the capitalist system, can be none

---

1 Louis-Adolphe Thiers (1797-1877) was a historian who served as Prime Minister of France and was instrumental in the suppression of the Paris Commune in 1871.

other than the process which takes away from the labourer the possession of his means of production; a process that transforms, on the one hand, the social means of subsistence and of production into capital, on the other, the immediate producers into wage-labourers. The so-called primitive accumulation, therefore, is nothing else than the historical process of divorcing the producer from the means of production. It appears as primitive, because it forms the pre-historic stage of capital and of the mode of production corresponding with it.

The economic structure of capitalistic society has grown out of the economic structure of feudal society.[1] The dissolution of the latter set free the elements of the former. The immediate producer, the labourer, could only dispose of his own person after he had ceased to be attached to the soil and ceased to be the slave, serf, or bondman of another. To become a free seller of labour-power, who carries his commodity wherever he finds a market, he must further have escaped from the regime of the guilds,[2] their rules for apprentices and journeymen, and the impediments of their labour regulations. Hence, the historical movement which changes the producers into wage-workers, appears, on the one hand, as their emancipation from serfdom and from the fetters of the guilds, and this side alone exists for our bourgeois historians. But, on the other hand, these new freedmen became sellers of themselves only after they had been robbed of all their own means of production, and of all the guarantees of existence afforded by the old feudal arrangements. And the history of this, their expropriation, is written in the annals of mankind in letters of blood and fire.

The industrial capitalists, these new potentates, had on their part not only to displace the guild masters of handicrafts, but also the feudal lords, the possessors of the sources of wealth. In this respect their conquest of social power appears as the fruit of a victorious struggle both against feudal lordship and its revolting prerogatives, and against the guilds and the fetters they laid on the free development of production and the free exploitation of man by man. The chevaliers d'industrie,[3] however, only succeeded in supplanting the chevaliers of the sword by making use of events of which they themselves were

---

1 Feudalism was the basis of medieval society from the eleventh through the fourteenth centuries. According to its principles and practices, a lord gives tenure, not possession, of land to a lower nobleman in return for services that are largely military. In turn, this nobleman can subinfeudate, that is, give a portion of his tenure to still lesser noblemen in return for service. This subinfeudation may be repeated.

2 Medieval trades guilds severely limited access to most crafts. The rise of the medieval trades weakened and thus superseded feudalism to a certain extent.

3 "Knights of Industry," a sarcastic equation of capitalists with feudal lords.

wholly innocent. They have risen by means as vile as those by which the Roman freedman once on a time made himself the master of his patrons.

The starting-point of the development that gave rise to the wage-labourer as well as to the capitalist, was the servitude of the labourer. The advance consisted in a change of form of this servitude, in the transformation of feudal exploitation into capitalist exploitation. To understand its march, we need not go back very far. Although we come across the first beginnings of capitalist production as early as the 14th or 15th century, sporadically, in certain towns of the Mediterranean, the capitalistic era dates from the 16th century. Wherever it appears, the abolition of serfdom has been long effected, and the highest development of the middle ages, the existence of sovereign towns, has been long on the wane.

In the history of primitive accumulation, all revolutions are epoch-making that act as levers for the capitalist class in course of formation; but, above all, those moments when great masses of men are suddenly and forcibly torn from their means of subsistence, and hurled as free and "unattached" proletarians on the labour market. The expropriation of the agricultural producer, of the peasant, from the soil, is the basis of the whole process. The history of this expropriation, in different countries, assumes different aspects, and runs through its various phases in different orders of succession, and at different periods. In England alone, which we take as our example, has it the classic form.

2. From John Ruskin, *Pre-Raphaelitism* (1851)

[Morris first started reading Ruskin as an undergraduate, shortly after *Pre-Raphaelitism* appeared. The enthusiasm of the young painters who termed themselves Pre-Raphaelites, described so well by Ruskin, was soon to infect Morris; he and Burne-Jones became the central figures of the second wave of Pre-Raphaelite artists. Morris was also to become Ruskin's friend.]

But is there to be no place left, it will be indignantly asked, for imagination and invention, for poetical power, or love of ideal beauty? Yes; the highest, the noblest place—that which these only can attain when they are all used in the cause, and with the aid of truth. Wherever imagination and sentiment are, they will either show themselves without forcing, or, if capable of artificial development, the kind of training which such a school of art would give them would be the best they could receive. The infinite absurdity and failure of our present training consists mainly in this, that we do not rank imagination and invention high enough, and suppose that they *can* be taught. Throughout every sentence that I ever have written, the reader will find the same rank attributed to these powers,—the rank of a purely divine gift, not to be attained, increased, or in any wise modified by teaching, only in various ways capable of being concealed or quenched. Understand this thoroughly; know once for all, that a poet on canvas is exactly the same species of creature as a poet in song, and nearly every error in our methods of teaching will be done away with. For who among us now thinks of bringing men up to be poets?—of producing poets by any kind of general recipe or method of cultivation? Suppose even that we see in youth that which we hope may, in its development, become a power of this kind, should we instantly, supposing that we wanted to make a poet of him, and nothing else, forbid him all quiet, steady, rational labor? Should we force him to perpetual spinning of new crudities out of his boyish brain, and set before him, as the only objects of his study, the laws of versification which criticism has supposed itself to discover in the works of previous writers? Whatever gifts the boy had, would much be likely to come of them so treated? unless, indeed they were so great as to break through all such snares of falsehood and vanity and build their own foundation in spite of us; whereas if, as in cases numbering millions against units, the natural gifts were too weak to do this, could any thing come of such training but utter inanity and spuriousness of the whole man? But if we had sense, should we not rather restrain and bridle the first flame of invention in early youth, heaping material on it as one would on the first sparks and tongues of a fire which we desired to feed into greatness? Should we not educate the whole intellect into general strength, and all the affections into warmth and honesty, and look to heaven for the rest? This, I say, we should have sense enough to do, in order to produce a poet in words: but, it being required to produce a poet on canvas, what is our way of setting to work? We begin, in all probability, by telling the youth of fifteen or sixteen, that Nature is full of faults, and that he is to improve her; but that Raphael[1] is perfection, and that the more he copies Raphael the better; that after much copying of Raphael, he is to try what he can do himself in a Raphaelesque, but yet original, manner: that is to say, he is to try to do something very clever, all out of his own head, but yet this clever something is to be properly subjected to Raphaelesque rules, is to have a principal light occupying one-seventh of its space, and a principal shadow occupying one-third of the same; that no two people's heads in the picture are to be turned

1 Raphael Sanzio (1483-1520) was one of the great artists of the Italian Renaissance. The British establishment painter Sir Joshua Reynolds (1723-92), against whose work the Pre-Raphaelites were particularly set, was an enthusiastic proponent of Raphael.

the same way, and that all the personages represented are to possess ideal beauty of the highest order, which ideal beauty consists partly in a Greek outline of nose, partly in proportions expressible in decimal fractions between the lips and chin; but partly also in that degree of improvement which the youth of sixteen is to bestow upon God's work in general. This I say is the kind of teaching which through various channels, Royal Academy[1] lecturings, press criticisms, public enthusiasms, and not least by solid weight of gold, we give to our young men. And we wonder we have no painters!

But we do worse than this. Within the last few years some sense of the real tendency of such teaching has appeared in some of our younger painters. It only *could* appear in the younger ones, our older men having become familiarised with the false system, or else having passed through it and forgotten it, not well knowing the degree of harm they had sustained. This sense appeared, among our youths,—increased,—matured into resolute action. Necessarily, to exist at all, it needed the support both of strong instincts and of considerable self-confidence, otherwise it must at once have been borne down by the weight of general authority and received canon law. Strong instincts are apt to make men strange, and rude; self-confidence, however well founded, to give much of what they do or say the appearance of impertinence. Look at the self-confidence of Wordsworth,[2] stiffening every other sentence of his prefaces into defiance; there is no more of it than was needed to enable him to do his work, yet it is not a little ungraceful here and there. Suppose this stubbornness and self-trust in a youth, labouring in an art of which the executive part is confessedly to be best learnt from masters, and we shall hardly wonder that much of his work has a certain awkwardness and stiffness in it, or that he should be regarded with disfavour by many, even the most temperate, of the judges trained in the system he was breaking through, and with utter contempt and reprobation by the envious and the dull. Consider, farther, that the particular system to be overthrown was, in the present case, one of which the main characteristic was the pursuit of beauty at the expense of manliness and truth; and it will seem likely, *à priori*, that the men intended successfully to resist the influence of such a system should be endowed with little natural sense of beauty, and thus rendered dead to the temptation it presented. Summing up these conditions, there is surely little cause for surprise that pictures painted, in

---

1 At the time of Ruskin's writing of this piece, the Royal Academy of Art was vigorously teaching principles valued by Sir Joshua Reynolds, outlined by Ruskin immediately above.

2 William Wordsworth (1770-1850) was one of the great English Romantic poets, author of *The Prelude* (1850).

a temper of resistance, by exceedingly young men, of stubborn instincts and positive self-trust, and with little natural perception of beauty, should not be calculated, at the first glance, to win us from works enriched by plagiarism, polished by convention, invested with all the attractiveness of artificial grace, and recommended to our respect by established authority.

We should, however, on the other hand, have anticipated, that in proportion to the strength of character required for the effort, and to the absence of distracting sentiments, whether respect for precedent, or affection for ideal beauty, would be the energy exhibited in the pursuit of the special objects which the youths proposed to themselves, and their success in attaining them.

All this has actually been the case, but in a degree which it would have been impossible to anticipate. That two youths of the respective ages of eighteen and twenty, should have conceived for themselves a totally independent and sincere method of study, and enthusiastically persevered in it against every kind of dissuasion and opposition, is strange enough; that in the third or fourth year of their efforts they should have produced works in many parts not inferior to the best of Albert Dürer,[1] this is perhaps not less strange. But the loudness and universality of the howl which the common critics of the press have raised against them, the utter absence of all generous help or encouragement from those who can both measure their toil and appreciate their success, and the shrill, shallow laughter of those who can do neither the one nor the other,—these are strangest of all—unimaginable unless they had been experienced.

And as if these were not enough, private malice is at work against them, in its own small, slimy way. The very day after I had written my second letter to the *Times* in defence of the Pre-Raphaelites, I received an anonymous letter respecting one of them, from some person apparently hardly capable of spelling, and about as vile a specimen of petty malignity as ever blotted paper. I think it well that the public should know this, and so get some insight into the sources of the spirit which is at work against these men—how first roused it is difficult to say, for one would hardly have thought that mere eccentricity in young artists could have excited an hostility so determined and so cruel;—hostility which hesitates at no assertion, however impudent. That of the "absence of perspective" was one of the most curious pieces of the hue and cry which began with the *Times*, and died away in feeble maundering in the Art Union; I contradicted it in the *Times*—I here contradict it directly for the second time. There was not a single error in perspective in three

1 Albrecht Dürer (1471-1528) was a great German painter and woodcut maker.

out of the four pictures in question. But if otherwise, would it have been anything remarkable in them? I doubt if, with the exception of the pictures of David Roberts,[1] there were one architectural drawing in perspective on the walls of the Academy; I never met but with two men in my life who knew enough of perspective to draw a Gothic arch[2] in a retiring plane, so that its lateral dimensions and curvatures might be calculated to scale from the drawing. Our architects certainly do not, and it was but the other day, that talking to one of the most distinguished among them, the author of several most valuable works, I found he actually did not know how to draw a circle in perspective. And in this state of general science our writers for the press take it upon them to tell us, that the forest trees in Mr. Hunt's *Sylvia*,[3] and the bunches of lilies in Mr. Collins's *Convent Thoughts*,[4] are out of perspective....

For it is always to be remembered that no one mind is like another, either in its powers or perceptions; and while the main principles of training must be the same for all, the result in each will be as various as the kinds of truth which each will apprehend; therefore, also, the modes of effort, even in men whose inner principles and final aims are exactly the same. Suppose, for instance, two men, equally honest, equally industrious, equally impressed with a humble desire to render some part of what they saw in nature faithfully; and, otherwise, trained in convictions such as I have above endeavoured to induce. But one of them is quiet in temperament, has a feeble memory, no invention, and excessively keen sight. The other is impatient in temperament, has a memory which nothing escapes, an invention which never rests, and is comparatively near sighted.

Set them both free in the same field in a mountain valley. One sees everything, small and large, with almost the same clearness; mountains and grasshoppers alike; the leaves on the branches, the veins in the pebbles, the bubbles in the stream: but he can remember nothing, and invent nothing. Patiently he sets himself to his mighty task; abandoning at once all thoughts of seizing transient effects, or giving general impressions of that which his eyes present to him in microscopical dissection, he chooses some small portion out of the infinite

---

1 David Roberts (1796-1864) was a Scottish painter and member of the Royal Academy.

2 Gothic architecture, a medieval style in effect from the twelfth through the early sixteenth centuries, was characterized by pointed arches.

3 William Holman Hunt (1827-1910) was one of the founders of the Pre-Raphaelite Brotherhood. His *Valentine Rescuing Sylvia from Proteus* (1851) depicts a scene from Shakespeare's *Two Gentlemen of Verona*.

4 Charles Allston Collins (1828-73) was also a founder of the Pre-Raphaelite Brotherhood. His *Convent Thoughts* (1851) depicts a nun in a convent garden.

scene, and calculates with courage the number of weeks which must elapse before he can do justice to the intensity of his perceptions, or the fullness of matter in his subject.

Meantime, the other has been watching the change of the clouds, and the march of the light along the mountain sides; he beholds the entire scene in broad, soft masses of true gradation, and the very feebleness of his sight is in some sort an advantage to him, in making him more sensible of the aerial mystery of distance, and hiding from him the multitudes of circumstances which it would have been impossible for him to represent. But there is not one change in the casting of the jagged shadows along the hollows of the hills, but it is fixed on his mind for ever; not a flake of spray has broken from the sea of cloud about their bases, but he has watched it as it melts away, and could recall it to its lost place in heaven by the slightest effort of his thoughts. Not only so, but thousands and thousands of such images, of older scenes, remain congregated in his mind, each mingling in new associations with those now visibly passing before him, and these again confused with other images of his own ceaseless, sleepless imagination, flashing by in sudden troops. Fancy how his paper will be covered with stray symbols and blots, and undecipherable short-hand:—as for his sitting down to "draw from nature," there was not one of the things which he wished to represent that stayed for so much as five seconds together: but none of them escaped, for all that: they are sealed up in that strange storehouse of his; he may take one of them out, perhaps, this day twenty years, and paint it in his dark room, far away. Now, observe, you may tell both of these men, when they are young, that they are to be honest, that they have an important function, and that they are not to care what Raphael did. This you may wholesomely impress on them both. But fancy the exquisite absurdity of expecting either of them to possess any of the qualities of the other.

I have supposed the feebleness of sight in the last, and of invention in the first painter, that the contrast between them might be more striking; but, with very slight modification, both the characters are real. Grant to the first considerable inventive power, with exquisite sense of color; and give to the second, in addition to all his other faculties, the eye of an eagle; and the first is John Everett Millais,[1] and the second Joseph Mallard William Turner.[2]

---

1 John Everett Millais (1829-96) was also a founder of the Pre-Raphaelite Brotherhood; his most significant Pre-Raphaelite work is arguably his *Christ in the House of his Parents* (1850). Five years after writing this piece, Ruskin's marriage broke up and his wife Effie married Millais, whom he had befriended.

2 J.M.W. Turner (1775-1851) is the great English Romantic landscape painter whose work anticipated that of the later Impressionists.

They are among the few men who have defied all false teaching, and have, therefore, in great measure, done justice to the gifts with which they were entrusted. They stand at opposite poles, marking culminating points of art in both directions; between them, or in various relations to them, we may class five or six more living artists who, in like manner, have done injustice to their powers. I trust that I may be pardoned for naming them, in order that the reader may know how the strong innate genius in each has been invariably accompanied with the same humility, earnestness, and industry in study....

3. From Robert Buchanan, "The Fleshly School of Poetry: Mr. D.G. Rossetti" (1871)

[Buchanan, a minor Victorian poet, first published this attack on Rossetti and Pre-Raphaelite poetry in the October 1871 issue of the periodical *The Contemporary Review*, publishing an expanded version in book form in 1872. Morris is a secondary target; Buchanan allows him at least some talent in crafting a story.]

If, on the occasion of any public performance of Shakespeare's great tragedy,[1] the actors who perform the parts of Rosencranz and Guildenstern were, by a preconcerted arrangement and by means of what is technically known as "gagging," to make themselves fully as prominent as the leading character, and to indulge in soliloquies and business strictly belonging to Hamlet himself, the result would be, to say the least of it, astonishing; yet a very similar effect is produced on the unprejudiced mind when the "walking gentlemen"[2] of the fleshly school of poetry, who bear precisely the same relation to Mr. Tennyson[3] as Rosencranz and Guildenstern do to the Prince of Denmark in the play, obtrude their lesser identities and parade their smaller idiosyncrasies in the front rank of leading performers. In their own place, the gentlemen are interesting and useful. Pursuing still the theatrical analogy, the present drama of poetry might be cast as follows:

---

1 Buchanan means *Hamlet*. Rosencrantz and Guildenstern are minor characters in that play. Hamlet is the "Prince of Denmark" referred to below.

2 "Walking gentleman," a theatrical term, denotes a minor character who is a confidant of the lead character.

3 Alfred, Lord Tennyson (1809-92) was Britain's Poet Laureate from 1850 until his death. Morris was briefly considered as his successor. Among Tennyson's many well-known works, *Idylls of the King* (1859), his version of the King Arthur narratives, was particularly influential. Morris issued Tennyson's *Maud: A Monodrama* at the Kelmscott Press in 1893.

Mr. Tennyson supporting the part of Hamlet, Mr. Matthew Arnold[1] that of Horatio, Mr. Bailey[2] that of Voltimand, Mr. Buchanan[3] that of Cornelius, Messrs. Swinburne[4] and Morris, the parts of Rosencranz and Guildenstern, Mr. Rossetti[5] that of Osric, and Mr. Robert Lytton[6] that of "A Gentleman." It will be seen that we have left no place for Mr. Browning,[7] who may be said, however, to play the leading character in his own peculiar fashion on alternate nights.

This may seem a frivolous and inadequate way of opening our remarks on a school of verse-writers which some people regard as possessing great merits; but in good truth, it is scarcely possible to discuss with any seriousness the pretensions with which foolish friends and small critics have surrounded the fleshly school, which, in spite of its spasmodic ramifications in the erotic direction, is merely one of the many sub-Tennysonian schools expanded to supernatural dimensions, and endeavouring by affectations all its own to overshadow its connection with the great original. In the sweep of one single poem, the

---

1 Matthew Arnold (1822-88) was an influential cultural critic as well as a poet. His most famous work is arguably "Dover Beach" (1867). Horatio is Hamlet's friend.

2 Philip James Bailey (1816-1902) was a Victorian poet whose best known poem was *Festus* (1839), a long work in which theological and philosophical themes are treated. It was more widely read in Victorian Britain than it is today. Voltimand, a courtier at the Danish court, is another minor character in *Hamlet*.

3 Robert Buchanan (1841-1901), the author of this piece, was a minor though prolific Victorian writer. His most famous work is this essay. Cornelius is another courtier in *Hamlet*.

4 Algernon Swinburne (1837-1909) was a Victorian poet best known for his *Atalanta in Calydon* (1865). As young men, Morris and Swinburne were friends.

5 Dante Gabriel Rossetti (1828-82), Morris's friend and rival in love, was a great painter, one of the founders of the Pre-Raphaelite Brotherhood, as well as a poet. Morris published at the Kelmscott Press his *Sonnets and Lyrical Poems* in 1894 and his *Hand and Soul* in 1895. Osric is a particularly foppish and obnoxious courtier in *Hamlet*.

6 Robert Bulwer-Lytton (1831-91) was an English statesman who served as Viceroy of India in the late 1870s. He was also a poet who published under the pen name of Owen Meredith. His most famous poem was "Lucile" (1860). There is a courtier at the Danish court in *Hamlet* whom Shakespeare terms "a Gentleman." Buchanan is likely referring to Bulwer-Lytton's public anonymity when assigning him this part.

7 This is the great Victorian poet Robert Browning (1812-89).

weird and doubtful "Vivien,"[1] Mr. Tennyson has concentrated all the epicene[2] force which, wearisomely expanded, constitutes the characteristic of the writers at present under consideration; and if in "Vivien" he has indicated for them the bounds of sensualism in art, he has in "Maud," in the dramatic person of the hero, afforded distinct precedent for the hysteric tone and overloaded style which is now so familiar to readers of Mr. Swinburne. The fleshliness of "Vivien" may indeed be described as the distinct quality held in common by all the members of the last sub-Tennysonian school, and it is a quality which becomes unwholesome when there is no moral or intellectual quality to temper and control it. Fully conscious of this themselves, the fleshly gentlemen have bound themselves by solemn league and covenant to extol fleshliness as the distinct and supreme end of poetic and pictorial art; to aver that poetic expression is greater than poetic thought, and by inference that the body is greater than the soul, and sound superior to sense; and that the poet, properly to develop his poetic faculty, must be an intellectual hermaphrodite,[3] to whom the very facts of day and night are lost in a whirl of aesthetic terminology. After Mr. Tennyson has probed the depths of modern speculation in a series of commanding moods, all right and interesting in him as the reigning personage, the walking gentlemen, knowing that something of the sort is expected from all leading performers, bare their roseate bosoms and aver that *they* are creedless; the only possible question here being, if any disinterested person cares twopence whether Rosencranz, Guildenstern, and Osric are creedless or not—their self-revelation on that score being so perfectly gratuitous. But having gone so far, it was and is too late to retreat. Rosencranz, Guildenstern, and Osric, finding it impossible to risk an individual bid for the leading business, have arranged all to play leading business together, and mutually to praise, extol, and imitate each other; and although by these measures they have fairly earned for themselves the title of the Mutual Admiration School, they have in a great measure succeeded in their object—to the general stupefaction of a British audience. It is time, therefore, to ascertain whether any of these gentlemen has actually in himself the

---

1 "Vivian" is one of the poems that comprise Tennyson's Arthurian *Idylls of the King*. "Vivian" is Tennyson's way of spelling the name of Malory's character "Nimue," who figures prominently in the selection "Pelleas and Ettard," included above (Appendix A3). Tennyson's poem centers on her dealings with the prophet Merlin.

2 Of common gender.

3 A person having the characteristics of both genders.

making of a leading performer. When the *Athenaeum*[1]—once more cautious in such matters—advertised nearly every week some interesting particular about Mr. Swinburne's health, Mr. Morris's holiday-making, or Mr. Rossetti's genealogy, varied with such startling statements as "We are informed that Mr. Swinburne dashed off his noble ode *at a sitting*," or "Mr. Swinburne's songs have already reached a second edition," or "Good poetry seems to be in demand; the first edition of Mr. O'Shaughnessy's poems is exhausted;" when the *Academy* informed us that "During the past year or two Mr. Swinburne has written several novels" (!) and that some review or other is to be praised for giving Mr. Rossetti's poems "the attentive study which they demand"—when we read these things we might or might not know pretty well how and where they originated; but to a provincial eye, perhaps, the whole thing really looked like leading business. It would be scarcely worth while, however, to inquire into the pretensions of the writers on merely literary grounds, because sooner or later all literature finds its own level, whatever criticism may say or do in the matter; but it unfortunately happens in the present case that the fleshly school of verse-writers are, so to speak, public offenders, because they are diligently spreading the seeds of disease broadcast wherever they are read and understood. Their complaint too is catching, and carries off many young persons. What the complaint is, and how it works, may be seen on a very slight examination of the works of Mr. Dante Gabriel Rossetti, to whom we shall confine our attention in the present article.

Mr. Rossetti has been known for many years as a painter of exceptional powers, who, for reasons best known to himself, has shrunk from publicly exhibiting his pictures, and from allowing anything like a popular estimate to be formed of their qualities. He belongs, or is said to belong, to the so-called Pre-Raphaelite school, a school which is generally considered to exhibit much genius for colour, and great indifference to perspective. It would be unfair to judge the painter by the glimpses we have had of his works, or by the photographs which are sold of the principal paintings. Judged by the photographs, he is an artist who conceives unpleasantly, and draws ill. Like Mr. Simeon Solomon,[2] however, with whom he seems to have many points in common, he is distinctively a colourist, and of his capabilities in colour we cannot speak, though we should guess that they are great; for if there is any good quality by which his poems are specially marked, it

1 A leading Victorian periodical, as is *Academy*, mentioned immediately below.

2 Simeon Solomon (1840-1905), was a Pre-Raphaelite painter, whose most famous work is arguably *Shadrach, Meshach, and Abednego* (1865).

is a great sensitiveness to hues and tints as conveyed in poetic epithet. These qualities, which impress the casual spectator of the photographs from his pictures, are to be found abundantly among his verses. There is the same thinness and transparency of design, the same combination of the simple and the grotesque, the same morbid deviation from healthy forms of life, the same sense of weary, wasting, yet exquisite sensuality; nothing virile, nothing tender, nothing completely sane; a superfluity of extreme sensibility, of delight in beautiful forms, hues, and tints, and a deep-seated indifference to all agitating forces and agencies, all tumultuous griefs and sorrows, all the thunderous stress of life, and all the straining storm of speculation. Mr. Morris is often pure, fresh, and wholesome as his own great model [Chaucer]; Mr. Swinburne startles us more than once by some fine flash of insight; but the mind of Mr. Rossetti is like a glassy mere, broken only by the dive of some water-bird or by the hum of winged insects, and brooded over by an atmosphere of insufferable closeness, with a light blue sky above it, sultry depths mirrored within it, and a surface so thickly sown with water-lilies that it retains its glassy smoothness even in the strongest wind. Judged relatively to his poetic associates, Mr. Rossetti must be pronounced inferior to either. He cannot tell a pleasant story like Mr. Morris, nor forge alliterative thunderbolts like Mr. Swinburne. It must be conceded, nevertheless, that he is neither so glibly imitative as the one, nor so transcendently superficial as the other....

4. William Hurrell Mallock, "How to Make a Modern Pre-Raphaelite Poem" (1872)

[This delightful parody of Pre-Raphaelite verse is applicable as well to the Pre-Raphaelite prose of *The Wood Beyond the World*. It is a section of Mallock's *Everyman His Own Poet, or the Inspired Singer's Recipe Book* (1872).]

Take a packet of fine selected early English, containing no words but such as are obsolete and unintelligible. Pour this into about double the quantity of entirely new English, which must have never been used before, and which you must compose yourself, fresh, as it is wanted. Mix these together thoroughly till they assume a colour quite different from any tongue that was ever spoken, and the material will be ready for use.

Determine the number of stanzas of which your poem shall consist, and select a corresponding number of the most archaic or most peculiar words in your vocabulary, allotting one of these to each stanza; and pour in the other words round them, until the entire poem is filled in.

This kind of composition is usually cast in shapes. These, though not numerous—amounting, in all, to something under a dozen—it would take too long to describe minutely here; and a short visit to Mr.—'s shop, in King Street,[1] where they are kept in stock, would explain the whole of them. A favourite one, however, is the following, which is of very easy construction. Take three damozels, dressed in straight night-gowns. Pull their hair-pins out, and let their hair tumble all about their shoulders. A few stars may be sprinkled into this with advantage. Place an aureole[2] about the head of each, and give each a lily in her hand, about half the size of herself. Bend their necks all different ways, and set them in a row before a stone wall, with an apple-tree between each, and some large flowers at their feet. Trees and flowers of the right sort are very plentiful in church windows. When you have arranged all these objects rightly, take a cast of them in the softest part of your brain, and pour in your word-composition as above described.

This kind of poem is much improved by what is called a burden. This consists of a few jingling words, generally of an archaic character, about which we have only to be careful that they have no reference to the subject of the poem they are to ornament. They are inserted without variation between the stanzas.

In conclusion, we would remark to beginners that this sort of composition must be attempted only in a perfectly vacant atmosphere; so that no grains of common-sense may injure the work whilst in progress.

5. From May Morris, *The Collected Works of William Morris* (1913)

[William Morris's daughter May, an artist in her own right who was the leading embroiderer of her day, edited her father's works, publishing them in 24 volumes from 1911 to 1915. Her rambling introductions contain much valuable information about her father and his methods of crafting his stories, essays, and poems.]

The Wood Beyond the World

My father had written some sixty-five pages of a tale called The King's Son and the Carle's Son[3] before he threw it aside and made a fresh

1 In 1872, Morris's shop, where he displayed Morris and Company items for sale, was at 26 Queen Square, in the Bloomsbury section of London.

2 A halo.

3 Son of a peasant.

beginning with The Wood beyond the World. As we remember from the early days of his narrative poetry, once he was dissatisfied with the work in hand, he rarely made any attempt at trimming or reforming, but consigned the manuscript to the waste-paper basket and started again with no idea of incorporating this material. In the case of The Wood beyond the World, as the plot of the remainder of The King's Son and the Carle's Son is extant, sketched out at some length, one can compare the two schemes and see what he has used over of the first ideas, what rejected and what transformed.

It is delightful to watch the story-maker at his craft, and for my own amusement I have made a double column of the two plots. Here one can see how the peasant's son, entering straightway into the wood to seek adventure, is transformed into the young merchant who breaks away from home and a bad wife and reaches the Wood beyond the World in a skillfully wrought atmosphere of wonder and romance. In the earlier form one may read of the Pleasure-Palace and its environs, thronged with wanton folk who come to picnic outside the Forester's Cot where Michael the Carle's Son is lodged, ostensibly to make him good cheer, but in reality maddening him with their heartless lewd beauty and their mask-like faces: in the published story one has far more sense of "reality" in the enchantment both of the Wood and of the Palace oppressive in its splendour and emptiness and the cloud of Evil that broods above it. The King's Son is transformed from a weak and not ill-meaning young man into a person of craft and low instincts; the Dwarfs, originally colourless and rather tiresome, have become the fantastic horrors we know, pervading the tale but not dwelt upon too much. All through, in comparing the unfinished manuscript and its plot with the finished work, one can feel how the story took hold of the writer as he progressed, with what zest he rounded off the incidents, concentrated the action, visualized the scenes; one can watch how the atmosphere grew around his personages as he moulded them, till behold the written word is transformed into a series of pictures before our eyes, and the story lives.

When The Wood beyond the World came out some reviewers exalted the sweet romance into an allegory. My father but rarely made public comment on his critics; but this was not the first time that allegory and a "lesson" had been read into his stories and poems, and on this occasion he wrote the following letter to the Spectator:[1]

---

1 *The Spectator* is a British magazine first published on 6 July 1828 that is still in operation.

Sir,

I make it a rule not to answer any criticism of my literary work, feeling that the writers have formed their opinions on grounds sufficient to themselves, and that they have a full right to express those opinions. But I think I might break this rule in the case of your very kind and generous notice of my "Wood Beyond the World" (for which I beg to thank you heartily), and, for the benefit of your readers, correct what is matter of fact, and not of opinion.

I had not the least intention of thrusting an allegory into "The Wood Beyond the World;" it is meant for a tale pure and simple, with nothing didactic about it. If I have to write or speak on social problems, I always try to be as direct as I possibly can be. On the other hand, I should consider it bad art in anyone writing an allegory not to make it clear from the first that this was his intention, and not to take care throughout that the allegory and the story should interpenetrate, as does the great master of allegory, Bunyan. Asking pardon for taking up your valuable space by writing even these few words about myself,

I am, Sir,

Yours faithfully

William Morris.

Select Bibliography

Alexander, Michael. *Medievalism: The Middle Ages in Modern England*. New Haven: Yale UP, 2007.

Arata, Stephen, ed. *News from Nowhere*. Peterborough, ON: Broadview Press, 2003.

Baker, Derek. *The Flowers of William Morris*. Chicago: Chicago Review Press, 1996.

Bolus-Reichert, Christine. "Aestheticism in the Late Romances of William Morris." *ELT: English Literature in Transition* 50.1 (2007): 73-95.

Boos, Florence S., and Carole G. Silver, eds. *Socialism and the Literary Artistry of William Morris*. Columbia: U of Missouri P, 1990.

Calhoun, Bruce. *The Pastoral Vision of William Morris: The Earthly Paradise*. Athens, GA: U of Georgia P, 1975.

Campbell, Lori. "Where Medieval Romance Meets Victorian Reality: The 'Woman' Question in William Morris's *The Wood Beyond the World*." In *Beyond Arthurian Romances: The Reach of Victorian Medievalism*, ed. Jennifer A. Palmgren and Lorretta M. Holloway. Basingstoke: Palgrave Macmillan, 2005. 169-90.

Corbett, David Peters. *Edward Burne-Jones*. London: Tate Publishing, 2004.

Dunlap, Joseph R. *The Book That Never Was*. New York: Oriole Editions, 1971.

Fitzgerald, Penelope. *Edward Burne-Jones*. Revised edition. Stroud: Sutton Publishing, 1997.

Hamilton, Jill, Duchess of, Penny Hart, and John Simmons. *The Gardens of William Morris*. New York: Stewart, Tabori, and Chang, 1999.

Hilton, Timothy. *The Pre-Raphaelites*. London: Thames and Hudson, 1970.

Johnson, Fridolf. *William Morris: Ornamentation and Illustrations from The Kelmscott Chaucer*. New York: Dover Publications, 1973.

Lewis, C.S. "William Morris." In *C.S. Lewis: Selected Literary Essays*, ed. Walter Hooper. Cambridge: Cambridge UP, 1969. 219-31.

MacCarthy, Fiona. *William Morris: A Life for Our Time*. London: Faber and Faber, 1994.

Mackail, J.W. *The Life of William Morris*. London: Longmans, Green and Company, 1899.

Marshall, Roderick. *William Morris and his Earthly Paradises*. New York: George Braziller, 1979.

Mathews, Richard. *Worlds Beyond the World: The Fantastic Vision of William Morris*. San Bernardino, CA: Borgo Press, 1978.

Mendelson, Michael. "*The Wood Beyond the World* and the Politics of Desire." *Essays in Literature* 18.2 (1991): 211-34.

Morris, May. *The Collected Works of William Morris with Introductions by his Daughter May Morris*. 24 volumes. London: Longmans, Green and Company, 1911-15.

Parry, Linda, ed. *William Morris*. New York: Abrams Publishers, 1996.

Parry, Linda, ed. *William Morris: Art and Kelmscott*. Woodbridge: Boydell and Brewer, 1996.

Parry, Linda. *William Morris Textiles*. New York: Crescent Books, 1983.

Peterson, William S. *The Kelmscott Press: A History of William Morris's Typographical Adventure*. Oxford: Clarendon Press, 1991.

Plotz, John. "Nowhere and Everywhere: The End of Portability in William Morris's Romances." *ELH* 74.4 (2007): 931-56.

Robinson, Duncan. *William Morris, Edward Burne-Jones, and the Kelmscott Chaucer*. London: Gordon Fraser, 1982.

Salmon, Nicholas. "A Friendship from Heaven: Burne-Jones and William Morris." *Journal of the William Morris Society* 13.1 (1998): 3-13.

Salmon, Nicholas, with Derek Baker. *The William Morris Chronology*. Bristol: Thoemmes Press, 1997.

Sparling, H. Halliday. *The Kelmscott Press and William Morris, Master Craftsman*. London: Macmillan, 1924.

Thompson, E.P. *William Morris: Romantic to Revolutionary*. Stanford, CA: Stanford UP, 1955.

Vallance, Aymer. *The Life and Work of William Morris*. London: George Bell and Sons, 1897.

Watkinson, Ray. *William Morris as Designer*. London: Trefoil Publications, 1990.

Wilhide, Elizabeth. *William Morris: Decor and Design*. New York: Abrams Publishers, 1991.

Wolfshohl, Clarence. "William Morris's *The Wood Beyond the World*: The Victorian World vs. the Mythic Eternities." *Mythlore* 6.21 (1979): 29-32.